Eviscerate

Book 3 in the Ronos Trilogy

Tyler Rudd Hall

Also Written by Tyler Rudd Hall

The Ronos Trilogy

Catalyst

Beacon

Eviscerate

King and Wakefield

The Death of Jonas Wakefield (Short Story)

.skinz (Short Story)

For Rosie, for giving me something to look forward to.
For Alderson, for helping the healing process.
For Maddy, for not letting me give up.

CONTENTS

Choose to hope.

TYLER RUDD HALL

Chapter 1
Lendrum

Before Lynn accessed the power of Ronos to time travel, before Mac brought dozens of people there to give them new power to fight the Invaders, before he discovered the truth about the war—that aliens were attacking and that General Zinger was incapable of defending humanity—before Mac found the hidden planet that became their only hope at survival, before leaving the military, before finding out his family was murdered by Zinger, before the city of Northgate was destroyed, before he even joined the military, Mac Narrad was a Luddite from Passage who was falling for Janelle Stewart.

Nearly five years later Mac felt no closer to finding Janelle or winning the war.

The pull from the beacon in the crust of Ronos activated for three minutes every ten minutes and twenty-two seconds. Out floating amongst the space garbage above Ronos, it was hard for Mac to tell when the pull would begin. More than half of the hundred or so spaceships in orbit were mangled. At the pull point where everyone was forced, was a giant ball of congealed metal. Mac could see Zinger's ship, the *Rundle*, which had massive burn marks along the hull. It was the biggest ship above Ronos and could take more of a beating when the pull happened. Smaller vessels were flying away from the scrum but it was a futile effort. When the pull happened there wasn't an engine in the universe that was powerful enough to escape.

He couldn't see Lynn, or the ship that had picked her up, from where he was floating freely in space. What did time travel look like? Had she done it yet? She had left Ronos to find a ship to take back with her. Her ultimate goal was to travel back to the time of the generation ships and get them to colonize Ronos earlier, so humans could be more prepared for the alien invasion. If she was going to use her power she needed to do it soon, because the pull was about to start.

But that wasn't even the worst part. The *Rundle* might have been the biggest ship right then but something bigger was on the way. The pull from the beacon was reaching farther each cycle and had taken a hold of the space station *Lendrum*. It would be there any second.

Broken ships started to bang against each other as they all were pulled in the same direction. The ships that had been streaking away to save themselves were now forced back. The pull had started.

Mac was out in the open. The transformation he had undergone on Ronos allowed him to be able to survive the cold vacuum of space, but it would not stop two ships colliding and turning him into human paste. He would be nothing more than a bug on a windshield. The only thing he had going for him was that the pull wasn't as strong for him as it was for the ships. He could feel it a little but it was designed for holding ships in orbit, not for holding humans floating through space.

Turning away from the lodestar, he focused on what was coming at him. It was like running uphill while someone threw sticks of dynamite at him. Half the time he couldn't see everything that was coming because ships blocked his way. A derelict ship ran into him; he got around it only to almost get bashed by another ship. He pushed himself away just as the two ships smashed into each other. Now he was flipping end over end until he hit against another vessel. It looked like it was operational. He landed against the window of the cockpit. There were five people inside and they all looked horrified to see him. Mac smiled and waved. That didn't help anything and they screamed even more. They probably had no idea what was going on. Maybe Mac would explain it to them—if they survived.

Laser fire lit the dark space. At first Mac thought it was an explosion. But then he saw that the *Lendrum* had arrived. General Zinger's futile reaction to the newcomer was to try and blow it up.

The *Lendrum* was bigger than Mac had imagined. It was two massive cylinders that were connected by a bridge in the middle. That bridge was minuscule compared to the rest of the station, and that bridge was twice as big as the *Rundle*. Zinger didn't stand a chance of defending himself, but that wasn't stopping him from trying. Lasers shot out of the capital ship as its engines burned to try and get out of the path of the space station. It wasn't working.

This was it. This was the moment that Mac had been dreading. Nothing would stop the *Lendrum* from slamming against every remaining vessel and killing them all. Mac was sure that this was his end. The only consolation he found was that he would at least see General Zinger—the man who murdered his family—die first.

There was a flash of light behind Mac, bigger than any of the explosions so far. The light intensified as it reflected off the metallic surfaces around him. It was bright enough that he felt like the explosion had come from nearby, but he hadn't felt it and none of the ships around him had moved. A few seconds passed and the light hadn't dimmed, as a normal explosion would have.

Just as the space station got to the capital ship the pull ended. The *Lendrum* was still moving forward on momentum but Zinger's ship veered out of the way while still blasting at the space station. Those laser strikes were slowly stopping the *Lendrum*'s progression. Mac was confused. Had the pull ended early? It hadn't been long enough. The light was still glowing behind him and he climbed over the ship to which he was clinging to get a better look at what had stopped the pull.

The vast blue oceans and green continents of Ronos, once very similar to Earth's, were gone. Mac couldn't see anything distinct anymore. Instead the entire planet was covered in clouds. But not normal clouds—clouds shining with a subtle purple light. Ronos had undergone another transformation. It was glowing now. What did that mean for the people still on the surface?

Lynn, Mac called out in his mind.

There was no answer.

Lynn, are you seeing this? Something is happening down there.

No answer.

Was that you who did this?

Either she couldn't hear him or she was ignoring him. He looked around for her ship but he couldn't see it anymore. The last he had seen of her she was in her ship getting ready to time travel. Is this what time travel looked like? Was she responsible for turning Ronos into a big glowing orb?

Mac studied the glowing planet beneath him but could not see Lynn's ship anywhere. It had vanished. Whatever she had tried to do hadn't worked. The only good thing to come out of it was that it looked like the pull was done.

Sneed? I mean Quentin.

Nothing.

Miss White?

Nothing.

Tayma? Mr. Somerset? Is there anyone down there who can hear me?

No answer. All communication had been cut off with the planet. He had brought the Passage people to Ronos to change them to be like him, so they could fight the Invaders. They had arrived at Ronos on two ships. One ship and its crew was on the *Rundle* with other refugees from the pull. The other ship had crashed on the surface of Ronos. Zinger had sent men down with Raymond Tysons to kill them all; there had been a showdown in the cavern with the pull machine. Raymond was dead but his men were likely still fighting the people from Passage. Was there anyone left alive on Ronos? Had Mac led the Passage people to their deaths?

He wondered if he could fly down there to see what was happening. There was enough space garbage floating around that it wasn't long before two pieces collided. One of them streaked towards the planet and was caught in its gravity. As the hunk of metal entered the atmosphere Mac thought that it might make it, but then it started breaking apart. It was shrinking as little bits of it broke off. Before long it disintegrated into nothing.

That was different, Mac said to himself. If something were to go wrong he would have expected an explosion, or burning, or something. Instead it just broke apart like it had turned to sand. Going down to the surface wasn't an option. If there was nothing he could do to protect the people on the surface then he would have to turn his attention to the Passage people who were still trapped on the *Rundle.* He was responsible for them being there; he couldn't leave them in Zinger's hands. He had no idea how to save them or where they were going to go now or how to stop the Invaders, but still—he couldn't abandon them.

Mac jumped from ship to ship towards the *Rundle.* Getting to Zinger was going to be difficult. His ship was full of loyal soldiers. Not to mention his android bodyguard who might be strong enough to tear Mac apart. He wasn't sure if his being transformed on Ronos was enough to take on the android one on one, but he would soon find out.

While he was thinking of it, he reached into his pocket to look for the small disk that Mr. Smith had given him in Passage. Being an android himself, Mr. Smith knew how to take one out. He had given Mac the disk and told him if he put it in Zinger's android bodyguard, then he wouldn't be a problem anymore.

Mac was one jump away from getting to the *Rundle* when a voice came into his mind. He used mind speak so often now that any new voices in his head didn't faze him. Except this voice was frighteningly familiar.

Mac? Can you hear me out there? said General Zinger.

You can mind speak? asked Mac.

I can do all kinds of things, Mac.

Did you drink the liquid rock or did you inject it?

I looked at you and Raymond. Raymond was burned and he and his men had to constantly drink that filthy liquid in order to keep their powers. You and Lynn, on the other hand, were never drinking that filth. So I figured that you found another way to get the rock into your system. You only had to inject yourself once and you were good for a lifetime—as far as we know. Plus, neither of you were burned. I decided to go with an injection. I'm like you now.

The threat of Zinger's android bodyguard paled in comparison to what Zinger was capable of now. Zinger and Mac were on the same level, evenly matched. The general didn't need to eat, he could survive the cold vacuum of space, and he was stronger and faster now than he had ever been before. Mac was in trouble.

What happened to Lynn? asked Zinger.

I don't know.

I still have some of your friends up here, Mac. Don't make me threaten them.

Mac didn't say anything right away.

Your silence means you don't care anymore, said Zinger. *That's fine. I wouldn't care either if I were you. Bunch of Luddites. Don't know a good thing when they see it.*

You don't get to hurt them.

They are on my ship.

We can't afford to lose anyone else.

They aren't soldiers. They have nothing that I want.

Stop killing other humans.

Tell me what I want to know. What happened to Ronos?

I don't know.
Where is Major Tysons?
Raymond's dead.
Guess I don't have to worry about losing my lunch over his ugly face. Where is Lynn?
I don't know.
The general wasn't going to be patient anymore.
You're a waste of life, Mac Narrad. Just like the rest of your family, and every Luddite. I have only ever tried to do what I can to save us and you went ahead and screwed us all. You have brought about our destruction. My destruction. You have killed me. Does that make you happy? Will you finally go away now that you know there is nothing I can do to survive what is coming? Will you stop being a wannabe hero and just die now?
I'm not going anywhere, said Mac.
No? Then I'll help you out, because it's time for the boys to stop pretending they're men. You're done, Mac Narrad. I wish I had done this a lot sooner.
Mac didn't like the sound of that. He jumped from the ship he had been hanging onto just as the lasers shot out of the *Rundle*'s cannons. The explosion propelled Mac back towards Ronos, back towards the highest concentration of ships. That was a place he could try and hide for a moment.
He met up with another hunk of garbage but didn't wait around to find a hiding spot. He kept jumping from ship to ship, all the while looking for where to go next. Every time he jumped, the ship behind him exploded as lasers shot out of the *Rundle*. There was no way he would make it to safety. His best bet was to head back towards the *Rundle*, but how was he supposed to do that with them shooting at him constantly? Mac wondered if there were any ships out there that he could fly back to the *Rundle*. He saw a mid-sized science vessel. It was smaller than the *Terwillegar*. Before Mac could even think about

implementing his plan Zinger turned the science ship into a ball of flame that was quickly snuffed out.

You aren't getting away that easily, said Zinger.

Don't you have something better to do than go around killing humans? asked Mac.

I'm not doing anything else until you stop existing.

Mac needed to distract Zinger.

If I stop existing then you will be getting rid of the one human who knows the most about the aliens, said Mac.

The laser blasts stopped momentarily. This was it. Mac looked across the vast field of floating garbage. He started propelling himself closer to the *Rundle*. It was easy at first but the closer he got to the capital ship the less jump-off points there were. The lasers could start again at any moment. Without a ship there was no way Mac could move fast enough to cover the distance.

What do you mean? asked Zinger.

I'm the only human who knows how many alien ships there are. I know how the emulators work. I know the best way to take them out. I know how to get around on their ships. If anyone is going to lead the army, it's going to be me.

You have to be joking.

More lasers. They missed Mac but he felt the heat from it. And he was thrown clear of his perch, flipping end over end again. Zinger fired repeatedly but it was difficult for such a big ship to hit such a small target. Either that, or Zinger had taken controls over himself and he was just bad at it.

Mac? Zinger said.

Mac didn't answer.

You still alive out there or did that last one finally get you?

Mac kept quiet. Maybe Zinger was dumb enough not to know if Mac was alive or not. Maybe the sensors had been damaged in the pull scrum. The *Rundle* couldn't be operating at a hundred percent. Above him Mac saw his getaway.

It was a two-person ship. The cockpit had been torn in half. It might still work and it would fly under the radar of Zinger's suspicion. Mac just had to drift over there naturally so that Zinger wouldn't think he was still alive.

Mac hit his target and got a better look at the vessel. The cockpit was completely smashed. There were no controls. He pulled himself around to the engines. They were still functional but Mac would have to hotwire them to get them to start up. It was still possible to use, but with no steering wheel, the best he'd be able to do was turn the engines on and hope the ship was pointed in the right direction. Mac looked at where the ship was headed. It wasn't right at the *Rundle* but it was in the general direction. Maybe if Mac pushed against another ship he could get it more on track.

Thought you could fool me, did you? said Zinger.

He had spotted Mac scurrying around the ship. More lasers shot from the *Rundle* just as Mac's ship—which had the name *Calder* painted on the side of it—drifted behind the main cluster of garbage. He started digging around in the engine's control panel to find the ignition wires. There was a cringe-worthy explosion every second or so as the *Rundle* blew up more ships and garbage, trying to get to Mac.

Mac sparked two wires together and the engine started warming up. Without a nav computer the ship would just take off in whatever direction it was pointed. Quickly, he pushed at the garbage that floated in front of him. That would leave him exposed but any second now the engines were going to kick in and he couldn't afford to crash into anything. The *Calder* started moving just as Mac kicked free the last junked ship. He was thrown back into the cockpit as the vessel sped up.

He needed to be ready to jump off before the *Calder* sped past the *Rundle*. He picked himself up and looked around for the *Rundle*. It wasn't hard to miss. They were headed right for it now. A collision was imminent.

Didn't think a suicide run was your style, said Zinger.

Mac jumped. He wasn't as close as he wanted to be but Zinger knew exactly where he was. When he jumped the dark space behind was momentarily lit up as the fuel in the *Calder* was ignited by the *Rundle*'s lasers. He was speeding right for the *Rundle*, faster than he'd expected. The lasers hadn't stopped.

You'll never make it, said Zinger.

The ship was getting bigger as Mac caught up to it. Zinger was still having trouble hitting Mac as he flew through space. As long as he could stick his landing he would make it. He looked unsuccessfully for a place to grab onto the ship's smooth surface. He hit against the side of the ship, shoulder first. The pain was incredible—it took a lot for Mac to feel pain, so if he hadn't been transformed then he probably would have been dead—and momentarily distracted Mac from trying not to float back out into space. Sliding along the pearly hull of the ship, he reached out to grip an edge but there was nothing. As a last resort he tried punching into the ship to get a handhold, but when he swung he found out he was already floating too far away from the ship to even reach it. He had missed his mark by mere inches. Since he was on the far side of the ship, away from Ronos, there was no more space garbage. He would be floating out there for a long time. He strained again to reach for the *Rundle*. The ship was passing in front of him. Soon he would pass the engines and it would be gone forever.

Then his back hit against something. Instantly Mac reached out and desperately held onto whatever it was. It was a piece of twisted black metal, the remnant of a smaller ship that had smashed into the *Rundle* and was now wedged in the hull. Mac could see into the general's ship through the jagged hole. He pulled himself along while breathing a huge sigh of relief. There was a chance now to force himself onto the ship and come up with a new plan—as if there was still hope. Mac had to keep believing but at this point he wasn't sure that humanity would survive. One step at a time. First, he was going to make sure the Passage people were safe. Nothing on Ronos could help them now. They were worse off than before.

Chapter 2
Mr. Smith

Depending on where the rupture in the hull was, the vacuum of space was sealed off by either a force field or by large steel doors. One of those doors is what Mac needed to find. The crater created by the small, now unrecognizable ship was covered in black metal and random debris. Once Mac thought he found a door but it turned out to be a surviving part of the little ship. After several minutes of searching nothing turned up. Mac took a moment to decide if he should force his way into the ship. Back on Ronos he had been able to climb a cave wall by punching and kicking places to put his hands and feet. It would take a lot of hits but eventually he could tear open the metal hull and get inside.

It was possible, but it wouldn't be quick, and whatever was on the other side would be sucked out into space. There was no way for him to guarantee that it wasn't going to be an innocent person.

He thought about all this while he continued to search for an access hatch. Just when he was about to give up, his foot slid against an uneven segment. He looked down and saw a door.

"Finally."

Mac braced his feet against the ship and used his hands to force the door open. There were no handles and the crack where the door was supposed to slide open wasn't wide enough for his fingers to slip through. He tried gripping it with his fingertips and pulling with everything he had in him. The door didn't move, but he did create ten little indentations where each finger had been straining. He pushed straight down in each dent until they were deep enough for him to easily grip. Then he forced the door open.

As the ship's atmosphere rushed against his face he realized his plan of avoiding unnecessary casualties was flawed. Whatever was on the other side was still losing oxygen. The only difference with this plan was as soon as Mac was inside the doors would snap shut and the atmosphere would return. But that wasn't going to do anyone near him any good if they got sucked out into space.

He opened the door wide enough to look inside. The door led to a hallway. If someone were to be sucked out into space they would be passing through a hole smaller than their body. Not a pleasant way to go, to say the least.

He pulled the door open wide enough but now faced a new problem. There was no way for him to hold the door open and crawl inside the ship. If he let off on the door even a little bit then it would slam back shut again. And the atmosphere was still rushing out; as soon as he let go he would be propelled through space.

There was a banging noise coming down the hall. All the stuff that wasn't bolted down was bouncing off the walls. A computer pad hit Mac in the face. It was so sudden he almost let go. He watched for further garbage so he wouldn't get surprised. A chair was tumbling towards him. There was no way he would be able to dodge something that big without the door slamming shut, so he simply braced himself for impact. The chair hit against his chest and leg, and then out into space, never to be seen again. Mac was able to keep the door open.

Sliding down the hall was something bigger, the desk the chair had been behind. From what he could see it looked like it was about the same size as the door. If Mac could open the door all the way and then let it shut when the desk passed through, it might hold the door open long enough for him to get inside.

The desk was moving fast. He repositioned himself to have his feet on one side of the door and his hands on the other, and then forced them apart. It was difficult to get a grip on the door with his feet, but he managed. Before the desk hit him he let the door slam shut. The door was designed to cut through any debris and close as soon as possible. The initial slam cut halfway through the desk. Mac had to quickly climb over it. By the time he was inside the door had closed and the desk was half as long as it used to be.

Mac sat with his back against the desk. The atmosphere was returning to that part of the ship. He noticed that his body no longer needed to pretend he could breathe. Many times he would breathe heavily after almost dying but it wasn't happening this time. He was starting to get used to his new abilities. Instinctually he was starting to realize that as long as he had enough Mac Gas in his system then his new altered blood didn't need the oxygen that breathing normally supplied.

"Should have known it was you." The voice came from the end of the hallway where there was a lift. General Zinger was standing there with his nameless android body guard. The robot had an extreme widow's peak, so that's what Mac mentally called him.

"Hey there," said Mac, getting to his feet.

"Two against one. You won't get out of this one alive."

"I'll take my chances."

"What did Lynn do to Ronos?"

"I honestly don't know."

"You came back here to make sure I wasn't mistreating your people, I imagine."

"We'll talk about that after you try to kill me."

Mac started walking down the long hallway to where they were standing. Zinger was shaking his head and laughing. It was disturbing to see the powerful purple glow around his body.

"No, I've changed my mind. My bodyguard here will easily be able to handle you. I'm going to take care of some of the other people on this ship. It's time to clean house. This is a military ship and all non-military personal will be personally removed by me."

"No!" Mac started running but there was no way he would be able to get there in time. Zinger was already in the lift and out of sight.

Mac kept running anyway. When he reached Widow's Peak he jumped and went heel first into the chest of the android. They both fell over but the android was merely dented—no real damage. They both immediately got to their feet. Mac swung but his punch was caught and he was thrown back. The android was strong and didn't feel pain.

Widow's Peak came over and tried to kick Mac but Mac caught his foot and tried to twist it off. He managed to break the foot but was unable to take it off completely. To stop him, Widow's Peak punched Mac in the arm repeatedly. Mac heard a bone crack so he let go and rolled out of the way. He waited a moment while his body healed itself. He had enough Mac Gas in him that he could manage to heal a few broken bones. Widow's Peak was also taking a moment. When he started walking again Mac realized the machine could self-heal as well.

"Oh, come on," said Mac.

Widow's Peak, as always, said nothing.

Hoping that Widow's Peak was designed like a human and that the most important mechanism was in the head, Mac attacked again. He faked a punch and then ducked under the android's attack; he struck with the hard palm of his hand under the jaw. With his new power it would have killed a normal human. He did hear some cracking noises but the machine was still very much mobile.

Widow's Peak grabbed Mac by the arms and started hitting him against the ceiling and floor. It happened so fast that Mac was caught completely off guard. Widow's Peak must have caught on to Mac's healing abilities because he didn't let up on his attacks. Mac hit the ground again. The android straddled him and started feeding him punches to the face. It was working. There wasn't enough time between blows to heal himself.

The damage to the floor had exposed the wiring running up and down the hallway. One of the thick tubes had broken open; blue sparks were shooting out of it. Through the fog of pain he realized that if he could reach that, then maybe he could get away long enough to fully heal. Mac strained for the electrical tube—it was an inch out of reach. He tried to shuffle his body over but Widow's Peak was too heavy and too powerful.

There was a break in the blows as Widow's Peak noticed what Mac was trying to do. He stopped to slam his fist down into the wrist reaching for the electrical tube. The bones broke on contact. Mac used his other fist to hit the side of Widow's Peak's head. After three blows there was a dent in the side of the android's head. His weight shifted enough that Mac could kick his way free.

He tried to roll but Widow's Peak didn't let him get far. They were now tangled up on the floor, neither of them able to fully pin the other and both landing solid attacks. More bones were broken; more dents were delivered. This fight was going to go on forever and there was no guarantee that Mac would win. Plus Zinger was already on his way to kill the Passage people and all the other refugees. Killing for the sake of killing—the man had gone fully crazy.

That's when Mac remembered what Mr. Smith had told him: The only way to defeat Zinger's android bodyguard was to put the disk in the port on the back of his neck. Mac was already on top. He let Widow's Peak flip over and stopped him from crawling away. He used one hand to bat away the failing arms and fished the disk out of his pocket with the other hand. The port was under the hair at the base of the neck. When Mac pulled the hair up

Widow's Peak realized what was happening and really started to struggle. Mac was almost thrown off.

There was already a data disk in the port. Mac pulled it out and the bodyguard went immediately limp. Mac had no desire to deal with him again. He crushed that disk with his fist and threw it away. Then he put in Mr. Smith's disk.

Slowly, Mac got off the android. He backed away and let his body heal. Bones snapped into place and bruises slowly dissipated. For a moment it looked like nothing was going to happen to the android. Maybe Mac had accidentally damaged the disk. Or maybe it was working perfectly—maybe its only purpose was to remove the android's drive to kill him.

But Mac didn't think so. He had his suspicions about what was on that disk.

The android groaned. It was the first vocalization that Mac had heard from him. He couldn't decide if that was a good sign or a bad sign. The metal body started to move. Mac backed farther away. Slowly Widow's Peak got to his feet and started looking around. When he turned and saw Mac he said, "Mac?"

"Yes?"

"What are you doing here?"

Mac waited a moment. The voice was foreign. It was deep and menacing. It sounded like the voice of someone who wanted to hurt him.

"Where do you think you are?" asked Mac.

"Well, obviously it's a ship, but the last thing I remember is being back in Passage."

"So it *is* you, Mr. Smith."

"Of course it is. Who else would it be?" said Mr. Smith.

"Check out your new body."

Mr. Smith took stock of his new robotic home. It was a lot younger than his last body, yet he still looked disappointed.

"This means that I told you about my secret, right?" said Mr. Smith.

"You don't remember?"

"No. I gave you a data disk?"

"Yeah."

"I make a backup at the end of every day. I'm not going to remember anything between then and now."

"Then I have a lot to catch you up on."

"Go for it."

"Not now. We need to stop Zinger. He's going to kill the Passage people."

"Where are they?"

"Last I saw they were in the docking bay."

"Okay, one sec."

It looked like Mr. Smith was just standing there, gazing at nothing in the distance, but Mac knew he was using the android's Imp to access something on the ship. It was moments like this where Mac realized having an Imp was incredibly convenient. If it had just been Mac he would have had to run around until he found a terminal.

"There might be something we can do to stall them," said Mr. Smith.

"What?"

Mr. Smith reached down to his arm and pulled back the synthetic skin to reveal another port. He pulled out the disk to examine it.

"No good."

"What?"

"The replicator has been broken. I was going to copy myself."

"That's my bad. We were in the middle of a scrap before I put the disk in."

"Who was winning?"

"Obviously, I won. We aren't fighting anymore."

"But my android body gave you a run for your money."

"Are you rooting for the android?"

"What? Maybe. I was just curious what this machine could do."

"I saw it repair itself. So why can't the replicator part get fixed?"

"The repair mode doesn't fix everything. You hit this arm pretty hard."

"In my defence, you were trying to kill me."

"In my defence, it wasn't actually me."

"Why do you need to replicate yourself?"

"So I could be in the ship and this body at the same time."

"In the ship?"

"Yeah. Then I can control the doors and lifts. Slow Zinger down while you go save the people."

"Okay. Let's do that."

"You need to take the disk out of me again and find a place to put it. If I get in, I'll find a way to communicate with you. You go get everyone Zinger wants dead off this ship."

Mac nodded and walked around Mr. Smith to pull out the disk again.

"Wait," said Mr. Smith.

"What?"

"If something goes wrong and I don't see you again—I want to say, it's been fun knowing you."

"I'll see you again. You're still back on Earth, remember?"

"Right." Mr. Smith almost said more but then held back. There wasn't time for Mac to ask what was on his mind.

"You ready?" asked Mac.

"Yeah."

"I'll talk to you soon."

Mac pulled out the disk and the android body shut down, its metal body locked into an inert but upright position. Mac, no longer having access to the android's Imp, started running around looking for a terminal.

He found one in a room off the hallway but it didn't have the port he was looking for. He went back to the lift and went up one floor. He quickly found an empty room full of terminals. It looked like a lab. Zinger wasn't the type to keep a lab for learning and research fully staffed at all times. Everyone was probably at battle stations until they figured out what had happened to Lynn and the planet Ronos.

Mac put the disk in the port and waited for something to happen. Like before, it took a couple minutes, but eventually the lights in the room started to blink and a message appeared on the screen.

I've never been a ship before.

Mac didn't know how to talk back to Mr. Smith. "There's no key pad."

I can hear you. Zinger has listening devices in half the rooms on the ship.

"That's overly paranoid for someone who can easily monitor Imp feeds."

Well, he's been walking down the road to mental breakdown for a long time now.

"Where is he?"

I have him pinned in a lift. There are soldiers with him and with the refugees. Right now no one realizes that I have complete control of the ship.

"Good, I'll get there first and help them."

Help them how?

"Contact the *Lendrum*. If the pull starts again then that's the only place where everyone will be safe."

Pull?

"Oh, right. I guess it's time to catch you up on things."

The ship had been through a lot, Zinger understood that. There were lots of things that weren't working properly. Every time they collided with another ship something else broke and there weren't enough spare parts anymore to fix everything. But they were in the middle of the ship now. Why had the lift stopped suddenly?

He was calm at first.

"Why are we stopped?" asked Zinger. Since injecting himself with Lynn Rock his Imp had stopped working. Without an Imp, he had to always have someone close to him who did. Spacer Quake was that person.

"Technical problems. Something is going haywire in one of the labs," said Quake.

"The labs? I thought I had those shut down."

"They are, sir. A team is investigating."

"Is Mac still alive?"

"Um…" Quake didn't want to give the bad news. "We are unable to reach your bodyguard."

Zinger didn't say anything. He knew this was possible. He also knew that because he and Mac were now equal in strength the only leverage that he had over him were the refugees. Zinger had already separated the Passage people from the others. Once Zinger got there and started shooting lasers through them, there was nothing Mac wouldn't do.

But to do that, the lift needed to start moving. Zinger was pacing back and forth now. With each pass he became more and more annoyed. Why did the soldiers in this elevator smell so bad? Had they always smelled this bad? Or were Zinger's senses simply becoming stronger after having injected himself?

"Sir," said Quake.

"Yes."

"There's something wrong with the ship."

"I know that already."

"No. We are completely locked out of everything. We have no control."

Mac. He had done this. Zinger didn't know how, but Mac was the one responsible. If he got to the refugees first then there was nothing Zinger could do to control him.

"Bring down a cutting torch. I want every door between us and the refugees removed. Do it now!"

Mr. Smith was all caught up on what had happened. While Mac filled him in, Mr. Smith was trying to smooth things over with the *Lendrum*. It was the safest place to be right now, but Zinger had been trying to blow it up. Mr. Smith spun a yarn about a mutiny and something about a cash reward, anything he could think of to get them to let the refugees on board. It was taking longer than Mac had hoped—but then again, they had just been attacked by the *Rundle*.

They are going for it.

"Good."

They're probably going for it.

"Probably?"

Zinger did try to kill them all. Would you trust us?

"No."

That's why I said probably. But we don't have time to get the answer we need. Let's go.

Mac found a computer pad he could carry with him so he could still communicate with Mr. Smith. The lift was out of service so Mac had to take the long way. Mr. Smith was directing him.

Once you get up these stairs, turn left and stop when you get to the big bay doors. Be careful. There may be some guards on the other side.

"May be?"

I don't know. I'm reading over some old orders to have some men stationed there, but it doesn't say how many.

"No cameras?"

I'm working on it. I removed your picture from the network so hopefully you're less likely to be recognized.
Normally the doors would have been locked but because Mr. Smith was in charge, they opened as soon as Mac got there. He had picked up a gun on the way there but wasn't prepared for what was on the other side. There were a dozen soldiers, all with laser rifles. They all turned toward Mac as the door opened. Behind the soldiers were hundreds of innocent civilians and their ships. They had been brought there by the pull and now had no choice but to stay until someone offered them a better way. When they saw who had come through the door some of them recognized him as one of the Passage citizens; he hoped they wouldn't give him away. He lowered his gun.

"Zinger sent me," said Mac. "There's something wrong with the ship. He's unable to communicate with you down here."

The leader of the squad stepped forward. His ID tag said Cutter.

"We've been having troubles ourselves. What's going on out there?"

"I don't know exactly. The planet is interfering with the ship's systems. The general doesn't want to have these people using up resources and manpower. We are to let them back on their ships and send them over to the *Lendrum*."

"General Zinger said to let them go?"

"Yes."

"Who are you? What is your rank?"

"I'm Spacer…" Mac hesitated. "Michaels."

"Why aren't you in uniform?"

You should shoot first. At least you'll kill a few before they attack back.

Mac saw that some of the refugees—the stronger ones, carrying whatever heavy objects they could find—were slowly moving in on the soldiers while their attention was on Mac. Most of them could be clubbed within a few seconds. The only ones the refugees couldn't get close enough to were the three out front, Cutter and the guards on either side of him.

"He wrote the orders down," said Mac. He handed over the pad.

As it switched hands and their eyes lowered he shot each of the three men in the chest. At the same time the refugees struck, disarming and bludgeoning the other nine guards. Their weapons were gathered and distributed.

"Thanks for the help," said one of the men who had helped in the clubbing.

"Mac. My name is Mac Narrad."

"We know who you are. The people from Passage told us about you. I'm Ian Cally."

"Thanks, Ian."

"You going to help us take this ship?"

"No."

"What?"

"You don't need to worry about that," said Mac. "You need to make sure all these people get over to the *Lendrum*."

"Why?"

"It's a space station. Bigger than everything else here put together. If the pull returns it will be the safest place."

"Zinger will destroy our ships if we try to leave here."

"No, he won't."

Mac went and picked up the computer pad he had handed over. With Mr. Smith he would be able to keep control of the *Rundle*, including its weapons. At least Mac hoped Mr. Smith still had control. There was a hole through the pad now.

"I have control of the ship," said Mac, tossing the broken tech aside. "Trust me."

"We might have a better chance of taking the ship. If we get out there and the pull happens again..."

"Where are the people from Passage?" They would help Mac lead these people to safety.

"They were taken away by the guards a few minutes ago. We don't know why."

The door behind Mac opened. He couldn't communicate with Mr. Smith, but he had to believe that he was being led to where he needed to be. There was no more time for discussion with Ian. Mac shouted out so everyone could hear him.

"I have taken control of the ship," he said to the cheers of the crowd. "But if the pull starts again it's not safe here. Everyone get in a ship and fly over to the *Lendrum*. They are expecting you. If you stay, there is a chance you will die. It's your choice. Go as soon as you can. I only ask you leave one ship behind for the Passage refugees."

There was a big rush for people to get back to their ships. Ian hesitated at first, seeming to think about going after Mac, but decided not to and went back to his ship. It was a wise choice. Once Mac freed the Passage people he was going to destroy the *Rundle*, with Zinger on it.

Chapter 3
Shoot the Hostages

Mac wanted to grab another computer pad to talk to Mr. Smith but it didn't look like that was the plan. As Mac ran through the ship doors opened and he charged through. None of them had the supplies he needed and he still hadn't found the Passage people, but he was heading in a steady direction and it still felt like he was being led somewhere. He kept going without knowing where or why, only hoping that it would all work out. He began to get nervous as he began to pass increasing numbers of soldiers. The first group was very suspicious of the man not in military uniform running through the halls. The Lynn Rock hadn't changed them so they were easily taken care of. One even happened to be his size, so he was able to switch clothes to blend in more.

There were more and more soldiers around. Most of them were confused when they saw Mac come through the door.

"How did you do that?" most of them asked.

"Do what?"

"The doors weren't opening for us."

"Oh, I don't know. It just kind of opened."

Mr. Smith let the soldiers out so Mac could keep going alone. He was eagerly running down a hallway when a side door opened unexpectedly. There weren't any monitors in there so he had no way of knowing what Mr. Smith had opened that door for. When Mac poked his head inside he saw that it was an armory. The walls were lined with guns and ammunition. He figured Mr. Smith could see some challenges ahead.

As he went in the room the door closed behind him. Mac picked a couple weapons up and went back to the door but it remained closed.

"Mr. Smith?" Mac said, hoping this was one of the rooms wired for surveillance. It was an armory, so why wouldn't it be?

The door opened and closed so fast that Mac didn't have time to get through it. Maybe he wasn't supposed to leave? He looked around for another door but couldn't see one. There were stacks of boxes in the middle of the small room. When he opened them he saw that they were full of explosive charges. That might come in handy. The charges were attached to an oversized belt that Mac hung across his torso like a sash. Then he went to the other boxes. Instead of weapons, they were full of tranquilizer guns. None of those boxes had been opened before—Zinger must not have had a need for them. Mac couldn't think of a need either. He left them and went back to the door. It opened and closed again before he could get through. The only other thing he could carry with him was a tranq gun, so he went back and got one. Now the door opened. Mac walked out with a belt full of explosives, a rifle in either hand, and a tranq gun in a hip holster. Whatever was coming, Mr. Smith thought it was going to take a lot of firepower. How many men did Zinger have guarding the Passage people?

Another door opened. As he entered Mac's first thought was of some kind of nature preserve in the middle of the ship—assuming they were in the middle of the ship. Mac really had no idea. Nature preserve or not, this room was nothing like the rest of the ship. The ceiling, walls, and floor were all covered in rock. There was a hole in the rock ceiling with a ladder so people could climb up. He had no idea what was up there but was pretty sure he could see a purple hue coming from above.

The room below where Mac was had a desk with a terminal on it and shelves of small samples of black liquid—Mac realized what this room was for. He walked over to the liquid vials, passing the terminal, and saw that Mr. Smith was trying to get a hold of him.

MAC MAC MAC MAC MAC MAC MAC MAC MAC MAC MAC MAC MAC

"What?"

Took you long enough. Use the charges in this room.

"I can't do that. I need this room. If Zinger is going to start killing hostages then this stuff might be able to keep them alive. I've survived laser blasts before with this stuff flowing through me."

But you need the injection AND the gas, right?

"Yeah."

Well, the Passage people are nowhere near this room and Zinger isn't going to bring them here for you. If you want them alive then you need to destroy this room. Release the gas into the ship and let it find the Passage people.

"But they still need to be injected."

That's what the tranq gun is for. Bring lots of ammo.

"You sure about this?"

Don't have any other options.

Mac, I know you are behind this, said General Zinger.

I don't know what you're talking about, said Mac.

We found out how you took over the ship. It's only a matter of time before we get control back.

I look forward to it. Maybe you'll try to stop me yourself instead of sending your goons.

I have the power to make you do what I want.

Mac needed to get the charges set and get out of there. But if Zinger really was about to get control of the ship back then was it a good idea to blow the room up before Mac could get to the Passage people?

"We have a problem, said Mac.

What?

"Zinger's going to get control of the ship back soon."

Yeah. I felt someone poking around.

28

"Really?"

It's very strange, being a ship. I don't recommend it.

"So what do we do?"

They won't be able to take me completely out of their system without removing the disk. I'll let Zinger know where it is and then he'll head in that direction. You meet him there and save the hostages.

"That'll work?"

It's right above this room. When you release the gas it's going to burn right towards you. It'll work. Once you shoot them you only need to buy some time before the gas gets to you. Use the remote detonator.

"Okay."

The liquid rock vials were compatible with the tranq darts so Mac loaded up. Then he set the charges and made sure the remote detonator was armed. Zinger must have figured out that the gas didn't burn things that were native to Ronos and had the entire room lined with rock. Mac had no idea how they got the gas inside. Maybe they had put it in containers that lasted long enough to get it from Ronos, to the transport ships, up to the room. That's the only thing he could think of. Hoses and pumps would have failed quickly and spread to the rest of the ship. He also wondered how many people Zinger had managed to change on the ship. Lots of the soldiers Mac had passed in the hall had canteens clipped to their side with liquid rock inside. None of them had the slight purple glow that Mac and Zinger did. Maybe this was another example of the general trying to control power.

You need to go. They are headed to my disk now.

"Okay."

Don't let them destroy it. It's the only version of me I have.

"You're still back on Earth, remember?"

As far as you know.

"You'll be fine."

Mac took off for the room with the disk in it. He didn't know how long it would take to get there but as he ran it already felt like it was taking too long. He didn't know the ship as well as Zinger did but Mr. Smith was still in control and he was still opening the doors to lead Mac in the right direction. If it weren't for that Mac would have been totally lost. Another door opened and Mac kept running.

Except that nothing looked familiar. Sure, most rooms and hallways on war ships all looked the same, but Mac didn't remember there being so many stairs. He was starting to doubt he was heading in the right direction and he couldn't figure out why Mr. Smith would lead him somewhere else.

Unless it wasn't Mr. Smith doing the leading. Mac stopped running. Mr. Smith said they wouldn't be able to completely get him out of their system without removing the disk. But what if they had gotten back control of the automatic doors and were herding Mac into a trap?

He had three weapons on him—two laser rifles and the tranq gun. The second rifle had been over kill; he felt powerful holding it but needed the tranq gun ready. He dropped it as he run and pulled the tranq gun out. If Zinger and his men popped up then he'd use the rifle. If they were holding the Passage people hostage then he would shoot them with the tranq gun and blow the charges. The remote detonator was tucked into the back of his pants.

Mac wasn't running anymore but kept moving through the opening doors. One more door opened and Mac's suspicions were confirmed. Zinger stood there with two dozen guards and the all the Passage people who hadn't gone down to the surface. There weren't very many of them but they all looked terrified.

The most scared was the family. Mac recognized them as Natasha and Jonathan Glover; he'd saved them from the grove of trees right outside of Passage. The father was trying to put on a brave face but the mother was a second away from a breakdown; the kids, all young, were already crying. Mac didn't know their exact ages but the oldest, Miles, couldn't have been more than eight. The other two kids were Sofia and Kendra. Miles held his father's hand and wept softly. The daughters clung to their mother. Darren and Clarissa were also there, obviously in shock. Being newly engaged they had been preparing for the rest of their lives but now that future was in jeopardy. Mr. and Mrs. Parkington, in their seventies, looked angry more than anything. Mac suspected if anyone threatened the children the Parkingtons would use themselves as human shields. Not that any of the weapons were pointed at any of the hostages—they were all levelled at Mac.

The only one threatening the hostages was Zinger. He had a gun pressed against the head of Scott Ryder. Scott looked content, almost glad he was going to be the first one to go.

"Looks like you fixed your ship," said Mac.

"The important parts, anyway."

Mac took note—they didn't have the disk yet. It was time to put his plan into motion. He stepped fully into the room and let the door close behind him. To set off the charges all he had to do was press the button by pushing the detonator tucked in the back of his pants. He couldn't reach around and press it without them shooting him but if he leaned his back against something it would push the button and set off the charges.

"You need to put down your weapons or I'll shoot them," said Zinger.

"That goes without saying," said Mac.

"And yet you're still holding them."

"If I put down my weapons you're going to kill us all anyway."

"Well, maybe."

Mac needed a distraction. He needed the charges to go off. He took a step back to hit the button against the door. But the door opened. Zinger hadn't locked it. Mac walked forward and let it close again. Then stepped back and it opened again. A couple of the soldiers looked at each other, confused. No one could figure out what Mac was doing. Even General Zinger cocked his head to the side in confusion. Mac kept going back and forth, the door opening and closing.

"Stop that. Lock the door," said Zinger.

The door slammed shut and wouldn't reopen.

"Thank you," said Mac.

He took another step back. The detonator button depressed and the room full of Mac Gas exploded. The ship rumbled. One of the soldiers spoke up.

"There was an explosion," he said.

"Where?" said Zinger.

"Doesn't matter," said Mac.

"You're right," said Zinger. "If you don't give me back my ship then I'm done with you and your friends. Say goodbye."

"Let me do the honours."

Mac pulled the trigger and shot Scott in the neck with a dart full of the liquid rock. The rock quickly emptied into his body. Scott quickly realized that although he'd been shot, he wasn't dying. He looked disappointed. Mac couldn't figure out why Scott would want to die. He had come too far to give up.

Before General Zinger could figure out what was going on, Mac went down the line, shooting each hostage. The hostages didn't know what was going on either. Jonathan and Natasha yelled at Mac to stop and shoved their kids behind them. The dad got three darts and the kids still didn't have any. The kids were now the only hostages that hadn't been changed. Darren and Clarissa pulled the darts out to examine them. They wouldn't feel the full effect of the liquid rock until the gas got there.

Which wouldn't be much longer. The ship was shaking. The lights were flickering. There was obviously something wrong going on. The soldiers weren't even paying attention to Mac anymore. They were wondering if it was time to start running for the escape pods.

Mac took the opportunity to remove some of them from the equation. His rifle lit up and the four men closest to the hostages dropped. The gas was now close enough Mac could hear the hissing. Any moment now and the floor underneath them would start to turn purple, then black, then vanish. Everyone on the ship who hadn't been changed would die. In that room the only people that included were the kids. The parents did not know what to do. They were all huddled together to protect each other. Zinger took aim at Mac and fired. The shot was easily avoided but the volley kept coming and Zinger kept yelling.

"What have you done to my ship!"

A blast hit Mac in the chest and tossed him backwards. It burned but it wouldn't be enough to take Mac down. He tried to get up but another laser hit him in the side. The ship was shaking so violently now it was hard to stand. The *Rundle* was tearing itself apart from the inside. With his head down on the ground he expected to hear a louder hissing noise, but he didn't.

Maybe the room they were in wasn't exactly above the gas room. Maybe they were going to miss the cloud altogether. But it had to be close. The hissing was dim but it was still there. Some of the soldiers had abandoned hope and gone running, but the few that stayed had joined Zinger in trying to gun down Mac.

Darren stepped up to help. He picked up a discarded weapon and started firing at the soldiers. His aim wasn't the greatest but it was good enough for a distraction. The soldiers turned their attention to him while Zinger walked right up to Mac.

"It's done. You're done," said Zinger.

Mac rolled over and kicked the gun out of Zinger's hand. It went flying. Zinger screamed in rage.

"I blew the gas room up. It's leaking into the rest of the ship and there's nothing that can stop it. You and your ship are done."

Zinger finally realized why the ship felt like it was shaking itself apart. He didn't care about Mac anymore. The general only ever cared about survival. Not the survival of humanity—his own personal survival. He ran out the room.

There were only a few soldiers left. Most them were shooting at Darren and the hostages, who were taking cover behind tables and chairs that weren't laser-proof. Mac joined in the battle, shooting the last remaining soldiers. When it was just him and the hostages the family and the old couple started running away from him.

Now he could see where the gas was coming from. The wall behind them all was changing color. The hissing was getting louder. It would come through any moment now and the kids still hadn't been changed.

"Wait!" said Mac.

"You tried to kill us," said Jonathan Glover while trying to stay between Mac and his family. The kids were now the closest one to the wall that was about to give way.

"Yeah, Mac. What did you inject us with?" asked Darren. He wasn't angry, just confused.

"Where's Lynn?" asked Scott. "Is she still alive?"

Mac ignored that last question. There were more relevant problems—also, he didn't know the answer.

"I injected you with something that will save your life. This ship is being eaten away by a highly corrosive gas. If those kids don't get injected they will die," said Mac.

"What?" said Jonathan.

"Trust me."

"Don't let him shoot me, dad," said Miles. The mother hid the two girls behind her. They were all still walking backwards. Mac could see the top of the wall was dark black now. Gas might already be leaking through.

"We don't have a lot of time," said Mac.

He walked over to the family and pushed the dad and mom aside. The kids were screaming but Mac ignored it. He wasn't going to hurt them. He pulled the trigger on the tranq gun three more times. The kids stopped screaming, in shock. They didn't know what to do. They weren't dead and it hadn't felt like anything more than a little prick. Mac took Miles by the hand.

"See? I was just giving you some medicine."

"Why were you using a gun?" asked Miles.

"It's the only way I could get it done fast enough. Here, let me show you something cool."

Mac could have held his hand and led him to the wall but they didn't have a lot of time. Instead he picked the kid up and walked over.

"Touch the wall," said Mac.

"Why?"

Mac didn't answer. He grabbed the kid's hand and pressed it against the wall. The hand started to glow purple. The glow was moving through his body like the gas was being sucked up through his hand.

"Oh wow!" Miles kept saying over and over again.

His whole body was glowing now and he was buzzing with energy.

"This is what happened to me. This is how I'm able to do everything you've seen. Remember what I did in Passage? It's because I was injected, just like you guys, and then exposed to this gas, just like Miles. It's the only way we can survive. Everyone get up here and touch the wall. Quickly, before it collapses."

The Glover family came up immediately. If one of them had been changed then they were all going to be changed. Darren and Clarissa weren't too far behind them. The Parkingtons hesitated, no doubt wondering how it could possibly be a good idea to touch the gas that was powerful enough to destroy a warship from the inside out. They didn't move forward until they saw nothing happened to any of the other people. Now they were all glowing purple, except for Scott.

"Scott, hurry," said Mac.

"Is it permanent?"

"As far as I can tell."

"Is Lynn alive?"

"I don't know."

"What?"

"It's hard to explain."

"Try me."

There was a massive crack. Mac saw a fissure opening in the side of the wall. It was about to come down. Scott was about to not have a choice about touching the gas or not.

Mac ignored him. He would be exposed eventually. "Do you know how to get down to the docking bay?"

"Yes."

"Lead these guys down there. I left one ship behind for us. Go down there and wait for me. If the gas gets there before I do or if the *Rundle* is going to explode or something, take off and I'll meet up with you later on the *Lendrum*."

"Where are you going?"

"I need to get one more person before we leave."

"Then you'll take me to Lynn?"

"Get these guys out of here and then we'll talk."

Scott led them down to the docking bay. Mac hoped that part of the ship hadn't been destroyed yet. There was only one terminal in the room. He ran over to it but there was no message from Mr. Smith waiting for him.

"Mr. Smith?"

They took back partial control of the ship.

"I know. I blew the charges. We're getting out of here."

Don't leave without me.

"I know. I need a map. I don't know how to get to you."

A map popped up. The room where Mac had left the disk wasn't all that close to where he was now.

"How much time do I have before we lose atmosphere and artificial gravity?" asked Mac.

Not long.

"I don't know if I can get to you."

You need to.

"We keep saying the same thing. You are still alive. You are still back on Earth."

That's what you don't realize. I don't know what you said or what I found out but there is no way I would have given you that disk if I thought my body on Earth was going to survive. I'm not the only android out there. We police ourselves and unnecessary replication is against our laws. I gave you that disk because—

"Because you think Earth isn't going to survive the war."

That's what it seems like to me. I don't know why I would think that. Do you?

Mac thought back to the alien fleet. Janelle had warned him that they were without number and they would not hesitate to kill every single human in order to get back to Ronos. When the beacon went haywire it revealed a clear path for the fleet to follow, one that led right through the human colonies. Mac didn't know how Mr. Smith realized the harsh reality of what was going to happen but there was a strong chance humanity— let alone Earth—wouldn't survive.

The lights flickered as the *Rundle* trembled again. Mac memorized his route through the ship and was about to head off when he got a message.

It's too late.

"What do you mean?"

Everyone's abandoned ship except you guys.

"That sounds like a good thing. Means no one is coming to destroy your disk."

You won't be able to get here. The ship is torn apart. We are on opposite sides. The gas is still burning. I won't last long enough for you to come get me.

"I can still try."

You need to get out of here. Make sure Zinger doesn't do any more damage.

"I can still come get you."

I've had my time. Trust me.

"I'm sorry."

Thanks for being a good friend, Mac. I was hiding in Passage to stay out of the way of history but I had no idea someone as critical as you would be raised there. There's always a chance that another version of me survived. So let's not get too mushy.

"Is there more than just your copy on Earth?"

There was no answer. Mr. Smith really didn't want to drag out the goodbye. Mac took off for the docking bay.

Chapter 4
Standoff

The ship was a newer model Arrow and it could fit a dozen people inside so there was more than enough room for everyone. The Glover kids had enough space to burn off some of their new energy. The name of the ship was the *Glenora* and, true to its model name, it was shaped like an elongated arrowhead. With enough speed the ship itself could be used as a weapon, but hopefully it wouldn't come to that. The important thing was it had a hyper drive that could get them far away, fast.

Everyone else was inside the ship waiting for Mac to get there so they could take off. All of them except the kids were strapped in because the *Rundle* was jostling around so much. The Glover parents tried to tell them to strap down or they would get hurt, but the kids knew that wasn't true anymore. The only real danger any of them faced was still being on the *Rundle* when it finally exploded.

The door to the docking bay opened and Mac came running through at full speed. His approach was accompanied by the most violent shaking of the ship yet.

"I thought you were bringing someone with you?" asked Scott.

"I'll explain later," said Mac.

"Where are we going?" asked Scott, who had sat down in the pilot seat.

"You're in my spot."

"You're flying?"

"Yeah. I've been trained."

"I used to build ships."

"Just move."

"You don't know where we're going, do you?" said Scott as he vacated the seat.

Mac didn't answer him. He and Scott were alone in the command deck. The pilot sat in the very tip of the arrowhead; the commander's seat was elevated in the middle of the command deck, flanked by two lower chairs and consoles. All the other passengers were in the *Glenora*'s common area in the middle of the ship. The common area had six living quarters off of it. In the back of the ship was the engine room.

"The first thing I'm going to do is take these guys over to the *Lendrum*," said Mac.

"Did you ask if that's where they want to go?" asked Scott.

"Nope."

Mac lifted off of the *Rundle*'s docking bay floor and headed away from the dying ship. The space around Ronos was still crowded from all the busted-up ships. He had to constantly dodge the drifting derelicts.

"I changed my mind," said Scott. "You were right to fly."

"Told you."

Mac still didn't know what to think of the glowing orb that was now Ronos. He didn't notice any more changes since he had seen it last. The glow was still there, bright enough to be a sun but without the expected heat— otherwise they'd have been burned alive. This was the first time that Scott and the others had seen it. There were view ports in the common area but the best view on the ship was in the tip of the arrow. The door opened and they all came in to look at what had happened.

"That's...Ronos?" asked Darren.

"Yes," said Mac, answering all their questions as best he could.

"What happened?"

"I don't know."

"Everyone else from Passage is down there, right?" asked Natasha.

"Yep."

"Are they alive?"

"I don't know."

"Lynn went down there," said Scott.

"Not only that. She caused this to happen."

"What?" Scott looked genuinely hurt by this—like he couldn't believe what he was hearing. He pulled Mac out of his seat by his shoulder and dragged him to the back of the room while everyone crowded at the front.

"I need to pilot the ship," said Mac.

"She used her power?" said Scott.

"Yes."

"She thought she was time traveling?"

"She was trying to go back to the time of generation ships. Thought she could lead them here and build an army."

"What did she think was going to happen?"

"No idea."

"No hint about the planet turning into a glowing orb?"

"Nope."

"So it was all for nothing."

"We're not out of this yet."

"You know how to stop the aliens?"

"No. But we're still alive. So that's something."

Scott didn't look comforted. Probably because it didn't matter if he was alive if the woman he loved wasn't.

"Scott, you can't give up," said Mac.

"Lynn's gone forever."

"We don't know where Lynn is."

"She's gone."

The ship rocked as it struck some garbage.

Now that they were a ways away from the *Rundle* they had a clear view of what the Mac Gas had done to it. It looked like the ship had been struck by a cosmic cleaver but the blade had only made it halfway through. Sparks were exploding all along where the gas had burned the ship away.

"Look there," said Darren.

Mac looked where he was pointing. There was a stream of escape pods heading for the *Lendrum*. Zinger was bound to be on one of them.

"Do those things have weapons?" asked Mrs. Parkington.

Mac looked back at her, shocked at her bloodlust.

"What? After everything he's done?" she said.

"They don't have any weapons but we aren't going to attack them. I'll tell the *Lendrum* not to let them on board. They can figure out their own way to survive."

"After you take us to the *Lendrum*, where are you going?" asked Scott.

"I'll probably meet up with our fleet. See what I can do to fight from there. Maybe I can slow them down."

"Giving up on stopping them?"

"Slow them down until we can think up a better plan."

"Better than sending Lynn back in time?"

Scott was angry with Mac for letting Lynn use her power. Mac didn't have time to tell him that he was against it. That Lynn had done it, over his objections, because she couldn't see another way out.

"Guys, look," said Darren.

He was pointing back at Ronos. It was changing. The glow was still there but it was dimming. The swirling clouds of light were slowing down. As they slowed the light decreased. Once the clouds stopped rotating they started to thin out. The new Ronos was about to emerge from its cocoon. Now they would see if using Lynn's power had been worth it.

Soon landmasses were visible. He didn't immediately recognize any of them—he was too distracted by what he saw on them. There were cities. Big cities. The kind that were found on Earth. Millions of people. Going to and from the different cities were ships flying through the air. Highways cut through the hills and mountains.

"What?" asked Darren.

"This is a civilized planet," said Scott. "How is this possible?"

"I don't know," said Mac.

"Did you know this would happen?"

"Of course not."

"Did Lynn?"

"How would I know? I don't even know what is going on."

"Well, she *was* time travelling. It hasn't even been a day yet so some kind of time traveling must have happened for all these cities to pop up."

In the north ocean there was an archipelago of rocky islands. It wouldn't have been noteworthy except that there were so many islands. It would have been its own continent if the ocean waters had dropped just a little bit. There had to be some people living on those islands because of all the air traffic around them. The closest landmass to those islands was a long skinny continent that was mostly green. It was hard to tell the topography from where Mac was, but the color was hard to miss.

"How many people are down there?" asked Clarissa.

"It looks like Earth. There must be billions of people," said Darren.

The escape pods were all veering away from the *Lendrum* and towards Ronos. The lights from their engines were leaving streaks in the black of space. Zinger had given an order. With billions of people down there he had a whole new audience to indoctrinate. His chance for power was greater there than on the space station. Mac changed course.

"Where are you going?" asked Darren.

"We have to follow Zinger," said Mac.

"Good," said Scott.

"Bad," said Jonathan and Natasha at the same time.

"I don't know what's going on or where these people came from. But that's where Zinger is going," said Mac.

"So?" asked Jonathan.

"We can't let him go down there and have him speak for us."

"Speak for us? You think they can speak Earth Common?" said Natasha.

"We have kids. You are not taking my family down there," said Jonathan.

"I'm sorry," said Mac.

"Who do you think you are?"

"I don't really know anymore."

He punched the engines into high speed and dashed after the escape pods. Maybe there was a chance he could get to them before they landed. Zinger had a head start but Mac had the faster ship. They were moving against the spin of the planet. More continents were coming into view. The biggest landmass was the most familiar, the horseshoe continent. So far every experience on Ronos had happened on that continent. It was where he, Lynn, and Raymond had crash landed. It was where Zinger's secret military base was set up. It was where Mac had taken the Passage people. It was where Zinger was heading now.

"I thought you said you weren't going to shoot them out of the sky?" said Scott.

"It was all talk," said Mac. "This ship doesn't have any weapons. Otherwise I totally would."

"So what's your plan?"

"I don't know."

"Do you ever have a plan?"

"I usually do better than this."

"Well, try ramming one of those pods."

Mac figured he could at least try. Ronos was getting bigger and soon they would all be in the atmosphere. The *Glenora* moved next to the nearest escape pod and Mac jerked on the controls to smash into it. The escape pod spun out of control and hit another one. They both exploded in momentary flames before being added to the space garbage already orbiting the planet. It had worked but slamming into other ships wasn't going to be an option for taking them all out. Red lights were flashing and the engines were fidgety now.

"We aren't going to be doing that again," said Scott.

"Maybe we got lucky and Zinger was on one of them," said Mac.

You managed to pick the one ship without weapons, Mac, said Zinger.

Why are you going to the surface?

Ram a couple more of those pods and I'll tell you.

Any more collisions would be mean disaster for the *Glenora,* and Zinger knew it. There was nothing Mac could do but follow them. They all entered the atmosphere.

Mac desperately wanted to know who had built the cities on Ronos but for some reason Zinger was heading towards the one continent devoid of life. Recent life, anyway. Ruined cities were scattered across the continent. The most predominant ruin, a toppled tower, stretched across a mountain like a giant finger had traced a straight line in the landscape. It was also possible that Zinger wasn't headed where he intended. The power was fluctuating on Mac's ship—the Mac Gas was eating away at the *Glenora.* The small escape pod Zinger was on had to be powerless by now. Mac had to shout above the hissing.

"We need to jump!"

"What?" said Clarissa.

"The gas is going to ignite the fuel. Jump or die. Trust me. The other Passage people survived."

"But then what happened to them?" asked Scott.

Zinger's pod exploded. A purple glow fell to the ground.

"Jump now. We all meet up at the fallen tower," said Mac.

He walked through the ship and started pushing people out before joining them as the final no-parachute skydiver. Mac landed in a shallow pool of foul-smelling liquid—rancid and slimy. Even though he could feel several broken bones in his body, the smell was worse than the pain. He forced himself out of the pool. As his body snapped back into place he looked around to get his bearings.

The night was darker here than on Earth. The only light Mac had was the subtle purple emanating from his own body interacting with the atmosphere. At first glance it looked like he was in the aftermath of a landslide. Except the rocks had all been cut to the same dimensions—most of them anyway, like giant bricks. Some of the white stone had designs chiselled into them. The stones were simply the things that jumped out first in the dim light. As his eyes adjusted to the darkness he saw metal beams, probably used as structural support in whatever building the rubble used to be.

Mac stumbled through the remains, avoiding the toxic pools. If this had ever been a city there was nothing left now. It reminded Mac of Northgate after the attack that had killed his family. Shadows danced on the white rock as Mac walked, reminding him of the monsters murdering the survivors of Northgate. He kept seeing monsters of his own and had to calm himself by remembering that Zinger glowed as well, so he wouldn't be able to sneak up. However, Mac still thought he saw shadows moving. He stopped. Listened. There were voices.

Quickly he looked around in the dark for a place to hide. There was a large stone with a carving of a tree on it. Leaning against it was a smaller block, forming a cave. Mac entered, but it wouldn't stop his glow from being seen in the dark. He listened to the voices, getting ready to attack. There were footsteps and then the sound of a rock being kicked and skipping across the ground.

"Stop it," said Clarissa. Mac heard them clearly now.

"What?" said Darren.

"When you disturb the water it smells even worse."

"I don't think it's water."

"It smells like decomposing remains."

"You think it'll make us sick?"

"We just survived falling out of the sky. I think we'll be okay."

Mac left his hiding place and saw them instantly. They were holding hands and avoiding the rock piles while they made their way to the tower rubble. They hadn't yet learned to mind speak. Mac hadn't had time to teach that yet.

"Guys."

Darren saw him first, "Mac. Where are the others?"

"Let's get to some higher ground and see if we can see them."

"Do you think the kids are all right?" said Clarissa.

"Yes. We only need to find them."

The farther they walked the higher they got up the side of the mountain. Every so often Mac looked back to try and spot the glows of the other people of Passage, but there were none. He had jumped out of the ship right after Darren and Clarissa, which is why they had found each other so fast. But the Parkingtons and the Glover family had gone first, so they could be anywhere.

"Stop. Let's wait here and see if we can see anyone's glow," said Mac.

The three of them waited in the remains of a small building. They climbed a wall and looked down the mountainside. Mac wondered why anyone would build a city on the side of a mountain. He knew this continent. There were plains next to jungles. They could have built on the plains, using the lumber from the jungle forest. Sure, there were trees on the mountains as well, but the terrain was steep. It was impractical to build a city here. The only thing more impractical was to build a tower at the top of a mountain. Yet there it was, and the abandoned city they were in looked like it was built around the tower. Maybe if they had settled somewhere else there would still be people living here.

Mac scanned the darkness. He was struck by the absence of any plant life. There must have been trees on these mountains at one point, but in the dark he didn't see any. Was it possible they had landed above the tree line? He didn't think they were that high up. And even above the treeline, there should have been other plants. But there was nothing. No moss on any of the rocks. No grass. No shrubs. Not even any dried-out remains of plant life.

"I don't see anything," said Darren.

"It's better if we stay out in the open in case they can see us," said Mac.

"But if they can see us then someone else might be able to."

"I don't think there's anyone else here."

Clarissa and Darren gave each other worried looks.

"Did you see someone?" asked Mac.

"No. But we thought we heard something," said Darren.

"Someone talking. It wasn't Earth Common."

"You didn't see anyone?"

"No. And when we stopped to listen the voices went away."

Mac looked into the darkness. The combined glow from the three of them made it more difficult to see. Their eyes were prevented from adapting to the dark. He saw nothing but could sense that they were being watched. There were two ways to be able to survive the atmosphere of Ronos without being burned up: injecting the liquid rock into the blood stream once—the side effect being the slight purple glow when in contact with Mac Gas—or drinking the liquid rock continually and not having a glow. Mac and the Passage people glowed. Raymond and his men did not. If there were still those two divisions on the planet then there could be dozens of men watching them right now.

"Did you hear that?" said Clarissa.

"What?"

"Screaming."

They all listened. When the wind blew in their faces they could hear the soft panicked scream of children. They were close.

"Why can't we see the glow?" asked Darren.

"They must be over the ridge." Mac pointed to his left. Instead of going up the mountain they needed to run across it.

After jumping down from the wall he started running. The screaming was getting louder. Darren and Clarissa struggled to keep up with him. They kept calling for him to slow down but there was no way Mac was going to do that. The Glover kids were still screaming. Where were their parents?

Mac got up to the next rise and looked down to see the three glowing figures of the kids. They were huddled together in an open area that must have been a park once, but now was spotted with pools of stomach-curdling liquid. He could also see two glowing people being dragged away by dark figures.

"Go keep the kids safe!" Mac said and charged after the nearest parent. He was too far away to tell who it was but ran with everything he had. It was his fault—he had brought them here. He hadn't been thinking clearly; he should have taken them to the *Lendrum* first. They were kids.

As he ran Mac picked up a rock and threw it at the attackers. One of the shadowy figures dropped the glowing person's leg momentarily. The others left him behind.

When Mac ran past the man tackled him to the ground. It was a man. Or at least it was a human. He had no hair, not even eyebrows. His face was completely white and he wore all black clothes. In his hand was a long blade. The memory of Raymond using a knife to stab Mac through the heart flashed in his mind. It was slightly more difficult to kill an enhanced human with a knife but it was still possible. He punched at the bald head but the ghostly figure used the blade to slice at Mac's limbs and then stabbed Mac through the chest.

Mac screamed in pain. The blade missed his heart but went all the way through his body, pinning him to the ground. That was the point—Mac enjoyed the pun but would have enjoyed it more if he wasn't going to die—he was pinned to the ground with his attacker on top of him. The attacker took out another blade and was now trying to separate his head from his body. Each slash was aimed at the neck. Mac fought him off. Each defensive block cut through his arms. They healed, but the man was moving so fast that he was getting more cuts than could be healed before the next blow came.

Mac had no other choice but to strain against the pain in his chest and get out of there. He couldn't pull himself up with the attacker on top of him. With his legs Mac rocked back and caught him unexpectedly around the neck. The pasty shadow rolled away but no real damage had been inflicted. Mac had to act quickly to survive. The children's distant screams were joined by his as he gripped the handle in the middle of his chest and pulled. Once it was out he wanted to take a moment to recover his energy but knew his attacker would be there any moment. When he looked back to see how much time he had he didn't see anything.

Mac started running. Now he had a weapon. The abductors would be able to see him coming. There was no way to avoid it. There were three glowing people being carried farther up the mountain. The closest one to Mac was one of the parents. He assumed.

He ran and once he was close enough he launched himself off a rock wall and stabbed his blade into the skull of a hairless spectre who screamed and fell to the ground. The person they were pulling away wasn't either of the Glover parents. It was Zinger. All six attackers dropped him and charged Mac. He ran. If he had noticed who it was sooner he never would have attacked them to begin with. Maybe they would leave him alone if he could get far enough away.

They didn't. While he couldn't see them in the dark he could hear their bodies moving across the stonework, crunching the pebbles, and splashing through the pools. The only thing interrupting the sound of their approach was the scattered screams coming from the Passage people being taken.

Mac was tackled to the ground. They weren't trying to kill him—not right away, at least. He couldn't understand why. Two people held each of his limbs and carried him. As much as he struggled there was nothing he could do to free himself. Once he thought he might be able to free one of his legs but one of the ghostly white abductors held a knife against his throat. The meaning was clear. Though cutting wouldn't be enough to stop Mac, decapitation would.

The group was heading up the mountain. That was as much as Mac could tell. He couldn't look around so he had no idea if they had left the ruined city or if they were being taken to a ship. The sound of footsteps increased and there was more of a dull light. He assumed he was being grouped with the others and if their lights were still there they hadn't been killed yet, which good. None of them made any noises. The farther along they went the faster their pace became, as if they were anxious to get to where they were going. If Mac didn't know any better it almost seemed like they were afraid.

Another noise echoed through the darkness. They all heard it. The people carrying him didn't stop, but moved even faster. The sound was similar to an engine. Mac knew the sound of most common engines used by the military, but this was something else. It was very low. Almost inaudible, he felt it more than heard it. He scanned the skies, but saw nothing.

Mac felt a rush of air—there was something up there. But it was running with no lights, or at least no lights that could be seen from the ground. There were a dozen snapping sounds—like whips going off above his head— and then several thumps on the ground nearby. More deep engine noises approached. It sounded like an army was coming.

The night was suddenly lit up by laser fire. It felt like Mac was going to have a seizure. There were a dozen men in armor from head to toe—almost like mech units. For all Mac knew they could have been robots and not men. It was hard to see in the flashing lights of their weapon fire.

The newcomers fired off lasers that vaporized their targets. Rocks were turned to ashes. Mac saw one of the bright blue lasers strike an abductor. It burned a hole in the man's chest and he fell backwards, dead on the ground. No one cared about Mac anymore. The shadow men didn't strike back with their blades. They each had long rifles. When they pulled the trigger a barrage of glowing orbs scattered and shot towards their targets. At first it seemed like there was something wrong but then each orb exploded. It was like shooting a dozen grenades at once. The shadows had much more destructive power.

Mac didn't know who he wanted to win. The newcomers were wearing so much armor that he couldn't tell if they were glowing or not. If they were glowing then he definitely would be on their side. It almost felt like they were coming to his defence.

There were battle cries coming from both sides of the fight. None of them were in Earth Common. Mac tried to find familiar words but couldn't hear any. It was also strange how there was so little communication back and forth. The sounds he was hearing were being repeated, the same phrase being yelled. He had never actively served on the front line but he had been on missions with the military and there had been a constant line of communication. Through Imps, yes, but there was still a lot of vocal chatter. He figured they must be using mind speak to communicate.

My name is Mac Narrad. I'm from Earth.

There was a brief pause in the battle—so brief that at first Mac thought he had imagined it. But then the battle continued, and around him it intensified. He had been heard and now the battle was centered around him. More snaps were heard coming from the ships above him. The ground shook when the objects landed. Something much bigger than soldiers had arrived. The shadow fighters were concentrating their firepower on the new target, which looked like a massive tank with a cannon on one end and a drill on the other—why would it need a drill?

An electric hum was coming from the drill tank as it powered up but it never got the chance to fire. A loud voice was broadcasting to everyone in mind speak. Mac heard it and could tell everyone else could too, because they all looked up.

Cease Fire! Cease Fire!

A light came on. Several lights, from ships high up in the clouds, showing the lay of the land clearly to Mac for the first time. He had been right—there was no foliage of any kind. The water he had fallen into looked green—like the plant life had melted together. The ruins he thought had been nothing more than rocks and girders were more sophisticated. He saw terminals and circuits, furniture, clothes, windows, and even books.

The fighting had stopped the second the lights came on from high above them. Mac couldn't see the source but he did have a clear look at the two sides of the conflict now. The ones who had abducted him—he hesitated to say men because he still couldn't tell the genders apart, or if they even had genders—wore all black. They had blades strapped to their backs and a leg holster for their guns. They were the whitest, most pale people he had ever seen, as if they had grown up never seeing the sun. That may have been accurate because when the light turned on they all reached down and put on heavily tinted glasses. Even then they still covered their eyes with their hands. Before their glasses were slipped on he had noticed their widely spaced eyes and how little they blinked. It creeped him right out. They had all the characteristics of humans, but there were little things that put them just left of normal.

The other side still looked very robotic, but at least one of them had taken off their helmet. Underneath was a woman with shoulder-length hair covered in sweat. She was looking at her enemies and making sure none of them made a move. There was definitely a glow coming off of her. Now that it was quieter Mac could hear a mechanical whirring noise every time she moved. Their suits were more than just armor. He wanted a closer look to see what they were really capable of, but figured that now wasn't the time.

The pasty army—there were three dozen soldiers revealed by the floodlights—were slowly backing away from the woman in the robotic suit and her friends. None of them were paying attention to Mac anymore. Everyone was looking up. He couldn't tell where the mind speak was coming from but he could hear the flapping of wings coming from above him. At first it caught him off guard but then he remembered what Vlamm, the alien impersonating Jace Michaels, had changed into.

Mac could see giant winged creatures circling the area. There were hundreds of them, maybe more. It was hard to count them while they moved. They were massive creatures, several feet taller than humans, and their wingspan was three times as long as their bodies. They had thick grey skin and monstrous heads, longer than it was wide, with a mouth that had multiple rows of teeth. Their eyes were wide and were placed so that Mac guessed the creatures had 360-degree vision. They looked like wild animals, made for hunting much larger game. The fact that they were wearing clothes helped Mac realize these creatures were intelligent enough to build a civilization alongside both the glowing and the pasty people.

Three winged creatures landed and folded their wings in behind them. The one in the middle—Mac had no idea what the differences between the males and the females were—had dark blue pants on with a yellow stripe up the outside of each leg, and no shirt. When his wings had been fully outstretched Mac had seen markings on them that resembled tattoos, but they were hidden now. Their wings were long but it was easy for the creatures to fold them tight against their backs. When they were folded up the wings looked like a fleshy board strapped to their backs, with two claw-like hands at the top. The other two Almics were dressed the same. If it was a military uniform it was much different from the armor of the other two civilizations. One of the Almics had black tattoos, some pictures, some words, over his entire torso. Mac thought that he spotted one depicting an Almic tearing apart another creature with his bare hands. He hoped that wasn't a depiction of an actual event. If the tattoos were meant to be intimidating, they were working.

The woman who had already removed her helmet stepped forward with a man who had also taken his off. He had a square head and inch-long hair that stuck straight up from his scalp even though he had sweat pouring down his face. The woman didn't look too impressed by the Almics, but the man looked like he might be a little afraid. His armor was different—the coloring was a little darker. Mac wondered if that meant he was the commanding officer. The man was looking straight at the lead Almic but said nothing. He was using mind speak and wasn't letting anyone else in on the conversation. The lead Almic roared.

The rest of the Almics landed, surrounding everyone— five for every other soldier. There were creatures surrounding each glowing person, pasty person, Passage person, and even Mac. He had no way to defend himself against so many. But they didn't attack. No one was attacking. No one was saying anything. There was a tense moment while everyone waited for someone else to make the first move. There were still sounds of flapping wings from above. Did these gargoyles have ships or did they fly everywhere?

What is your name?

The message had to be coming from one of Almics who had just showed up but Mac didn't know who was talking or if they were talking to him. It felt like it was a message for him, but when he hesitated he could hear others shouting in the distance.

"Darren."

"Miles!"

"The general of the armies of Earth."

The others must have replied but Mac couldn't hear it. He hoped, anyway. The other option was that they were dead.

What is your name?

That message was not broadcasted. Mac felt it echo inside his head.

"Mac. Narrad." Mac answered in Earth Common.

Macnerrad? The voice sounded expectant. They were looking for Mac. Hundreds of Almics had showed up to find him.

"Close enough. Do you know me?"

Are you Macnerrad?

"Who is looking for Mac Narrad?" Mac asked.

I am Volmere, leader of the Almics of Ronos. Are you Mac Narrad?

They knew him. Mac had no idea who this Volmere was or why they were looking for him. What interest could they have in him? They hadn't been responding to him because he was talking in Earth Common. He decided to respond in through mind speech.

I am Mac Narrad. And these are my friends. We didn't come here to harm you. We came here to stop the general.

That is not for you to decide right now.

Please. They're here because of me.

Mac heard a growl directed at him and stopped talking.

You will do as you are told, said Volmere. The "or else" was implied.

Volmere spoke again, broadcasting to everyone. *There are one hundred and fifty Almic warriors on the ground right now. There are five hundred in the skies and four thousand on their way. We will have more soldiers here faster than either of you. Your options are to either give us the interlopers or die. It is a simple decision and you have thirty seconds to make it.*

The pale soldiers didn't hesitate. They all dropped their weapons and ran back into the dark. The glowing soldiers hesitated. The large Almics surrounding Mac prevented him from seeing exactly what the glowing soldiers were doing but he could see them all gathering to the same spot. What was over there? Mac stood up but that made the Almics stand closer to him. One of them put a giant clawed hand on his shoulder to keep him from moving around too much. It was terrifying—Mac still didn't know if they were friend or foe. Their crocodile smiles and monstrous forms were not at all comforting to him.

You do not get them all, said a new voice.

Who are you? said Volmere.

I am Kallen. Leader of the Passengers.

Where is Taynner?

Killed three weeks ago in a Ray attack.

He was a good man.

He was. And he wouldn't leave here with nothing. We will take the general with us.

It is not safe.

Since when are you worried about the safety of the Passengers? You just threatened to kill us all if we didn't do what you asked.

This man is a threat to us all.

One man cannot destroy an entire planet.

Do not take the general.

Neither leader was in the mood to compromise. Mac could see the position that Volmere was in. Whether he admitted it or not, Volmere did care about the fate of the Passengers, which Mac figured were the glowing people. If he didn't care, he would simply kill them all to get to Zinger.

Mac shuffled his position and caught a glimpse of the two leaders. Volmere towered over Kallen. The Almic had his wings fully extended even though he had his feet firmly planted on the ground. It was a sign of intimidation. There were tattoos all along his wings, dark waves that didn't depict any scenes of carnage like Mac saw on some of the creatures around him. It gave Volmere a more animalistic look, like the stripes of a tiger.

The young leader of the Passengers was trying to be brave in his new position. Willing to put it all out there to show he was a real military leader. Looking at him, Mac knew he would not go back empty handed.

It was foolish to risk the life of his men to keep Zinger. Why him? Why did the Passengers need anyone? How did these people know Mac's name? There were so many questions banging around in Mac's head that he needed to start writing them down just so he could remember them.

More ships could be heard coming. The standoff was reaching a critical point. Kallen and the others were itching for their weapons. Mac figured pride ran thick on Ronos—they refused to go home with nothing.

Volmere roared. If he gave an order to his people Mac didn't hear it. The Almics all lifted off the ground, one of them grabbing on to Mac. The rest of the Passage people were taken as well. Only one was left behind. As Mac rose through the clouds he looked back and saw Zinger with a wicked smile on his face, as if he knew more than Mac and was happy to go with Kallen and the Passengers. A happy Zinger was never a good thing.

Chapter 5
Archipelago

The wind rushed against Mac's face as the ground rapidly disappeared behind clouds. The lights from above had been turned off and the world became dark again. Now it was easier to see the glow of the other Passage people being carried away to the same unknown destination. The lights had to be coming from somewhere. Ships, maybe. They had to have their own ships; there's no way they could travel the world on only their wings.

"Hey Mac!" Darren's voice stretched across the sky between them.

"What?"

"Are these the good guys?"

"I don't know."

"They don't look like good guys."

They didn't. But none of them had been hurt yet. The kids were even having fun, yelling and cheering as they went higher and higher.

"They can hear you," said Clarissa from even farther away.

"I don't think they can. They only talk in their heads," said Darren. "Can you understand me?"

He was looking up at the creature who was gripping him around the arms with its long claws. The creature didn't say anything back. Mac remembered Vlamm. He could only talk to humans in mind speak so Darren was probably right. When there was time the Passage people would need to be taught the same skill. Right now Mac was the only one who could speak for all of them.

Where are you taking us?

To the council, said Volmere.

Why?

To judge your worth.

That didn't sound good. What would happen if they didn't have enough worth? Did the kids have a chance? Were they all being judged, or just Mac? They knew who he was but he wasn't sure they knew all the human newcomers.

Do you know me? asked Mac.

We cannot speak of it right now.

And there was no more information coming out of Volmere. He had said *cannot*, not *will not*. As if he wanted to say something but couldn't. Was Volmere not the leader of the Ronos Almics? Maybe he wasn't the one who knew Mac and Zinger.

They flew through another cloud and the massive Almic ships were revealed. Their design was meant to imitate the look of their outstretched wings—like a giant, metal, bodiless bird. All along the wings were cannons glowing with energy; they were ready to fight. When they got closer, Mac could see there were ridges and creases every few feet. He wasn't why it looked like that: because there were a lot of moving parts to the ship that could be hidden away, if smaller ships could break off of it, or if the entire thing could transform into something else. One thing was sure, though—the whole vessel was built for war.

There were three of these ships. Volmere and the others flew over top to the landing pad along the spine where the two massive metal wings met. There was a party of Almics waiting. The landing group split into two. The dozen or so that were carrying the Passage people landed near the front of the craft while the hundreds of other troops landed nearer the rear. The landing process was executed with military precision. Stairs leading down into the ship opened up. The soldiers landed twelve across—the maximum width they could safely land in a line—and promptly entered the ship so as not to clog the landing area. They were so efficient at it that there was never a moment when a soldier was standing still. They were either flying, landing, or marching into the ship.

The Passage people were pushed together and surrounded by Almics. No one talked to them. It was the first time that Mac got a really good look at the others since the *Glenora*. Jonathan was holding his family close and watching the Almics vigilantly. He was ready to die protecting his family. He knew it wouldn't be much of a fight, but he was still willing to try. Natasha kept comforting her kids, telling them not to be scared and that everything was going to be okay. It was more for her than for them—the kids looked excited, like it was all a big adventure. Darren and Clarissa looked nervous but also excited. Mr. and Mrs. Parkington were trying to act natural, but they mostly looked awkward. If the Almics could speak Earth Common then the Parkingtons would probably be trying to make small talk with them, because that was the polite thing to do.

Scott walked over to Mac.

"Lynn was down here, wasn't she?" Scott said.

"She was in a ship headed towards Ronos. She must have been caught in the glow."

"Then she's gone," said Scott. "Why did you let her go?"

"I didn't do anything."

"You let her go."

"She went on her own, Scott. I tried to stop her."

"You should have never let her use her power. There's no way it would have worked," Scott looked around at all the creatures escorting them. "Where do you think these guys came from?"

"I don't know. They were here before but they were— unevolved. Animals."

"Less than a day under the glow and now they have war ships?"

"Yeah."

"Not to mention those other human-looking things out there."

"Human-looking?"

"I don't know if I would count them as human."

"You glow in the dark too, Scott."

"You made me like that. I didn't want to glow. But those other guys. They looked like they lived underground. Their skin was almost transparent."

"Yeah. They called them Rays and Passengers. It kind of makes me wonder."

"About what?"

"If the Passengers have anything to do with the Passage people."

"And the Rays?"

"Raymond Tysons. He was the leader of the soldiers who came down here to kill everyone."

Scott didn't know what to say. He looked at the passing clouds, trying to process what was going on, before finally saying, "How much time has passed?"

"What?"

"How long would it take to build a ship like this? Several months depending on how complicated it is on the inside—and it looks very complicated. Could be as long as a year. But that's nothing compared to how many people and creatures—"

"They're called Almics," said Mac.

"Right. Almics. We have seen hundreds of them. And a whole lot of Passengers and Rays. Did you recognize anyone?"

"No."

"How long does it take to build up a population like we've seen? Not just those people but also the cities we saw from the ship. There could be millions here, maybe billions. How much time has passed for that kind of population to build up?"

"You think...you think the time travel worked? You think that Lynn did it?"

"Do you think she is still alive?" said Scott.

"I hope so," said Mac.

Scott shook his head and gave Mac a dark look. It was clear that Scott would blame Mac if she wasn't alive.

When Mac looked at how much time had passed and how much Ronos had changed he didn't have very high hopes. Both men were grim. The youngest, Kendra, saw all the solemn faces on the adults and piped up.

"Don't be sad."

"Quiet, Kendra," said Natasha. "It will all be okay. Don't worry."

"I'm not worried."

"Yeah, didn't you guys hear?" said Sofia.

Mac turned to the kids and crouched down. "Hear what?"

"They're nice guys."

"How do you know that?"

"Those monsters told us," said Kendra.

"They aren't monsters," said Sofia. "Her name was Sellet. She was carrying Miles."

"She was nice," said Miles.

"She told us stories. She said that we were going to see the island leaders and that we were honoured guests. Kings and queens."

"Which one is Sellet?"

Miles pointed. The female Almic's back was towards them. Of course there had to be a difference between the males and females of this species but he couldn't immediately tell what it was. They wore the same clothing. Neither of them had hair. The grey color of their skin might have been a little different. Sellet had slightly darker skin, but other than that Mac couldn't tell any difference. Maybe it was in the wings. But she—like the rest that surrounded them—had her wings tucked in behind her, so he couldn't be sure.

Sellet? he asked.

I am not permitted to speak to you, said a feminine voice in his head, very soothing. Mac could see why the kids felt better about what was going on than their parents did.

But you spoke to the children.

I am not permitted to speak to you.

Mac turned to the Passage people—was it too much to assume he could call them Passengers as well?

"How many of you guys know how to mind speak?" he asked.

"Talk with our minds? Like they're doing to us?" asked Darren.

"We can do that?" asked Clarissa.

"Yes. Let me teach you."

Before Mac could start the lesson something about the ship changed. There was a buzz of electricity. The hairs on his arms were standing on edge and the air felt different. Thicker and still. He looked over at Clarissa, whose hair was full of static. She was brushing at it with her fingers, frustrated. Chairs rose up out of the floor.

Sit, said Volmere.

Each of the humans sat down and automatic safety belts pinned them to their seats. The Almics continued to stand around them, facing away, looking for outside threats. They weren't making sure the humans didn't attack; they were making sure nothing attacked the humans.

The ship started moving faster. Clouds were whooshing past but Mac felt no air on his face. No one's hair blew in the wind.

"We can't be moving," said Jonathan.

"We'll fall off! They need to let us in the ship," said Natasha.

"There's a force field. I felt it activate. As long as they keep flat we'll be okay. Notice how you can't even feel the air on your skin? That's the force field blocking it," said Scott.

"You seem sure about yourself."

"I've worked with them before. We're fine."

"I thought you made ammunition?" asked Mac.

"Before that we made ships. We used force fields for emergency hull breaches. It's good tech, but we weren't allowed to research much."

"Figures."

"You going to teach us to mind speak?" said Darren.

"Yeah."

They were quick to catch on—the kids especially. They figured it out way before the adults did. Once they had a firm grasp Mac asked them to try and talk to Sellet and get some more information out of her.

Kendra stared at Sellet and thought the words Mac had coached her to say. *Why did you take us?*

You are special, young one, said Sellet. Kendra relayed the messages.

What makes us special?

You are from beyond the glow.

How much time has passed? asked Kendra.

Since what?

Since the glow started.

These are not things you need to worry about, young one.

"She's not answering me anymore," said Kendra. "She keeps saying the same thing over and over again. 'These are not things you need to worry about.' "

"At least ask her how long until we get to where we're going," said Scott.

After a moment Kendra reported back, "We'll be there soon."

"Soon" was relative. It was several more hours before the ship started to descend out of the clouds. Night had turned to day. Mac could see a visible change in Volmere, Sellet, and the others when the light touched them. They relaxed. Their muscles loosened up and they moved around instead of staying in one spot. Mac had thought that Sellet would be more open to giving the kids information but she stayed silent. Her role had been to comfort the kids and make sure they weren't scared, but now it was obvious they were fine.

The belts held them in their chairs but they were near enough the edge of the ship that they had a little view of what was underneath them. In the daylight all Mac could see was ocean, miles of water in every direction. When the ship started to slow and move out of the clouds he could see what he thought were little islands. He thought they would quickly fly over the tiny landmarks but the archipelago was their destination. There were thousands of islands. A dozen of them had tall mountain peaks jutting into the sky. There was steam coming out of one. None of them had snow. Below the tree line was a jungle green so dense that Mac couldn't see the ground. The most obvious—and confusing—thing was that there were no cities. Yet he could see Almics flying around the volcanic mountain peaks—thousands of them. The absence of buildings or infrastructure made them look like a wild tribe of gargoyles.

"There's no buildings," said Scott.

"I don't see any either," said Mac.

"Maybe they all live on this ship."

"But there's thousands more down there."

The ship descended toward one of the largest islands. Lower and lower. The volcano was towering over them now and the ship was still moving down. Then they were landing, underground. For every Almic up top, there were ten times as many below. As the ship rested on the landing pad and the island closed up above them, Mac could see into corridors and rooms that were packed with Almics. It was a massive underground city. The ceiling wasn't made up of dirt and roots; the sun was still shining through. Mac didn't know how that was possible and he couldn't stop staring at it.

Not all is as it seems, said Volmere.

"You can talk to us now?"

No. Not many humans have seen what you see right now.

"How many humans?"

Before you? Only one.

It was hard to tell if the monster with the crocodile face was smiling, but the corners of his mouth were vibrating and his lips were tight, as if Volmere was proud. The force field was turned off. The safety belts were released and everybody stood as the chairs sunk back into the ship. Volmere, Sellet, and the other Almics picked up Mac and the other Passage people and carried them off the ship, then escorted them down one of the corridors. The newcomers gawked at everything as they passed and the gawks were returned. Everywhere they went they were never alone, never secluded. All the walls were partially transparent in the public areas of this city. Mac instantly understood why—these were creatures that could fly. For some reason they were hiding underground and so they were trying to make the best of it. Letting sunlight in somehow—he still didn't understand how that worked—and creating the illusion of wide open spaces in a cramped underground city by using translucent building material.

The material wasn't completely translucent so it wasn't possible to see straight from one side of the city to the other. Mac could only see through five walls before it became too difficult to make out details. There were some private areas—they passed rooms that no one could see through. Plus there was so much going on around them that it was hard to stay focused on one thing.

It was so odd to see Almics doing human things. They passed a room where a meeting was taking place. The large creatures sat around a table in oversized chairs built to accommodate their wings. One of them stood away from the table, pointing at an image being projected on a non-translucent part of the wall. In another room a couple Almics were preparing a meal. It was heavy on the meat. The red chunks looked uncooked from where Mac was—simply pulled from a drawer and cut up. One of them mixed the meat with some greenery. The other slathered it with some yellow paste. They both ate with their hands.

Mac also noticed that not all the Almics dressed the same. There were still a good number of them who wore what he now figured was a military uniform—the dark blue pants. The ones not in the military wore as wide a variety of clothes as was ever found on Earth. Pants and shirts, all different colors. Some clothing covered their wings as well, but the more popular choice was to keep them free and have the shirt button or zip around them. About half of the civilian Almics were wearing brimless hats in soft tones. There was less style variation in these hats. The only change he could see was the color and the type of stitch around the bottom of the cap. The hat was big enough to cover their ears, but it wasn't cold enough to warrant such clothing. No one in the military wore a hat.

They got to an elevator but when the doors opened Mac realized it was only the shaft. Almics were flying up and down it. Mac and the other humans were each picked up by a gargoyle. There were so many creatures in the shaft it was amazing that there were no collisions. Mac wondered if the Almics had to take flying lessons, liked he'd had to take hover car lessons. The first time he'd gotten into a car accident—which was technically Janelle's fault, he had protested to his parents—the car keys had been taken away from him. What happened when an Almic teenager got in trouble flying? The parents couldn't take their wings away. Maybe the Almics who had their wings covered were younger and didn't have permission yet to fly whenever or wherever they wanted.

They were flying up into the volcano. There was no way it could be active and Mac was starting to doubt it was even real. How many of the islands in the archipelago were artificial? At the top of the shaft they stood on a landing platform. A short—still taller than any human—Almic sat on a stool. One of his wings was taller than the other. When he saw Volmere he stood up and started walking towards them. With each step he limped on the same side as the drooping wing. This was a crippled Almic, yet he still wore the military uniform of dark blue pants. He had a thin computer pad in his hand that he was now touching, looking at Volmere occasionally. No words were said out loud beyond the growl of hello—Mac guessed—they had given each other. Everything was in mind speak.

Did you see that pad? Scott asked Mac.

What about it?

The limping guy, he has a computer pad so thin and flexible he can roll it up like a piece of paper. He had it rolled up when we first got up here.

Seriously?

Yeah. I saw it. Incredible.

Scott was a tech guy and was now completely surrounded by new technology. At least he wasn't still brooding over Lynn's fate. Mac didn't have much hope for her. Too much time had passed—somehow, even though it had only been less than a day.

The lame Almic started walking to the big double door at the other end of the landing pad. Volmere and the others followed. The walls on this level, the highest level the shaft went to, were completely opaque. There were lights recessed into the walls and ceiling. The door opened into a cavernous room. In a semicircle around them were tables and chairs, stadium seating with at least a dozen levels. Every seat was filled with Almics. There was plenty of room for some of the Almics to fly around, but none of them did.

This was the council that Volmere had been talking about. Mac suspected that the reason they didn't fly was because they were much older than any other gargoyles they had seen so far. They had the same signs of aging that humans had. Loose, sagging skin, wrinkles, shaking in some, discoloration and spots—several of them had canes leaning against the tables and chairs.

The lame Almic held his hands wide and broadcast to everyone in the room.

Honorable and wise council of the Almics of Ronos, the leader of our flying army has returned with strangers from outside of our planet. They were being attacked by our enemies, the Rays and the Passengers. Volmere freed them and brought them back here to have them share their knowledge with us. The truth about the disappearance of the glow will soon be revealed. Oh honorable and wise council, if it be thy will. Please allow these humans to stand before you to be questioned, their worthiness to be determined.

A fist pounded against a table and an Almic dressed all in black, with a large scar around his left eye and a clawed hand missing from one of his wings, growled and roared.

Another voice spoke. It was a new voice, not the voice of the lame Almic.

Zaxxer, speak for all to hear.

The scarred Almic responded but Mac still didn't hear anything.

They are already in the room. They have already seen our faces. The damage you are worried about is unavoidable at this point.

To all our folly, said Zaxxer. His whiny voice did not match his rough-and-tumble exterior.

The lame Almic continued. *Do you accept these guests, oh honorable and wise ones?*

We accept, Lew. Return to your post, said the Almic who had been arguing with Zaxxer.

Lew bowed and spread his wings as far as he could in a sign of respect, one of his wings less extended than the other. Then he stood up and walked out the room to stand guard on the platform. What one Almic would be able to do against a group of attackers determined to get in, Mac did not know. Volmere pushed the humans from behind, getting them to move into the middle of the room where they would be in full view of the council.

Mac got a better look at the creatures that were about to judge his worthiness. The scar on Zaxxer's face was not unique. More than half of the council had visible scars. All of them were wearing shirts so there were probably more scars that couldn't be seen. The leaders of the Almics had seen a lot of conflict in their days. They were not a soft crowd.

One of the Almics spread his wings and landed in front of the humans. He wore a long red cloak that dragged on the ground behind him. He held a spear in one hand. By far he was the youngest-looking one in the council but he still had more wrinkles and spots than Volmere.

I am Glinter, speaker for the council. What are your names?

Mac stepped forward. He made sure everyone in the room could hear him. *I am Mac Narrad*—there was a murmur through the audience but Mac continued—*This is Darren and Clarissa. This is the Glover family, the father Jonathan, the mother Natasha, and their kids Miles, Sofia, and Kendra. This is Mr. And Mrs. Parkington. And this is Scott Ryder.*

A Ryder and Macnerrad. Does this give them validity, Zaxxer? Glinter asked.

Their information will determine their fate, said Zaxxer.

Indeed. Macnerrad. You speak for them?

Mac looked back at the group and got nods. None of them wanted to be responsible for what was happening.

I do, said Mac.

Then we shall begin. There is a certain amount of anonymity desired by the council. If desired, their questions will be filtered through me and I will broadcast to everyone. First question: where do you come from?

Here we go, thought Mac. *We come from the planet Earth.*

Glinter had to wait a moment before he asked his next question because he was getting so many questions from the council at the same time.

Another planet, like Ronos?

Yes, said Mac.

Outside of the glow?

Yes.

We cannot not see another planet.

It's billions of miles away.

Zaxxer growled again and yelled so even Mac could hear, *He is a liar. That is impossible. All we have known is the glow. There is nothing beyond it.*

Volmere spoke up. *And yet it is gone. It is time to know more.*

This is a plot by our enemies. These people are Passengers. They cannot be trusted.

The glow was always meant to end.

That is not what the colony ship teaches us.

Colony ship? How could a colony ship have landed on the planet with the glow? Mac or Zinger or somebody on the space station would have seen it. What colony ship were they talking about?

This is not a debate on the purpose of the colony ship. We are determining the worth of the humans before us, said Glinter. To Mac he asked, *Why are you here on Ronos?*

I came to stop another human, a man named General Zinger, from hurting other people.

Why did he come to Ronos? Who does he want to hurt?

Honestly, he doesn't think he's hurting anyone. He is the military leader of our people but he thinks to save us he needs to forcibly bend all of us to his will. He would kill us all if it meant saving himself and those loyal to him.

You are actively plotting against the leader of your people?

He has killed millions of humans, including my family. If we lose the war it will be because of him.

The war with the Rays?

No. I do not know the Rays.

There are no Rays on Earth?

No.

Who are you at war with?

Well, this was complicated. Mac was about to blurt out that they were at war with the Almics but he wasn't sure he was at war with the Almics in the room. Did the council know there was an invading fleet on the way?

There is a fleet of ships entering our space, billions of soldiers who are killing or capturing every human they come across. They're fighting through us...to get here.

The council members, though Mac expected them to all be squirming in their seats at this news, were calm and collected. The news he had delivered did not faze them.

Why do they want to come here?

They believe this is their home.

It is their home, said Zaxxer.

You are here to stop them? asked Glinter.

This was the pivotal question. They knew about the other Almics. Mac had just admitted to being at war with Almics so did that mean he was at war with all Almics? He was starting to feel like he had led the Passage people to slaughter.

I'm here to make sure no more humans have to die, said Mac.

What happened to the glow? asked Glinter.

I don't know.

Do you work for the Passengers or the Rays?

Neither.

Who is Linryder?

You know Lynn? broke in Scott.

There was a flurry of movement in the council. Zaxxer screeched and flapped his wings. Glinter spoke loudly in everyone's ear.

Macnerrad speaks for you. You are a guest here. No human has addressed the council before. This is unprecedented. Macnerrad speaks for you and no one else will. If you speak out of turn again you will prove you are of no worth, incapable of respect, and you will be silenced permanently.

Scott's eyes went wide. His desperation to find out what happened to Lynn was no match for the fear these monstrous creatures could instill in him.

Who is Linryder? Answer the question, said Glinter.

A friend. Ally. She is not our enemy.

Why would she help us? We are Almic.

She…must have realized that we're on the same side. The other Almics. The Invaders. They are coming here and they have destroyed civilizations across the galaxy to get here. They're not going to want to share this planet with anyone.

Are the Almics of Ronos in danger?

Yes.

Can you prove it?

No.

Are you our enemy?

No.

You said yourself, you want to stop the Almics. We are Almics.

I came down here to stop Zinger. I didn't even know you were down here.

Now you know. Are we enemies?

No. We are on the same side of this conflict. Stop the Invaders before they kill everyone between them and this planet.

Zaxxer couldn't take it anymore. He flew out of his seat and circled the room while flapping his massive wings. The whole time he was growling intimidation. If he was mind speaking—and Mac had no reason to doubt it—then the Passage people were not privy to it. The aged Almic smashed into the ground and started to violently point his finger at each human as if accusing them of some great travesty. Then he stormed out the room towards the shaft.

Glinter spoke. *The council will reconvene when all its members are present. The prisoners will be left in the hands of the military. Keep them close, Volmere.*

Yes, sir, said Volmere.

The humans were led away from the council, like prisoners being escorted back to their cells. As they flew down the shaft—going from the very top to the very bottom— Mac asked Volmere a question.

Did they decide our worth? Asked Mac.

Most of them have made up their minds already but they haven't come to a unanimous decision, said Volmere.

They knew Lynn, said Scott.

Linryder.

Yes! Do you know her? Is she still alive?

It's complicated.

How can it be complicated? Dead is dead. She is or she isn't.

That depends on how you define being alive. Be patient, Ryder. All will be explained soon.

76

Volmere was more open to talking now so Mac decided to ask some more questions. *How long has it been since the glow started?*

The glow has always been.

The glow hasn't even been going on for a day yet. You're older than one day, right?

Yes.

Mac had him. *How long is a day?*

Volmere only laughed. *You are not as clever as you think. I am one of the few Almics who knows your customs.*

Because Lynn taught you, right?

You should hear it from her.

Chapter 6
There is a Plan

The look on Scott's face was a mix between confusion and jubilation. She was alive—somehow—at least enough to pass on information. He might be able to talk to her. The Passage people were still being carried down the shaft. Once they reached the bottom all the Almics but Volmere and Sellet left. It was still hard to tell the difference between them but Mac knew Volmere had been carrying him and the only other Almic was staying with the children. She was holding two of the kids' hands and even had her wings slightly extended to almost wrap them. It was a comforting gesture. Natasha was starting to lighten up but she still kept a nervous eye on Sellet. Jonathan was starting to catch his children's excitement.

We wait here, said Volmere.

They weren't anywhere. It looked like a lobby of an underground building. There were several large doors leading inside but none of them, or the walls, were transparent. There was writing above the main double doors. Mac recognized the writing but not what it said. It looked similar to what was carved into the walls around the beacon. For a moment he thought that maybe the beacon was on the other side but that was impossible—it was in two pieces way back on the horseshoe continent. One segment was significantly smaller but it was still trapped underground in a lake of Lynn Rock. It wouldn't be easy to move across the ocean to the archipelago.

What are we waiting for? asked Mac.

Behind those doors we keep unwanted guests and traitors. That is where you are supposed to be but that is not where you are needed.

There was a hum and then a ship came out of the shaft and landed. It was big enough for all of them to get inside, even the two Almics. It was cylindrical with a shiny silver skin. Its engine ran on a track that moved around the entire ship so that the ship didn't have to move around in the shaft, making it easier to get through the crowds. As they boarded Mac noticed there were no windows—no one would be able to see Volmere sneaking the humans around. Mac felt like that was a good sign; Volmere was willing to take risks for them and was defying his orders.

How much farther? said Scott.

We have to go to another island. This ship is fast. We will be there soon.

The Almics were obsessed with keeping secrets, Mac was starting to realize. He thought the ship would shoot outside and fly quickly to another island but they travelled underwater. The ocean was crowded with other ships. From the air the Archipelago looked wild and primitive. Did anyone really know what the Almics were capable of?

They stopped their ship in the middle of the ocean. Volmere didn't move a muscle. The kids were talking back and forth and Volmere turned and growled at them. The ship fell completely silent. He pushed some buttons on the console in front of him and turned a dial. Over the ship's speakers there was a loud buzzing. No one made a noise. Sellet and Volmere both had the nose of their long heads straight in the air, listening. Mac didn't hear anything.

You were a soldier, Macnerrad? said Volmere.

Yes.

Do you hear anything wrong?

All Mac could hear was the buzz of the volume being turned all the way up.

No, he said.

Do you see anything?

No. What's wrong?

I thought I saw a ship out there.

There's lots of ships out there.

Our ships run with the current as a disguise. Our people can see the movement of the water. There was something out there that didn't move with the current.

No fish out there?

Yes.

Big fish? Whales?

I'll send a ship to confirm.

Volmere didn't want to say any more. Mac looked to Sellet. *It's the ocean. Shouldn't there be fish all over the place?*

Yes. It's just one of his paranoid theories, said Sellet.

About what?

An attack. He's the leader of our military and he is dividing his time between a dozen different projects and divisions. Ever since the glow disappeared he's been preparing for the Rays or the Passengers to try and make a move. He's thinking about moving the colony ship.

Colony ship?

It's what the fighting is all about. Don't worry about him and his theories. He already sent a ship out to investigate. They'll find a whale pod and come back. Everything will be okay.

Okay.

The island they were going to was much smaller than the one they left but it was still heavily guarded. The underwater door—with a force field that kept back the water—had two laser cannons on either side. The barrels pointed at the ship as it entered.

The docking bay was small, barely enough room for the ship to fit. There was an Almic waiting for them. He wore dark pants and his wings had been dyed red. Mac didn't know if it was a tattoo or something that could be washed off.

Where is she? Volmere asked when they all got off.

In her office, said the red-winged Almic.

Thank you, Witt. Ryder.

Scott stepped up to Volmere. *Yeah?*

She's not the way you remember her.

Lynn is here then!

Prepare yourself.

How bad is it?

She will not look how you think she should look.

Enough, I need to see my wife. Scott took off through the door, yelling for her. "Lynn! Lynn!"

Volmere's strides were so long he could easily keep up with the scampering man. Scott threw open every door but there were only empty rooms. This new island wasn't anything like the last one. The only Almic they had seen so far was Witt. The last room wasn't empty—inside was lab equipment. Tables of supplies. Computers. Lights. Junk stacked against the wall. The room was so busy and cluttered it was difficult to focus in on any one thing, except for one human female with her back to them.

"Lynn!" Scott yelled out as he ran towards her.

Mac could spot the differences. The hair was platinum blonde and long. Her body was much thinner—like eat-a-sandwich-already thinner and through her tight shirt he could see muscles crawling across her back and the definition in her arms. She was much taller but the length was all in the torso. This was not Lynn's body.

And yet she turned when Scott called. Her thin face still erupted into a smile and her wide eyes were still full of recognition. She opened her arms to invite him in for an embrace but he stopped short.

"Who are you?" asked Scott.

"Lynn. It's me, Lynn. You have no idea how excited I am that I can—"

"Who are you?"

Scott was starting to back away. He had been told she would be different but he had been expecting battle scars. She was supposed to still be recognizable, not a completely different person.

"I can explain everything. Just let me say one thing. I need to tell you one thing," said Lynn.

"What?" asked Scott.

"I love you. I've been waiting so long to tell you that. I love you, Scott. After all this time I never forgot you. Never. I was so worried that it had been too long. That maybe we would never see each other again and when we did, I'd realize I'd forgotten what you looked like, but I didn't. I still remember."

Mac stepped out from behind Volmere and asked, "You're Lynn?"

"Mac. Yes. It's me. Thank you for bringing Scott."

"You're not Lynn."

"Ask me what only she would know."

"Where did we first meet?" asked Mac.

"What did we eat at our wedding?" asked Scott.

Lynn—the woman claiming to be Lynn—didn't hesitate, "Mac, we met in the ruins of Northgate. And I didn't have a bite to eat at our wedding. The first thing we did when we left was go through the drive-thru. I know how I look and there's no easy way to explain things to you so…I'm just going to have to show you. Remember that I'm on your side."

Then she dissolved and became a cloud of particles swirling in place but taking no form. Mac instantly knew what she was talking about.

"You're a swarm," said Mac.

I had to do it to stay alive, said Lynn.

"You've become exactly what we're trying to stop."

Come on, Mac. Just because I can swarm doesn't mean I'm one of them. I'm still human. I'm still on your side.

Lynn came back together. She was smiling but it was a tentative smile, hoping that the people she cared about weren't about to grab their pitchforks and storm the castle.

Scott threw up his hands and shrugged his shoulders, defeated. "It's not like we have much of a choice anyway. You might as well tell us everything. Start from the beginning. Tell us how you became a swarm."

Lynn started, "It all comes back to the beacon. It's the reason for everything. It's the reason I was able to start the glow in the first place—although it wasn't what I thought it was. It's the reason the aliens want to come back here, and through it I was able to learn to swarm. Swarming is a technology—remember that. Generations ago—when the Ryder family was trapped on Ronos—they found the beacon. The pull had been activated and they couldn't leave the planet. They thought they were trapped there until one of them figured out a way to reprogram it to obey a certain genetic code. It had been programmed for Almics but he changed it to respond to his own genetics and was able to create a way off the planet.

"The beacon is entirely organic. It looks like a machine, looks like a ship that runs on electricity, but it doesn't. So when my ancestor, the first Ryder, reprogrammed it he unknowingly solidified his descendants as some of the most important people in the galaxy. We are the only ones who can control it. That's how I was able to utilize its time-travel abilities."

"But you didn't time travel," said Mac.

"What I thought was activating the time travel power was actually starting the glow. Have you heard what the Almics call the beacon? We call it a beacon because the aliens are following its signal to get to Ronos but that's only a small part of its abilities. The Almics call it a colony ship. It was sent to Ronos to turn it into a new Almic home world. Ronos was supposed to be terraformed, able to support life. The time travel was real but it didn't do what we thought: it could only wrap the planet in a cocoon to protect it from outside harm until it could fully develop. I started the glow. I started the time cocoon."

"How much time has passed?" asked Mac.

"As far as I can tell, 20,000 years."

"You've been alive for 20,000 years?" said Scott.

"Technically less but the details aren't important anymore now that the glow is gone. For a while I was stuck in the upper atmosphere just watching what was happening down here. Time didn't move as fast for me when I was there. The clouds had different layers. But then the Almics came up and rescued me. They could see my ship and wanted to know what it was. Their journey to get to me was like the humans' first journey to Mars. It took decades of preparation and years of travel. But they found me and expected answers from me.

"I told them everything I knew about the war, Zinger, and the alien Invaders. Back then they believed me. But enough time passed and eventually the story of the end of the glow and the coming of the aliens faded. I was allowed access to the colony ship before I fell out of favor and was able to learn how to swarm."

"Wait a sec," said Mac. "Where did the Ronos Almics come from?"

"The colony ship," said Lynn.

"The Almics I saw before the glow were primitive animals, not a highly advanced society. They were trying to eat us."

"The colony ship had two contingency plans for population development. One was naturally, through evolution. One was through clones. The important thing to remember is nothing on Ronos is going as planned. You remember how the ship looked when we first saw it, Mac; that thing was a mess. It's no wonder it didn't work like it was supposed to. When it landed it was supposed to completely transform the planet into something the Almics could survive on. But it didn't work. It made the gas but it didn't get properly distributed into the atmosphere. There's other evidence. On the Dead Continent—what you would know as the horseshoe continent—there's an unnaturally straight line cut into the ground. Remember that from when we first got here? That was part of the first stage of the terraforming. I don't know what Ronos was supposed to end up looking like but the colony ship is too broken to finish it now. Because it's broken, the evolutionary development of the Almics started first and was happening for a few thousand years before the cloning started."

"Evolution takes longer than 20,000 years," said Scott.

"The glow was supposed to last for longer. Either way. The evolution of the Almics was stopped a long time ago when the clones took over. The colony ship also gave them a boost in knowledge and technology. It is the source of all knowledge on the planet. All three civilizations rely on the information learned from it, but they don't use it to better their lives—they all use it to find new ways to kill each other."

"The Rays are descendants of Raymond and his men," said Mac.

"Yep. That man's hate has inspired all the Rays to think they've been hard done by and are the only ones who deserve to live on Ronos. Right now they all live underground. They would be at an extreme disadvantage if they didn't have the largest section of the colony ship."

"Who has the other part?" asked Mac.

"We do. Or, the Ronos Almics do. Volmere snuck me back in here after they stopped believing me useful. I've been studying it covertly. Because of me Volmere was one of the few Almics who wasn't surprised when the glow ended."

"The Passengers? Are they—"

"Descendants of your hometown? Yes."

"From what I saw they're obsessed with war like everyone else."

"Only out of necessity. If they were shown that were was no more threat they would drop their weapons in a heartbeat. The same with a good portion of the Almics. Soon enough."

"Soon enough what?" asked Scott.

Lynn looked surprised, like she just realized that Scott didn't know what this conversation was all about. "Soon the wars will all be over. I know how to stop the Invaders."

Apper and Mennick were two of Volmere's most trusted soldiers, which is why they couldn't understand why they were the ones who were sent out to chase down the fish. Their ship—shaped like a wide flat ribbon that moved with the current, with a powerful but silent engine on the back that wouldn't disturb any animal life—streaked away from a military island and out to where Volmere claimed to have seen something suspicious.

He always sees something when they let him pilot his own ship, said Mennick.

You saying they should keep him under lock and key on his own island? asked Apper.

No. But he would like that, I think.

There might actually be something out here.

Mennick checked the scanners. The reason they had taken the ribbon ship, which was almost like piloting a flattened eel, was because it had the widest and most precise scanners. Whatever Volmere had seen out here, they would be able to find it. Unfortunately, right now there was nothing on the scanners.

As long as we're doing what we're ordered to do. That's what counts. Even if there's nothing out here, said Apper.

You didn't hear then, I take it.

They made a decision?

Yeah.

Apper knew what that meant. As soon as the glow had gone down, Volmere—who had somehow been preparing for this—announced that a scout ship was being sent off planet. That word, off planet, barely even registered with the soldiers who had been there for the announcement. Some of Volmere's soldiers were going to be the first Almics—the first anyone—to leave the system. More than anything Apper wanted to be on that ship. But they had already made their choice. No doubt the crew had already been notified, and Apper had received no notification.

Do you know when they leave? asked Apper.

No. All the details are being kept under wraps. If I were Volmere I wouldn't even tell the council. I would just launch.

Then they've probably left already.

Probably.

Do you know who he chose?

I have my guesses.

Vissia?

If he can't go then I think he would at least want part of that honor to stay in his family. His daughter will be more famous than he is.

The sensors started beeping and Apper studied the screen while Mennick took over piloting the ship. At the very edge of the sensors a group of whales were being picked up. It felt like a double blow. Not only had Apper not been picked for a career-making mission but now his wild goose chase had been nothing more than a wild whale chase.

Whales, said Apper.

Let's just turn around, said Mennick.

It's not procedure. We need to get closer and see if they've been tagged. Or, at the very least, see what kind they are.

We'll go see what kind they are but I'm not tagging whales today. I want to be close to the Archipelago.

Fine.

Apper knew that part of the reason that he was on fish duty was because he was the animal expert in his unit. He would be able to tell what was going on with these whales, whether they were looking for some grub or just passing through on their way to somewhere else. They were close enough now that he could count them. It was a big pod— over a hundred whales. They were spread out, but according to the sensors, they were coming closer together, slowly.

Hmm, said Apper.

What?

It's the biggest pod I've ever seen. Especially in this part of the ocean. This is cooler water for big mammals like them. Not a popular destination.

So what?

I don't know. Their swimming pattern is a little odd as well.

Should we call it in or should we just blow them out of the water?

I don't want to fill out the paperwork for the missing ammunition because we decided to shoot a suspicious whale.

We're far enough away that no one would see us.

They'll count the shells when we get back.

We'll use lasers. What kind of fish are they, anyway?

They're whales. Fish don't get that big. And I think they're...spotted whales. Maybe.

Maybe?

Get closer.

The pod was still moving closer together. Whales didn't normally do that; they needed room to swim. They were behaving so strangely. Warning bells were starting to go off in Apper's head. Something was wrong.

Kill the engine. Quick. Turn off all the noise on our end.

Mennick turned everything off and Apper switched on the sonar. If these were whales then he wanted to hear whale songs. He turned the volume up and waited. At first, that was exactly what they heard, whale songs. But Apper recognized the problem immediately: If these were spotted whales then they should have a much deeper tone. The sound he was listening to right now was lilly whales.

There's something wrong. These aren't whales, said Apper.

They look like whales to me.

Trust me, they aren't. Open a channel back to base.

Mennick turned the communications back on and tried to radio base. But all he got was static.

What's wrong? Apper asked.

I had a connection and then it vanished.

We're being jammed.

Over the speakers there were clanging noises intermingled with the lilly whale song.

These aren't whales, said Mennick.

Get us back to base. Now.

As soon as the engines turned back on the masquerade was over. The whales were now moving like ships. They all turned towards the ribbon ship and fired. Lasers surged out of the mechanical whales and boiled the water between the two enemies. Apper and Mennick hardly had time to process what was going on, let alone prevent it, before their ship was torn apart and their remains sent to the crushing depths of the ocean.

"You can end the war?" said Mac.

"Yes. I figured it out a long time ago, actually, but it's tricky. There's a plan but I wanted to be sure about everything. I couldn't implement it until after the glow ended. We'll get started in a few hours; I just have to set some things up."

Mac couldn't be happier to hear that. He felt an intense weight lift off his shoulders. Up till now it had felt like humanity's fate depended on his actions. Now Lynn was in charge. She was the one with a plan. She was the one who knew how to end the war before the Invaders even got to Ronos. It would all be over soon enough and Mac couldn't have been happier. A sudden noise caught everyone's attention—a stack of bundled wires toppled over as the Glover kids stood sheepishly near it. They saw the looks of everyone around them and ran back to their parents. Scott went to help Lynn pick them back up.

"What is this room?" asked Scott.

"My lab-slash-workshop. It's where I try to utilize what I learn from the colony ship," said Lynn.

Mac was walking around the room when he noticed the body floating behind a rack of metal scraps. It looked exactly like Lynn's new body and it was floating above a lit-up blue platform. This was her emulator.

"Is this her?" asked Mac. Lynn looked over.

"That's just the emulator. Her body is somewhere safe."

"Who is she?"

"A friend. I didn't force her to do this. She volunteered. I take a ship over to the Passengers' territory when needed. Volmere helps me sneak back here. The volunteer actually gets a sweet deal out of this—the emulating process preserves the body for an extended amount of time. But I guess that won't pay off. She's only been in there for a few years. My last emulator was in there for three hundred years. He lived a hundred years longer than he would have otherwise."

"People live for two hundred years?"

"Passengers, yeah. I don't know about the Rays. You got a long life ahead of you, Mac."

"And when these volunteers come out—it's like they never left?"

"Physically. Mentally they've been living in their own heads the whole time. I was worried at first but it turns out it's not that bad. It's like living two lives. Plus, the volunteers believe the same thing we believe."

"What's that?"

"The glow will end and the war going on down here is not important, because there is an army coming to kill us all."

Volmere spoke up. Since they had all been talking in Earth Common he hadn't been in on the conversation. *Is everyone caught up? Because we need to evacuate.*

Evacuate? said Lynn.

A scout ship has gone dark. Follow me.

Volmere led the way out of the room. As Mac crossed the threshold the ground started to shake. They all remained still for a moment while the shaking passed.

"What was that?" asked Darren.

Something attacked the island, said Lynn, and she took off running.

It's not safe. We need to get to the bunker, said Volmere.

Nally! I can't leave her. I promised.

Volmere had turned to Lynn and was ready to fly after her and drag her to safety, but he hesitated. Scott was already running after her.

I'll go get them, said Mac. *Get these guys to safety.*

Witt will go with you, said Volmere.

The red-winged Almic was running towards them. He was breathing heavily and his large round eyes were straining out of either side of his head.

Rays, sir. A hundred ships, said Witt.

Call for reinforcements.

They're on their way. But they wouldn't attack the Archipelago with only a hundred ships.

I know. More are on their way. I'll send out an order to mobilize everyone. Go with Macnerrad and protect Linryder. This is all for nothing without her.

The ground shook again. Volmere ushered everyone down one end of the hallway while Mac and Witt went the other way after Lynn and Scott. This building wasn't trying at all to go for the illusion of open spaces. The walls weren't transparent and the rooms weren't wide open. The biggest room they had seen so far, besides the docking bay, had been Lynn's lab.

Lynn had been moving up the island, towards the surface, but because she couldn't fly she had taken the stairs. Witt got to the shaft and picked up Mac, flying like he knew where she was going. Bits of wall were shaking loose and falling down the shaft.

You know where she's going? asked Mac.

To save her volunteer. She's defenceless and Lynn promised to protect her, said Witt.

But then Lynn won't have a body.

She will be able to possess the volunteer until she can arrange to get a new one.

The island was struck with such force that Witt slammed into the wall while flying and Mac fell down the shaft. Witt swooped down and picked him up before he hit the ground. Wires had torn apart at the top of the shaft and the sparks created a fire. The fire was rapidly expanding. Flames and smoke was something Mac didn't know how to deal with. Would he get burned in the fire? Would the smoke choke him? He doubted it but he still didn't feel a compelling urge to jump through flames.

Witt landed on the floor below the flames and made for the stairs. There was flickering light from that doorway but the stairwell was empty. Mac started taking the steps two at a time and launching himself up with the handrail, but that wasn't fast enough for Witt, who picked him up. There was enough room for him to fly but he had to curve around the stairwell.

There was an explosion one floor down. A missile crashed through the wall. Mac thought it must have been a dud because it didn't instantly explode.

Buzz bomb! yelled Witt. He flew as fast as he could, banging against the wall in a panic to put space between them and the bomb.

The cylinder exploded like a firework. Each individual piece—each the size of a fist—turned bright orange and buzzed as it streaked through the air. Several went through the wall, right through the wall, like it wasn't even there. They glowed orange because they were hot enough to burn through anything. One zipped past Mac's head. He dodged, but it burned through Witt's wing and they fell onto the stairs.

Mac fell a couple of steps and turned to look. The buzzer hadn't burned right through. It was lodged in the wing. Witt clawed at himself, drawing blood, removing the weapon and throwing it just as it exploded. The buzzer could burn through anything, but it stopped and exploded when it hit a person. When he threw it another one lodged itself in his abdomen. He started clawing at it but his hands were too big for a bomb so small. Mac sprinted up the steps to his side and plunged his hand into the bloody wound. Almic blood was thick, black, and stinky. Once he felt the metal he yanked and tossed it down the stairwell, where it exploded. There were no more buzzers zipping around. They had been lucky to only encounter two of the two dozen buzzers from the bomb. Every time the island shook Mac worried a buzzer was going to burn through the wall and into his body.

Witt was very slow to get back up. One hand was on the thick handrail, the other holding his bloody black stomach.

Where is she? I'll go, said Mac.

I can go with you.

No. Look at yourself.

The buzzer's heat cauterizes the wound. Give me a moment and I'll make it.

Tell me where to go and then you can catch up. If not we'll come back down here and get you.

Three humans won't be able to carry me. If I'm not there leave me behind.

We'll wait as long as we can.

Don't be foolish, said Witt. *If I'm not there when you're ready to go, you go.*

They were wasting time. The island shook again. *Fine. We'll ditch you. Where do I go and how do we get out of here?*

Scott and Lynn were running as fast as their bodies could carry them. Lynn was confident about where they were going. Scott had lost track of how many floors they had passed. Down endless hallways and through countless doors, they were heading into the heart of the island. One more door opened and they were in a room the size of a gymnasium that had a massive, strange-looking ship in it. It was dark, almost black, and had tubes and wires everywhere. It almost looked like it had been gutted but then Scott realized it wasn't a complete ship. Part of it had been broken off—or they were still building it. But that didn't make sense; the room wasn't big enough to finish the ship. Either way it was ugly and didn't look all that significant.

Lynn ran to a control console and started feverishly typing away.

"What are we doing here?" asked Scott.

"I'm downloading all my information so we don't have to start over."

"What do you mean?"

"There was only partial information in my lab. All of my research—everything—is here. I have a plan to win the war but it's not going to work if this island gets destroyed with all my work."

"The island's going to be destroyed?"

"This is a floating artificial island. Judging from the vibrations from the explosions, I'm guessing the Rays are attacking with buzz bombs. If there's enough of them this island will start to sink and it'll be crushed under the weight of the ocean."

"You're saving your work? I thought you were trying to save you and your volunteer."

"That doesn't matter as much as this."

"I just found you and now you're ready to kill yourself?"

"I'm ready to win the war."

A buzz bomb crashed through near the high ceiling. It exploded before it hit the ground. Lynn grabbed Scott and threw him to the ground while the buzzers burned through the room. Lynn acted quickly enough to avoid any of them. Half of them exploded when they hit the large ugly ship in the room but they left no mark on it. Scott wondered what it was made out of.

"What is that thing?" asked Scott.

"The colony ship. We have to destroy it if we are going to win the war."

It had just been hit by a dozen buzz bombs that didn't even blacken the hull.

"How are we supposed to do that?" asked Scott.

Lynn had been typing into the console again but stopped to look straight ahead. She was hearing something through mind speak. There was a look of terror in her eyes.

Mac went where Witt had directed him. The room was solid—reinforced like a bank vault. Mac had to enter a code to get inside. Witt and Lynn worked side by side so he knew the code. Inside was a mini pool with green water—like someone put too much spinach in the smoothie. The room wasn't big and it was empty. Lynn was supposed to be in there.

Lynn, where are you? asked Mac.

I'm backing up my work.
Where!
The colony ship. Scott and I are at the beacon.
We need to get out of here.
Not yet.

Mac heard footsteps in the hallway outside of the door. It was not the hard clawed footsteps of an Almic. It was a human—Passenger or Ray. He had a pretty good guess which it was. Three Rays came through the doorway. They didn't have the same rifles they did back in the ruins of the tower. Their new weapons looked more like grenade launchers; each had an ammunition belt slung over their shoulders. As soon as they saw Mac—his glow was impossible to hide—they each fired. The grenades were buzzers. They burned through the air almost faster than Mac could dodge. When he looked back at what had almost hit him he couldn't believe how easily they had burned through the wall and tried not to imagine what kind of damage that would do to him. Quickly he closed the bank vault–like door.

I'm trapped, Lynn. There's Rays on the island, said Mac.

Where are you? said Lynn.

Where Witt thought you would be. A room with a green pool in it.

My volunteer is in that pool! Jump in and get her. If she dies, then I die.

Okay, but we're going to need a way out of here.

Mac jumped in the pool. It went up to his waist. When he jumped three more buzzers came through the solid metal door. They flew over his head and went through the opposite wall. Three more came right behind them. The Rays figured if they shot everywhere they would be able to get him. Mac got lower into the muck and started feeling around. He felt something and recoiled—it felt like a body. Then he remembered that's exactly what he was looking for. It was a foot and a leg. He felt around for the hands and then pulled the woman out of the muck. The green goo stuck to her body and her clothes. Even through all of that Mac could tell it was exactly the same way Lynn looked right now. Even the clothes were the same.

She wasn't breathing. Mac tried to wipe away the goo from her mouth and nose but she opened her eyes before he finished. She smiled, but when she noticed who was holding her she frowned and pushed him away.

Who are you? she asked.

I'm a friend of Lynn's.

Where is she?

She's okay.

The volunteer shook her head. *If I'm not being emulated then she doesn't exist anymore. If I'm awake then she can't use me as an emulator.*

Chapter 7
Signs of Life

Scott was firing off questions—about the beacon and what was going on and where Lynn had been and what she was doing and what they were supposed to do now. There weren't any breaks between the questions. He wasn't interested in the answers; he simply had to get them off his chest. She kept shaking her head and trying to interrupt him but he was a runaway train of dialogue and Mac's actions in the vault-like room were about to cut everything short.

She shouted, "Stop! Listen!"

"What?" said Scott.

"You need to tell Mac that the beacon needs to be destroyed."

The subtlety wasn't lost on Scott.

"Why can't you tell him?"

"I'm going to try but—"

That was the last thing she said. One moment Scott was holding her hand, looking into her eyes, and the next she was gone—broken into a million pieces and then nothing. It was so sudden he didn't know how to react. He looked on the ground for a pile of dust that was once her body but even that didn't exist. She had vanished. Worse, she had known that might happen and had passed on the only helpful information she could think of: Destroy the beacon.

Scott, is Lynn okay? asked Mac in Scott's head.

No. I mean I don't know. She vanished.

We need to get out of here.

I don't even know where I am.

Mac still had the volunteer woman wrapped in his arms. The green goo had been a strain on her body. She was still flexing her arms to get them working again. Her legs weren't yet strong enough to support her body.

"How long have you been under for?" asked Mac.

She rolled her eyes and pointed at her ears. Even though she looked human she didn't understand Earth Common.

How long have you been under for?

What cycle is it?

I don't know. I'm not from here.

How could you not know what cycle it is?

For starters, I don't know what a cycle is?

Wait. What's going on?

She was blinking her eyes repeatedly and apparently just realized that buzzers were attacking them and that something had gone wrong which is why a stranger was waking her up. The Rays were done shooting randomly and were now shooting the hinges of the door off so that they could kick it down.

Who are you? she asked.

I'm Mac Narrad. I'm a friend of Lynn Ryder's. We're under attack by the Rays and we need to get out of here.

Well, Mac Narrad, I'm Nally. You need to get me out of this pool and then we'll go.

We have no weapons and you can't walk.

I said, get me out of here. Can you handle that?

She wasn't going to take any grief from Mac. He picked her up and walked over to the edge of the pool to set her down. The buzzers stopped coming through the door; now the soldiers were kicking at it. The door was a foot thick. They wouldn't get through right away but Mac was going to need to be ready to defend them.

Nally's upper body was recovering faster than her lower body. The goo that still clung to her was what was slowing her down. She knew that. Under normal circumstances she would have been taken right to a shower, but this was not normal. Using her hands, she scraped off as much of the green liquid as she could. Her toes were moving now and she worked to get her legs under her as the door thundered under the blows of the Rays.

Mac went and stood next to the door so that he could jump the Rays when they entered. If they focused on her he might be able to surprise them. The door was only two inches away from coming completely free of the wall. Mac crouched, ready to spring into action. Nally was against the opposite wall, tapping, looking for a secret compartment. She touched a segment of the wall and a door slid open revealing a weapons cabinet with three laser spears inside. They were Almic weapons but she knew how to use them.

The door came free of the frame and fell into the pool. The wave of goo completely splashed the far wall and knocked Nally off her feet before she could arm herself. The tip of a launcher came into view and Mac jumped, shoving the barrel aside as the buzzer screamed free. Another buzzer skimmed Mac's shoulder and spun him around but he still gripped the first weapon and ripped it free of the attacker. He flipped it around and pointed it at the three Rays trying to come in the room.

They had two buzz bomb launchers and Mac had one. It was a standoff, neither side willing to kill the other for fear of dying themselves. The fatal blow came from Nally. She shot one of the armed Rays in the face, completely removing the head. The body fell to its knees and then toppled on its side. The unarmed Ray fled and got a shot in the back from the spear Nally had grabbed. The last Ray made a move to shoot her but Mac fired first. The man exploded when the buzzer entered his chest.

You hesitated, said Nally.

I was waiting for them—

To kill you. When you hesitate with a Ray it will cost you your life.

I guess I owe you one.

Don't owe me one—just try not to kill yourself next time.

Sure thing.

Witt stomped up to them. Mac was startled and almost shot at him but then Nally recognized that an Almic was approaching, not a Ray.

Lynn is not responding, said Witt.

This one woke me up. We don't know if she made it, said Nally.

Come with me. There are escape ships on the surface.

What about Scott? asked Mac.

Where is he? asked Nally.

He was with Lynn. She went to the colony ship to make sure her work wasn't destroyed. I was supposed to go to you and make sure she could hold her form long enough to get that done, said Witt.

And? asked Nally, looking at Mac.

She told me to pull you out so she must have finished.

Nally shook her head. Clearly she was not impressed by what Mac had done. Maybe someday he would get to tell her about his high scores in the military, how he and Lynn were able to escape the cave without dying, how he figured out the truth about the war, or how he was able to save his home town from being completely destroyed by the military. Then maybe she would be impressed. Maybe, but not likely.

Witt, you are too injured to come. She handed him one of the laser spears. *You go to the surface and get out of here. We'll go see if Lynn died in vain or not.*

You do not give the orders around here, said Witt.

No. I don't. But I can point out the obvious.

Witt barked—was that the Almic equivalent of laughing out loud? Mac figured it could be. Witt was also shaking his head a lot.

I will go. Good luck. If the worst happens then we meet on the Dead Continent. You know the place, correct? said Witt.

I do. Lynn showed me, said Nally.

Without saying anything else, Witt the red-winged Almic left. Nally went back into the room and grabbed the other spear. It was made for an Almic so it was much longer than was comfortable for her to use.

You can use the launcher if you want, said Mac.

I will not use the weapon of a Ray.

Mac didn't have the same hangups. He let Nally lead the way.

There weren't any breaks between the explosions anymore. The island had to be under attack by more than just buzz bombs. It felt like a shuttle constantly going through turbulence. More buzz bombs had broken into the room. Scott had wedged himself under the only thing that could protect him from the buzzers—the indestructible beacon that Lynn had said they needed to destroy to win the war.

Accompanying the shaking was a low rumble. Water was now leaking into the room. Scott had to move out from his hiding place. When he got out from under the beacon he stumbled a bit and slipped in the standing water. At first he thought it was from standing up too quickly but now he could tell that the whole room was tilted. How was this possible? Did islands sink? He was pretty sure back on Earth islands were just the peak of mountains sticking out of the ocean.

Mac, we don't have a lot of time. This room is filling up with water. I need to meet you halfway, said Scott.

No. Nally says no. Just wait there. Don't get lost in the island, said Mac.

Who's Nally?

Lynn was backing up her information on the beacon. Do you have it? asked a new female voice. Scott correctly guessed that it was Nally.

Hold on. I'll check.

Scott went over to the computer console Lynn had been working on. The water hadn't gotten to it yet. The leaks were in the walls, not the ceiling. It looked like the room was sweating. The amount of liquid steadily increased but the room was big. The water wasn't even up over his feet yet. They still had time.

He tried to figure out what Lynn was doing on the computer but it wasn't in Earth Common. Over the last few thousand years she had learned whatever language they spoke on this planet and used it to run the computer. He tried to see if there was a pattern. There was a status bar that was all the way full, like when data was transferred somewhere. That could have been what Lynn was doing. She had put something in the computer. He felt around with his hand for the protruding device. It was hard to tell where it was. The cold water was making his fingers on one hand feel numb. He rubbed his hand on the side of his pants to warm them up and then slapped his two hands together. The feeling did not return. It was the strangest sensation— the closet thing he could compare it to was when his leg fell asleep, but even that wasn't completely accurate. It was numb but he still felt something there.

While he was trying to muster the finger dexterity to pull the small disk out of the computer the wall in front of him started creaking. Along the seam of that wall the water was no longer lazily dripping out—it was shooting out like a water cannon. If he had been a few feet to his left he would have gotten it right in the chest. The wall thumped, the seam opened even more, and the wall bulged. It was going to blow.

Before he could take the disk out the wall tore apart under the force of the water. Part of the wall smashed the console and then smacked Scott in the face. He fell back into the water. It was almost enough to cover him while he was laying down now. With the wall missing the room was filling even faster. He stood up and used his good hand to feel the side of his face, expecting to see blood in the water and maybe a missing eye. In all the chaos he had forgotten about his new healing abilities. Other than a little dizziness, he was doing okay.

Everything in the room was moving now. He could feel a current in the water. All the water was pooling near the wall that had blown apart from the water pressure. There was a loud metallic scraping noise as the beacon started to shift.

You underwater yet? asked Mac.

Not yet, but it won't be much longer.

If Scott was going to avoid getting crushed by the beacon he was going to have to climb up and over it. The ship was three stories tall; it wasn't going to be a quick climb. It was already starting to move. He reached up and started climbing. The water had been up to his chest when he started. The slope of the room was increasing. The water was pouring out the ceiling now. The room was too big, too spread out to keep all the water back. It was only a matter of time before everything came crashing down on him.

He wasn't even climbing fast enough to keep himself out of the water that was rising up. A buzz bomb broke into the room again, a torrent of water behind it. One of the buzzers hit the beacon right beside Scott and exploded. The force of it threw him completely off of the ship and into the churning water. He was caught in the current and couldn't tell which way was up. He could see several different sources of light through the bubbles and started swimming, hoping it was the surface. But it wasn't. Now he was too far away to get there and he was going to drown.

Don't sweat the water, said Mac. *Now that you glow in the dark you don't need oxygen to breathe. You can hold your breath forever.*

Scott wouldn't have believed it if he hadn't been experiencing it for himself right then. He had been under for several minutes now and his lungs weren't burning for a fresh supply of oxygen. He was fine.

There were two other figures in the water now. It was Mac and...Lynn in her new body? How was that possible?

I thought you were dead, Lynn, said Scott.

I'm not Lynn. I'm Nally. Lynn was using my body.

Catch up later. Let's get out of here, said Mac.

You have her information?

No, said Scott. *It was destroyed. She said we needed to destroy the beacon but she didn't say how or why.*

The what?

The colony ship, said Mac.

Impossible, said Nally.

I know. It was hit dozens of times and not even a dent appeared. I don't know how to destroy it.

That can't be her plan. We need to figure it out before we leave here.

Mac shook his head underwater, *This artificial island is full of holes. If we don't get out we are going down with it.*

But we can breathe underwater, said Scott.

I doubt we would survive being crushed by the ocean.

If they had been able, getting off the island could have been as easy as swimming against the current but there was an entire ocean trying to push its way in. There was no way they would be able to swim out that way. Nally led the way but the second time she hit a dead end and made them turn around Mac started to question if she really knew where she was going.

I've been under for a long time. It's not like it's fresh in my mind, she said.

How long has it been? asked Scott.

I take it you don't know how long a cycle is either?

Twenty-eight days?

Not that kind of cycle, said Mac.

Mac's ears were popping. The air pressure was changing but had they sunk too low to escape now? Or was all the water just pushing the air up? The leaks were coming from all directions. Nally found the staircase that she and Mac had come down and took it all the way to the top. They were following Witt's blood trail now. It was in clumps, not puddles like human blood would be—well, human blood that hadn't been injected with Lynn Rock and enhanced by Mac Gas—so it wasn't being washed away as easily.

She threw open the door at the end of the stairs and they were all bathed in sunlight. The island hadn't sunk completely yet, but it wasn't very big anymore. Mac stepped out into the sunlight. The water all around the island was broiling and bubbling, sneaking up on them. They had made it to the surface just in time. There were supposed to be ships up here they could use for an escape but all Mac saw was one tree, and some grass. There was debris floating in the churning water at the edge of the island.

The skies were full of Ronos Almic ships, dozens of them the same size as the one that had brought Mac and the others there. The Rays had ships up there as well, attacking. But they were smaller and weren't doing enough damage for it to be worth it. The big push for their attack had come from the sea—where the Almics were the most vulnerable. The distraction of the end of the glow and the arrival of the newcomers had been the ideal opportunity for the Rays.

Nally was looking up into the blue sky; she couldn't believe what she was seeing. For a moment it was like she didn't know they were about to sink into the ocean.

There's no ship up here, said Mac.

The glow is over, said Nally.

That's right. We come from a place beyond the glow. That's why we don't know what a cycle is.

She looked at Mac and Scott with new understanding. A lot had happened while she had been under. Overwhelmed, she plopped down on the ground. There were several underwater explosions that threw water into the air. One of the smaller Ray ships exploded and crashed into the ocean. The Almic ships were venting something that created cloud cover. Mac looked at the other clouds that were already up there. How many of those hid ships inside?

What are you doing? We need to get out of here! said Scott.

There's nowhere to go. The ships were hidden in the landscape of the island but unless there's a ship hiding in that tree over there we are stuck.

Even if the tree was a ship in disguise, it was too small for one person to fit inside, let alone three.

Volmere, come pick us up. We are on the surface of your island, Mac said.

An Almic ship ducked out of a cloud and moved closer to the ocean. Rockets burst out of the water and homed in on it. That's why the ships were staying so far above—if they got any closer they would get bombarded with missiles. If the Rays patrolled the Almics' flight path there was no way the fleet would be able to land. The Rays had driven them out of their homes and were now playing the waiting game.

Volmere's ship was moving fast. It dove towards the island. On the back of it, a dozen soldiers took to the air. Three of them scooped up the humans and flew them back to the ship. The rest grabbed cables and attached them to the island. They were trying to keep the island from sinking.

Why would they do that? asked Mac.

The colony ship is sacred to them. They won't let it fall into the hands of the Rays, said Nally.

They should just let it fall into the ocean. Lynn said we need to destroy it, said Scott.

I doubt that.

She said that just before she died.

She said those exact words?

Yes. She told me to tell Mac that we need to destroy the beacon to win the war.

All three of them stumbled and almost fell as the ship jumped after being hit by a missile. There was smoke rising into the air. The Almics who hooked up the cables returned—most of them returned. In the mix of bodies an Almic with red wings emerged with a bandage around his stomach. He grabbed all three of them and dragged them below.

The ship is separating, said Witt. *We'll meet Volmere at the rendezvous.*

It didn't take long for Mac to learn what Witt meant by separating. The large Almic ship was composed of smaller versions of itself. Now that the ship was broken and about to crash into the ocean, the healthy segments could break off and make a run for it. The smaller version Mac and the others were on couldn't have fit another human inside, and certainly not an Almic. Witt was piloting.

He pointed the ship straight up but Mac could still see what was happening to the island. Half of the dozen cables had been severed and none of the island was visible anymore. There were over a hundred little ships scattering into the sky. Rockets were consistently emerging from the ocean. Most of them hit a target just because there were so many to hit. Witt made it to the clouds and then started jumping from cloud to cloud, moving away from the Archipelago.

Do you think the weight of the ocean is strong enough to crush the beacon? asked Scott.

I don't know. I don't even know how we'll find out if it's still working.

Not more than an hour passed. They were still flying high above the ocean. Out of the cockpit window Mac could see other ships like theirs flying with them. One of them was Volmere, who reassured Mac that the other Passage people were safe. Mac breathed a sigh of relief. If he had known that Ronos had turned into three civilizations each trying to conquer the world he never would have brought the Glover kids or any of the others down there.

A shock wave expanded outward from the Archipelago. It moved so fast it dispersed clouds. The wave it caused in the ocean was several hundred meters high. Their ship was thrown off course and the electronics were momentarily thrown out of whack. Witt had to act quickly to get them back online and to level off the ship.

What was that? Volmere said to everyone.

It originated in the Archipelago, said Witt, looking at his instruments.

A weapon?

It was an explosion of some kind but different than a weapon. There were several ships still hovering around the Archipelago. They are sending info now. The explosion didn't come from the surface. It displaced an incredible amount of water. There is no weapon known that could do that. This didn't come from us so it must be the Rays.

It wasn't a bomb. If it was they would have used it before the evacuation.

What about the colony ship? said Scott.

It slid into the ocean, said Witt. *Trapped on your sinking island, Volmere. The coordinates line up with the source of the explosion. If it wasn't the colony ship it could have been something else Lynn was working on.*

What weapons was she working on? asked Volmere.

None at the moment. She hasn't worked on anything since the excavator and she made sure it wasn't on the island. It would have destroyed the whole thing.

What would happen if the colony ship exploded?

We were never sure. I didn't even think it was possible. The ocean is deep. It probably slid into the Val Valley. We don't have the technology to go that deep yet. Anything we send down there gets crushed. No one is even sure exactly how deep it is and your island was suspended right above it.

It's not too far of a reach to assume that if it can't be explained, then the colony ship is the cause.

That was mine and Lynn's motto for a lot of years, said Witt.

Scott let out a massive sigh of relief and had a grin on his face. Lynn had known what they needed to do and now it had been done. The beacon had been destroyed.

"What's up, chuckles?" asked Mac.

"The war is over if the beacon is destroyed," said Scott.

"Because of what Lynn said?"

"Yeah."

"You think the beacon is the reason the aliens are coming here?"

"I don't know. I just know what Lynn said."

Scott flexed his left hand again. The numbness was still there. It had been an hour and there was still nothing there except a tingling sensation, so maybe it wasn't numb, but it sure wasn't right. At first he thought it had been from the cold water but his hand should have warmed up by now. He looked for something that might be cause it but he didn't even have a scratch. At the very worst it might have been a little more red than normal but that might have just been because he kept rubbing it to get some feeling back.

"Hey, can I ask you something?" said Scott.

"Yeah," said Mac

"You've been changed the longest out of any of us. You ever feel numb for no reason?"

"No, but these people down here have been changed so long they don't know what it would be like to not have the glow."

Mac turned to Nally. *Scott feels numb. Is that normal?*

Nally's eyes went wide and she rushed to Scott's side. *Where?*

He held up his hand and she examined it as closely as he had.

There's nothing wrong with it. It doesn't hurt; it's just numb. I don't know why, said Scott.

How long has it been like that?

An hour or so.

Back when we were on the island?

I guess so. I didn't really notice it at first. It's subtle. I thought it was from the cold water.

It started when Lynn disappeared, Nally said. It wasn't a question; it was statement. She knew what was going on. *You were holding Lynn's hand when I was pulled out of the emulating pool. She didn't have an emulator so she threw herself into you.*

What? asked Scott.

Lynn preserved her life by moving into your body. Your hand is numb because there is another person inside you and your body is having trouble processing what's going on in there. She did it to me once in an emergency.

Mac and Scott were both looking at the hand like they had never seen one before. From what he could see it was a normal-looking hand. There was nothing special about it; nothing had changed. How was this even possible? If there were two people inside of Scott then wouldn't he be twice as big now? To Mac he looked relatively the same size. Only his hand was numb—did that mean that her entire body was in his hand? Should his hand be the size of a person?

Scott was thinking the same thing.

How come I don't feel the weight of an entire person in me? he asked.

Because she might not have had time to move all of herself into your body. If it's just your hand that's numb then there's only a part of her inside of you, said Nally.

Where's the rest of her?

Floating out in the ocean probably. If we can build an emulator again then we can get her back and she can tell us her plan.

Scott smiled. *Her plan already worked. She wanted the beacon destroyed and it's been destroyed. We need her back so we can finally be together.*

She said the beacon needed to be destroyed? asked Witt.

Yeah.

You hear that, Volmere? We need to destroy the colony ship, said Witt.

What? said Volmere.

That's what Lynn said just before she disappeared, said Scott.

That's impossible.

It's already done. It got crushed by the ocean. That's what the explosion was.

That was only part of the colony ship. A small part, actually.

Where's the other part? asked Mac.

The Rays have it.

Well, that narrows it down, said Scott.

I thought you knew where it was, Nally said to Volmere.

I only have theories. When the glow first started the colony ship pieces were in the same place, a massive underground cavern controlled by the Rays. It was their capital, where they all gathered. And since they are all killers, eager to wipe out Passengers and Almics, there was no way anyone would be able to walk in there to retrieve the colony ship. That ship is the source of all knowledge on the planet. It was built to teach colonizers how to advance their technology. Since the Rays were the only ones who had access to it they were advancing faster and killing more. They were becoming unstoppable.

The Passengers repeatedly tried to storm the caves and take over control of the colony ship but it never worked. They never even got close—the Rays were too powerful. The Almics learned from the mistakes of the Passengers. Instead of attacking from the top down, as expected, we attacked from the bottom up. We snuck thousands of troops in through an underground river system and attacked. The battle was bloody. The Rays were still incredibly powerful even though they had been caught off guard. We used explosives to widen the underground river and escaped with a portion of the colony ship.

I think the colony ship is still there, in that cavern where it has always been. It's too big to move without someone noticing. And since they have kept it in the same place they can defend it more easily. That Almic raid happened thousands of years ago. The Rays have had all that time to build their defenses around it. It is the thing that matters most to them. It will not be easy to get to it.

Mac spoke up. *They've had thousands of years to reinforce and build defenses against an attack on the beacon. Forget about easy. It's going to be impossible to get to it.*

Lynn wouldn't send us on a fool's errand, said Scott. *She had a plan.*

What was it?

I don't know. But she told me she had a plan.

Does anyone know Lynn's plan? Mac made sure to broadcast to all the ships that were flying with them. There were a lot of the little ships flying around but there were also a few larger winged ships keeping up with them.

I know part of it, said Witt.

I think I can figure out part of it, said Nally.

What have you got, Nally? said Mac.

I wasn't randomly selected by Lynn to be her body. She needed me. She said she was going to use my connections to hide something among the Passengers for when she needed it. I asked her what it was and she said it was safer if I didn't know. I could go back home and try and track down where she went and maybe what she hid there.

What was it?

There was always a plan for when the glow ended, said Witt. *She always knew how she was going to destroy the colony ship. The thing that she hid among the Passengers was a bomb.*

I've seen the colony ship get hit by bombs. That's not going to work, said Scott.

Well, your wife knows a way. She had this plan a long time ago. She could have implemented it at any time.

Then why didn't she?

I don't know. She said she was waiting for the right moment but I never understood why. It doesn't matter. I'm telling you that she hid a bomb using Nally, in a place that no one would look and a place that no one would accidentally blow up. Which is important, if you think about what that bomb is capable of.

They now had part of her plan. There was a bomb and Lynn was going to use it on the beacon. But how were they going to even get to the beacon? If it was where Volmere suspected it was, then it was in the Rays' most secure location. The Almic home had been decimated. Mac didn't know if there was enough Almic firepower left to take on the Rays and fight to the beacon to set the bomb off. Volmere was their military leader but no one would listen to him if the council didn't agree. This might be a futile effort but they had to try. No one else but Lynn had a plan for ending the war.

Chapter 8
Arrival

The Archipelago had been completely abandoned by the Ronos Almics. The artificial islands—like the one Lynn had been working on—were sunk to the bottom of the ocean. The real islands were in flames or swarming with Ray soldiers. The Almics who had survived took to the air and regrouped in the clouds while the council tried to figure out what to do next.

Volmere—as leader of the Ronos Almic military—should have been with the council planning their next move, but instead he was making his own plans. The original plan had been for all those loyal to him to meet on the Dead Continent but he changed his mind and instructed all the ships flying with him to avoid the Dead Continent. His second in command, Lemnell, questioned his wisdom.

No. The Dead Continent is too unpredictable, said Volmere.

You are worried that the Rays will attack us there as well? said Lemnell.

They have always been active on the continent. We simply have no way of determining how many there are there or any way of stopping them. Thinking we are safe there is a trap.

Then where are we going? asked Lemnell.

We will swing around the northern part of the Dead Continent and head towards Sanctuary.

The Passengers?

Yes.

You think we will be safe there?

We won't be safe anywhere.

Sir, I will follow you anywhere and I will execute any order you give, you know this. But how are we supposed to trust the Passengers after all these years?

They may not trust us but there are some among us that they might.

And the council?

We will meet up with them later. This is more important than them right now.

The greatest sign of trust Volmere was showing was not having any private conversations. Their conversation was being broadcast to everyone. Secrets had a way of undermining everything. As long as they were all on the same page they could all be confident in the choices Volmere was making.

Obviously the people he was banking on being able to help them were Nally, Mac, and the other humans. Mac went to sit over by Nally.

You are key to this plan, I'm assuming, said Mac.

You assume right, said Nally, but she didn't look comfortable with the thought.

So are we going to have a welcoming party or get blown out of the sky?

No one is answering my calls.

What do you mean?

I've been trying to get in touch with my family and friends—one by one—no one has answered me yet.

Maybe they're busy.

That might be true of my dad but the others should answer me.

Is it possible they can't answer? Is it possible to block mind speak?

No.

When Lynn and I were first here she got trapped in the caves and it blocked our communications.

The Rays rarely take prisoners.

If they weren't answering they were either dead or ignoring Nally.

Who is your father? asked Mac.

He is the president of the Passengers.

Taynner, right? Mac remembered the name being mentioned when he had been on the Dead Continent. The Passengers had told Volmere that he had been killed in a Ray attack three weeks previously. No one had told Nally yet.

Yes.

I have heard news about him. I'm sorry but it's not good.

Nally scoffed, *You know what happened to my father? Unlikely.*

We ran into some Passengers when we first arrived. Volmere asked about your father because there was a new president there. Your father died in a Ray attack three weeks ago. I'm sorry.

You don't know what you're talking about.

I hope I'm wrong but that's what I heard.

You don't know what you are talking about. He is one man. Why is no one answering? Are they all dead? Everyone I loved? Why is no one answering me? Nally was getting worked up now. The frustration was showing on her face. She strained with each word and tears were forming in the corners of her eyes. In her mind she screamed out to any of the Passengers for some kind of answer. *Is there anyone out there!*

Then she waited for someone to answer. She had desperately reached out to anyone in her species. There should have been an answer right away unless there was some kind of protocol for answering such a widely broadcast message. Despite all the emotions in the air, Mac couldn't help but wonder how many spam messages were sent to people's minds. Mind speak really was the ultimate spamming tool. Since it couldn't be turned off the message would always get through. Maybe Passengers were too distracted by war to worry about advertisements.

There was an attack. Stay away from Sanctuary, said a male voice. It sounded young.

What happened? None of my friends or family has been answering, said Nally.

It's not safe for anyone. I can't believe you don't know about it.

The royal family, where are they?

There was no immediate answer. She called to him again but there was nothing.

Did you know that boy? asked Volmere.

No.

How long until we reach Sanctuary? Volmere asked.

An hour. We are well within their sensors and we still haven't been contacted.

Mac asked Volmere a question. *Is the Ray military big enough to attack both the Almics and the Passengers?*

I had hoped not but that no longer appears to be our reality. We have never come this close to their capital without being contacted. There is something wrong.

Mac was given a brief history of the Passengers and the Dead Continent. All three civilizations had developed first on the Dead Continent, but their wars had destroyed all plant life there and none of them could live close to each other. The Almics were the first to leave and set up in the Archipelago, thinking it the least desirable land and that no one would follow them or fight them for it. The Passengers left the Dead Continent for a snake-shaped landmass—thin and in the shape of an elongated S. The letter shape and their hope to be free of the Rays and Almics led it to be called Sanctuary. That's where the Passenger government was located and that's where Volmere was headed.

Half an hour later, Sanctuary appeared on the horizon and they were finally contacted.

Almic fleet, state your intentions. It was impossible to determine race simply by the voice. Mac couldn't pick up any cultural differences anyway, and a Ray could easily imitate an accent.

We need to speak to the president of the Passengers. We have urgent information and seek an alliance with them.

An alliance. The voice sounded caught off guard—as if that was the last thing they expected.

Yes. Are you willing to accept us in peace?

Proceed to the Government Block.

Volmere looked back at Nally, *You know where that is?*

Yes, said Nally. *I used to live there.*

The landmass was much closer now and Mac could see buildings. And smoke. Nally gasped and stood closer to the front window to get a better look. The capital city had been attacked. The destruction was limited to a few key buildings but Mac didn't know their significance and he was distracted by the familiarity-yet-strangeness of the city. There were several skyscrapers—if it had a density similar to a city on Earth then it would have a population of about ten million, the same size as Northgate. The tall buildings were organized into blocks and had roads and sidewalks between them, but the structures themselves were alien. They were ugly—no windows, no sense of cohesion. All the buildings were clad in thick armor that looked like it was cobbled together with whatever metal was available. The color was not consistent. There were no billboards on them, no logos. On top of each building was a cache of heavy weaponry. The Passengers had come to Sanctuary hoping to avoid war, but they had been prepared for an attack.

The buildings that had been damaged had giant holes blown out the side. The holes in the armor exposed the underlying windows and more visually appealing architecture. Mac could see blast marks in the armor where weapons had failed to break through. In fact, it looked like all the attacks from the outside had failed. The buildings with broken armor all showed evidence of an explosion from the inside.

There were no vehicles or pedestrians on the road. The entire city looked abandoned. Or maybe that's how it always looked. Mac didn't know, but the look on Nally's face said there was something wrong.

Nothing can get through that armor, said Nally, trying to dispute what she could plainly see.

The explosions came from inside, said Volmere, who had noticed what Mac had.

That doesn't make sense either. There's no way the Rays could have gotten that far in.

Maybe it wasn't the Rays.

You confessing something? said Nally.

No. But there are other players in the game now.

If Mac had been the easily-offended type he could have latched onto that last comment but he knew that Volmere was referring to Zinger. If anyone could make all this destruction happen in such a short amount of time, it was the general. Mac didn't know how it was possible—but when bad things happened it wasn't too far off to think that Zinger had something to do with it.

Follow the main highway to the center of the city. There will be a party there to meet you. It was the same mysterious voice. They didn't know if it could be trusted.

Is everyone okay? We have ships if you need them.

All will be explained once we meet in person. I look forward to it.

None of them believed it. Whoever was talking to them was not their ally. Mac scanned the skies and saw nothing other than the Almic ships. If this was the capital, then there had to be Passenger ships somewhere. Unless the attack had happened so fast none of the pilots had been able to get to their ships. To Mac that meant the attack had come from below, not from above. Rays.

Did the Rays leave the Dead Continent as well? Mac asked.

Yes. There are Rays under every landmass on Ronos. The treaty we all signed, the only thing that any of us could agree on, said no one was to settle the Dead Continent. But it is long believed that the Rays have not obeyed that treaty and have a city there, said Volmere.

It has to be the Rays that attacked the Passengers then.

Agreed. We are not going to stay here much longer, said Volmere. *Well, not all of us.*

You still want me to find the bomb, said Nally. It wasn't a question. She was hoping she would be able to do that.

Yes.

Good.

Do you know where it is?

I'll find it.

It was comforting to see her confidence.

We'll keep a ship standing by to pick you up. It won't be pretty down there, said Volmere.

Stop. Head over to that group of towers, said Nally. *Three together, connected at the top by a pedway.*

As soon as we move off course they'll know something's up, said Mac.

It'll be quick. If the bomb is where I think it is then it shouldn't be too bad. Especially if the city is as abandoned as it looks.

The Almic fleet flew away from the main highway that ran through the center of the city. The reaction to their new flight path was immediate and came from unexpected places—laser blasts from the three towers they were headed towards. There were turrets at the top of each tower but parts of the armor also opened up to reveal more cannons. None of the towers had been damaged yet. The Passengers had been hiding out there. As soon as they saw the Almics head towards them they panicked and started shooting.

The Rays also responded. There were several explosions on the ground right by the towers, creating holes in the street. Streaming out of the holes were Ray soldiers heading straight for the three towers. They hadn't completely taken the city—yet.

Target the Rays and fire, said Volmere.

A steady stream of lasers burned the bodies coming out the ground, preventing them from getting to the towers. More explosions opened new tunnels underground. Some were much larger. But nothing came out. Mac figured they were decoys until a loud boom shook the ship and a thick laser burned through the sky, destroying one of the Almic ships in a single shot. There were a dozen of these holes now, with more appearing every second. That explained why there were no Passenger ships in the air anymore. Another Almic ship was destroyed; the burning remains fell onto the broken city.

You need to get out of here, said Nally. *Let me off.*

You can't go alone, said Mac.

It's my city. I know what I'm doing.

I'm a soldier. Plus I know Lynn. I can help.

Scott stepped forward. *I literally have Lynn inside of me. Maybe I should go.*

No, Nally and Mac said at the same time.

You're not a soldier. It's too dangerous for you, said Mac.

Having Lynn inside you isn't going to help anything, said Nally. *You can't communicate with her and she can't communicate with you. As soon as we can we will set up an emulator pool but first I need to find the bomb.*

We *need to find the bomb*, Mac corrected.

Fine, said Scott.

Volmere ordered the ship brought low on one of the side roads leading to the towers. There hadn't been any Ray activity there yet. The side door opened and Nally and Mac jumped out. There was a loud boom. Rocks and dirt were thrown into the air, hitting Mac. He had been falling but the force of the explosion threw him back up into the air. He was flipping end over end. The debris prevented him from seeing anything.

He was falling again but instead of hitting the ground he fell through the hole and onto the weapon now targeting Volmere's ship. The weapon was a large cannon on four mechanical legs. The barrel of the cannon was six feet across and Mac landed right in it, right where the laser came out. There was a light coming from inside it. It was about to fire.

Mac jumped out right as the laser fired. He looked up to see Volmere's ship duck behind a building and out of sight. When he looked back down at his surroundings he found he was at the end of a tunnel. There were two machines. The weapon—which looked like it was folding up and getting ready to move since there were no targets anymore—and a drilling machine that must have made the tunnel. The only light came from the opening to the surface. It was enough light to see the machines but not who operated them. There had to be Rays there, hiding in the shadows.

Nally, where are you? said Mac.

In the alley. Where are you?

Fell in the hole.

On my way. Watch out for Rays.

The shadows started moving. They were wearing all black clothing and had long rifles as well as blades, just as they had on the Dead Continent. Mac reached for the weapon holstered at his side, but it had fallen out. He had no way to defend himself. They all raised their weapons to fire.

Then the big cannon sparked back to life. It had picked up another ship and was charging to fire. It buzzed with energy and adjusted its aim automatically. That action was enough to divert the attention of half of the men. Mac knew he wasn't going to get another chance. As the cannon fired, deafening everyone for a moment, he leapt into action, grabbing the rifle barrel of one of the distracted Rays. That Ray started firing madly but Mac thrust the barrel away from him and towards the other pale-skinned attackers. Three of them went down. Mac flipped around the man he had attacked as lasers tore through the tunnel. None of them hit Mac. All the casualties had been Ray-on-Ray.

Mac was fully exposed now. The man he'd jumped at was a burnt mound on the ground. His weapon was not close enough for Mac to get to before the others attacked. They were about to pull the trigger when Nally shot the lead attacker in the head with a laser. She was up top picking them off one by one. As they moved to focus on her Mac picked up a weapon and finished them off.

Thank you, said Mac.

Let's get out of here before more come.

The ground was vibrating from a nearby digger. They needed to find a place to hide. Mac climbed out of the tunnel and followed after Nally, who seemed to know where she was going. His instinct had been to run into one of the buildings and go up a couple floors so they were off the ground. But it was impossible to get inside any of the buildings. They all had armor right down to the ground.

Nally kept running. The buildings around them were so tall he couldn't see the three-tower target they were heading for. She knew where she was going. There were no signs or markers that told him what street they were on but he was looking where the signs would normally be on Earth. There must have been a different setup here.

There was panic in her eyes when she stopped running a few minutes later. She stood still listening and watching the ground down each street in her view. Mac looked as well and couldn't see anything. They were in the shadows now. The sun was starting to set.

They didn't follow us, said Nally.

Maybe they're focusing on getting into the capital building.

Impossible. They won't be able to.

Then how were we going to get in there?

I didn't really have a plan.

Just run around until something happens?

We don't need to get to the bomb; we just need to get the bomb to where it's going.

Mac had no idea what that meant. Bombs couldn't think for themselves. Someone was going to have to take it to the beacon. Nally was still spinning around in a panic, as if waiting for someone to attack them.

What's wrong? Mac asked.

It's getting dark. I don't do well in the dark.

Mac had forgotten that they hadn't had day and night down here. All they'd had was the constant glow. Now that it was gone they were experiencing night regularly. The Rays were built to survive the dark of the caves. Nally's eyes had not developed the same level of night vision.

Once it gets dark, the Rays will attack. She looked down at her own body, glowing slightly as it reacted to the Mac gas. *We can't hide from them.*

We still have time to try and get in the capital building. How much farther is it?

But I don't know how to get inside.

Let's get there first.

Nally closed her eyes and concentrated, then started running again. *This way.*

Volmere trusted Lynn. He was the reason she had been able to set up shop on the Archipelago and given access to the colony ship. No Almic, outside of Volmere and Witt, knew there was a human on that island—two humans, if Nally was included.

The truth about the glow and the war with Invaders had been passed down for many generations among all three of the civilizations on Ronos. But given enough time, truth fades into fiction. Legends are scoffed at as superstitious. The glow would never end. There was no fleet coming to Ronos. There was nothing beyond the glow. The truth was forgotten by almost everyone.

The Almics had seen Lynn's ship in the upper atmosphere. They used her ship to mark the passage of time—each time her ship circled the planet became known as a cyle. They believed that her ship had answers for them. That maybe she would be able to tell them the truth about the glow and why they were there and what was coming— if the Invaders were real. It took several lifetimes to get to Lynn. There were different levels of atmosphere that each moved at a different pace, making the task difficult. By the time she was retrieved the people who had sent for her had been long dead. Lynn explained that the different levels in the atmosphere experienced time at different speeds—the higher up the less time went by. This was why no one would ever be able to leave the planet.

Lynn had come into Volmere's life at exactly the right time. His career in the military meant he had devoted his life to defending the planet from invasion—something that might not happen during his lifespan, if at all. She was fresh—she remembered life outside of the glow. She was able to teach them all about life off of Ronos. She knew words like system, sun, star, space, Earth, and light year.

Volmere—with Lynn's help—started preparing for the end of the glow. He had built ships that would help the Almics survive in space. As soon as the glow ended he sent a crew up to scout out what was out there and let them know if—no, not if—there was an enemy fleet on the way. Volmere wanted to where it was and how much time he had left before the attack started.

How far have the scouts gotten? said Volmere, thinking about his daughter Vissia on the scout ship.

They are almost out of the...system.

Lemnell—Volmere's top lieutenant—wasn't sure of his words. They were ones he never needed to understand before. None of them had. It had always been a requirement in the Almic society to study the old ways of space travel but not everyone took it seriously. Generations had gone past with no one ever needing to use it. Some had advocated dropping it as required study. If the glow trapping them on Ronos had lasted a few more hundred years it was probable that the Almics would be like everyone else and have no knowledge of what had happened off-world.

Right now there was a ship full of brave volunteers heading away from Ronos. Their job was to act as an early warning system. Volmere needed to know what was on its way.

Have they anything to report? asked Volmere.

Nothing. There are human ships in orbit but they did not attack, said Lemnell. *You should know the council is waiting for the moment that they can take your power away from you.*

They are too quick to side with an invading fleet.

The Almics fell into two groups: those who believed they were there to colonize the planet and prepare it for the rest of their people to arrive, and those who believed they were there to defend the planet from anyone who wanted to destroy it.

The council of Almics was made up of the rulers of each main island. Together they made decisions for the entire civilization. They still thought that peace was an option. They believed that the invading fleet coming to Ronos was coming to liberate them. That went against what Volmere believed and what the colony ship had taught them. The colonization had failed. The fleet was coming to wipe them all out, regardless of species, and start fresh. Ronos was a failed experiment.

The council won't do anything until the fleet makes the first move. Prepare anyone still alive and loyal to us to mobilize. I want them ready to form up at a moment's notice, said Volmere.

You only command a quarter of our military resources.

What!

The council blames you for the attack. They know the colony ship was lost. You have been branded a traitor.

And only a quarter remain loyal?

Yes, sir.

Then have them mobilize.

A new voice entered Volmere's mind. It sounded distant and panicked but he recognized it straight away. It was his daughter, Vissia, the captain on the scout vessel.

Father, we found a ship on the sensors. Unknown origins. It will arrive at Ronos in an hour and a half.

Has it engaged you? asked Volmere.

No, our stealth technology was able to hide us. We will keep moving away from the planet to give us as much of a warning as we can.

Volmere didn't think it was the stealth technology. Maybe the Invaders were more interested with getting to the surface than dealing with one ship. He looked at his top officer. *The first ship is on its way.*

Now?

Soon. The scouts are tracking it. Hopefully a quarter of the military is enough. The council is about to find out how wrong they are.

Is there something we can do to change their minds?

Keep no secrets. Pass along all this information. Tell them the meeting site.

They will arrest you.

It doesn't matter.

What?

The first invading ship will be here soon. Then we will know their intentions. If I'm wrong, I'll gladly surrender to the council.

And if you're right?

If I'm right then in an hour and a half hour the real war will begin.

Lemnell stayed in the clouds above the Dead Continent, awaiting the arrival of the first enemy ship, while Volmere waited on the ground with the ground troops, as he preferred. Each of them was armed with a cutter and a blade. The cutters were long spear-like weapons that had a powerful electrical charge going through them. Depending on how the weapon was held, the charge could be released as a power bolt that would turn the enemy into ash, or it could charge the sharp edge so that it could cut through almost any material. The blade they all kept strapped to their backs was more ceremonial than anything since their main weapon already acted as a blade. Of course, Volmere had won battles with his blade when his cutter was destroyed in combat, so it wasn't completely useless.

The ship is approaching your position, Lemnell reported.

The enemy ship? asked Volmere.

No. One of ours.

It was a massive warship. Instead of landing it hovered below the clouds near the other ships loyal to Volmere. Three dozen soldiers took flight from the ship and swooped down to meet Volmere. Zaxxer was leading them. He held a cutter in his hand, indicating he was ready to fight.

Volmere, you have been relieved of duty, said Zaxxer.

You do not dictate my duty, said Volmere.

You will be arrested for destruction of the colony ship. Don't act surprised or betrayed. We left you in charge of the colony ship because you promised you could uphold the covenant to keep it safe. There can be no forgiveness for its loss.

I do not ask for forgiveness.

Lemnell interrupted, *The first ship is entering the atmosphere.*

And soon, Zaxxer, you will see how wrong you and the council have been, said Volmere.

Zaxxer threw back his head, pointing the tip of his snout into the air, and then said, *You have already made up your mind. You are welcoming them with an army. They will consider us enemies because you are treating them like enemies. I will make first contact, show them friendship.*

The skies were spotted with clouds. Lemnell was hiding in one of them. The black dot indicating the approaching ship grew. Its flight pattern changed as it moved to land where Volmere and his men had gathered on the ground.

Land was a generous word. As the ship got closer the men on the ground could see smoke and debris falling. A great hissing sound could be heard emanating from the vessel. It was damaged.

It's not going to be able to land, said Volmere.

The ship was picking up speed. It was going to slam into the crust of Ronos. Zaxxer looked at this as an opportunity to show their willingness to work peacefully with the newcomers.

Fly, soldiers! Zaxxer commanded.

Not all of them took to the air—those loyal to Volmere stayed on the ground.

If I am wrong then you will be following the council's orders after this. Do as he commands, said Volmere to his men so that Zaxxer couldn't hear.

All the officers spread their wings and took to the air. They flew defensive patterns that made them look like a massive, man-made, slow-moving tornado. The soldiers would fly in slowly descending circles until they got to the ground and then they would fly up the middle of the formation until they got to the top and repeated it. This was a standard Almic formation and the soldiers could hold it for weeks if needed.

Yelven, Tevitt, bring your men with me. We are going to catch that ship and give it a safe landing, Volmere commanded two of his most trusted soldiers.

Zaxxer was giving the orders, but remained on the ground. Fifty soldiers broke formation and followed Volmere up to meet the falling ship. Instead of meeting the ship head on, Volmere let it fall past him and reached out to it from the top. Normally the Ronos Almics wore thick boots on their feet but during a battle it was more important to have another couple of limbs that could grip a weapon and fire while flying. Volmere gripped the ship, extended his wings as far as possible, and flapped as hard as he could. The other fifty soldiers followed suit.

The ship was massive; it could have held a thousand men. It looked like a dark metallic sea creature, with tentacles spinning in a futile effort to slow its descent.

Everyone flapped their wings as hard as they could to slow the fall. It was working. Now that Volmere was closer to the ship the hissing was almost deafening. He could see the ship slowly disintegrating in front of him.

Once or twice a soldier went flying off because the piece of the ship he had been gripping fell off. Quickly, the soldier flew back to the ship and gripped a more secure section.

It's falling apart, said Yelven.

Volmere, you need to see this! said Tevitt.

Volmere let go of his section and flew over to Tevitt. From where Tevitt was holding on to the ship he could see inside through a tear in the hull. Inside there were no people, no bodies, no intelligent life. All they could see were billions of tiny purple lights.

I don't understand, said Tevitt. *Zaxxer, these are not Almics.*

Let them speak for themselves.

The ship was breaking up more rapidly. The bottom of the ship was dissolving. The lights were falling out now and it looked like the fifty winged soldiers were shaking bright dust onto Ronos.

Then the Mac Gas–atmosphere got to the fuel tanks. What remained of the ship exploded. Men, chunks of the ship, and purple specks were thrown in every direction. Volmere tumbled end over end. His head was foggy and he couldn't concentrate enough to flap his own wings. He hit the ground, landing face first in a pile of the tiny lights.

Once he rolled over and had taken a moment to let his body recover he was able to look more closely. The lights went out once they touched the ground. When he stood up and looked out over the vast area the where the lights were falling, he saw that there was some sort of intelligence to them. They weren't just drifting lazily to the ground. Once they got within a couple feet they zipped across to a specific place. Each little speck had a place to be.

There's hundreds of them. Maybe a thousand! yelled Tevitt.

Of what? asked Volmere.

Bodies.

Tevitt wasn't on the ground. He had taken to the air and had a different perspective on things. Volmere and Zaxxer joined him and immediately saw what he was talking about. As more lights got to the ground it was easy to see the rough outline of bodies. Not human bodies, but Almic bodies with their wings extended. It was close to a thousand.

It isn't taking long for their bodies to form again. In a few minutes they will all be complete, said Tevitt.

Volmere issued an order to all of his men, *Take to the sky.*

Zaxxer cut in. *Do not draw your weapons.*

Everyone took off, including Zaxxer this time. Volmere kept a dialogue open with the wing leaders.

How is this possible? he asked.

It's not. This is an alien illusion. The enemy is trying to imitate or intimidate us, said Yelven.

The colony ship taught that there are others like us. Maybe they are further along the evolutionary scale than we are, said Tevitt.

This could come from the missing section. If they are the ones who sent the colony ship here then they would have more technology than we do, said another wing leader, Riv.

This could have something to do with swarming, said Volmere. But he wasn't sure if any of his men knew about that besides Witt, who wasn't there because of his injuries.

From his position on the ship in the clouds Lemnell spoke up. *We tried to gather a sample of the light but they are impossible to keep contained. We tried an airtight container, a force field—there was nothing that would keep it in the ship.*

How is that possible? said Volmere.

It can divide itself until the pieces are so small it can get through anything that is restraining it.

Then there is no way to stop their progress?

We can't contain them, but the closer they get to the surface the weaker they become. It might be possible to destroy them. Do you want me to target the gathering points on the surface?

No! said Zaxxer. *We do not know their intentions!*

The first of them, now completely formed, stood up. He stretched his limbs and wings as far as they could go and let out a massive growl of pleasure. It looked like sheer happiness, maybe even excitement. He started spinning in a circle, his wings slicing through the lights that were falling around them all, interrupting their path to the surface. Then he crouched down and took off into the air. After a couple flaps he fell back to the earth and let out another primal roar.

Once the creature was done it finally took in his surroundings, realizing he was standing in a field of lights with a cloud of creatures flying above him. All his muscles tightened and it looked like he was ready to take off again, but instead he waited. Other creatures came together and stood next to him. No one said anything, each waiting for someone else to make the first move. Zaxxer made the first contact. Tucking his wings behind him, he dove to the ground and landed in front of the first invader.

I am Zaxxer of the Almics. State your intentions.

I am Jevik. I am an Almic and this is my home.

Welcome to Ronos.

You are an Almic? said Jevik.

Yes, said Zaxxer.

You were with the fleet?

No. We were here already.

You came from the colony ship that was sent here?

Yes. The colony ship created us.

And we *created the colony ship. This is our home. You are not an Almic. You are a failed experiment. This is our home. Not yours.*

Failed? Zaxxer couldn't believe what he was hearing.

This planet has not been properly terraformed, you have allowed other life forms to develop civilizations, and there have been no preparations made for the arrival of the rest of the fleet.

It is possible to live in peace with the humans, said Volmere. Lynn had promised that it was possible.

We alone deserve to make this our home and grow our empire from this throne.

Jevik leaped at Zaxxer with such speed that Zaxxer didn't have time to react. Jevik kneeled on both arms and used his wings to keep Zaxxer's claw wings pinned to the ground. With both hands he squeezed his neck.

You do not have the means to stop us. This planet is primitive compared to our power. There is nothing you can do to dam our progression.

Tevitt used his cutter to slice off Jevik's head. The body went limp. Zaxxer threw it off of him and took to the air.

Back to the ship! Zaxxer ordered his men. Volmere and his men were going nowhere. This is what they had been preparing for. This is what they had been expecting. The war had begun.

The Ronos Almics, led by Volmere, flew through the crowd of newly formed beings, their cutters out in front of them. Each shot disintegrated an invader. They cut through the newly formed and still-forming Invaders.

The Invaders weren't going to die that easily. Ones that were already formed burst into the air. The call travelled through their ranks, *Pull their insides out! Grab their weapons!*

The initial sweep through the crowd was supposed to come out through the other side but the counter-attack bogged everyone down. The Invaders struck fast and hard. Weapons were changing hands. Both sides were taking losses. It was quickly evident that the best way to strike a killing blow was to remove the head or completely disembowel the enemy. Maiming or injuring simply made them angrier and more determined to kill.

Volmere hadn't lost his cutter yet. He struck again and again. He had been pulled out of the sky—as many of his men had—and was whipping around on the ground, striking as many Invaders as he could reach. Because of the close proximity he used his weapon to chop rather than shoot. There were a few moments of hesitation when he wasn't sure if the Almic he faced was from Ronos, or one of the Invaders. The only difference was that the Ronos Almics wore clothing.

Get the leader! Avenge the death of our brother!

Four enemies latched on to each limb and pulled Tevitt out of the sky. Desperate, he struck out with his wing claws. Going for the eyes, he stabbed the one holding his left leg. The creature stumbled back, completely blind but not out of the fight. Now he swung wildly, wanting revenge.

Volmere was near. He ran and jumped. In the air he held the cutter out in front of him and pulled the trigger. One of the attackers holding Tevitt turned to ash. That was enough for Tevitt to reach behind his back—he had already lost his cutter—and grab his blade. The other two assailants were easily taken care of. Tevitt looked for more targets.

It was a free-for-all now. The formations had all fallen apart. It was all about killing whoever was closest. Volmere tried to get his men organized again. He ducked in and out of the melee, sometimes running along the ground, switching to flying when needed. They outnumbered the Invaders, so as long as they didn't panic they could get through this with minimal casualties.

All troops move in. Lemnell, I need you to pick out the targets from the sky, said Volmere. *Then I need—*

Volmere was struck from the top and forced to the ground. His face filled with dirt and rocks. He could feel more bodies piling on top of him. Along with the loud roars and growls he could also hear the hum of attacking ships and the sizzle of their lasers. He was attacked by two Invaders. One was an ugly, heavy Almic with blood already coming out of his mouth. Volmere spread his wings and shoved them both off. The ugly attacker was run through by one of Volmere's men who had come to his aid. The other attacker was already in the air and diving back at his target.

You think you can defeat us? You think that you can kill us and be done? Pathetic. You are no Almic. We are stronger than death. Our existence is not dependent on you or your weak weapons. If we want this world then we will take this world.

Volmere unleashed a laser bolt with his cutter and dropped the Invader out of the sky. It struck him a glancing blow so he wasn't immediately incinerated. He landed with a thud on the ground. His chest was burned and his face was torn from the rough landing. Volmere walked over to put him out of his misery.

You do not have a say in my existence. I will…see you …again.

Volmere was too stunned to deliver the final blow. The Invader died anyway. Volmere flew off to make another attack but the words haunted him. "I will see you again." That soldier knew he was going to die but he was more than confident that didn't matter and he would be back to fight again. His confidence was unsettling. The distraction of that soldier's final words was enough. He was attacked by another group of Invaders, too many for him to count. He tried to fight but it was too many for him to handle all at once.

None of the people attacking him had any weapons but they still had their razor claws and he could feel them digging into his back. Two of the Invaders held Volmere's wings while the others frantically clawed at him. Some were at his neck, others at his side. The pain was almost overwhelming. He let loose a scream, both out loud and through mind speak.

The rest of the army of the Ronos Almics were moving in. The Invaders were vastly outnumbered and were being quickly cut down but they were desperate to add one more casualty. The Invaders lifted Volmere into the air and started shaking him by his wings as they clawed at him.

A lightning bolt of pain climbed up his back and paralyzed him momentarily. The Invaders tore Volmere's wings from his body. The removed appendages were tossed aside but before the death blow could be dealt Lemnell's attack ship swooped in and took them out.

Volmere hit the ground again, face first. He held still, too afraid to roll over onto his raw exposed back. Tevitt landed beside him.

Volmere!

Volmere was in too much pain to answer but he tried to get to his feet.

Stay down. The enemy is defeated. We are going to take you back to base.

No... Volmere managed to whisper in Tevitt's mind.

Don't move. You were almost killed.

Volmere shook his head. *No...the enemy has not been defeated.*

Chapter 9
Passengers

Nally led them to the courtyard surrounding the building. The courtyard, a grassy space with benches, trees, and flowers, was really a beautiful green area in the middle of a city—except that it was now pockmarked with hundreds of holes. Obviously it was the work of the Rays but there were no soldiers emerging from underneath. No heavy artillery was trying to break through the armor around the three capital towers. Not that Mac blamed them. This armor was the most secure-looking in the city, not patchworked like the rest. The pieces of metal were bigger and they were all the same shade.

What are they waiting for? Mac asked about the Rays.

Instead of answering Nally pointed up. The sun was setting and the city was getting darker by the minute. The Rays were waiting for the cover of night. The way it was looking they could strike any minute.

This is Nally. I'm trapped outside of the building. Is there a safe way for me to enter?

The message was directed at the building but she kept her eyes on the holes. As the sun set Mac realized that there wasn't much ambient light, especially with the buildings all covered up. A few of the openings in the ground were glowing. The heavy artillery was powering up, the attack about to start.

Whoever was speaking with Nally wasn't broadcasting it so that Mac could hear but Nally was letting him in on her side of the conversation.

Yes. I have the president's code word for you…The old president…We need to get in there! The Rays are about to attack…There is a great weapon hidden in that building…

Mac turned to Nally. *This battle is going to start any minute. We won't be able to get in that building until the*

Rays do. We need to hide so they don't kill us on the way in.

Nally wasn't done making her case. *This is bigger than the conflict with the Rays. There's a fleet coming to destroy our planet…Our only hope of survival is to get in that building and find the hidden weapon.*

Who are you talking to in there? asked Mac.

It's Kallen. My father's vice president. No doubt he is the one in charge now.

Mac knew she was right. He had met Kallen on the Dead Continent when he first landed. He had been dumb enough to take Zinger back with him and dumb enough to think that was some kind of victory because he hadn't gone home empty-handed.

Let's find a place to hide, said Mac.

They looked around. There was some loose rubble from an explosion on the side of a building. They were able to move enough of it to be able to wedge themselves inside and cover themselves up except for two small peepholes so they could watch the Rays' progress and wait for their chance to break inside.

Almost every single hole in the ground was glowing now. No soldiers were streaming out. They had to break through the building's armor first. It was getting darker by the minute. The glow from underground was easily the brightest thing in the city now. Mac hoped that because they weren't hiding between the holes and the three towers that no one would look back and see his and Nally's purple glow coming from their peepholes.

One by one, thick lasers began to fire from each hole, scorching the side of the closest tower. It was a slow process. There was a delay between each shot. Mac figured they were working on their aim and figuring out which parts of the building were in range of which holes. Once they figured that out they would unload everything they had until that armor was gone.

They are trying to find a weak spot in the armor that they can all aim at, said Nally, confirming what Mac already suspected.

Are there weak points? said Mac.

Must be. They think they found something.

The blasts were becoming more frequent, aimed directly at the center of the building thirty feet off the ground. Five laser blasts at a time hit it in waves. There was never a moment when the now-night sky wasn't lit up in the glow of laser fire. The side of the building was heavily scorched. Little bits of armor were burning off. Some chunks fell to the ground. The Rays were going to make it into the building without the Passengers even fighting back.

The Passengers must have realized they were in trouble. From the top of the massive building came laser fire. Several of the Rays' heavy artillery lasers exploded, rocking the ground. This just spurred the Rays to attack more. They doubled their efforts, never taking a break from pulverizing the armor. Soldiers were now streaming out of the ground.

There was a loud crack and a big explosion on the side of the tower. The armor was ripped open. The Rays let out a cheer and charged. The tear in the armor was thirty feet off the ground but the Rays had lifts in their boots. When they got to the side of the building they just pressed a button, their boots lit up, and they were propelled into the air just high enough to get into the building.

The heavy artillery stopped and even more Rays charged for the building. This was the center of government for their enemies. This was the big battle they had all been waiting for. They ran for the towers, shouting and cheering, believing the war was at an end. The Almics had been driven out of the Archipelago and now the Passengers were about to lose their capital. It was a good day to be a Ray.

Do you know where to go once we're inside? asked Mac.

Yes. But only if the bomb is where I suspect it is.
Care to share that information?
Not yet.
What are you waiting for?
I can't say yet.
Why keep it a secret?
You'll understand soon enough.

Mac looked at the Rays' glowing boots as they flew up to the gap in the building. There was also the problem of how they were going to get inside. They would have to wait until all the Rays were in there or they would get shot trying now. But the longer they waited the more Rays were going to be between them and their goal.

We need to go now, said Mac.
No, wait.
Every moment we wait makes this harder for us.
I have a plan; just wait.
For what?

Nally pointed out her peephole, smiling. She had seen what she was waiting for. Mac looked across the field of soldiers and saw it immediately. There was a new kind of soldier. He was tall. Gigantic. A foot taller than anyone else there. The soldier was also very thin and had a long head. It wore dark body armor, similar to the other Rays' black armor, but dark red. As the red soldier got to the surface it was surrounded by Rays who had their guns pointed in every direction, as if protecting this soldier was the most important thing they could do. Like winning or losing this battle was based on whether the red soldier survived. Why did Nally want to wait for him to show up? With how heavily guarded that soldier was, making a run for it now was sure to get the two of them shot.

What is that thing? asked Mac.

Nally's eyes went wide, and she covered Mac's mouth without saying anything. He couldn't figure out why she was worried that someone would overhear them? They were using mind speak!

The soldier in red pointed directly at them and three soldiers broke off from the group to investigate. The red guy could eavesdrop on conversations that were supposed to be secret. No wonder he was so important to the Rays. That's how they could know what the Passengers were going to do ahead of time.

The three soldiers headed right for the pile of rubble that Mac and Nally where hiding in. They must have noticed the purple Passenger glow. Before they even got close they started to open fire. Their hiding spot was collapsing in on them. Mac burst free holding a slab of cement in his hand. He threw it at the closest attacker. It struck him in the head; at the same time Nally jumped forward and grabbed the man's gun. He pulled the trigger to shoot her but she spun around and the lasers cut through his friends instead. Nally may not have been a soldier by trade but she still knew how to fight. Mac was impressed.

They picked up the weapons and pointed them back towards the three towers. No one else was headed their way. The red soldier was entering the building and the cheering and surging army was passionately following behind him. It was only a matter of time before they turned around to see the two glowing Passengers. Nally started dragging one of the bodies around the corner. She needed to hide but she also needed the body. Mac wanted to ask what she needed but was too afraid to mind speak now so he helped her drag the body. Once they were around the corner she pulled the boots off and switched them with hers. She pointed at one of the other bodies—that's how they were going to get in the tower.

Once they both had their boots on she showed them how they worked. To activate them Mac simply had to tap his feet together. He flew straight up into the air. How was he supposed to aim himself towards the towers? He saw

Nally lean her body forward, her feet out behind her, propelling herself forward over top of the Rays running for the towers. She had used boots like this before and knew what she was doing.

Mac had to be quick so she wouldn't get to the towers by herself. He leaned forward—too far—and was propelled hard into the ground. He spit out some dirt and looked up to see Rays turning to see the idiot who didn't know how to fly with rocket boots. They fired as Mac got his feet under him and leapt again into the air. He didn't go straight up this time. Instead he aimed himself straight for the crag in the tower's armor. Lasers cut through the air around him as he flew over the army.

As far as he knew there was no way to regulate the speed. There was simply stop and go. Right now Mac was going. In seconds he was at the building. The Rays were too distracted by something inside to stop him from entering. He couldn't bring his feet together fast enough to turn the boots off and he smashed into a wall inside the building, colliding with a group of Rays in the process. The corridor was bright with laser fire as the Rays fired down the winding staircase at Nally's fleeing figure.

Mac still hadn't turned his boots off and was still slammed against the wall. Instead of turning them off he needed to point himself towards Nally to catch up with her. Of course that wouldn't do any good if the Rays were going to shoot him before he got there. When he looked down he saw his solution. One of the Rays he had landed on had a grenade on his belt. There was no pin but there was a sliding button. Mac picked it up, activated it, then dropped it. There was panicked shouting as everyone made a run for it. No one was worried about Mac who flew down the spiral staircase.

He caught up to Nally and picked her up. She was in the middle of taking her boots off when he grabbed her. His boots weren't powerful enough to keep them both up so they slid lightly down the stairs as the explosion above them echoed through the walls.

Nally was still afraid to say anything in mind speak. She tapped his arm and Mac let her go. Then she reached up and tapped his boots together to turn them off.

"These are pretty cool," said Mac.

She started to undo her laces but Mac stopped her.

"You should keep them."

She frowned and shook her head, but didn't try to undo them anymore. It must have been an unethical thing for her to use Ray technology. Mac didn't have the same qualms.

"You won't use Ray boots or Ray guns, eh?" He knew she couldn't say anything but he needed to talk out loud so he wouldn't accidently mind speak. "Ray guns. If we were speaking the same language right now you would be impressed with my puns."

They ran down the staircase for several floors until Mac was sure they were underground. He figured the Passengers had to be pretty brave to add basements to any of their buildings, especially the capital building. The Rays were the rulers of the underground and basements were essentially invading their territory. Why hadn't the Rays come up through the basement?

They ran until they got to the very bottom and then Nally led him through a maze of doors and corridors. She knew exactly where she was going. The entire Ray army had been heading up through the building. Why were they heading down? Wasn't she worried that Rays were going to follow her?

Okay, I think we are safe to talk now, said Nally.

Because before that soldier in the red could hear our conversations?

Yes. Some of us have gifts to hear things we aren't supposed to hear. The Rays have utilized selective breeding to strengthen this quality in their military. They are very dangerous soldiers. In battle it is always a risk to mind speak. We must be careful about what we say.

So we shouldn't talk about where we're going.

No. But don't worry. I grew up in this building. I know exactly where I'm going.

What about—the thing?

The bomb?

I thought you said we have to be careful.

I think we're far enough away to not be overheard. I think I figured out what Lynn has planned for it, said Nally as they continued moving through the sub-basement of the tower. *She needed to emulate me in order to hide it and I have access to this building. So I believe it is in here somewhere. She knew that she would need it once the glow ended so it needed to be something that wouldn't accidentally be thrown out or modified or discovered.*

Why did she have to wait until the glow ended before the bomb was set off?

Setting it off early would have started a vendetta that killed everyone on this planet. Think about how fanatical the Rays and the Almics are about the colony ship. They consider it sacred and wouldn't have stopped attacking until all the Passengers were destroyed. I'm guessing she hoped that something from outside the glow would help them see that the colony ship needed to be destroyed.

So where is the bomb?

Everyone says that the Passengers don't have any part of the colony ship. You've heard that, right?

Right. The Almics have—had—a small section and then the Rays have the rest of it.

Well, that's not accurate. The Passengers have a small slab. A foot long, three inches wide, an inch thick. She pantomimed the size of it to Mac. *Very small. It's a treasured possession of the Passengers. Our people have only been in the colony ship's chamber once. And during that battle only that small piece of the colony ship was taken.*

Mac had been at that battle. The Passage people, the people he had grown up with and who had trusted him and followed him to Ronos, had fought against Raymond Tysons and his soldiers. The battle had been brutal and part of the beacon had broken off with Mac on top of it. He had been saved by Vlamm the Almic. Mac hadn't seen the end of that battle, but if the Passengers and the Rays were still fighting then the battle hadn't ended yet. That fight in the caves had been the start of a war that never ended. When the beacon had broken apart many smaller pieces had gone flying.

The colony ship is supposed to be indestructible. No one remembers how we got that small piece but it symbolizes the great power of our ancestors. If we could do it once we could do it again. That piece is on display at the top of one of these towers.

And that's where you think Lynn hid the bomb?

Yes. Only certain people are even allowed to touch it. As the daughter of the president I am one of those people. She could have used my body to switch out the real piece for the disguised bomb.

Lynn wouldn't have had the same reverence for a chunk of metal—organic substance that looked like metal; Mac didn't really know what it was made out of—that the rest of the world had so she would have had no problem violating something everyone else found sacred. She had been at that first battle as well. Once she had successfully hidden the bomb there it would be one of the safest objects in the world. She had access to the Almic beacon so she knew how to make a good copy. Not enough people had access to it that she had to worry about her copy being discovered. Plus, if she had Nally's body and memories at her disposal she could take all the time she needed to make the change and make sure no one was suspicious. Even though Lynn had never said where the bomb was Mac was sure that Nally was right.

So what's the plan? asked Mac.

Getting the bomb will be the easy part. Activating it will be significantly more complicated.

Why?

The only way to activate the bomb will be to get it to the colony ship. She had planned to use the Almic segment to activate it and then get it close enough to the Rays' portion to destroy it. But now the Almics have lost theirs, we have to go right to the Rays. It's been a long time since any Passenger made it there.

The bomb is activated by the colony ship?

Yes.

And the only colony ship left is underground with the Rays?

Yes.

She was right that it was going to be nearly impossible for them to get to the beacon. But that didn't matter if they didn't get their hands on the bomb.

We also have to make sure the Rays don't get to it first or even find out it exists. They could easily activate the bomb and then detonate it in any major Passenger city, killing millions.

Then we probably shouldn't talk about it anymore, said Mac. He wasn't convinced that the red soldier wasn't eavesdropping.

Right. No more talking about it. Just in case.

But just to settle my own curiosity, why on Earth would a government building have a basement?

It's complicated and probably shouldn't be said out loud. Let's just say that the Rays were wise not to attack from this part. They must have been given inside information because the trap is a closely guarded secret. This way. There is a lift to the top over here that requires a presidential password to use. Hopefully my father's still works.

The elevator was hidden in a wall. The code to enter the elevator had to be given through mind speak to a computer. Mac couldn't believe that kind of technology existed. If computers could pick up mind speak then it was possible that the Passengers could listen to conversations with technology like the Rays' red soldiers.

Nally ran through the list of secret phrases she had memorized when her father had been president.

Nally.

There was a negative beep from the other side of the wall.

The Welcome Home Party.

Negative beep.

Nally's Welcome Home Party.

Negative beep.

I thought you said you knew the password, said Mac.

I don't know the exact words. Just a general idea. It has something to do with his child and his favorite memory, said Nally.

You think it's going to be something as simple as a phrase?

Or what? Numbers?

Or a combination of the two.

This might take longer than I thought.

General Zinger couldn't have been happier. Everything was bending to his favor and his instincts were all following through. When the glow had first vanished and the new Ronos had been revealed he had immediately announced who he was and sought out allies through mind speak. The first people to respond were the Rays. Specifically, their leader Bellin of Sacred Lake, as he was called. Zinger was instantly able to see the influence of Raymond Tysons in the Rays and knew they would be not only powerful allies, but also a powerful weapon. The Rays, mixed with the military that Zinger already had control over, might be enough to stop the war.

Those were Zinger's initial thoughts—he'd had good intentions. But then he was taught the true power of the Rays and what they were able to do. There was no one on Ronos who was as powerful as the Rays. They had twice as many underground cities as anyone suspected. There were billions of Rays. They controlled more territory on Ronos than the Passengers by a long shot, and the Almics and their Archipelago didn't even come close. The Rays had agreed to abandon the Dead Continent like everyone else, but they hadn't. Now it was a stronghold for them. They flourished in the dark of the caves. Most of the Ray population had never seen the sun and were disgusted by the thought of living on the surface. They preferred the dark damp caves.

Zinger threw his support behind the Rays and wanted refuge with them. They were willing to grant it, for a price. They wanted information from the Passengers. After he landed on the surface he was supposed to end up with the Passengers who would take him to the capital city for questioning. Then he was supposed to relay all the information he could to Ray spies situated around the city, just below the surface.

Everything was new to him so he just narrated it all and parroted everything he was told. The Passengers were too trusting of him because he had the same glow. It didn't take long for the Rays to get the information they needed. Combining what Zinger was able to observe from the surface and what they already knew about the Passengers' preparation for attacks from the basement of buildings, the Rays struck with such speed and skill that everyone was thrown off guard.

It happened so fast the Passengers didn't even have time to suspect that it had been an inside job from the newest member of their group. Zinger was still with President Kallen and his men when they all evacuated to the government center.

Now he stood on the top floor of the main tower, pretending to be frightened about the recent attack on the towers, when really he was excited to finally move to the Rays' side of things. He was curious about their underground cities and how powerful their weapons were. Thoughts about ending the war were far from his mind now. Instead Zinger was thinking self-preservation. The Rays were the rulers of the underworld. No one could best them below the surface. Not the Passengers, not the Almics. The invading fleet wouldn't be able to do anything either. The humans of Earth didn't have a chance to survive the war but if he went with the Rays and lived underground with them, maybe Zinger would have that chance. Maybe eventually he would be able to work his way up to rule over them. It had been hard work to get to the top on Earth—it took a lot of conspiring, murdering, blackmailing, and political maneuvering—but right now he had never felt more energized in his entire life, had never felt so healthy. He could do it again. He could rule on Ronos like he had on Earth.

The top floor of the room had partially been an observation deck. The glass windows were laser-proof and explosion-proof. But that protection wasn't enough. Once they all entered the building the armor descended and covered the entire building. Now the windows looked out onto thick metal. There were offices on this floor for all the workers that ran the different segments of the government, including Kallen's office. But they were now all in the observation deck, a big open space that had windows around three quarters of the room. There were tables and chairs, as well as important monuments from the long history of the Passengers—mind-bogglingly long. Zinger still didn't understand how it was all possible; he just knew he needed to end up on the winning side.

There were a dozen government workers in the room and ten guards for each official. Even Zinger had his own guards, which was nice because he was used to that back on Earth. You don't make it to the top without making a few enemies.

The Passengers around Zinger spoke in their native tongue, which Zinger could not understand, but they all received updates from soldiers elsewhere in the building via mind speak.

The armor has been breached on the fifth floor.

This caused a flurry of nervous chatter around Zinger. He had to remember not to smile. It wouldn't be long now.

It's Nally! She entered the building! She's fighting Rays. There's someone with her but I don't recognize him. He pulled a grenade and killed a dozen Rays!

There was a cheer. Zinger had a funny feeling about the mystery person. For the last little while one person had repeatedly been a thorn in his side. Once Zinger was safely in the hands of the Rays he would make sure that Mac Narrad got what was coming to him.

The Rays are splitting up. Half of them are fighting their way up the tower. We have them pinned down at floor ten but a group has gone to the basement. We don't have any men down there to stop them.

This was grave news for Kallen. He went pale. There was something important in the basement.

Kallen nodded his head repeatedly as his top advisors laid out the situation for him. A decision was being made. Seeing the approval of their leader the advisors went to the console on the wall and tried to implement the plan.

It's not working! said Lorn Sneedman, Kallen's vice president. His announcement in mind speak caused everyone to switch over momentarily.

What do you mean it's not working? asked Kallen.

Something went wrong when the armor was ruptured. We won't be able to take off from this tower.

Then we evacuate to one of the other ones.

We can't get to the pedway with the armor up. Safety protocols. We should have taken off before they arrived.

You told me there was no way the Rays could get through. Now we're trapped.

An urgent voice broke through the fight between president and vice president. It was the soldier on the tenth floor giving updates.

They hacked into our controls. They're deactivating the armor!

There was a loud shuddering noise and the entire building shook. The armor was pulled back up into the storage areas every ten floors. All three towers were totally exposed. It would be a lot easier for the Rays to gain control now. They could move in like a flood and overwhelm the Passenger forces. That didn't faze Kallen or his advisors. They saw their opportunity to survive.

Everyone head for the pedway. We are launching the third tower!

That's when Zinger got his new instructions.

Jennyzinger, said Bellin.

Zinger hated being called that but had already corrected them so many times he didn't see the point in continuing.

What? said Zinger.

There is a weapon we need you to retrieve.

Right now?

Yes. It is with you somewhere in the main chambers of the president. It is disguised as a metal slab from the colony ship, further proof of the Passengers' lack of respect for our holy machine.

A metal slab?

Yes. A bomb in disguise.

The crowd was already moving towards the stairs to go down a floor the pedway. No one was paying attention to Zinger anymore outside of his armed escorts. They had an eager look in their eyes but were waiting for Zinger to move first. They were used to guarding dignitaries and politicians they knew. Zinger was an outsider and they didn't know how to react to him. If there had been less of them Zinger would have killed them to get them out of the way.

Go without me, said Zinger.

We can't do that, sir; we have our orders, said the lead soldier. Zinger hadn't bothered to remember his name.

Now you have new orders. Get out of here. I have other things I need to do and your ride is about to leave.

The soldiers were all glancing at their leader, waiting for permission to leave. The president and the others were probably at the pedway by now. They weren't going to wait before they took off—whatever that meant. Was there an escape ship in the other towers?

While the soldiers were looking elsewhere Zinger grabbed the closest weapon and ripped it from his hands to point it at the others.

Now the choice is easier for you, said Zinger. *A free ride out or a couple of you get shot before you're forced to shoot the man you were ordered to protect.*

Several of the younger soldiers took off. The remaining ones edged away with their weapons focused on Zinger. They didn't understand what was going on and knew there was more to the story than they were seeing. They were right but Zinger still needed them to leave. He fired a warning shot over their heads and they moved faster to the door.

Now that he was alone it didn't take long to find the slab of metal he was told was a bomb. There were several displays in the room but only one fit the description he'd been given. It was encased in glass on a pedestal. He blasted through the display case with his stolen weapon and grabbed the bomb. It was much heavier than he expected. He heard a ding behind him as an elevator arrived.

I have the bomb, said Zinger.

Good. There will be men up there shortly to retrieve it from you.

The elevator doors opened up but there were no Rays inside. It was an unknown girl and Mac Narrad.

Chapter 10
Detonate

Zinger was waiting for them when the elevator doors opened. With one hand he pointed a gun at Mac. With the other he held the bomb out in front of him to remind Mac what might happen if he pulled the trigger and hit the wrong target.

"Stay right where you are, Mac," said Zinger.

Mac stopped moving forward but didn't lower his gun.

"Do you know what you're holding?" Mac asked.

"A weapon. A powerful bomb that caught the interest of me and the rest of the Rays."

"We need that bomb."

"You've wanted to kill me for a while now. This bomb would be a nice opportunity for you."

"We are going to use it against the Invaders. The Rays are going to use it against the Passengers. Millions of humans will die."

"The only ones powerful enough to fight the Invaders are the Rays."

"You caused all this, didn't you? You brought the Rays to the surface."

"We all have our part to play."

Let him go, said Nally. *It's not worth it.*

You're kidding, right? said Mac.

Trust me.

There's nothing worth more than that bomb. If Lynn's right it could win the war.

Zinger was using the bomb as a shield so Mac shot at his legs. To keep the bomb in his grip Zinger dropped the gun. As Mac ran towards him he kept firing. The general was quick and dodged the first few shots but one clipped his leg and he fell. As he fell he threw the bomb to try and distract Mac while the general healed himself.

The three of them tensely waited, still, to see if an explosion would follow.

"You were defending yourself by blowing us all up," said Mac.

"You were burning my legs off," said Zinger. "I'm unarmed. You still want to kill me?"

"My family was unarmed."

"Very unarmed, considering they were Luddites. Couldn't even call for help."

Mac fired again, hitting Zinger in the chest and sending him flying backwards towards one of the doors leading out of the observation area. Ray soldiers ran through that door as he hit the ground.

They have the bomb! Zinger yelled.

He clutched his chest. He was badly burned but it wasn't a fatal hit—not quite. If Mac would have gotten two shots in it would have all been over. But now that was impossible with the Rays there, defending Zinger.

The whole building started to shake. He grabbed the bomb and started running, pulling Nally behind him, who was strangely reluctant. Laser fire rained down around them. Only the displays set up in the middle of the room, between them and the Rays, saved them.

Pick it up! We need to go! said Mac.

No. My leg. I'm hit, said Nally and fell to the ground.

As she fell she knocked the bomb out of Mac's hand and kicked it across the room to the advancing Rays.

What are you doing? said Mac.

It was an accident.

That's the best weapon we have.

It's too late now.

No.

Mac said it but he didn't believe it. There were a dozen Rays in the room now and more coming through the door. If he and Nally didn't start moving now they wouldn't survive. The whole building was shaking and swaying.

Something big was happening and they needed to get out of there.

We need to get to the other tower before it takes off, said Nally.

Takes off?

You'll see.

Mac would interrogate her about her lack of interest in the bomb later. She had apparently healed enough to get back to her feet and start running. This time she was pulling Mac behind her as if she was worried he would go back for the bomb, but why would that worry her? They weren't headed for the stairs. They were headed for the window facing the other tower. She ducked behind a display, pulling Mac close to her.

Trust me, okay? I know what I'm doing.

About the bomb?

No. The glass window in front of them exploded under heavy fire from the Rays. A burst of air shot into the room showering them briefly with tiny shards of glass. *About this.*

She grabbed his hand and started running. They leapt out the window. Mac fully expected to fall all the way to the ground but they only fell two floors before they hit the top of the pedway that linked all three towers. Nally was more prepared than Mac was. She hit the top of the pedway, rolled, and kept running towards the second tower, which looked like it was vibrating more than the others.

Mac hit the pedway and rolled off of it. At the last moment he reached out and gripped the edge to stop himself from the quick trip to ground level. He looked down at what could have been. There was smoke and fumes coming up from the bottom of the second tower. The Rays on the ground, confused, were running away—if they could; the ground was shaking so much that none of them could run in a straight line. It finally clicked for Mac. He knew what was happening. The second tower was a ship and, just like Nally had said, it was getting ready to lift off. If they didn't get inside it was going to leave without them.

Mac pulled himself up and started running. Nally was already at the second tower, pounding on the side, trying to get the attention of the people inside. It wasn't working. There was a loud explosion under the ground. A shockwave threw the remaining Rays clear of the building and shattered the ground as the massive tower started to take off. There was a metallic grinding sound as the moving tower pulled against the pedway.

Nally had pounded herself a handhold and gripped it with every ounce of muscle strength she could summon. Mac hadn't even gotten to the ship yet. The pedway broke off the building behind him but was still—for now—connected to the tower taking off. He ran up the pedway, its angle getting more and more extreme as the lift off continued. The engines of the massive ship were scorching anyone dumb enough to hang around down below. The remaining Rays were decimated.

Mac ran. As the pedway broke free and started to flip end over end down to the surface of Ronos, Mac kicked off the pedway towards the tower. He reached, but there was no way that Nally would be able to hang onto him. She was too busy trying not to fall herself. Mac felt the weightlessness in his stomach as he apexed and started to fall. There was no giving up. The floors of the tower were flying past him but he didn't stop reaching for the ship.

The tower was no longer moving straight up. It was dipping away from him. The ship was getting farther and farther away. Until he looked down—the bottom of the ship was getting closer. But the bottom, where the engines were, would burn him to a crisp just like it had the Rays. The ship wasn't even close to horizontal yet but the trajectory was heading in that direction. Mac kept his arms extended and looked for a handhold.

There was some damage to the ship about the tenth floor. It wasn't much but it would give him a chance at gripping it. He was falling fast. Reaching desperately, he felt the chink in the hull beneath his hands.

He was moving too fast to get a firm handhold. He bounced along the ship, waving his limbs in every direction, looking for a way to stop. He noticed the ship's flared fin at the bottom; beneath that was the flame of the engines. It was his only chance—if he could slow himself down enough he might be able to avoid skipping off of it and either falling to the ground or getting burned alive.

His feet collided with the fin. The force of the fall made his legs collapse. He fell to his hands and knees and started to slide off—the heat was incredible. As the ship's trajectory levelled off Mac was able to stop his slide. He couldn't believe he was still alive. He scrambled back up the side of the ship. The tower ship was high in the air now. There was no way the Rays would be able to get to them from the ground now.

Mac felt stupid for thinking that when the first missile hit. An explosion, out of sight from Mac, sent a tremor through the ship. The Rays had not finished their attack.

Nally, you okay? said Mac.

Yeah. Did you make it?

Barely.

I thought you were a goner for sure.

Thanks.

That's not something that needs to be thanked. I'm glad you're alive.

Parts of the armor opened up and laser cannons emerged to shoot the missiles out of the sky before they could make their target. The ship turned to become fully horizontal and now Mac could walk across the top of it to get back to Nally. He walked with his hands out on either side, afraid to lose his balance. The wind was intense and he felt he could be blown off at any moment. The ship shuddered slightly every time one of the cannons went off. That was starting to slow down as the ship got out of range of the Rays' assaults.

How do we get in this ship? asked Mac when he finally caught up to Nally.

We don't. We need to meet up with Volmere again.

We need to find a new way to get the bomb. Or maybe make our own.

Lynn's the only one who knows how to make a bomb like that so unless we find her schematics, that's not going to be an option.

But—

I left the bomb behind deliberately, Nally interrupted.

What?

Those guys could hear everything we said in mind speak. I told them all about the bomb but lied to them about it needing to be taken to the colony ship to be activated. I have the detonator. As soon as they take the bomb there I'll blow it up. They'll do the hard part for us.

And you couldn't tell me any of that because they could hear everything we were saying.

Yeah.

Okay. So now we go back with Volmere?

That's the plan. We just need to wait for Volmere to come pick us up.

You don't want to stay here with your people? asked Mac.

They don't know enough about the Rays. I need Volmere and the Almics' intel so that I know how much time to wait before I set the bomb off.

Wait, you don't have a tracking device on it?

The Rays would have seen that.

And you don't know how long to wait before you push the button?

I have a guess. It takes four hours to get from Sanctuary to the Dead Continent where the colony ship is, but that's by air. I'm assuming that it takes much longer underground, even if most of it is by water. My best guess is seventeen hours, give or take ten hours.

Give or take ten *hours? That's not precise at all. We should have just taken it there ourselves.*

That would have cost millions of lives, if *it worked. And that's a big if. There hasn't been a successful assault on the Rays' stronghold in thousands of cycles. It may be the most heavily defended place on Ronos. The only way that bomb was ever going to make it there was if the Rays took it there themselves. This is the best plan we have.*

Does Volmere know about your plan?

He will soon enough.

They could see a group of Ronos Almic ships coming closer. They were smaller bird ships that could easily weave in and out of the laser cannon fire coming from the Passenger ship. There were a dozen ships. All but one kept flying around the tower ship, distracting it, while one landed on top and lowered the ramp so Mac and Nally could quickly jump on board.

Scott's hand was getting more out of control. It felt like it was possessed. He had to concentrate hard to make sure it did as he commanded. What started out as numbness had transformed into spasms. Every so often his hand would lunge and start tapping whatever was close with his knuckles. Witt the red-winged Almic was giving him weird looks—which for the alligator-faced creatures meant that he would snap his jaw shut three times and then look at him out of one eye. Scott knew this was the Almic's suspicious body language because Witt asked him more than once if he was okay.

Now Scott was gripping his left hand with his right to keep it from moving. He was concentrating so hard that he wasn't helping Witt much at all. They were supposed to be trying to figure out what Lynn's real plans were, trying to find notes or backup drives—anything that could help them figure out how she had planned to get the bomb down to the beacon. They couldn't even find any evidence that she had designed or built a bomb. Or why the beacon needed to be destroyed.

We need to go back to the lab, said Scott.

The ocean pressure crushed the lab. There's nothing left.

What if something floated to the surface? What if there's something on one of the other islands?

The Rays have taken the Archipelago. We can't go back unless we know it's there. It would be a waste of manpower. Maybe a waste of lives.

Scott slammed his fist on his armchair. Witt gave him another suspicious look. The clicking of his teeth unnerved Scott.

Was that you or her? asked Witt.

A combination.

Maybe instead of trying to guess what she was trying we could just ask her.

Ask away. I don't think she has any ears right now.

Hmm…None of this would be a problem if we could just get her to tell us her plan.

How do we get her a body?

Try moving her to another part of your body, said Witt. *Put your fingers in your mouth.*

It was too simple to work. All five fingers were in his mouth but the numbness and spasms didn't move from his hand to his mouth.

You're assuming that she is trying to say anything, said Scott once his fingers were out. *What if she doesn't know what's going on?*

There has to be a way for her to get out of you or she never would have latched on to you in the first place, said Witt.

Well, I'll let her do her thing and you tell me if you can see a pattern or message or something, because I can't figure it out.

He let the hand run wild. It rapped his knuckles on the arm of the chair he was sitting in. It rubbed the fingers on his leg. It made a fist then released it. Each time it was in a different order and each time it was a slightly different move. There was no pattern. None of it made sense.

Do you know her history? asked Scott.

My family has known her ever since she came to live with the Almics. My ancestors were on the ship that went up to save her.

And she was with the Almics the whole time? All her info was with you guys, on your computers?

No. There's Nally and the Passengers. Lynn was over there for a time.

Any access to their systems from here?

Good idea. I'll see what comes up.

Witt worked on that while Scott went back to focusing on his hand. Despite the randomness he was still certain there was a message in it somewhere. He let the hand go free to do whatever Lynn wanted. There were spasm and swipes, knocks and fists, but Scott refused to restrain her anymore. Witt had been at the computer for more than an hour when Scott noticed that the spasms weren't happening as often anymore. She was calming down, it seemed.

There was a sudden bustle of activity as the ship picked up Mac and Nally. Scott and Witt had been in a makeshift office in a supply room. All they needed was a console that had access to the all the Almic networks. Supplies for the ship surrounded the two of them. The door didn't even close all the way—they could see people running to meet Mac and Nally and to see the bomb.

We better go get an update, said Witt.

He went out the door but headed to the infirmary instead of the docking bay.

Why are we here? asked Scott.

This is where they are going to come. They will want to know that Volmere is okay.

They went in the infirmary and walked to a room flanked by guards. Everyone recognized Witt—who had almost as much clout as Volmere—so no one stopped him from bringing Scott into Volmere's room. Almic hospital beds were huge, mostly because there were times when the wings needed to be fully extended for proper healing. Volmere wasn't going to have that problem. He was lying face down on the bed. His long head went through a hole in the top of the bed. His back was covered in bandages.

Who is there? asked Volmere.

Witt and Scott Ryder. Mac and Nally are back.

They have the weapon?

They should. They sent the signal to be picked up.

Just then Mac and Nally came into the room, accompanied by another Almic that Scott couldn't distinguish. Mac and Nally were empty-handed.

They don't have the bomb, sir, said the new Almic.

What? Where are they, Lemnell?

We're here, said Nally. *Listen. We were never going to get that bomb to the Rays' colony ship so I tricked them into taking it there themselves. They know it's a powerful weapon and they think they need to take it to their colony ship to activate it. Once it's there I'll detonate it.*

Good, said Volmere. *I needed some good news.*

Are you okay? said Mac.

I'll live. I'm well enough to still be in charge of repelling the invasion. Any news from Vissia? Volmere asked Lemnell.

Yes. Her long-range sensors have shown that the Invaders are preparing a ship on the outskirts of our system for an attack on Ronos. She doesn't know what kind of ship it is or what it can do but it is heavily guarded so it has to be important. Some kind of weapon or massive transport.

If they can get enough soldiers here at the same time we won't have a chance.

We will destroy that ship before it can land. Other Almic forces have abandoned the council and joined our cause. Now with the Passengers under attack from Rays we might have their attention as well.

Their leaders are on board the ship you picked us up from, said Nally. *Talk to them. Tell them everything and beg them to help us.*

We were already going to do that, said Lemnell. He turned to leave. There was no reason for him to be there to receive orders. He had just been escorting Mac and Nally.

There's one other thing, said Mac, giving Nally a nervous look. *We don't know exactly when the bomb will get to the beacon.*

What?

Well, I wasn't able to put a tracking device on it, said Nally. *We need to time it out. According to your intel, how long does it take to get from Sanctuary to the colony ship?*

Scott wasn't listening to the conversation. He was worried about his hand. He thought he had calmed Lynn down but now that he was walking around his hand was really freaking out, pulling away from his body and flopping around. Mac, though heavily invested in the conversation between Nally and Volmere, noticed Scott's weird behavior and sent him a questioning look. All Scott could do was raise his shoulders. It's not like he could control what Lynn did to his body.

Scott's hand unplugged the IV going into Volmere. Blue liquid shot out everywhere. Volmere's bandages were soaked and the floor was smeared. Scott didn't know what it was or if it was dangerous to humans but he got down on the ground and tried to wipe it up.

Mac ran over to him with some towels. Before he started wiping he looked at the pattern Lynn was making in the blue liquid.

"Stop," said Mac.

"It was Lynn. I should've been paying more attention," said Scott.

"Stop wiping it up."

Scott's body stopped moving except for his left hand. It was repeating a pattern now. Like Lynn could feel the liquid in under the fingers.

"She's trying to tell us something," said Mac. He bent down and grabbed Scott's arm. He put the arm down for a moment, then moved to the side so she could make another symbol, and then moved it again to continue.

"T. E. K," said Scott, reading the letters.

"Tek? Does that mean anything to you?" asked Mac.

"No."

Does anyone here know what Tek means or why Lynn would be trying to tell us about it? Mac asked the group.

I'll check our system, said Witt. He moved to a nearby console and started typing. Mac moved beside him, curious about what he would type—mind speak acted as a universal translator, but this was writing. The Almic alphabet was vastly different from the human alphabet. The keys and symbols that Witt was inputting had no relation to the letters that Mac knew. There was no way the Almics would know anything about Tek. Witt changed the display and then traced the three letters onto the screen with the knuckle of his longest finger and searched again. Nothing came up.

If it means something, said Witt, *then it comes from her time before she came here.*

"That means there could be information on the Imp networks," said Scott.

"There are no Imp networks on Ronos," said Mac.

"What about up there?" Scott pointed up to the space station *Lendrum*. It would be easy enough to go up there and do a search.

We're going to leave the planet, said Mac. *We might be able to find out what Lynn is trying to tell us. But we need a ship to take us up there.*

We have been converting our ships to survive in space. There are several that are available, said Volmere.

How much longer before you detonate the bomb?

Less than twelve hours. We'll keep you in the loop while you are gone.

Thanks.

Be careful of the fleet massing on the edge of this system. If they all come at once there might not be anything we can do to stop them from destroying your ships up there.

Well, hopefully we'll get our answers before that happens.

Zinger had expected to be hailed as a hero among the Rays but instead he was being treated like a prisoner. His demand to be the one who escorted the bomb to the beacon to activate it had been happily obliged. They taped the bomb to his hands and bound him to a seat in one of the drill machines that the Rays used to travel underground. He didn't know what the tape or the bindings were made of but even with his enhanced strength there was nothing he could do to break it. The only reason he could think that they would be fine with him holding the bomb all the way to the beacon was because they never intended to let him drop the bomb—he was going to be holding it when they exploded it. That wasn't part of their agreement—or in his plan—so he started to look for an escape.

The long trip to the beacon started underground. The sound of the drill machine moving through the pre-made tunnels was loud, but not uncomfortably loud. More like a hover car that wasn't properly sound proof so the wind rushing against it could be heard inside, except that for the drill machine it was the rubbing of rock on the outside of the ship. All the drill machines he had seen had rough-looking exteriors.

The vibrating of the ship ended and was replaced with the sound of fluid bobbing. The engine clicked and started vibrating from the rear of the ship. They had moved to the ocean now. The drill ship had turned into a submarine. There were two dozen other soldiers in the ship with Zinger. It was a tightly-packed group, but not as tight as it needed to be. They were all avoiding sitting right next to Zinger. Bellin wasn't on the ship either, probably as a safety precaution.

The longer they travelled, the more it felt like a funeral procession and these Ray soldiers were his pallbearers.— except now he wasn't as big as he used to be so he didn't need quite so many. That didn't matter. What mattered was that Zinger had been in worse situations than this and had come out alive. He had worked his way from the bottom to the top of the military and in the process had changed the government from a democracy to a faux-democracy-military-dictatorship. He had done that, no one else. If he could do that, if he could lead the military to repel an alien invasion—which admittedly hadn't been successful yet, but would have if it hadn't been for Mac Narrad—then he shouldn't have a problem separating himself from the bomb before it went off.

He leaned back in his seat, smiling and closing his eyes, having convinced himself that everything was going to be okay, and fell asleep.

"How do you think the people on the *Lendrum* are going to react to us?" said Scott.

"Because we are glowing or because your left arm is possessed by an alien swarm?" said Mac.

"The glowing mostly. And Lynn isn't an alien, remember?"

"Sorry."

All the Passage people were on an Almic ship heading to the space station. The Glover family looked happy to be away from the war, and so did Clarissa, but Darren still had the yearning for adventure in his eyes and was disappointed to be so far away from the action now. He had tried to talk his way into staying but neither Mac nor Volmere felt comfortable with that. Not yet, anyway. There were real soldiers that could fight in the war right now. They hadn't become so desperate that they needed to arm civilians.

Mac opened a channel to the space station. "This is Mac Narrad. I'm a human from the surface. I was the one who stopped the *Rundle* from blowing you up. We need to come on board and access your Imp network."

"What kind of idiot do you think I am?"

"Excuse me?"

"Why would I let someone from the surface onto my station?" The voice was female and she sounded stressed.

"What's your name?"

"Asking for my name isn't going to change my mind. We have taken on refugees and our resources are already stretched."

"There's only three of us—"

"Two," corrected Scott.

"There's only two of us," said Mac. "I'm human. I'm the one who sent the refugees over. Confirm it with them. My name is Mac Narrad. I'm from Passage on Earth. All I need is to access your Imp network via a monitor."

"You don't need to be on our station to access the Imp networks."

"I don't have an Imp."

"What is a Luddite doing so far from home?" She, like most people, had the misunderstanding that Luddites truly hated all technology, including hover cars and shuttles.

"You can supervise the whole thing. Even if I have to do it at gunpoint, it doesn't matter, but I need to do it. Five minutes. Then we will get back on our ship and be gone."

She didn't say anything for a while.

"Five minutes," repeated Mac.

"I heard you the first time. Let me confirm your identity with the refugees."

There was a pause while she went to confirm what Mac was saying. He didn't stop moving towards the Lundrum. Sure, he may have been asking permission, but truthfully he was getting into that space station one way or another. All they needed to do was do a simple computer search.

"Head to the lower docks. We're having problems sending the coordinates to your ship so we'll leave the door open for you to see. Just go to the lowest point on the station and land inside. I'll be there personally to greet you and hold the gun to your head while you do your search."

Mac was piloting the ship. Scott could have done it as well but not with Lynn in control of one of his hands. Once he found the docking bay he skilfully flew the ship inside and landed. The doors of the Almic space ship, which looked like a pair of wings like all their other ships, opened and the Passage people led the way out.

"You are already lying to me," said the woman waiting there for them.

"They're kids and old people. They stay. We will go once our search is done. Can you handle that?" said Mac. He looked at her name tag. "Can you handle that, Miss Hunter?"

"Genny Hunter," she said as the kids walked past her. There was a security force behind her but they didn't know what to do about the children with the subtle glow. Mac wasn't sure how he would explain that the glow enabled them to survive on the surface of Ronos, so he ignored their stunned faces for now. There were more important things to talk about. He reached out and shook her hand. She hesitated a moment, wondering if anything would happen if she touched him, but decided it was safe and shook.

"Thank you," said Mac.

She nodded her head but was still unhappy about the strangeness of it all.

Then she reached for Scott's hand.

As soon as she shook Scott's hand she froze. The numbness in his body moved from his left hand, up his arm, across his chest, and down into his right hand before vanishing completely into Genny Hunter. Her eyes got wide and she collapsed into his arms. He was caught so off guard he almost dropped her. It was like she had fainted but was still fully conscious. Her eyes were wide and she looked around her as if lost.

"Scott," she said.

"Yeah. Scott Ryder. We really just need a terminal to—"

"It's me."

They didn't know what to say. Did she mean *me* as in Lynn? The security people in the docking bay were pointing their weapons at them and moving closer. Lynn realized what was going on and stepped back into place while giving her head a shake.

"I probably shouldn't have skipped breakfast," she said. "Sorry about that. You guys are dismissed. We have nothing to fear from these people."

The guards hesitated a moment, not sure if they believed what they were being told.

"Go now. I'll give you further orders from the command deck."

The guards left.

"Is that you, Lynn?" asked Mac.

"Yes. I knew pulling Nally out of the emulating pool would mean I couldn't hold my form so I put myself inside of Scott to save myself."

"But his arm just went numb. Why didn't you take over his whole body so we could talk to you like we are now?"

"Because that's as much as I could do to a human that's been changed by the Mac Gas and Lynn Rock. This Genny Hunter woman is a normal human—much easier for me to take over. Swarms can survive without emulators for a short amount of time."

"We got your message," said Scott.

"About Tek! Good. I had no idea if that was getting through or not. I just kept thinking the same thing over and over again, hoping you would understand. But obviously you did—that's why I'm here."

Mac and Scott looked awkwardly at each other.

"We didn't understand. You're here by accident. I shook her hand and you went over to her body," said Scott.

"You don't know who Tek is?" she said.

"No. Didn't even know it was a person."

"Tek was a man I was trapped with in the rubble of Northgate. He had an arm that was possessed by an alien. I was trying to tell you that's what I was doing to you and to try and get me a new body."

"Only his arm was possessed?" asked Mac.

"Yeah. My guess is that he didn't have a full swarm inside of him. If he did his whole body would have been taken over."

"We never would have figured that out," said Scott.

"It still worked out," said Lynn. "So what's going on?"

Mac looked down at his watch. "Well, Nally and I found your bomb on Sanctuary and it's on its way to the beacon now to destroy it."

Lynn—in Genny's body—had been smiling from ear to ear but at this news it vanished. Panic filled her features.

"My bomb?"

"Yeah," said Mac. "The bomb you designed to destroy the beacon. We found it."

"It wasn't designed to destroy the beacon."

"What?"

"It was designed to clear a path to the beacon. I was never able to build something powerful enough to destroy the beacon."

"But you told me—" Scott started to say.

"The only thing strong enough to destroy the beacon *is* the beacon. We use the bomb to clear a path to the Ray's beacon. Then we crash the Almic beacon into it, doing enough damage to stop the Invaders from being able to hold their swarm form."

"What? What does the beacon have to do with the swarm forms?" asked Mac.

"The beacon has been sending out a signal for millions of years. Maybe signal isn't the right word for it. Energy might be more appropriate. Something humans have never been able to see or measure. That energy is feeding the Invaders' abilities to swarm. I was able to harness that energy to slow down the deterioration of my body. It gave me nourishment. From the beacon I extracted some plans to build a machine that could harvest the energy and transfer it from one body to another—from an anchor to an emulator—from a human body to a fabricated body I could live through. This energy, as far as I could tell, is artificial. It *only* comes from the beacon. If we destroy the beacon, the swarms disintegrate into nothing and stop being a threat."

"Destroy the beacon. Win the war," said Scott.

"Yes. But it's not going to be easy."

Mac felt the emotional blow to his entire body. He was hoping for the weight on his shoulders to be lifted when they figured out Lynn's message, but now it was amplified.

"What's wrong, Mac?" said Lynn.

"There is no Almic beacon. It's gone."

"That's impossible."

"It got crushed by the depths of the ocean in the Ray attack."

Lynn wasn't deterred. "Then that's what we'll do to the Ray beacon. Detonate the bomb now. Expose the beacon. Then we'll go down, pick it up and carry it over the ocean and destroy it."

"Is that possible?" said Mac.

"It sure won't work with you sitting on the floor like that. Get up and tell Volmere what's going on. Get him to activate the bomb and then we'll try our next plan."

Mac didn't know how to explain it but deep in his heart he knew that whatever Lynn was planning, it wasn't going to work.

Zinger still had the bomb in his hands when he woke up. He didn't know how long he had been asleep but it must have been a while because the drill ship had stopped and everyone was getting out. Four guards stood around him with their weapons pointed at his head. These guys didn't take chances—every shot was a kill shot.

He walked out of the drill ship into a massive cavern that was a beehive of activity. There were thousands of Rays in the room, all moving around an especially massive machine. Zinger rightly guessed that the machine was the beacon. The plan was working. Soon the bomb would be activated and he would be in charge. He could hold all one thousand people there hostage, demanding they do whatever he wanted or the bomb would blow.

The guards escorted him to the beacon. As they walked they all heard a beeping noise. All the noises in the cavern were new to Zinger. Everything echoed and it felt like he was listening to a thousand whispered conversations at the same time. So he didn't give the beeping a second thought.

The soldiers, on the other hand, grabbed Zinger and inspected the bomb. The beeping was coming from inside of it.

You activated it! said one of them.

Yes. And I'll use it if you don't do what I say. Take me to Bellin. I want to stay in your most fortified city when the fighting starts up top. And I want—

The explosion tore through the cavern and instantly vaporized Zinger and all the Rays surrounding the beacon. The explosion surged through the underground tunnels, allowing the power of the bomb to get farther and vaporize more soil and rocks, until it burst through to the surface of Ronos in a glorious flaming ball of destruction. The crater from the bomb was bigger than that of any bomb the humans on Earth, or Ronos, had ever invented before.

Lynn hadn't designed the bomb to be exploded right next to the beacon, but as a tool to excavate it. The explosion hadn't created a clear line of sight. Looking to the bottom of the crater, all anyone could see was more rocks but the beacon was down there somewhere. And it was closer to the surface than it had ever been.

For Mac, ending the war, and maybe even finally finding Janelle, had never been closer. Now all he had to do was destroy one of the most powerful ships in the universe. Somehow.

Chapter 11
Mind Prison

Five Years Earlier

The light vanished as soon as Janelle Stewart was inside the alien ship. She expected to fall to the floor but instead was still suspended in the air. The room she was in didn't have a floor. She was floating in the middle—as if on display. There was a walkway all the way around, against the walls and above the bottomless floor area. On the walkway were aliens—tall purple aliens.

"This can't be real," she said to Mac, but there was no reply.

"Mac?"

She craned her neck to try and look around her but as far as she could see she was alone, unless Mac was right behind her. If he was, why didn't he answer? Hadn't he been sucked up with her? He had been right there. She could still look down, could still see the lights of Passage in the distance. Grass and crops. Hover cars on the highway. Mac on the ground, shouting up to her. She couldn't hear what he was saying. Then the engines of the massive ship hummed to life and the ship left Passage.

There was another city below them now—skyscrapers on either side of a wide river. It took her a moment to recognize the location as Northgate. She had never seen it from this angle. She was over a city park full of people running around, screaming and pointing. They were as confused as she and Mac had been. The light turned on. She could see it all happening. Five people were caught in the light and lifted off the ground. Mechanical arms extended from the beetle-like collector ship and dragged four of the people back to the ground. One middle-aged lady rose to Janelle's level and hovered in the air next to her.

"What's going on?!" she screamed over and over again.

"It's okay," Janelle tried to soothe her, but the lady wasn't having it. The purple creatures watching the abductions displayed no reaction to what either of them were saying.

The lady was flailing her arms and legs, trying to move out from the middle of the bottomless room, but she didn't go anywhere. The only thing she came close to was accidentally hitting Janelle.

"You almost kicked me in the head," said Janelle.

"Where are we?"

"I don't know."

"How do we get out of here?"

"I don't know. I've only been here two minutes longer than you have."

"Where were you?"

"Passage. South of Northgate."

"You're a Luddite?"

"No, but—"

"My Implant isn't working. I can't even call for help."

"This ship is the size of a small city. It's not going to go unnoticed."

"They have to come for us."

"They will."

"They need to save us."

"They will."

"I'm not supposed to be here."

She was breathing heavily and babbling randomly. Janelle realized she wasn't specifically talking to her, and why should she? Janelle was a high school kid. Sure, she would technically be an adult in a few months, but to many people she was still a kid. This lady had to be at least forty, maybe even fifty. She should be comforting Janelle, not the other way around.

"What's your name?" asked Janelle.

"Bernadette."

"I'm Janelle."

"They're going to kill us."

"They aren't."

"They are."

"If they were going to kill us then they would have already."

"My kids. My grandkids. They got left behind. What if they got hurt?"

They were both looking down. Northgate was long gone. The view was now all of North America. Because it was night on this side of the planet it was difficult to see any of the major landmarks, like the Rocky Mountains or the Great Lakes. The best she could do was guess from where the lights were. The collector ship was like a bouncing ball that abducted another person every time it hit the ground. The next time they came down and a giant black man was caught up in the light. He was screaming and flexing every muscle in his body. He was yelling at the purple men surrounding them, but did not get any reaction out of them.

"What is this! What is happening! What is going on!" Each shout was so loud and so desperate Janelle could feel it echoing in her chest.

There were five purple men—probably men—staring at them from the walkway. None of them said anything to the abductees or to each other. No official statement, no explanation, was ever given by the aliens.

The ship went back up. First the cities, then the lights, and then the planet disappeared. The stars stretched out below them. They were leaving everyone else behind. Humans had not come across intelligent life outside of Earth yet. They had built dozens of colonies in several solar sytems but had found no other civilizations. Whoever had just abducted them had come from a long way away. The farther they went the more she realized she probably wasn't going to see her home world, family, or Mac, ever again.

The ceiling rippled like it was made out of metallic water. Metallic arms—smaller versions of the one that had plucked her out of the air a few moments ago—emerged, each holding a needle with green liquid moving through it. Three arms for the three abductees. They were each injected. As they lost consciousness, they unknowingly said goodbye to the physical world and entered the mind prison set up for the emulated.

The last thing Janelle saw was the purple aliens' expressionless faces. Then her entire world turned green. She felt like she was floating—no, sinking—in a green ocean. The murky liquid was sucking her down. She had no control over her body, could not swim to freedom. She panicked, knowing she could only hold her breath so long.

Except, she realized, she didn't need to breathe. She couldn't command her body to swim because she couldn't feel her body. She couldn't even move her head to look down at her body. It was like she only really existed in her mind, and all her mind could see was endless shades of green.

There was no way for her to know how much time had passed unless she counted out the seconds in her head.

It got to the point where she became that desperate.

Then it got to the point where she got bored of counting.

She realized she couldn't get tired.

Sleeping wasn't an option.

All she could do was float.

Is this why she and the others were taken? The aliens wanted to see how long humans could exist in a green world before they went insane? It wasn't going to be much longer before that very thing happened to her.

Then, as suddenly as it had engulfed her, the green ocean receded. Janelle was lying on her back looking up at a clear blue sky. For a moment it felt like she had fallen asleep outside and that the abduction had been only a bad dream. But then she realized she couldn't feel the grass underneath her or the warmth of the sun on her face—none of this was real. She sat up and looked around. She was in what resembled a prison yard. Bernadette and the black man who'd been captured soon after her—she would later learn his name was Reggie—were there, as well as thirty-six other humans, all lying on the ground.

Janelle was the first to stand up. She could see a creature standing near the main gate leading into the prison yard. He wore thick, insulated white clothing and had purple skin. He looked exactly like the beings that had abducted her. Who were these guys?

Who is your leader? asked the purple man. His voice echoed inside of her head. His mouth did not move.

None of them said anything—first, because the humans hadn't even all met each other, let alone decided which one of them was in charge; second, this purple alien had played a part in their abduction, so why should they give him any information?

When no one moved he tried to soothe their worries by speaking to their minds again.

You have been taken captive by an alien race known as the Almics. They have taken everyone here—including me. No doubt you are having trouble trusting me because you saw me on the outside. Maybe I played a role in your abduction. I assure you they were using my body against my will. I mean you no harm. No one here will hurt you. I've unlocked the prison gates. When you are ready to learn more about what is going on here I'll be waiting in the field outside with the others.

Then he smiled and left. He walked to the gate and went through without closing it behind him. Janelle racked her brain, trying to decide if this was a trap of some kind. But she couldn't figure it out. She couldn't figure anything out. Why couldn't she feel anything anymore? Why was there no smell here? Her senses were all dulled and it made her uncomfortable. For that matter, where were they to begin with? Why put them in a prison and then leave the door open? Why were they all taken?

There were too many questions. She headed for the gate to get her answers.

"Don't go out there," said Bernadette.

"I need to know," said Janelle.

She ran across the field and through the gate. She stopped cold in her tracks. Reggie and a couple others had followed her but stood back to make it look like she was in charge.

There were other people in the field. People—not humans. It was the strangest collection of aliens— sometimes monstrous-looking creatures. One creature looked like a walking tripod. Where the three legs came together there was a mouth; on top of the mouth was a giant eye that could spin in every direction. The creature was only as tall as her. Each of the legs had a seven-digit hand at the end. When it sat at a table it used two of its hands to move around whatever was on the table while the third hand kept it balanced. When it got up and moved it used all three legs to walk. It was a disturbing sight. There were three dog-like creatures moving together as a pack. They had long alligator heads but were covered in fur. Their mouths had endless rows of teeth and their tongues were almost as long as their bodies, flopping in and out of their mouths. More than once she saw a tongue flop onto the ground. There were beings that could fly. There were beings that looked like they were made of jelly. Almost anything that Janelle could imagine was standing in the field.

The field itself was massive—no end in sight and the crowd went way back with it. There were more buildings, more prisons than the one the humans had come out of and, like the aliens in the field, none of them looked the same. From the outside the human prison looked very much like a prison back on Earth.

"My name is Janelle," she said to the purple man who was standing very near the gate, as if he knew someone would come right away.

My name is Rizzen. My people are the Bize. My ability to speak with my mind transcends language restrictions. I can talk to you but until I learn what you are saying to me this will be a one-sided relationship. I will talk to you but I won't be able to hear your replies. Is this acceptable?

"Yes," said Reggie, close behind Janelle.

Janelle laughed. So did Rizzen. This purple dude had a sense of humor—asking a question when he knows he won't understand the answer, and then laughing when it's answered anyway. He looked at her and smiled. For an alien abductor he was very nice.

You. Step forward if you are willing to help me learn your language.

Janelle didn't hesitate to step forward, and nodded her head.

The movement of your head is significant?

She nodded her head again.

It means "Yes"?

She nodded again and he nodded back, smiling. He must have been in charge because he liked to learn.

You are all the prisoners of the Almic people. We are all prisoners of them. Everyone here is in the same situation that you are, said Rizzen, repeating what he had already said in an effort to make the humans realize they were all on the same side. *We do not know how to leave the prison. The field you stand on goes on forever. Each species has a prison building that is their own. You are not permitted to go in another species' prison. There is no contact with the outside world. You are free to try but we have not been successful. Communication is the biggest problem here. Your best chance is to memorize these two simple gestures that are universal.* He opened his six-fingered hand, with fingers twice the length of Janelle's, and raised it into the air. *This means "Yes."* Then he flipped his hand palm down and lowered it. *This means "No." No one else can communicate with you with their mind like me. These gestures will help me to learn your language.*

Rizzen frowned—assuming that turning the edges of your mouth down meant the same thing to the Bize as to humans—like there was other bad news he was holding back.

Enough time had passed for Rizzen to learn to effectively communicate with the humans. It helped that he had a similarly-shaped mouth and tongue. It wasn't long before he told Janelle the bad news. The Almics didn't just attack and move on: They destroyed civilizations. Captured as many as they could to use for emulators and then moved on. The words he said were without hope, but the way he said them still comforted Janelle. That was his gift and it was why he was one of the most popular people in the prison. That, and he could communicate with almost anyone there.

The Almics didn't have a home world but they did have billions of ships. Each time they destroyed a civilization they added the fallen people's ships to their fleet and became more powerful. They were virtually unstoppable now. The only thing that kept them from barrelling through the human's territory was that they weren't sure exactly which way they were going—they were looking for something but none of the prisoners was exactly sure what.

That's not to say they didn't know anything about the Invaders. Janelle was told all about emulators and swarms and how to stop them. She knew that the aliens could read the minds of all their prisoners so there were no secrets.

When the aliens encountered a new species they always abducted a few dozen of them. The first round of abductees were split into two groups: one for learning how to emulate the new species they had encountered, and a second group for experimenting and dissecting to understand their weaknesses. Janelle had been lucky enough to be in the first group.

All the prisoners agreed that the Almics were not to be trusted. Once they had decided to attack they attacked, and nothing could stop them. They didn't stop until everyone was dead or emulated. They were an unstoppable wave of destruction. Rizzen gave hope but the others knew that it was only a matter of time before the humans were in the same boat as them.

"Why do you learn everyone's language?" Janelle asked him.

Because it's what a good host does.

"So...you were here first?"

Yes.

She had never seen any other purple people. He wasn't just the first—he was the only Bize left.

"I'm sorry."

No need for being sorry. It was a long time ago. I have new people to serve now.

"Has anyone ever broken out of here? In all the time you've been here. I mean, I know you say it's impossible but...in all this time and with all these people, has no one even come close?"

They can read our minds. They will know what we do before we do it.

"So it is impossible."

Rizzen hesitated. Janelle prodded him.

I made it out once.

"Really?"

It was not worth the price I paid.

"How did you do it?"

Almics are very good at learning from their mistakes. I would not be able to do it again.

"You're sure of that?"

Yes.

"If it were your civilization on the brink of extinction would you give up trying?"

No. I do not give up hope. But there are other ways to prepare for the day we leave this prison. On that day there are going to be billions of prisoners free, without a clue what to do or how to survive. If I can get everyone to be able to communicate with each other then maybe we can avoid another war when this all ends.

"Then you do think we will get out of here."

I think it's outside of our control. But we have a lot of time on our hands to prepare for the worst.

"The worst thing being that we get free and then immediately start killing each other."

Right now we are all united because we have a common enemy. But if that enemy didn't exist anymore, then what would keep us all together? There are dozens of civilizations imprisoned here. What if two of them have conflicting goals when the Almics are gone?

Janelle was about to ask about which groups were prepared to go to war when the feeling returned. She had been feeling it for the last little bit. A familiar feeling—which wasn't a good way of describing it, because it wasn't something she had ever felt before. It was more of a feeling of being recognized. Like someone was watching her. But they were in a field full of billions of people—of course she was being watched. It was so strange and she could never accurately describe it to Rizzen so she just called it her familiar feeling.

"It's back," she said.

What?

"My familiar feeling. Do you see anyone watching us?"

They both spun in a circle, taking in the massive crowd. The two of them had been standing. Everyone was standing. One of the good things about their minds being trapped was they didn't have bodies that needed rest so no one needed to sit, rest, or even sleep. It felt weird at first but she got used to it. It was interesting, the things she had gotten used to, not sitting, not eating, not being aware of the passage of time.

No one was looking at them. They did this every time she got this feeling and no one was ever paying them any attention, or at least not paying her any attention. Then she heard a familiar voice.

"Janelle, where is Janelle?"

It was Mac. Janelle could hear his voice as clear as day. It came from inside her head, like when Rizzen talked to her. She closed her eyes to focus on the sound, to try and figure out where it came from. When she opened them again she was somewhere new.

She was on a collector ship with Mac—talking to him. She spoke quickly, telling him everything she could. A few moments later she was back in the field with Rizzen. A group had formed around the two of them. Whatever had happened, it must have looked weird to them. Nothing different ever happened in the mind prison so they were all captivated.

"I'm fine. I'm back now," said Janelle.

Where did you go?

"I was inside a swarm body. One of their leaders. I was talking to one of our men. A friend of mine."

Rizzen was nodding his head, as if he understood.

You kept vanishing and reappearing. Your mind was moving between bodies. What did you learn?

"Mac knows where the Almics are headed. He's going to try and stop them. I told him about the emulators."

"That's huge," said Jace Michaels. He had bright orange hair and was one of the earliest human soldiers to have been emulated. "No human outside this prison knows anything about the emulators—other than that they're being used."

"I told him as much as I could but I didn't have enough time. The aliens weren't prepared for me to take over but they fought back quickly," said Janelle.

Janelle moving her mind outside the prison was the biggest thing to happen since Rizzen's time. There was nothing to do there but talk and now everyone wanted to talk to her—which didn't make sense to her because she didn't know how she had momentarily escaped or if she could do it again. Even if she could, that meant that only her mind was outside the prison. There was still her body to worry about. The answers weren't going to come from her or from Rizzen. The only way to get new information was from the new captives.

"Let's go back to the prison."

New captives always showed up in the prison designated for their species. Rizzen was the only being who was allowed to enter any species' prison—he was the unofficial leader and peacekeeper. The stream of new arrivals was getting more and more frequent but it was still sporadic. Bernadette had taken it on herself to welcome the human newcomers and orient them. Then Reggie and a couple other men would question them, trying to learn about the progress of the war.

Janelle and Rizzen walked over to Reggie, who was in the yard of the human prison. Reggie was talking to a soldier, younger than most, who had just arrived. His eyes were wide with shock. He was going to need a minute to wrap his head around what had happened.

"Something happened," said Janelle.

"What? Just come out with it. It's been a long day and I'm tired of asking questions." Reggie sometimes got depressed seeing all the humans coming. It wasn't ever good to see someone new there, even if it was the only way to get news from the outside world.

"I left the prison. Or my mind did."

"How?"

"I don't know. It kind of just happened," said Janelle, "I heard a voice calling me and then I was out."

"Does that mean you don't know how to replicate it?"

"I wish I did."

But no one's ever done that before. Has something changed in the war? said Rizzen.

"Nothing abnormal," said Reggie. "Capital ship got destroyed. The survivors are being emulated now. That's who Bernadette is talking to."

"What ship?" asked Janelle.

"The *Skyrattler*. And make sure everyone knows. I get too many questions as it is."

"The Almics haven't advanced?"

"No. They tried to lay a trap for them but it didn't work. Some kid screwed it all up." To Reggie all the young soldiers were kids. "We only get the bad news. When something goes wrong we can only talk to the losers. If the general found a way to weaken the Almics then we might not hear about it right away."

"If you hear anything about a guy named Mac Narrad can you come find me?" said Janelle.

"He the voice you heard calling you?" said Reggie.

"Yeah."

"Must have a powerful connection if he was able to pull you out of here just by saying your name."

"He was there when I was taken."

Reggie scoffed. "Probably more than that, but I won't pry. I'll let you know if I hear anything."

Waiting was hard. Janelle ached to hear Mac's voice again, but the Almics were champions at adapting, changing to make sure things went their way. Plus they could read the minds of all their prisoners. If she had escaped momentarily then they were already working to make sure that wouldn't happen again.

"Rizzen, do you have a plan for when we get out of here?" asked Janelle.

You think we're to that point already?

"Soon."

I've seen people get their hopes up before. It only gets harder for them when it ends badly.

"But no one's ever moved their mind out of the prison. This is different. If this ends before we're ready then it's going to be chaos on the other side. You should at least get all the leaders together to talk about it."

I can't make that kind of announcement without getting everyone's hopes up.

"Why are you so worried about that?"

I know what it feels like to see the light at the end of the tunnel and then to lose everything. I was broken for a long time. It makes everything here more difficult.

Word had burned through the crowd—most beings were hanging around the human prison, trying to learn what was happening—and reached Janelle, with a wave of curiosity behind it.

"A group arrived. They're friends of Mac's and they know you," said Jace.

"They know *me*?"

The only person she knew in the military was Mac. That might mean that the Almics had reached a planet and were taking civilians again.

"Apparently Mac sent them. Know anyone named Phillip Pilgrim, Nelson Koyczan, Ryan Rivers, or Jazlyn Oliver?"

Chapter 12
Eviscerate

Someone had arrived at the prison who knew Janelle. Jace had given their names but she'd never heard of them. She hoped that when she saw their faces it would jog her memory but it didn't. She would have run right past them if they hadn't been standing in the middle of a crowd. Two of the men were young, early twenties, no older than twenty-three. Then there was a middle-aged man and woman. All four were wearing military uniforms. Janelle hadn't seen many grey-haired women in uniform. But then, she wasn't sure if the hair was naturally grey or if it had been dyed that color. That hadn't been the trend when she had been abducted, but trends changed and who knew how long she had been there? The four captives didn't recognize Janelle either. She had to introduce herself.

"I'm Janelle Stewart," she said.

"I'm Dr. Phillip Pilgrim. This is Jazlyn Oliver, Ryan Rivers, and—"

"Nelson Koyczan. It's nice to meet you. Mac sent us," said the youngest-looking of the group. He shook her hand and smiled. It had been a while since he had seen a pretty face. She had seen that look before in soldiers from the front.

"What do you mean, Mac sent you?" Janelle asked.

"We went behind enemy lines to free the prisoners."

The humans gathered around started to cheer. That only made Phillip grimace. He shouted at everyone to be quiet and held up his hands to get their attention.

"You're celebrating too early," he said. "We're in prison with you now, understand?"

"Does that mean you've found a way out?" asked Jace, who was standing beside Janelle.

"No. It means we were captured before we could make our move."

There was a collective groan through out the group. Seeing the disappointment on everyone's faces, Nelson shouted, "But we are going to figure out a way to get us all free. Don't worry. We're on it."

No one bothered to tell them that it was pointless to try. Most people now believed that Janelle's brief mental sojourn outside of the prison was a fluke, not likely to be repeated at will. Nelson could see that no one in the crowd believed him. Many turned to leave.

"It's true. We can do things that no other human can do. Well, no one other than Mac, but he's the one who gave us these abilities," said Nelson.

"What abilities?" asked Janelle.

"Show them, Ryan."

"Does it work in here?" asked Ryan.

"Yep, I can still hear people," said Jazlyn.

"Okay, here goes," Ryan said out loud. Then in everyone's head the same voice said, *We can mind speak. No other humans can do that. It's how the aliens communicate with each other. It's how we were able to sneak around under their noses.*

Janelle shook her head. "Being able to mind speak doesn't make a difference here."

"How would you know?" asked Nelson.

"Don't be a jerk," said Phillip. "If she says it doesn't help, then it doesn't."

"But if we're the first humans to come here that can mind speak then how would she know?"

"There are more than just humans here," said Janelle.

As if on cue, Rizzen forced his way through the crowd and demanded, *Who sent that message?*

Ryan raised his hand.

You?

Yep, said Ryan in his head just to prove it.

How?

It's kind of like thinking to yourself but projecting the words towards other people. I can also just float them out there so everyone can hear them. It's kind of cool.

I did not know humans had this ability, said Rizzen, looking directly at Janelle.

"They don't. These guys learned it somehow," said Janelle.

"From Mac Narrad," said Phillip. "He can do this too. He changed himself. Something to do with his blood. He injected us with the same stuff and that's how we got his abilities. We can all mind speak but Nelson can send pictures with his mind, I can use alien technology easier than anyone else, Jazlyn can overhear all the mind speak going on around her, and Ryan can talk to people who can't normally hear mind speak."

What do you hear? Rizzen asked Jazlyn.

"Nothing right now. I think they've realized what I can do and are keeping talking to a minimum while I'm in here. When we first woke up I could hear them trying to figure out how to break into our heads to read our minds and keep us emulated."

Nelson shot Phillip a worried look. "If our minds are already being read then that's not good news for Aleeva and Durgan."

"Probably not."

"So," Nelson said to the crowd. "Where are we and how do escape?"

Through the crowd barrelled a tall man with hair cut short, almost bald. He was yelling and running right for Phillip. He hadn't been there much longer than these four but everyone knew who he was—General Roy. He launched himself at Phillip, flung him to the ground, and started punching him in the face. Each blow should have let loose a gush of blood but in here there was no change.

General Roy wasn't attacking his actual body so there could be no harm inflicted.

"You have killed us all," said General Roy.

"I didn't do anything. And you're not even hurting me. Get off," said Phillip.

General Roy and Phillip got to their feet. The general pointed his finger in Phillip's face.

"I was the best chance we had at winning the war. We had everything organized. The enemy was losing ground. But the second you decided to help that idiot spacer, Mac Narrad, my ship gets attacked and now our military is leaderless."

"*We* were the best chance of winning this war," said Phillip.

"Then what are you waiting for? Win the war and we'll all go home," said General Roy sarcastically, his arms stretched out, inviting him to save them all.

"We'll find a way out of here."

"You won't. But you're welcome to try."

"If anyone can figure it out, we can."

"Sure. I'll just wait here and hope that my family gets emulated instead of murdered so at least I get a chance to see them again."

The general was being overly pessimistic—it hadn't got to the point where civilians were being taken again. The Almics could have gone to any of the colony worlds whenever they wanted—that's where the war had started, after all—but they were still only attacking military targets. That had to be a good sign. Janelle was optimistic about the new humans who could mind speak. There was no one else there who could mind speak other than Rizzen. This could change the way things worked around here.

Newcomers were always coming fresh from battle and were ready to keep fighting, desperate to find a way to get back at the aliens who had taken them. But they didn't realize that there were creatures who had been here for years, lifetimes. It was hard to measure, because none of them ever aged. But Rizzen had said that there were some people who simply vanished due to old age. Their bodies eventually rejected the preserving process and the Invaders executed them, seeing no need to keep them around. Rizzen, who had been there the longest, was lucky—the Bize lasted long as emulators.

Janelle tried to offer Phillip and his friends a comforting smile but they still had that desperate look in their eyes. It would be a while before they adjusted to their new surroundings. She tried to distract them with questions.

"How was Mac when you saw him last?"

Eventually they lost the desperate look in their eyes. But unlike everyone else they never lost the need to escape.

Jazlyn had been distracted since they had arrived in the prison. That wasn't accurate—she had been distracted since they had gone behind enemy lines. There was always another conversation happening that only she could hear. When they had been with the fleet it had been so overwhelming that she couldn't even function but here in the prison—where they knew her abilities—they kept their distance so that she couldn't find out their secrets.

But they weren't careful enough. There was one alien just close enough to wherever her real body was that she could hear one side of a conversation.

It is not known.

We are doing the best we can.

It is not known.

They can't get out.

We know they can't get out.

It is not known.

It was the same voice, the same words, every time. Jazlyn guessed that he worked alone because there would be long stretches of silence. Then someone would come check his progress and each time he gave what sounded like, at least to Jazlyn, disappointing news.

We are working on it.

The human model isn't working.

The Bize model isn't working.

We are creating a new one.

Soon.

We should not have emulated them so soon.

It was a mistake.

Yes. My mistake.

There was trouble with some emulators. The human model and the Bize model weren't working. Until then the Bize were the only prisoners who could mind speak. Now the enhanced humans were there and the invaders were having trouble emulating them.

I want to know what's going on in their heads as well.

I will.

I will.

I will not fail.

Jazlyn had spent most of her time in the prison walking around with Phillip. Nelson was with Janelle. Ryan was out in the mass of people, trying to learn as much as he could about who was there, hoping to find a way out. When she heard that last part of the conversation she realized the truth about what the Almics were struggling with. She called out to the other four.

We need to talk, she said. *All of you act normal. I heard something that will change everything.*

What's that? asked Phillip.

The Almics can't read our minds.

Seriously? said Nelson.

Act normal. If they can read everyone else's minds then they will find out that we know, said Jazlyn.

Janelle says that Rizzen has a plan for peace when we all get out of here. He is making sure that all these different aliens don't try to kill each other when we escape.

So? said Phillip.

So then it's up to us to make a plan for war. When we escape we make a plan to take back the fleet and destroy the Almics.

Ryan was already out among the creatures, talking to them and getting their stories, so it wasn't suspicious that he would also get information about their ships and weapons. When he learned more he passed it on to the group so they could plan.

The Hodders have smaller ships, he said.

What's a Hodder again? said Phillip.

The weird-looking dog things that never sit still and have a tongue as long as their bodies. I wouldn't have pegged them as actual intelligent life. But "animalistic" might be the best way to describe their ships. They call them "beautiful" and "the perfect union between pilot and machine."

I can't even picture them using machines.

The machine wraps itself around them and responds to their muscle movements. It can move as quickly and as accurately as they can—which is impressive because they are constantly moving and can turn on a dime without losing speed. Plus there's tons of Hodders here. You see them all over the place.

How many?

They said when they first got taken the Almics had a million Hodders in captivity but their emulators went out of vogue and now there are only a hundred thousand. They aren't very popular.

What are the chances the Almics kept their ships?

I don't know. But they would be useful. They're small so they do all their damage up close. Their weapons are short range. They'll scramble over the hull to expose the weak spots.

Tear at them like an animal.

Like I said. Animalistic.
What else did you find out?
The plan was coming together.

Nelson had stayed next to Janelle since he'd gotten there. She knew it was half an assignment from Phillip—who acted like the leader of the group even though he was only a doctor—and half because there weren't that many girls their age among the captives. He was just old enough to be in the military and she had been about to graduate when she had been abducted. Although, if what he was telling her was true, five years had passed since then. Years had passed and she hadn't physically aged a day.

Spending their time in the wide open field full of monsters got old. The only change in perspective they could have was to go back in the prison or to climb on top of it. They sat with their feet dangling over the edge of the top floor of the main cell block, looking out over all the mingling prisoners below.

"I kind of hoped to see something more up here," said Nelson. "But there's only prisons, a field, and a billion weird-looking aliens. Not much going on here."

"Just enough to keep our brains busy so they can use our bodies."

Their feet were right above the main doors to the human prison. There was a rush of people running out of the building. None of them were in military clothes. Once the other human prisoners noticed, a crowd gathered around the building.

"Looks like they hit a base," said Nelson.

"What makes you say that?"

"They aren't in uniform. The only place I was ever allowed to take off my uniform was when I was on base. Never on the ship—not even when I was sleeping."

"Military-grade pyjamas?"

"Wait," Nelson pointed down below. "Look. Kids."

Janelle studied the crowd more closely. There were no soldiers in the mix. It was young and old, male and female, a whole range of skin colors—an accurate cross-section of society. This was a group of random civilians. Rizzen had told Janelle that there was a clear tipping point in each war the Invaders started—when the Almics started capturing civilians rather than soldiers, the war could be considered over. The tipping point was here.

"What's the closest planet to the front?" asked Janelle.

"Sixbe, I think. Depends on the time of year. Just before I was captured it was Sixbe but if enough time has passed it could be Ople."

Janelle jumped off the roof. Nothing in this world was real so instead of splattering all over the ground when she landed, she rolled over and got back to her feet like nothing had happened.

The crowd was confused and sad. A couple looked relieved not to be dead, but also cautious, like the afterlife they had expected was nothing like what they were experiencing. Janelle grabbed a small elderly woman with a friendly smile by the shoulders and asked, "What planet are you from?"

"Mezzenick, darling. Mezzenick. Where are we right now?"

"They didn't explain it to you in there?"

"No."

"You've been captured. By the Invaders."

The elderly woman shrugged her shoulders. "It's not so bad here. I've never felt so young in my entire life."

Soon enough she would figure out it was because her mind and body were separated at the moment. Janelle didn't have the heart or the patience to explain it to her. There were hundreds of people coming out of the prison. Maybe even thousands.

Janelle walked upstream of the people coming out of the prison. She asked every few minutes where they were from. She got more than one answer. Eventually she did come across Sixbe and Ople, but it wasn't long before she got to even more familiar places. Titan—a moon in her home solar system.

A red-headed young man stumbled out into the sunlight where Janelle was waiting. He tripped and she helped him back up. He looked very familiar so she asked him where he was from.

"Mars."

Maybe it wasn't as bad as it sounded, but if the aliens were at Mars then it was close to the end. Soon enough she expected to see Mac coming through that door.

"What's your name?" asked Janelle.

"Daniel Michaels."

"Michaels?" she knew that name.

Then the man she was thinking about came up beside her, the orange-haired Major Jace Michaels. He grabbed his nephew and gave him a full hard hug.

"What are you doing here?" Jace asked.

"I don't know," said Daniel, "There were alien ships picking people up. I was visiting another dome and they sucked me up."

"What about your mom and dad?"

"I don't know. Do you think they're okay?"

"We'll find out. First tell me what happened. Tell me everything."

"A bunch of ships sucked us up. I was floating out in this room while we circled the planet. Then I saw another ship. Like a circle with a floating ball in the middle. The ball started spinning so fast it blurred and then the planet broke apart and the core was pulled out. They removed the core of Mars."

"You saw it?"

"Yeah, I saw it. Do you think mom and dad were still down there? Nothing could have survived that."

"We'll look for them."

"There's so many people."

"We're lucky we found each other."

"Why would they take some of us and leave some behind to die?"

"Don't worry about that right now."

Jace was giving Janelle a questioning look, like he wanted to ask her something. Or rather, that she should already know what he wanted to ask. She had no idea what he was trying to say.

"Janelle!"

Janelle snapped around, hoping and dreading to see someone in her family. It was only Nelson. He was standing on the wall overlooking the doors.

"We can watch the crowd from here. If we see someone we know we can jump down and talk to them," said Nelson.

Jace and Daniel followed her. They wanted to find the rest of their family. Jace moved closer to Janelle to have a whispered conversation.

"If they take Earth then it's all over," said Jace.

"Well, if they removed the core of Mars then there's a safe bet that the same thing will happen to Earth," said Janelle.

"Unless we stop them. And by we, I mean your friend Mac Narrad."

"If I'm being totally honest, I feel like it's only a matter of time before we spot him in this crowd somewhere."

They climbed up onto the prison wall beside Nelson.

"Phillip, Ryan, and Jazlyn are down there getting updates. They'll yell out if they find something. We're supposed to stay up here and look for Mac or anyone else from Ronos."

"Ronos? Not Earth?"

"Apparently the big showdown is happening on a secret planet called Ronos, not on Earth. We might still have a chance."

"Maybe, but I'd still like to go home when this is all over."

"I'd settle for just being alive."

Janelle didn't believe him. She knew he was just doing the tough-guy routine. They waited on the edge of the wall. There wasn't much room up there so they had to be careful not to knock each other off. Other prisoners saw what they were doing and climbed up to search the crowd as well. Soon the wall and the building rooftop were full of people calling down to the crowd. It was getting hard to hear Phillip and the others reporting back.

Phillip was talking to someone who was crying. Whatever was being said made him tear up. Janelle wondered if they knew each other. They didn't look related, but then again, neither did he and Nelson and they were uncle and nephew. Phillip turned to the wall and shouted something. There was too much noise and Janelle couldn't hear it.

He cupped his hands around his mouth and shouted the message over and over. It wasn't long before everyone stopped talking and listened to what he was saying.

"Earth! These guys are from Earth!"

The Invaders had taken Earth.

The humans' home world no longer belonged to the humans.

Janelle looked over at Nelson. He wasn't even trying to be tough. He was openly crying now. Janelle reached out to comfort him—awkwardly, because the wall wasn't wide enough for her to do it effectively—but he shrugged her off and jumped down. He ran into the field. In a place like this it was impossible to be by yourself. The best anyone could hope for was to run into a group of aliens that didn't understand anything you were saying and didn't care what you did around them.

I'm sorry, said Rizzen.

Janelle heard his voice in her head but didn't know where it was coming from. Then she saw him standing at the bottom of the wall. He had been through this many times before, the end of a civilization. The takeover of a home world. Janelle jumped down so she could talk to Rizzen face to face.

"It's over now?" asked Janelle.

It happened much faster than I expected. Usually there is more time between when civilians start showing up and when the home world is taken. As far as I can tell they broke up the fleet and hit multiple targets at the same time. Which actually makes the humans unique.

"Why?"

The Invaders took a risk with you. They divided their power to—sorry for saying it like this—eliminate you faster. They're scared of you for some reason. They've never been scared of anything.

"Scared. What do they have to be scared of?"

I don't know. This is not normal behavior for them. But if it's true that they are almost back to their home world then maybe this all has to do with their end game. Maybe from here on out we're in for a lot of surprises.

Janelle wasn't sure about that. Already she was brainstorming how they were going to fight back and retake the Earth once they escaped. A pipe dream, of course. They had no say in whether they got out of prison or not and there was no reason for the Almics to let them go.

Then everything changed.

One second she was standing outside the human prison talking to Rizzen, and the next she was lying on her back, covered in green goop and looking up at the stars and a strange-looking group of ships. For the first time in years her body was sore. For the first time in years she could feel something. It was almost overwhelming. She could feel the current of the green gooey liquid as it flowed past her. She could feel tubes and the slippery floor beneath her. She could feel her clothes against her skin. It had been so long since she had felt anything that she had almost forgotten what real life felt like.

Real life.

She sat up suddenly, as if a lightning strike and brought to her to life. Every movement took an incredible amount of energy. But now she could see where she was, where they all were. It was a massive lake with a drain in the middle. She had been up near the bank so when the lake of green goo started to drain she had been one of the first exposed. As more goo started to drain more prisoners were exposed.

Her whole body was shaking, like the beginnings of a panic attack. She could feel it there in the back of her head, the emotional avalanche that was waiting to burst out of her. This was real life. They weren't in the prison anymore.

If she had to guess they were on a ship, protected overhead by a dome that covered the entire lake and the walkway around it. The lake itself looked like it was big enough to have several thousand prisoners in it. All she could see were humans.

This was real life.

The dam burst and she started sobbing. She didn't understand why this had happened but they were free. It was over. They were out of the prison. Her entire time there, she had talked about getting out. When she had talked to Mac she had hoped it was possible. But truthfully, deep down, she was never sure that it was actually possible. Now that it had happened she had never felt so many emotions all at the same time.

By the time she was able to get control of her emotions again she could hear others around her still in the middle of their own cry fest. Janelle cleared the tears from her eyes and looked out over the lake. It was so big that it still wasn't done draining. Some people were starting to get to their wobbly legs. She looked to her side and saw Reggie struggling to his feet. He fell over and almost landed on someone else. That would have been devastating. Even though they had been in the green goo for years he still looked huge—like he hadn't lost any of his muscle mass. They were wearing the same clothes as when they were taken. Her shoes were still tied.

"What happened?" Reggie asked Janelle.

"I don't know."

"They let us go?"

"I don't know if they let us go, but this is real life."

Janelle looked around for Bernadette. The three of them had been the first ones taken. In this moment of confusion and disorientation Janelle needed the security of her oldest friends in the prison. But she was nowhere to be seen.

"Why wouldn't she be here? Everyone in this lake is human and we were some of the first taken. She should be here," said Reggie.

"If they let everyone go then they wouldn't have any bodies to fly the ships," said Janelle.

Janelle didn't point out that it didn't make sense why any of them had been freed. She struggled to her feet and started walking out of the slippery lakebed. The bottom of the lake wasn't muddy—it was slimy metal. There was no way she would have been able to walk on it if there hadn't been tubes she could wedge her feet between to keep some grip. Reggie was doing the same thing. He fell once or twice, distracted by what was happening in outer space above them. Janelle didn't think she had the coordination to look up and not fall on her face so she waited until she was on the metal grating walkway around the lake. Then she looked up to see what had so distracted Reggie.

There were thousands of ships up there, all different sizes, built by all the different civilizations that the Invaders had conquered. Janelle knew that they could only be seeing a small portion of the entire fleet. From what Rizzen had described, the fleet was millions of ships, not thousands.

They were near a planet with two moons. One moon looked very similar to Earth's moon but the other one was black and jagged. The planet itself looked dead. Parts of it had broken off and there was no water or plant life below— at least as far as Janelle could tell. It was a dead hunk of rock floating through space, orbited by two moons.

"The fleet has been abandoned," said Reggie.

"How do you know that?" asked Janelle.

"I saw at least three collisions up there while I was walking out. Watch."

They didn't have to wait long before a large ship drifting through space collided with a smaller one, completely destroying it. As the smaller one broke apart no bodies were sucked out into space.

"They left their ships behind and took off somewhere," said Reggie.

"Why would they do that?"

"I don't know. There are so many ships up there it seems like it would be crowded if they all got together into one ship."

"Maybe they needed to get somewhere all at the same time."

"What do you mean?" asked Reggie.

"All of these ships probably can't go the same speed. They were made by different civilizations. If the aliens needed to get somewhere fast they would have to abandon the slower ships and all get on the fast ones."

"You're assuming they needed to get somewhere fast."

"Yeah. I don't know why they would be in a hurry now. They've taken Earth. What do they have to be worried about now?"

"Earth? No."

"What?"

Reggie collapsed to his knees, looking up at the planet with two moons.

"That's the Earth. It's been destroyed. We have no home anymore."

Janelle looked at it. Of course that moon had seemed familiar—it was the Earth's moon. What she had assumed was the other jagged moon was the Earth's core. As the planet rotated the scar where the Almics had pulled the core out of the planet was more visible. The oceans were gone, the plants had all burned up. There was nothing on Earth left alive.

Chapter 13
Keep Hope Alive

Phillip was awake and aware of entering his body again. He was farther down in the lake than Janelle had been and was still mostly submerged in the green goo. But his eyes were open and he was looking around at the other humans trying to figure out what was going on.

"They let us go?" asked Jazlyn. She wasn't too far from him.

"No."

"But we aren't in the prison anymore. That's the fleet."

"It's not the fleet."

"It is."

"If it was, then you would be curled up in a ball on the ground with a billion conversations in your head."

She looked up at the mass of ships surrounding their domed ship. They were drifting aimlessly, some of them bashing into each other like the pilots had fallen asleep. Then they realized why she wasn't hearing any conversations.

"They abandoned the fleet," she said.

"They abandoned the fleet and let us go? That doesn't make any sense."

Phillip was still looking up. The movement of the ships wasn't all lazy drifting. There was a squadron of smaller ships moving through the fleet. The four of them hadn't been able to catalogue all the ships in the fleet but they had interviewed several species and had a solid base of knowledge to build on. Phillip tried to think who those ships belonged to.

Were they Hodders? Hodders had small ships but they were different—black metal, studded with spikes. These ships were small, smooth. Elongated, like a stretched-out raindrop.

He remembered Ryan talking to a group of flying creatures. They had wide thin wings, so thin they could fold up into nothing. Attached to the wings were small humanoid beings with pale blue, nearly transparent skin. They had described their ships as "nature-inspired"—like every hover car company said in their ads back on Earth, so he hadn't thought too much of it at the time—with impenetrable shields and a laser-targeting system that never failed. A force of nature. Rizzen had said the aliens were called Tamminla.

That's what Phillip was looking at now. He was sure of it. Someone was piloting the raindrop ships. Had the Tamminla already escaped? The squadron of a dozen ships turned and headed towards the ship Phillip and the other humans were on. Then they opened fire. There was a shudder and the goo sloshed around him.

"They didn't just let us go," said Phillip.

He stood up and almost fell over—the goo had a numbing effect. The ship shuddered again. The raindrop ships were zipping around the domed lake, firing as often as they could. It wouldn't be too much longer before the shield went down, the dome burst, and they were all sucked out into space.

Phillip stumbled to the edge of the lake. The humans were trying to escape but there was nowhere for any of them to go. All the doors surrounding the lake were locked. The consoles were useless—nothing was in Earth Common. People began panicking. The ship was rocking more and more. It was getting hard to stand. It wouldn't be much longer now.

Not all the humans were panicking. Some of them stayed where they had woken up in the goo and simply sobbed into their hands. Others just sat, stunned by what was happening. Phillip noticed Nelson sitting there, his eyes locked on something out in the fleet. Whatever he was looking at was making him cry.

Phillip looked up. It was a hunk of rock with two moons. He didn't know why that was significant to his nephew but now wasn't the time to figure it out. There were ships trying to kill them and they had no way to defend themselves.

Phillip Pilgrim. Have you escaped? There weren't that many people who could mind speak and who knew his name. He recognized the voice.

Aleeva! We got out of the prison but we don't know how or why.

All will be explained.

How come they didn't cube you?

We avoided detention. Some of us did, anyway. As I said, all will be explained.

We might not be around long enough to get the explanation.

We are coming to assist. We have taken control of a collector ship.

He kept an eye out for the rescuers. The raindrops kept firing; shaking, Phillip realized the metal of the ship was grinding and tearing. The ship was coming apart. They didn't have time to wait.

Where are you?

We are defending another emulating lake. It is taking longer than we expected.

How many swarms did they leave behind?

Not many. But more are turning around now that they realized we stopped the self-destruct and set the prisoners free.

We aren't going to last much longer.

There's nothing we can do.

The ship was shaking so hard now that Phillip was having trouble standing. His whole world was vibrating. Above him the raindrops moved back and forth. Their speed was incredible. It would have been more impressive if they hadn't been about to die.

It was pure chaos under the dome. People were running around in a panic. They didn't know what to do, but they had to do something, and running around and screaming was the only thing they could think of. Others were banging on the doors that refused to open, hoping there was something on the other side that would save them. Then there were others like Nelson who were still and looking up at the soul-crushing something that hadn't clicked with Phillip yet.

There was an explosion. The ship rocked wildly back and forth. Phillip was thrown into the air. He thought for sure the dome was breached and he would be sucked out into space. But he landed with a thud on top of the slimy tubes in the lakebed. The explosion had happened outside the dome.

There was another ship flying around up there. It was a human ship. Not a capital ship or a HAAS3. It was a gun ship—maybe a G22. Those ships looked like oversized HAAS3 but packed to the brim with laser cannons. There weren't very many of them in the fleet. It was a newer ship and the only reason that Phillip knew about it was it had been sent to the front to be tested out on the aliens. The pilot had been injured and Phillip had treated him. The ship hadn't been effective against the collector ships but it was doing wonders against the raindrops.

The space battle didn't last long. They were all gone now. The G22 had caught the raindrop ships off guard and cleaned them up nicely. Now that the shaking was over Phillip made his way out of the lake bed. Janelle was there. She looked just as shaken as Nelson did. Phillip still didn't understand.

Jace Michaels was standing with her. He was smiling.

"You're the only one around here who is smiling," said Phillip.

"I got my revenge," he said, touching his temple.

"What do you mean?"

"I never saw the G22s go into production but I was part of the team that was developing its weapon. We designed it to be operated by Imp."

"Imp? You were the one driving that thing?"

"Yeah. My Imp hooked up to a network as soon as we got out of the goo. Everyone's did."

"Mine got disabled when we made the transformation. What network are you on? Can you tell where we are?"

"There aren't any networks left on Earth but there are a few capital ships that were taken over and I signed on to one of those, then gained access to the G22. It's a sweet machine. Too bad—"

"Too bad what? Why are there no networks on Earth?"

Janelle pointed up at the lump of rock with two moons. As the realization sunk in he realized why Nelson was so distraught. He went back and held his nephew. While his nephew released his emotions Phillip reached out to the rebel swarms.

We found a way to defend ourselves.

Good. Now get off those ships and let's blow them up.

Why?

So they think you're dead. We must move quickly.

The rebel collector ship was going to be the center of their counteroffensive—whatever that was going to be. It took a while to figure out how to get out of the dome ship before the rebel swarms came to help. Now Janelle was included in the group heading towards the collector ship. She was considered important because she had been able to move her mind outside the prison. No had done that and since no one knew what was going to happen next they considered her a mysterious ace in the hole.

The rebel's collector ship was on the edge of the fleet, out of sight from what remained of Earth. She was grateful for that. What was left of her home world made her stomach sick. It was hard to focus on what they were fighting for. It wasn't for their home. They didn't have a home anymore.

Phillip, Ryan, and Jazlyn were trying to figure out their next step. There was much confusion as everyone tried to learn everything all at once. Jace was working with General Roy to organize the human side of things. Jace's nephew Daniel was with Janelle. Neither of them were happy about that—she wasn't here to be a babysitter.

"How old are you?" she asked.

"Why does everyone keep asking me that? I know how to use a gun. I can fight as well as any one of you," he said.

They were heading to the command deck of the collector ship. Nelson's gaze was hazy and he looked straight ahead without blinking. She didn't have to ask if he was upset—there were tear marks down his face—or why everyone else seemed to be on edge. Their home planet had been destroyed. Back in the prison Nelson had bragged that it wouldn't matter if the Earth was gone as long as they were alive, but that wasn't true. The Earth was no more and Nelson was alive, but it looked like he wished he were dead.

When they got to the command deck she saw a familiar face.

"Bernadette," said Janelle. "What are you doing here?"

"I'm not Bernadette. My name is Aleeva. I am an Almic."

"What? Where is she? How come we were all freed but you kept her?"

"Only a dozen anchors were kept. She has not been harmed."

"Where is she? Is she on this ship?"

Jace came up behind her and put his hand on her shoulder. "She's not on this ship. The prisoners that weren't set free are with the rest of the aliens in a smaller fleet heading to Ronos. Aleeva didn't choose to use Bernadette as an emulator; she just needs something to anchor her swarm or she can't help us." He leaned down and even more quietly whispered, "We tried looking for her. This swarm seems to be telling the truth."

Jace had been quiet the whole time, doing all his communicating via Imp. Nelson slumped into an empty chair continuing to look void of life. Ryan was nearby, a nervous, angry look on his face. His muscles were tense like he couldn't relax. Janelle went over to him.

"You don't trust them?" said Janelle.

"Swarm mentality. It's only a matter of time before they betray us. I tried to talk sense into Phillip but he doesn't believe me. Jazlyn's on his side. I'll go along but I'll be ready for when it happens."

"Can't Jazlyn read their thoughts?"

"She's trying to keep it together. It's hard to hear so many things at once. They know she can hear mind speak, so if they are plotting against us, they'll hide it."

"They set us free."

"They're waiting to see what we know."

"What do we know?"

"That none of us are going to give up until there is no hope left at all."

On the bridge Aleeva started to gather the information she needed on the command console in the center of the room. All the swarms in the room were still in the form of their emulators. Janelle recognized all of them. There were several Bernadettes, as well as five other types of human emulators. General Roy was not there yet.

Aleeva and Durgan are the leaders of this rebel band of Almics, said Rizzen. The two of them stood off to the side while everyone waited for Phillip and Nelson to come up.

"Can we trust them?" asked Janelle.

I have long suspected that there was a split in the Almics. She claims she will share all the information she has with us to give us the best chance at winning. We were supposed to all come up here so that she could give us our next target.

"What is it?" Janelle asked.

She didn't say.

There was a commotion at the command console. Ryan had his weapon pointed at Alveea's head while she punched in some commands. The ship's engines were powering up. She had plotted a trajectory.

"Where are we going? You said we weren't going anywhere until we discussed your new information," said Ryan.

"There's no time to wait for your leader. We need to hurry. They already have a day and half on us and this ship isn't as fast as the others," said Aleeva. "We are leaving now."

Ryan pulled the trigger. The laser left the gun, went right through Aleeva's head, and hit the wall on the other side of her. She didn't miss a beat.

"You done?" she said.

"I'll find a cube and put you in it," said Ryan.

"No, you won't."

Ryan kept pulling the trigger over and over again. None of them did any damage. He was acting emotionally. All soldiers knew that their weapons were no match for the aliens. Ryan was still trying to deal with his emotions over the destruction of Earth.

Rizzen walked over to Ryan and put a hand on his shoulder. He must have been speaking to him privately in his head. Whatever he said convinced Ryan to put his weapon away. He was still breathing quickly but he asked as calmly as he could, "Where are we going?"

"The Almic fleet has taken their fastest ships to the edge of the Ronos system. If they have kept to the timeline we were privy to before we were exposed, then they are preparing to land the emulator machine on the surface of the planet."

"What's the emulator machine do?"

"Once the emulator machine lands there won't be anything we can do to stop them."

"Will we get there in time?" asked Janelle.

Aleeva's hands flew across the controls as she prepared to intercept the fleet in the Ronos System. The results were displayed and she shook her head.

"No. Do you know of anyone there who can destroy it before it reaches the surface?"

Chapter 14
Possession

Lynn was still in control of Genny Hunter's body so she and Mac had access to everything the *Lendrum* was capable of. Right now they were on the command deck, the biggest command deck Mac had ever seen. There were five dozen people on the deck. Monitors and consoles lined the walls. Seven massive command consoles, spread around the room, were crowded with people. There were five slightly smaller rooms just off the main deck but because there were no doors separating the rooms—just open walkways—it could be argued that it was all one big room. The entire station could be controlled from here. Considering the size of the station, it was impressive that they were able to accomplish all this with so few people and without military precision.

Mac, Lynn, and Scott were the only people on the command deck who weren't supposed to be there. At first no one had given it a second thought, but that wasn't the case anymore. Lynn wasn't playing the part well enough and the ones who knew Genny Hunter well were growing suspicious. The most suspicious, Clayton Mentz, stood nearby watching everything the three of them did and said. His scowl deepened as the time passed.

The station's sensors were focused on the Dead Continent, specifically on the crater created by Lynn's bomb. They had spent the last hour watching Volmere fire every missile and explosive he had, trying to destroy the beacon. Nothing had made any difference.

Lynn looked especially frustrated. "This is pointless."

Use mind speak, said Mac.

This is pointless in mind speak and in Earth Common, said Lynn. *I already knew this wouldn't work. The only thing strong enough to destroy the beacon is itself.*

And the crushing weight of the ocean.

It's in the middle of the continent, surrounded by the last remaining Rays who have been in a murderous rampage ever since we attacked them. There's no way we could get to it, let alone pick it up and drop it over the ocean. It can't be done.

You were going to do it before.

I was going to bring the much smaller Almic piece of beacon to the Dead Continent, attach an engine to it, and send it hurtling to the Ray beacon that had been exposed thanks to the bomb I designed. None of that is possible now.

What if we crashed ships into it? If we got them going fast enough—

We don't have the technology to send it fast enough to do the damage we need it to.

Mac couldn't shake the feeling that he was missing something obvious. The beacon couldn't be completely indestructible. It had to have a weakness. Then he realized.

"It's broken," said Mac out loud.

"What?" said the half-dozen command crew members standing near him. They all went to the console to try and repair whatever Mac was talking about.

"Never mind. Just thinking out loud," said Mac, getting them to back away. "It's all good."

Try thinking to me instead of out loud, said Lynn.

The beacon is broken. When we first saw it parts of it looked like it had been sliced like a pizza. It's not indestructible. There has to be something that can destroy it.

Lynn rolled her eyes—or rather rolled Genny Hunter's eyes. *Thanks for showing up, Mac. Of course it's not indestructible. The entire time I was on Ronos it was broken into two pieces. I know it can be destroyed because it's already been broken apart. I just don't know how that happened. I don't know when it happened. I don't even know how long the beacon has been down there. For all I know it crashed on the planet and the damage we saw when we first got here is from that. But we'll never know. All we know is that there is a way to destroy it. We just need to find out how.*

If it broke because it crash landed then we should try and crash a ship into it and see if that does anything.

If you suggest that one more time—

We should try everything.

No ship is strong enough. It's like throwing a tissue paper at a hawthree. That tissue paper is never going to be strong enough to destroy the hawthree.

Then we drop it in the ocean.

It's like you aren't even trying anymore. We just talked about how that's impossible. I miss working with Witt.

I asked him. He doesn't know what to do either.

"Guys…um, commander, I mean," said Scott, pointing to another readout on the console.

There was more activity on the edge of the system. The Invader fleet had been mobilizing there ever since the first scout ship had been down to Ronos. Now it looked like the Invader ships were getting into formation. They were preparing to attack.

"What are they doing?" asked Clayton. Mac and Scott had gotten onto the command deck under the pretence of being experts on the Invaders—not a total lie.

"They're getting ready to move," said Mac, pointing at the readout of the ships. "They're going to attack in waves. See how they are organized here. The first wave is these smaller ships mixed with large transport ships. They'll want to get as many troops on the ground as they can, while at the same time preparing for the next wave to come."

"Won't the next wave be reinforcements?"

"Maybe. I can't figure it out. There is this one ship here—" said Mac. The ship was flat on the bottom and had several spires coming out of it. If it had been on the ground it would have looked like a factory. "It's part of the second wave but I can't tell what it is. It looks like they are trying to protect it—see the concentration of ships surrounding it—but why, I have no idea."

"If it's of value then we should target it," said Scott.

"You don't know what it is?" said Clayton.

"No, I don't know what any of these ships are. I'm simply judging them based on their flight patterns. The second wave is moving defensively to protect that factory ship. There's something else. There's this ship near the back. See it there—made up of flat cylinders stacked on each other. It almost looks like the hilt of a sword. It's building up energy, a lot of energy, and it's slowly moving to the front of the fleet. I think it might be a weapon of some kind."

"Know anything about that?" said Mac to Lynn.

Clayton cut everyone off. "How would Commander Hunter know anything about this?"

Mind speak, remember? said Lynn. *And no, I don't.*

Volmere sent up a message from the surface. He was still in charge down there but he was out of the action and recovering from his wounds. Of course he had been told to take it easy and leave the fighting—and the ordering of the soldiers—to someone else, but he didn't listen.

We're stopping the attack on the colony ship. There's no way for us to win the war that way.

Have you made contact with the Passengers? asked Lynn.

Yes, but they are still reluctant to aid us. They don't trust anyone right now and are too afraid to land their ships. They think they are safe in the sky.

"What is going on?" said Clayton. "Commander, you need to level with me."

"What?" said Lynn.

"You guys aren't talking normally. You say a couple words to each other out loud and then stare at each other like you're trying to read minds. You never did that before. Something has gone wrong."

"Relax. Everything is fine."

"Everything is not fine." Clayton took another step towards them. Mac looked around the room. There were more security guys there than before. Clayton had called them up with his Imp. "You haven't been responding to my messages and you are completely ignoring me. You keep talking about things like you know what is going on here, but until these two idiots showed up none of us had any clue how we even got here."

"That makes you the idiot, not me," said Mac. It slipped out. He knew that wasn't going to help anything.

"Tell me what's going on here."

Mac wasn't sure where to start. With the liquid rock that makes them glow in the dark, and gives them healing power and the ability to talk with only their minds? That wasn't likely to get Clayton to believe them. With the giant indestructible machine underground that pulled ships towards it and sent out a signal that the alien fleet was using to find this planet? Nope. That wouldn't work either. That his commanding officer was possessed by a human who was over 20,000 years old? There was nothing Mac could say that would make them sound sane *and* be an accurate description of what was going on.

The console started beeping. There were alerts going off. The lights turned red in the room. The command crew turned their attention back to their posts. Only Clayton still kept an eye on her.

"It's the hilt ship," said Scott. "It's stopped building up energy and now it's preparing to fire."

"It's a weapon?" said Mac.

"What else is it going to do with all that energy?"

"Let me see something," said Lynn.

She took over the central command console and started punching in information to recalibrate the sensors. After

20,000 years she had been able to figure out a way to scan for the swarms and track where they were. She brought up the readout. It showed that half the ships gathered at the edge of the system had been abandoned and those swarms had entered the hilt ship.

They're going to shoot swarms at us, said Mac.

Why? asked Scott.

To get as many soldiers on the ground as they can at the same time. Volmere and the others might be able to shoot down ships but if the swarms shoot themselves at high speed right to the surface Volmere won't have enough time to do anything.

"They're firing," said Scott.

They watched it happen on the sensors. The sections of the hilt ship stopped spinning and a stream of illuminated purple specks shot out. It looked like an impossibly thick laser—almost as wide as the *Rundle*. Scott tracked its trajectory.

"It's going fast. And it's really dense. There's a lot of swarms in there," he said.

Lynn looked at the readings. "Half their civilization, I'm guessing."

"The stream is going to pass right through this ship before it gets to Ronos."

Lynn's eyes grew wide—and Genny Hunter's eyes could go really wide, comically wide. "How much longer before it gets here?"

"At the speed it's going? Within the hour. I don't even know how that's possible but we need to get out of here before it gets here."

Mac put a hand on Scott's shoulder. The command crew was all looking nervously at the three of them. They were confused and worried about being caught in the stream. "We'll be fine."

Then in mind speak he said, *We—just the three of us—will be fine because they can't take over bodies that have been changed. I mean, I got attacked in Passage and they almost took over me but I had used up a lot of the Mac Gas inside of me. I had almost died a few hours before that. I was weak. But when I was on the front they couldn't do anything to me. I was more powerful then having just come from Ronos. Right now I'm fully charged. We will be fine. And once we destroy the beacon the rest of the people on this station will be fine.*

Lynn shook her head. *Nope. They can take over a changed body if there are enough of them, and there's billions in that stream. Plus, I'm in a body that hasn't been changed so I'm just going to get mixed up with all of the rest of them when they get here.*

So we are all vulnerable? We can all get possessed by the aliens?

Yeah. I'm sorry to say it, but yeah.

Any chance we'll be able to destroy the beacon in the next hour?

No.

Then get your crew together and figure out a way to move this space station.

Do we need to move the station? asked Scott.

Of course. They'll take over our bodies, said Lynn.

But the whole point of that stream is to get as many swarms to the surface as possible. They've been flying across the universe and destroying civilizations just to get to this point, and they're going to take some time to go on a side trip to kill all of us?

For the last few thousand years they have had two objectives. Get to Ronos and kill whoever gets in their way. Right now, we are in their way. Yes, we are momentarily delaying their journey to the surface, but that just means they will be that much more angry with us. When they get here they will kill everyone on the station and then move on.

There's billions of swarms in that stream, said Mac. *It's not going to take long to kill us all.*

An hour wasn't a lot of time to move a space station with no engines. The only way to get it out of the path of the swarm stream was to get out and push. But if they didn't push it in the right spot then it would just flip end over end instead of moving forward. A flipping space station was dangerous to the ships trying to push it.

It was getting close to an hour and the station had moved a bit, but not enough for everyone to be free of the swarms. Lynn had already ordered as many people as she could to get on ships and get off the *Lendrum* but it wasn't going to be enough. Everyone left was ordered to the side of the station that was going to be less affected. The stream was going to be there any minute now. The ships that had been trying to save the station were giving up now and making a run for it. No one understood exactly what was going on but they all saw Lynn's fear and worry when she spoke. Their leader may have been acting strangely, but they were still willing to follow her orders.

"What's going to happen when that...thing gets here?" said Clayton. The command deck was supposed to be clear of the swarm stream but it was right on the edge, so Lynn had said no one was obligated to stay.

"That beam of light moving through space is really trillions of tiny alien particles. If it touches you the aliens will take over your body," said Lynn.

"And the space station won't protect us?" asked Clayton.

"They'll find a way inside—even though we're airtight."

"How is that possible?" asked Mac.

"They can divide their particles so small they can get through a seal without breaking it. Trust me. I've done it before," said Lynn.

It took a moment for those words to sink in for Clayton. When they did he started to back away from the group. "You're one of them. You're an alien. You took over the commander's body."

"Yes and no. I did take over her body but I'm not an alien. I'm just borrowing her for a moment."

Clayton wasn't comforted by the truth. He pulled his gun out and pointed it at Lynn.

"Don't," said Lynn. "You can't hurt me without hurting her as well."

"You are giving them this space station and everyone on it. They'll kill us all."

The stream arrived. It enveloped half of the *Lendrum*. The tiny particles didn't immediately enter the ship but it didn't take long. Alarms started going off. Mac watched the abandoned sections of the station on the console and saw each room lit up by millions of the tiny little lights. Before they had been moving in only one direction—straight towards Ronos. But now that they were inside the station they shot off in every direction like a cloud dissipating into the atmosphere. Except this cloud was intelligent. It moved through the ship with purpose.

"We need to abandon ship," said Lynn.

Her hands flew over the controls of the ship. The alarms started sounding and a voice repeated on the loud speaker, "Please proceed to the nearest escape pod on all even-numbered floors. Do not panic. There is enough room for everybody. Please proceed…" and over and over.

"There isn't enough room," said Mac.

"What?" said Scott.

"We can't get to half the ships without going through the swarms to get there."

The room was starting to change. There was a buzz of energy and the lights were changing color. It felt like the air was moving. Mac's whole body felt like it was tingling and his glow was getting brighter as his body naturally tried to heal itself, as if something was attacking it.

Lynn was backing away from them, looking horrified at the front of the room. Swarms were coming through the cracks in the walls. The room was filling with alien swarms. Mac and Scott could hold off a certain number of them—on the front line Mac had taken on what felt like an entire collector ship full of them without being injured—but they wouldn't be able to hold them all off.

Scott ran to Lynn and took her hand. "Go inside of me. You aren't safe in that body."

Clayton ran for the door but didn't make it in time. He started screaming and clawing at his body before being ripped apart from the inside out. Lynn shook her head at Scott's suggestion, "I'm not going to do that. I need to stay in this body if I'm going to protect her."

"Lynn! You won't even make it to the door without them ripping through your body," said Scott.

Still she shook her head. "I'm protected in your glow."

"I don't know if that's a thing," said Mac.

"Well then, she's dead either way. Stop debating and let's go."

She wrapped herself around Scott and then Mac wrapped his arms around the other side of her and they ran for the door. It opened automatically and they stormed through. Lynn started screaming.

"I can feel them!"

They ran faster. As they moved away from the command deck, the tingling sensation all over Mac's body dissipated. But Scott wasn't about to let her go. They kept running.

"We won't get to an escape pod in time," said Scott.

"Try optimism. We didn't think we were getting off the command deck either," said Mac.

"You have a plan?"

"No."

Lynn led the way. She had never been on the *Lendrum* before but because she had access to Genny Hunter's memories she could easily lead them where they needed to go. The cloud wasn't following them. Mac guessed that the swarms could only move so far outside of the stream under their own power before they had to either go back or dissipate and become useless.

Mac! Where are you? asked Darren.

We are trying to get to an escape pod.

Forget that. Cross the bridge and get to the other section. I'm going to blow the bridge up. The momentum will push us away from the swarms and save everyone who couldn't get out.

Wait—what? You don't need to do that. Everyone who was vulnerable has been evacuated. As long as we avoid that part of the station we should be okay.

Nope. We've been watching the monitors. There's a bunch of people who underestimated the reach of the swarms and got possessed. I'm blowing the bridge to keep us safe from them.

How many is a bunch?

Twelve hundred.

Where are they?

It's a group of refugees who were hiding in the top docking bay, but because the angle of the station changed they got caught exactly where they didn't want to be. They are heading down right now trying to get to the bridge. You understand now?

Yep. We are running your way now.

Mac started running while he explained the situation to Scott and Lynn. Lynn looked especially terrified because she was the most vulnerable, but truthfully, Mac didn't doubt that twelve hundred people would be able to tear him and Scott apart as well.

The *Lendrum* was made up of two colossal, long, hexagonal structures, titled the *Chadwick* and the *Lefevbre*.

A bridge the size of the *Rundle* connected these two structures. The main command deck was in the middle of the *Chadwick*. Darren and the rest of the people who hadn't made it to escape pods were on the *Lefevbre*.

"How much farther?" asked Mac.

"We're on the right level. It's straight ahead," said Lynn.

They both spoke while looking up instead of looking at each other. There were pounding footsteps above them as the horde of swarm-infested refugees scrambled to get to the bridge so they could inhabit the rest of the people. Lynn stopped running and went to one of the doors lining the wall.

"We don't have time," said Mac.

"We will after I lock the doors," she said.

"What's the code?"

"011412. All these doors lead to lifts or stairs."

Mac and Scott ran to lock as many as they could. The footsteps on the floor above them only got louder. The sounds were starting to echo down the stairwell. There were too many doors. This was a high-traffic area for the station. It wasn't meant to be shut down.

"We need to go," said Mac.

He grabbed Lynn by the hand despite her protests. Once the swarm-possessed starting banging on the door she had first locked she realized he was right and stopped resisting. The bridge was right ahead of them.

I need to close the security doors to protect us from the explosion. Hurry, said Darren.

The doors behind the three sprinters exploded open from the force of the people behind it. The bridge was in front of them. It was as big as the *Rundle* but didn't have any rooms or hallways, just one big open space for people to move back and forth between the two structures. The lights were brighter here and the floor was so shiny it could double as a mirror. It was a flat-out race to get to the other side.

Genny's body hadn't been changed like Mac and Scott and she couldn't keep up with them. To keep ahead of the swarm of people behind them Scott picked her up. Mac wasn't sure if it would be enough.

They crossed the seam in the wall and floor where the security door would close on the *Chadwick* side. If only Darren and whoever was helping him—Mac was pretty sure some random dude he went to school with in Passage didn't know too much about explosives—had set up the explosives at that door.

You guys are losing ground.

Mac looked over his shoulder as they ran. Darren was right. He must have been watching on the surveillance system. They weren't going to make it. At least, not all of them were going to make it. He slowed his pace and let Scott and Lynn get ahead of him.

"Get Lynn to the other side. I'll try and buy you some time," said Mac.

Sure thing, said Scott without slowing down. It used less energy to mind speak than to yell while running.

"Let me know the second you cross the threshold," said Mac. *Darren, do not close the door until Scott and Lynn get there.*

What about you?

I'll be fine.

Darren didn't argue. Either he didn't care what happened to Mac or he really believed Mac could take on twelve hundred people at the same time. Truthfully, he was just hoping to survive until the explosion.

I'll be fine, Mac repeated. *Give me a heads up before you blow it.*

Sure thing.

Also, if you guys have any weapons over there start firing.

But won't that kill the humans the aliens are inhabiting?

They're goners as soon as you blow the bridge.

Right. Heads up then.

Mac turned around and met the crowd head on. Swarms had to practice being human so their faces didn't register surprise, but they did slow down and cock their heads to the side, wondering what was going on. From behind him came a volley of laser fire. Acting like a bowling ball to the swarm pins, he started running, surrounded on either side by laser fire. One person against a horde wasn't going to slow them down much, but he had to try.

The swarms weren't hesitating anymore. They realized there was something more going on and now more than ever they needed to get to the other side. Mac ran into the throng with his fists flying. His speed slowed down as soon as he hit the group but he didn't stop. The swarms were ignoring him for the most part, pushing him out of the way. If they all worked together they could have killed him but it was more important right now that they got across the bridge.

He didn't understand why none of them were attacking him. Not at first, anyway. Then the tingling sensation started to cover his body. Each time an infested crew member ran past him the tingling sensation increased. They weren't ignoring him; they were trying to fill him with swarms. He could feel his body buzzing now. They hadn't completely taken over his body but he could feel himself getting heavier as more and more aliens entered his body.

They're almost here, said Darren. *Get ready.*

Mac didn't want to get blown out into space when the bridge exploded. There wasn't much to hang onto but he figured an emergency security door would close with the drop in air pressure. He just had to make sure he was on the right side of it when it happened. Mac moved against the crowd like a salmon swimming upstream—except that he wasn't doing it nearly as effectively. Laser fire kept downing targets all around him and scorching the walls. He wasn't going to make it in time. If he was going to prevent himself from getting sucked out into space he needed to grab onto something.

Brace yourself, said Darren.

Mac wasn't ready. He jumped to the walls and frantically looked for something that wouldn't get sucked out. There was only the handrail. He wrapped his hands around it and waited for the boom. The entire station shook. He could feel it vibrating through his whole body. At the far end of the bridge there was an explosion and a whoosh of air. As expected the emergency security door came down to seal off the other section of the *Lendrum*, trapping Mac and the infested crew members on the bridge as the atmosphere failed. Everything not strapped down was sucked into space.

Bodies were flying past Mac. Several tried to grab onto him as they were sucked out. A woman latched onto his leg. He kicked at her with his free leg but was distracted by the chairs and vendor stands tumbling towards him. A chair hit his hand at the same time a vendor kiosk hit his body and he let go. Now he was tumbling through the bridge towards the gaping hole caused by the explosion.

Mac bounced off the floor and back towards the ceiling. His hands reached out for anything to stop him from getting sucked out. Now was not a good time to drift aimlessly in space. Someone might be able to come pick him up, but there was also a chance they would be too busy with the fleet coming.

The last of the atmosphere was sucked out of the bridge just before Mac was pulled out into space. The inside of the bridge was now like the vacuum of space, no air, no gravity. He wasn't in danger of getting sucked out now and could float freely. He was close enough to the other end of the bridge that he could see the hole caused by the blast. Stars were moving past it. The explosion had split the station in two and propelled the two sections in opposite directions. He didn't realize the consequences of this until the color of the room started to change—his half of the station was being pushed right into the swarm stream.

He already had some swarms in his body, but now that what was left of the bridge was becoming engulfed in microscopic purple lights heading to Ronos, even his movements were starting to slow down. There was no way to know how many swarms were in his body but it was more than he had ever had before. He was starting to lose control.

Chapter 15
Immortal

Volmere could still receive updates from his hospital room but the pain was so intense that he could hardly get out of bed. And that was just the physical pain. The emotional pain of having his wings—his gift of flight—taken away from him was enough to make him go crazy. The wings were long gone, completely destroyed, but he could still feel phantom pain and itchiness. He wondered if that was going to be there for the rest of his life as a constant, annoying reminder that if he was ever to go back into battle he would have to walk.

That was the wrong way to think of it. It was never *if* he was going to go back into battle; it was *when*. The invasion of Ronos hadn't gotten beyond a scout ship so far, but according to what his daughter Vissia was telling him, that wasn't going to last long.

His upper body was covered in bloody bandages and every bit of movement involving his back muscles sent pain coursing through his body. But he didn't care. He was the military leader of the Ronos Almics. Now was not the time to abandon them.

Pushing himself upright, he moved his legs to the floor and sat on the edge of the bed. The fact that he'd been able to do that without crying out in pain was a small victory for him. While he sat there, gathering his strength, he received a message from Vissia.

Father, they have fired a weapon aimed at Ronos.

What kind of weapon?

Our sensors show it is a dense beam of energy. Its destructive abilities are unknown. The fleet that's been gathering at the edge of the system was protecting this weapon until it built up enough energy to fire.

A dense beam of energy. Volmere felt like he should know what it was from his time with Lynn but the pain in his body was distracting his mind from making the connection. He passed the information on to Witt.

Swarms. The Invaders have reverted to their swarm form and have been super charged by that ship and shot at the planet, said Witt.

What?

Vissia has been sending me the information from her sensors. The beam is so dense because it's billions, maybe trillions, of swarms all packed together.

What do you mean by super charged?

I mean they will get here way faster and in much higher numbers than they would have if they had tried to come in ships. Hundreds of thousands could be formed almost instantly.

How long do we have?

An hour.

In one hour there will be a hundred thousand Invaders forming on the Dead Continent?

Yes, sir. And more forming every second. If we don't get control of the situation immediately then their numbers will overwhelm us.

There was no way that Volmere would be waiting in the hospital while his men fought an impossible war. It would probably lead to his destruction but he was going to keep fighting.

Stop attacks on the beacon. We need to save our ammunition and heavy artillery for the Invaders. Gather anyone who can hold a weapon. Get all the ships in the air. Contact the Passengers and tell them what's coming. Even if they don't believe us at first, they will once it starts. Contact the Rays as well, while you're at it. Might as well give them the chance to at least try to help.

Yes, sir. I'll pass that information on to Lemnell.

You can't do it yourself?

The door to Volmere's hospital room opened and Witt came inside holding a box full of bottles. His eyes were wide with excitement.

I thought I'd find you doing something stupid without any help, said Witt, seeing Volmere sitting on the bed.

I'm still your commanding officer.

I know. But I'm here to help you. I'm assuming you still want to fight.

I do.

Well, then I have something you need to take. Witt took out a bottle full of an innocuous-looking clear liquid. It was unlabelled. *This is a nerve killer.*

It'll take away the pain?

It'll take away everything. I hesitate to recommend it. I'm not a healer but a builder. And I built something amazing for you—but it won't work in your current condition.

What did you build me?

To be honest, I wasn't thinking about you when I built them, but they'll fit you just as easily as they will me. Lynn helped with the design. We've had them lying around for a while. Waiting for the need to arise. They're artificial wings.

Those have robotics. I need to heal more before I can use them.

I wouldn't come to you with only robotics. These wings are unique. They have mechanical enhancements to them but they are also partly organic. They can fuse with your body and the computer inside of them can be operated using your mind. It will be like having normal wings with a little bit more punch.

Why do I need the nerve killer?

The fusing process is too painful for you to handle on your own. Numbing isn't enough. The nerves need to not exist anymore. Of course, if we kill them now they are gone forever.

Do it.

You won't be able to feel anything in portions of your body. For sure your back, but I can't guarantee that it won't spread to other areas. This is all speculative—I'm not a healer, like I said before. But in theory.

Do it.

Witt nodded his long alligator head and flicked his tongue in and out of his mouth.

I'll get it ready, said Witt.

He filled a needle with the nerve killer and walked over to Volmere. Witt stood ready to inject the nerve killer but hesitated for moment while he asked, *You don't think we're going to survive this war, do you? That's why you don't care about the nerve killer.*

Just do it so I can fight.

Volmere let Lemnell command the ships circling the Dead Continent. They all had instructions to avoid making physical contact with the swarm stream at all costs. The swarms would be more vulnerable when they reached the surface so that's where the Almic fire power would be concentrated. The giant bird-shaped ships circled the crater Lynn's bomb had created trying to destroy the colony ship. The swarm stream was heading directly for that spot. The Invaders knew that it was their only vulnerability and were moving to protect it. They didn't know that Volmere and the others had no way of destroying it. Volmere was going to have to win this war the old fashioned way, soldier versus soldier.

Volmere stood near the crater with an army of Ronos Almic soldiers. A third of them were on foot with Volmere. Another third took to the sky. The last third were in tanks. The Almic tanks were rarely used. Since the Almics survived on the Archipelago it was easier to defend with ships and flying soldiers than with tanks, but Volmere always knew that there was a possibility they would need massive ground forces on one of the continents.

The tanks could stop on a dime and move in any direction. Its weapons included three laser cannons that could be independently aimed to take on multiple targets simultaneously. Each tank was also armed with two plasma grenade launchers that burned hot enough to melt metal—well, most metal; not the strange, indestructible, organic, colony ship metal. Volmere had launched several missiles with the same capabilities just to make sure that was the case, and no damage had been done. The tanks were also incredibly fast. Speed was always a key feature in Almic technology. The faster they went the more comfortable they felt.

Lemnell had tried to talk Volmere out of commanding the ground troops but that was impossible. The Almic leader stood at the edge of the massive crater and looked at the center. Not more than a foot of rock and dirt still covered the beacon. Ray tunnels, now abandoned, pocked the walls of the crater. It was possible that surviving Rays could still come through there. If they did, hopefully they would fight for the right side. On his back Volmere wore his new wings—more intimidating than the wings he was born with, mostly because they were infinitely uglier. Their biological features allowed them to mold into Volmere's body. The wings themselves were a metal frame, covered in a malleable organic material that was yellow, green, and bulging. They were as long as his old ones, and ten times as strong, but he was not an attractive Almic anymore. He knew how he looked but he didn't care—as long as they worked. He had decided to avoid testing them for as long as he could. In the dark recesses of his mind he still wondered if they would work at all.

The nerve killer had only affected his back so far. Witt warned that there was a possibility it could spread, especially during the battle when Volmere's heart was racing. The red-winged Almic who had given Volmere his wings back was right about one thing: The risk of the nerve killer was worth it considering they might not make it to the end of the day anyway. He needed his wings to fight. It gave him a chance—a slim chance, but still a chance.

We have visual, said Lemnell. *The swarm stream has entered the atmosphere.*

From the ground it looked like nothing more than a distant cloud, but it was moving rapidly. From the air, Lemnell and the others could see it stretched out across the sky and into space like a never-ending snake.

The Ronos Almic ships opened fire on the beam of light hurling through the sky. There were no explosions or dramatic yelling as particles of light were destroyed. The beam was so dense that it didn't even look like any damage was being done. That didn't stop the ships from firing everything they had. The orders were to aim for the section of the beam that was closest to the surface. That's where the swarms would be most vulnerable.

The swarm stream hit exactly where predicted, the dead center of the crater.

Fire into the crater! Volmere ordered.

Soldiers aimed their cutters and shot at the beings forming below. Tanks blasted grenades and the ground shook with explosions. The lights coming down were so dense that Volmere could no longer see to the bottom, or even the other side, of the crater. When the lights hit the ground they instantly turned into Invader soldiers.

Volmere aimed and fired at several enemies walking around on the crater floor and wall. They weren't trying to get out of the crater. As they came together began to stumble around like they were learning to walk again. There were more Invaders forming than the Ronos Almics could shoot down. The enemies that survived took flight and flew straight up into the swarm stream.

There had to be tens of thousands of Invaders fully formed, but they all stayed in the stream where it was hard to see them. Volmere realized they were massing to strike as a large group once they had enough numbers.

Before he could warn Lemnell the enemy soldiers burst out of the stream high above and surrounded one of the Ronos Almic ships. It looked like they were trying to force their way inside. The other Ronos Almic ships were cautious about firing on one of their own ships, even though Invaders were overtaking it. Another group of Invaders flew out of the stream and attacked another ship.

Back away from the stream, said Volmere. *Don't let them sneak up on you.*

The command was mostly for Lemnell and his ships but he motioned for the ground troops to back away as well. They kept firing into the crater as they moved but it was too difficult to aim at individual targets.

Incoming, said Lemnell.

Volmere looked up. The first wave of Invader ships had arrived. There were thousands of small, one-man fighters. The wings came out of the cockpit at a downward angle and the nose came to a sharp point, as if the ship could also be used to ram into bigger ships if the pilot had no other option. The tiny spear ships were fast—so fast it was difficult for the larger ships to target them.

The flying corps of the Ronos Almics took off in pursuit of the new threat. Lemnell also ordered one of their own large winged ships to break up into its smaller fighters to help with the newcomers. The massive Ronos Almic ship shuddered and then broke apart. It looked like it was going to crash to the ground in a hundred pieces but the individual pieces took off, heading for the spear ships. The small ships looked like miniature versions of the ship they came from. The ships could hold two to three soldiers inside.

A group of Invaders unleashed themselves from the swarm stream right in front of Volmere. He fired his weapon into the face of the leader, who fell dead to the ground. The blade on the end of his cutter was charged and the Invaders were flying close enough to the ground—attacking tanks and soldiers—that he was able to swing his weapon and slice through a dozen opponents before the group was out of range. He looked around him and saw many injured Almics. He realized he had been lucky.

In a normal battle there would be time for a medic to come and take away the injured but they had no such luxury now. The injured would be taking care of themselves and they knew it. The less injured took care of those more seriously hurt; they started forming a group and slowly moving away from the battle. If they could fly they would but most of them couldn't. The enemy seemed to know that taking away their wings was a pivotal blow.

More enemy ships entered the atmosphere. They were larger and completely decked out in weapons. They could fire out of dozens of different laser cannons at the same time. Lemnell's ship completely gave up fighting the one-man spear ships and focused entirely on the new battle ships that looked almost like porcupines—each quill was a laser cannon.

There was explosion after explosion above Volmere. Casualties on each side. Massive broken ships were burning and falling apart. He was going to have to keep one eye up to avoid getting smashed by falling debris.

A strange stillness, centered around the crater, grew. Invaders' group attacks, rushing around the swarm, became less. They looked like they were waiting for something. It couldn't be that they were waiting for everyone to get there—the swarm stream was still coming and would be for a while more. Not all of them would fit in the crater. He didn't know how they were all fitting already. No, they had to be waiting for something else.

The ground battle had come to a halt. There wasn't anyone attacking them so the Ronos Almic soldiers all shot into the stream, hoping that would do something. But truthfully they had no idea if it was making a difference. The air battle above them intensified. More and more enemy ships of all different shapes and sizes were descending into the atmosphere. Volmere thought he could see a pattern.

Back away, Lemnell, said Volmere.

We can take them. We can do this, said Lemnell. He did not want to back down now. They were all probably going to die anyway and he wasn't giving up.

They are leading you astray, distracting you. There is a bigger target. Move away and regroup for an attack.

Yes, sir.

The ships moved away from the heaviest number of Invader ships.

Do you see the large cluster surrounding the stream right now? said Volmere.

Yes.

They are moving down.

They are following something down to the surface.

Yes. Something vulnerable that they need to protect. We need to destroy it before it gets down here.

Yes, sir.

Lemnell organized his ships while Volmere arranged the attack from the ground. He kept most of the tanks firing into the crater with their grenade launchers but had each of them aim up at the cluster of ships with their laser cannons. The tanks hadn't yet engaged the incoming ships so he hoped this would catch them off guard. Then Volmere would move in, all his men taking to the sky, and charge the ships that weren't in the stream to draw their focus. Then Lemnell would target whatever they were protecting and destroy it.

We are ready, sir, said Lemnell.

Fire, Volmere commanded the tanks.

The sky was full of laser fire as the first volley leapt out of their cannons. The weapons targeting the crater realigned and shot up with the second volley. Dozens of ships exploded in a fury of fire.

With the second volley, every able-bodied Ronos Almic spread their wings and took to the sky as fast as they could. The Invaders were already targeting the tanks on the ground, who were scrambling across the hilly terrain to make themselves a more difficult target. The tanks never stopped firing.

Volmere commanded his artificial wings to extend. He heard them more than felt them. His balance changed as the weight on his back was distributed differently. The organic material spread thin but did not tear and the metal moved without hesitation. There was a laser cannon on his back that could only pop out when his wings were fully extended. He charged it up as he took to the air.

They needed to clear a path so that Lemnell would have a clear line of sight for whatever the Invaders were protecting. Hopefully it was would be more vulnerable than the colony ship—otherwise there was no hope. Volmere used his cutter to hit Invaders as they flew to intercept the army that had risen up from the ground, and used his laser cannon to find the weak spots on the ships. He hit a spear ship from below, at the base of one of the wings, and it exploded instantly. The laser shouldn't have been powerful enough to do that.

The spear ships are weakest where the wings connect underneath to the cockpit.

There was a hail of explosions as his men utilized this new information.

The explosion on the bridge connecting the two different sections of the *Lendrum* had thrown the station through the swarm stream. Now it was floating farther and farther from Ronos. Farther and farther from where the swarms were so desperately trying to go. They weren't going to kill Mac. They were going to use him to get to the surface.

Mac didn't have control over his body anymore—there were that many swarms in him. The exact number he didn't know, but they were telling him to move and no matter what he tried he was powerless to resist. He needed to escape somehow, but what could he do if he couldn't even make himself walk in the right direction? The swarms had him pull himself to the outside of the station and along the hull until he found an airlock.

They used Mac to open the airlock and he climbed inside the station without hurting anyone else. By now he had stopped fighting them. His mind wasn't strong enough to do anything about it. Although he had stopped fighting, his movements were still sluggish, either because he had so many swarms inside of him or because they couldn't all agree on which direction they needed to take. He was walking like he was impaired and stumbling his way home to bed.

Mac! Mac, can you hear me?

The voice was familiar but he didn't immediately place it. When he tried to answer the words couldn't form in his head. He could think to himself but he couldn't send messages to others. The swarms were blocking his mind from sending for help.

Mac? Are you there? We need your help.

Now Mac recognized the voice. It was Phillip Pilgrim—the doctor he had sent behind enemy lines with three other soldiers to rescue the human prisoners being used as emulators. With all his mental dexterity he willed himself to send a message to Phillip.

Did you find Janelle?

The message didn't get through. Phillip kept repeating himself.

Are you there Mac? I feel like you are. I almost heard something. Try again.

Did you find Janelle!

Mac sent the same message again, yelling it in his mind hoping volume would help it get through to Phillip. The swarms stopped his body, realizing that something was happening to their host. He could feel his head buzz more as his thoughts were attacked. There was no way the message would get through now.

We...need to...machine...before...surface.

The swarms were working so hard that the incoming messages were being screened now. Mac couldn't hear the whole thing. Why would Phillip be talking about machines? The surface of what? Where were Phillip and the others? If part of the fleet was at the edge of the Ronos system did that mean they were nearby?

Destroy...emulator...before...the surface. Please...way. You...machine!

Destroy the emulator? Mac couldn't figure it out. Even the words that did make it through were too hard to hear. More swarms entered his body and he was forced to continue down the hallway. They stopped once they got to the escape pods. The pods on this side of the station hadn't been used because they were in danger of being enveloped by the swarm stream.

Mac opened the door and climbed inside. They wanted to get to the surface and using his body would get them there faster, especially now that the station had been thrown clear of the swarm stream. He knew what happened when the Invaders got down to Ronos. They got their bodies back and didn't need emulators anymore. If all the swarms inside of him got their bodies all at the same time, it would tear Mac apart. Even one Invader inside of him would split him in half—or worse.

There was nothing he could do to stop himself. Whatever Phillip needed help with wasn't going to happen. Mac was being taken to the surface to die.

No matter how many Invaders were killed or how many of their ships were destroyed, they kept coming. More every second. The Ronos Almics were easily outnumbered now but they kept fighting. Whatever was being lowered to the surface was halfway there and Volmere had no idea if they had even done any damage to it. The sensors couldn't pick anything up other than the dense swarms surrounding it.

This isn't working, said Lemnell. His ships had been hit the hardest. They were the firepower of the Ronos Almic military, and the enemy knew it and had targeted them. Lemnell's lasers hadn't stopped firing but there was no way to tell if that even made a difference.

I'm abandoning ship, said Lemnell.

You're going down?

I'm going on a suicide run.

You can't.

I'm hitting the engines on full and flying this thing straight down their throats. Maybe the collision will destroy it.

No. I'm ordering you not to kill yourself for no reason.

Fine with me. But this isn't for no reason. I'll make sure the sensors are broadcasting to all the other ships. We'll find out what they're protecting, at the very least, and maybe even have a chance at destroying it. I'll program the course and then abandon ship so I still have a chance to survive.

Good. Do it.

Volmere watched Lemnell's ship. It didn't need to be abandoned but it also wouldn't have lasted much longer. It was one of the bigger winged ships in the fleet. Smoke was pouring out of several places. Lemnell must have seen there wasn't much time and made the decision. Escape pods blasted away from the ship in all directions. The escape pods had limited steering and no weapons. Their only hope was to be picked up by another ship. Volmere made the order to save as many as possible.

The engines on Lemnell's ship-turned-battering-ram glowed bright as they powered up. Volmere hoped the trajectory was correct. If anything was going to happen it needed to be a direct hit. One final escape pod shot out of the ship and straight down. Lemnell didn't want to be picked up by another ship. He wanted to join the fight on the ground.

There was a sonic boom as the ship's engines engaged and shot forward. There was a loud metallic scraping noise as the ship entered the stream. Two ships came out the other side. Lemnell's ship was spinning—one of the wings had clipped the hidden ship inside of the stream. It hit the ground and exploded. The hidden ship, visible now outside of the stream, looked more like a building than a vessel. It was flat on the bottom and had several spires and a large dish on top. Lemnell's ship had done some structural damage to the side of it but its engines were still working. The entire bottom of the structure was glowing to keep it afloat. It had no weapons. At first glance it didn't even look threatening.

But as soon as it was exposed the Invaders swarmed it. Volmere only caught a glimpse of it before it was covered by soldiers and ships circling it. Anyone who tried to get close enough to do any damage was immediately killed.

Bring that thing down! It needs to be destroyed! commanded Volmere. It could be damaged. It wasn't built like the colony ship. It was important to the Invaders and it could be destroyed.

All weapon fire was focused on that ship but not a single blast made it through. Ships and soldiers threw themselves in front of the blasts, willing to die rather than let the ship be destroyed. What could be that important? They acted like the fate of the war depended on it making to the surface.

One of the Ronos Almic ships wasn't being careful enough and drifted into the stream while they moved to fire on the ship. The ship stopped firing on Invaders and switched to firing on fellow Ronos Almic ships. It had been taken over by swarms. It quickly destroyed two other Ronos Almic war ships.

Lasers came from far off to cut through the taken Ronos Almic ship. Volmere looked at who had made the shot. It was a Passenger ship. They had finally come to their senses.

Don't go anywhere near that beam of energy. Alien swarms will possess your bodies, said Volmere.

What are they protecting over there? asked a human Volmere didn't recognize.

We don't know, but we need to destroy it.

All the Passenger ships targeted the mystery ship and fired. The Passenger ships were smooth wavy-looking vessels. They looked almost like flower bulbs that hadn't fully bloomed. The colors were even metallic florals—dark shiny colors in almost every variety. There were hundreds of ships coming to join the fight, and more on the way, if Volmere's intel about what the Passengers were capable of was any indication. This fight wasn't over yet.

As Mac's escape pod entered Ronos' atmosphere it was surrounded by the carnage of battle. There were explosions all around him as ships broke apart under laser fire. Almics flew and fired at each other. Others latched on to their enemies and simply tore them apart with their claws. As far as Mac could tell that was the only difference between them: The Ronos Almics had weapons and the Invader Almics were forced to kill with their own hands. Most of the fighting was taking place in the air but even from this high up Mac could see machines on the ground firing up into the stream and the enemies who had already formed. There was a glowing army moving closer to the stream. The Passengers were finally in the fight. Mac wondered if their armor would protect them from the Invaders' claws.

Mac still didn't have control over his body. The swarms inside of him piloted the pod to the thick of the battle. All the ships in the sky were targeting a clump of Invader ships and soldiers that were working to protect something. Mac didn't know what it was but that's where the escape pod was heading.

His body was vibrating even more intensely the closer he got to the surface. The swarms inside of him were getting ready to form their bodies again. It wasn't going to be much longer before he got ripped apart.

The ship he was heading towards reached the surface. Mac hadn't caught up to it yet but as soon as it touched ground his skin started to visibly vibrate. The ship that landed looked more like a building with a giant dish on top of it. The Invaders were still circling it but Mac could catch glimpses of what was inside.

Passenger ships and Ronos Almic ships were firing to destroy whatever that building was, but none of their weapons could get through the living shield the Invaders had created. Mac couldn't figure out what the Invaders held so dear that they would die to protect it.

Then he found out.

A white circular beam of energy exploded out of the dish without destroying it and streaked across the ground. Mac could see the Ronos Almics still on the ground freeze for a moment while they tried to figure out if they were hurt. They weren't.

The beam of energy emanated outward from the building, passing over the ground and moving through the air. As it moved over bodies that were dead on the ground

Mac saw them stand back up and join the fight again. Invaders who had been shot in half came together. Soldiers long out of the fight now had a chance to avenge their own deaths. The beam raised all the Invaders—and only the Invaders—back from the dead as it moved across the battlefield.

Instead of hurting their enemies, the beam healed the Invaders. It made them immortal. They didn't come here just to regain their bodies so they didn't have to rely on emulators anymore. They didn't want to die so they brought the technology to be able to keep the swarms together in their original bodies forever. The Invaders had figured out a way to transfer the way they had kept the swarms alive to their normal Almic bodies. The swarms had been around for thousands of years—enough time to build their own fountain of youth.

Down below, Volmere watched the first wave of the energy beam resuscitate nearly all the Invaders he and the others had killed. The Invaders had been expecting this and were now ready for a fight. Stunned Ronos Almics, suddenly surrounded by creatures thought to be dead, were easily hewn down and their weapons confiscated. Tanks were destroyed or hijacked. The tide was never really in Volmere's favor, but now there was no denying it. Unless they destroyed that dish building there was no way they could win the war.

Mac wasn't on the surface but some of the beam's residual energy was still affecting him. He could feel things moving inside of him.

Chapter 16
Evacuate

Mac started to spasm violently. His head smashed against the back of the chair and his limbs flew in every direction. For a while now he hadn't been in control of his own body, and now it seemed like the swarms inside of him weren't either. He felt like he was getting heavier as the bodies inside of him started to form. He was a man; he wasn't supposed to know what it felt like to have a body growing inside of him. The closer he got to the surface, the worse it got.

One of his legs kicked at the controls of the escape pod accidentally and changed course to shoot the escape pod straight up into the sky. Another wave of energy came out of the dish. Mac screamed in pain. There were things moving under the surface of his skin. It looked like a million worms stretching the epidermis and trying to break free. It settled down a little bit as he got farther from the dish but that wasn't going to be his answer forever. He needed to get the swarms out of him without tearing himself apart.

Volmere! Mac called out. The swarms were too busy building their bodies inside of him to screen all his thoughts.

Mac Narrad, where are you?

In…an escape pod…I'm possessed…swarms.

I see you and will send help.

Hurry.

The safety belt holding Mac in place strained as Mac grew. Either it would eventually break or Mac was going to get cut in half. The creatures inside of him were expanding. He looked out the window and saw the escape pod had tipped back towards the surface. He could no longer make out the dish building. It was completely enveloped with several layers of soldiers. There was nothing more valuable now to the Invaders' plan, and there was nothing Mac or Volmere could do until it was destroyed.

Skin has a lot of stretch before it begins to tear. Mac had never been overweight but when he caught a glimpse of himself it looked like he had doubled in size. How many swarms were inside of him?

The escape pod rocked as something latched onto the back of it, out of sight from the cockpit. It was being pulled upwards. The engines were shot and destroyed.

If you have swarms in you then it's not safe to be down on the surface, said Volmere.

Thank you.

I don't know how to get the swarms out of you.

I need them…out.

We will keep you away from the surface. The farther you are from the surface the better.

Volmere gripped the escape pod with his hooked hands and flew into one of his own ships, dropping Mac in the docking bay.

Take the ship into space, Mac heard Volmere command his men. *Seal everything up so we don't lose atmosphere.*

The swarms inside of Mac stopped forming. They broke apart and Mac went back to normal, his skin and clothes only slightly more stretched out. He couldn't mind speak anymore, and he still didn't have a say in how he moved, but his body was no longer flopping about like he was having a stroke inside of a washing machine.

The swarms could tell something was wrong. Calmly they made Mac stand up and go to a seat in the escape pod. Under the seat was a drawer. They opened it. Inside were medical supplies, which they tossed aside to reveal a gun on the bottom of the shelf. They knew that someone was coming to stop them. Mac could hear footsteps approaching the escape pod. They made him face the door with the gun out in front of him.

Mac, don't worry, said Volmere.

The door opened but there was no one in front of it. Volmere must have known it was a trap. The whole pod shifted a bit as something on top of it moved. The swarms made Mac look up. While they were distracted an arm reached inside, tore the gun out of his grip, and then pulled him out.

Mac thought he was going to get tossed through the air but Volmere didn't let go. The Almic stood on top of the escape pod and held Mac out like a fish hanging on a rod. At first Mac couldn't understand what Volmere was doing but then he felt movement inside of him. The swarms sensed the danger and started to leave his body to try and infest both of them.

Volmere was much larger than Mac was but he couldn't let all the swarms enter his body, just in case they had enough to take them both.

"Wait," said Mac in his own voice and without being forced to.

Wait, Volmere. I'm good now, said Mac.

Volmere put Mac down.

You have control again?

Yes.

Good.

You took some swarms inside of you. That means neither of us can go back down to the surface.

I know.

There was more than one reason why they couldn't go back down to the surface. The Invaders had pretty much won the war. It was impossible to defeat an army that could come back to life.

Is there any way we can destroy it? asked Mac.

We threw everything we had left against it. It didn't work. Every time we attack it sends out another wave and the soldiers we killed come back to life before we attack it again. We don't have the firepower we need to destroy it. We wasted everything on the colony ship.

That was pointless. We should have saved it for this dish building.

The dish building is utilizing the swarming ability from the colony ship. We picked up a link between the two. That's why it wasn't operational until it reached the surface. The two have to be in range of each other.

So now the Invaders have two vulnerable spots that we can't get to, said Mac.

If we can destroy the colony ship then we still have hope.

There is nothing strong enough to destroy it.

There has to be. If not, then we should just make a run for it now and hope they don't chase us.

Yeah, said Mac, *because we know these guys wouldn't go out of their way to run us down.*

Mac was being sarcastic but he didn't know if Volmere caught on. Volmere went off to talk with some of his other men. There was still a battle going on down below that he needed to coordinate. Since there wasn't a lot of hope, Mac wondered if he would simply call a retreat and get everyone off the Dead Continent.

It was while Mac was waiting for what to do next that he remembered Phillip trying to talk to him. He had said something about how to stop the aliens.

Phillip, are you there? said Mac, stretching his mind as far as it would go.

Yes. Did you get my message? I was worried when you didn't answer.

I got part of it.

Did you do it? Did you destroy the emulator machine?

Oh. So that's what that is.

Did you?

No. There's no way. They have hundreds of thousands of soldiers surrounding it. As soon as we kill a few it brings them back to life. There's no way to get to it.

Kill them all at the same time.

We don't have any weapons that will do that. We wasted them all trying to take out the beacon.

I take it that didn't work.

No, said Mac. *It's made out of too strong of material. We figured out that the only thing that can break through it is itself.*

And there's only one beacon.

Exactly.

Well, said Phillip, *on the plus side, we found Janelle.*

What?

Yeah. The swarms had rigged all the prisoner ships to explode while they made a run for Ronos as fast as they could. Some rebel swarms freed us before our ships were destroyed. She's with me right now.

Mac couldn't believe it. This had all started because he was looking for her and now there was a chance they could actually be reunited. The war on Ronos was almost a write-off but he couldn't have been more happy right then.

How is she? Did they hurt her?

She's fine.

I need to talk to her.

We haven't given her any of our blood. We wanted to wait until we got to Ronos to do it right. There's a few others with us.

I understand. Mac had almost died giving up his blood. It wasn't worth an accidental death to try and change Janelle just so Mac could talk to her.

Tell her I'm sorry it took so long.

She says that's okay.

Where are you guys right now?

General Roy is with us now and we're on our way.

Mac wasn't sure how to tell them that coming to Ronos would be a waste of time and that they should run away as fast as they could. They already knew the aliens could come back to life, that there was no way to make them stay dead. Why bother coming?

There has to be a way, said Phillip, as if reading Mac's mind. *We can't give up yet.*

Mac wasn't sure why he was still trying. He didn't even know what trying looked like anymore for him. He couldn't go back down to the surface with swarms in him and how was he supposed to fight the war from up here?

Come up here, said Volmere, as if reading his mind.

Where? said Mac as he left the escape pod behind.

Up to the command deck. If we can't help on the surface then we will fight from up here. We'll destroy as many of them as we can before we give up the ghost.

That's what it looked like to not give up—fighting like there was still a chance.

Phillip made sure that everyone was caught up on his conversation with Mac. They all looked depressed. Alveea hadn't been kidding when she said that the emulator machine needed to be taken out or the war was over. The swarms were invincible now. They had the best of both worlds: They had their own bodies, and could still swarm and come back together after they died.

If Nelson had been depressed before, he was completely done now. Devoid of all emotion, he was done crying, done feeling sorry for himself. He was past feeling. He slumped in his chair, unblinking, focused on nothing.

Janelle walked over to him and put a hand on his shoulder. He shrugged it off and got up and walked away. Jazlyn looked like she was in pain. Now that she was out of the prison she could hear all the mind speak conversations going on around her. It wasn't enough to completely overwhelm her but enough to give her a constant headache.

Ryan looked confused. Phillip looked exhausted. There had been a lot of blows that day. The entire ship was on the verge of a mental breakdown.

Almost the entire ship—Aleeva was at the console.

I want all the information you have on the colony ship, she said.

The colony ship? asked Phillip.

It's what you call the beacon. I'm going to find a way to destroy it.

Okay. I'll see what I can get from Mac.

Jace walked over to Janelle, Daniel close behind him. The younger Michaels was looking nervously at the multiple Bernadettes that occupied the command deck. It was unnatural to have so many of the exact person in the same room. So alien. There weren't many prisoners left to emulate now so there were multiples of them all.

"At the very least we can gather the humans at Ronos and make a run for it," said Jace.

"I think that's a good idea," said Daniel. "Mom and dad might still be out there. We just don't know yet."

"Yeah. Last resort."

Janelle shook her head, "We can't do that."

"Why not?"

"Once Ronos is taken they'll come after us. We can't run."

The course was already set for Ronos. The ship— named the *Kameyosek*—was a heavily modified collector ship. The engines and the weapons had been upgraded. Durgan had said that was one of the reasons they had chosen it as their last-chance ship. It wouldn't be much longer before they caught up with Mac and his group. But it still wasn't instantaneous travel and there was still down time.

No one was in the mood for conversation, at first anyway. Eventually Janelle decided that enough was enough and people needed to get their heads straight if they were going to figure this all out.

"Knock, knock," said Janelle.

"Not now," said Phillip. He was watching what Aleeva was working on, trying to offer input, but she wasn't telling him anything so he was actually just distracting her. General Roy stood nearby, soaking up all the information. His eyes were wide and wild, the look of a desperate man who needed a solution.

Jazlyn was rubbing her temples and looked like she was in pain but agreed with the need for levity. "Who's there?"

"Smell map."

"Smell map who?"

Jazlyn smiled as she walked into saying "smell my poo." Instead of smiling Ryan just nodded his head as if he approved of the word play.

"How do you catch a unique rabbit?" asked Janelle.

Ryan shrugged.

"Unique up on it," she finished. "Nelson, how do you catch a tame rabbit?"

"If it's tame you don't have to catch it," he said. It was the most words he had said since they had gotten to the command deck.

"Nope, the answer is, 'the tame way.' "

"I have one," said Jazlyn. "How did the dentist become a brain surgeon? His hand slipped."

Ryan actually smiled. Nelson shifted in his seat. Maybe he was more in the mood for dark humor, considering the circumstances. Talking out loud was distracting Jazlyn from the voices in her head.

"A man goes into a library to check out a book on suicide. He can't find any books about suicide anywhere so he goes to the librarian to complain. The librarian tells him that they used to have a ton of how-to books on suicide but none of them got returned."

Nelson was the only one who laughed at that. The rest were not amused. By the joke anyway—but they were relieved to see that Nelson was laughing. Not that one lame joke about a horrible thing was enough to make his depression go away but at least he was still capable of laughing.

They swapped jokes for a few hours. They all took turns, except for Nelson, and he only laughed when the joke was twisted or someone got hurt. If they did survive this war he was going to need some therapy. They were all going to need some therapy.

General Roy interrupted their conversation. He was smiling.

"Aleeva thinks she found an answer," he said. Rizzen and all the humans gathered around the command deck. The swarms had already been informed and continued tending to the ship. "She figured out what the beacon was made up of. She's never seen the beacon in person so she had to get help from someone on Ronos named Lynn Ryder. Lynn has been studying it for years so she was able to answer all of Aleeva's questions. The colony ship—or the beacon or whatever you want to call it—was built by the Almics a long time ago. Longer than any of us, including the swarms, have been alive. It is an Almic ship made out of unique Almic material. In their original home world the material is not unique. Lynn was right in thinking that the only thing that could destroy it was itself. Aleeva confirmed that. If we have another Almic ship we can ram it into the beacon and end everything."

There are no Almic ships left, said Rizzen. *That's why they take the technology of the civilizations they destroy.*

"No. There's one left," said General Roy.

He pointed at the console. The last Almic ship was on the display. Aleeva had pulled up the schematics. She had all the information about the ship at her fingertips. The ship was shaped like a claw or a crescent moon that was wider at one end. According to the scale it was a gigantic ship, more closely resembling a space station than a human capital ship. A lot of swarms could fit inside of it.

"It's too big," said Jace.

"Too big for what?" asked Phillip.

"We're going to crash a small moon into Ronos? You'll destroy the planet."

General Roy hesitated to answer but then said, "Yes. That's right."

There was a flurry of objections. Aleeva motioned for quiet and brought up a simulation on the console. The last Almic ship flew through the air towards the Dead Continent and collided with the beacon, destroying both of them and cracking the planet in half in the process.

"We can't destroy the only home we have left," said Ryan.

"All the calculations have already been done. We have been in constant contact with Narrad and his people. We have thought through every scenario we can in this short amount of time. Running won't save us. Continuing fighting the way we are won't save us. Destroying the beacon will stop them from being able to swarm so the emulator machine won't work anymore. Destroying the planet means the soldiers who have already formed will die with it. It will end the war."

"We're going to kill all of them?" asked Daniel.

"We're killing them before they kill us. They took everything from us and now we're going to take everything from them," said Nelson. He was standing next to them now. The plan would give him the revenge he thought he needed. "So now we need to take over the last Almic ship."

"Yeah, that's what's next for us."

"How do we do that?"

General Roy looked over at Aleeva and grimaced a little. "That's where it gets complicated. The last Almic ship is impossible for us to get to with only the *Kameyosek*. But there are reinforcements coming. Together we can fight our way to the ship and take it by force with numbers."

"How many swarms are defending it?" asked Phillip.

"The last Almic ship is a staging point in the Ronos system for swarms who were left behind or forced to stay behind," said Aleeva using Bernadette's voice.

"Like you?" asked Ryan.

"Like the swarms we saved you from. The ones left behind to kill all the prisoners. This ship can hold millions of swarms so getting inside and taking control of it is not going to be easy. We can't gain access."

"They have a way of telling which swarm is which?" said Ryan. He was being deliberately antagonistic. Aleeva didn't respond—obviously they did. Just like humans could tell each other apart, swarms could tell one from another. Whatever means of identification they used prevented the rebel swarms from getting on board.

"We can't gain access without a host," she finished.

"What?" said Ryan and Nelson at the same time.

"I can sneak on if I take over one of your bodies. It happens. There's procedure for it. They can't identify me as quickly if I'm in another person's body."

"What's the difference between an emulator and a body?" asked Phillip.

"The vibration. I'm asking you to trust me. Swarms can see it, you can't. Once the other rebels and I get on the ship we can secure an area and fight our way to the bridge."

"You said there were swarms on that ship. How are we supposed to fight them?"

"With cubes."

Ryan shook his head. "You just told me there were no cubes on this ship."

"I lied."

"How do we know you're not lying about this?" said

Ryan. "Maybe you just need our help to sneak onto Ronos. You're leading us into a trap."

"If I wanted you dead—"

"You don't need us dead. You need us to sneak onto the last Almic ship so you can get to the hilt ship and onto Ronos. He turned to all the non-swarms in the room. "Has anyone even stopped to think about why they are doing this? Helping us kill their own people?"

Aleeva was in someone else's body so it was easy for her to hide her emotions. She let Ryan talk without responding to the accusations being thrown around. Janelle was the one who figured it out.

"It's because she isn't going to die."

"What?" said Ryan.

"You say she wouldn't help us kill herself, and that must be right, but then that means she knows how to survive."

"Yes," said Aleeva.

"And?"

"If we possess a body when the colony ship is destroyed we can survive long enough…"

The bridge crew did not like the sound of this. They erupted with questions and arguments. Everyone started talking at the same time.

"You mean this plan isn't even going to work?"

"How many swarms will survive?"

"They wouldn't let any of us survive. Kill them all."

"Who are you going to take? You expect volunteers?"

"Cancel everything. We need to make a run for it."

Aleeva stood patiently and waited for all of them to stop talking. It took a long time but eventually they quieted down as they realized none of their questions were being answered.

"If we possess a body when the colony ship is destroyed we can survive long enough to figure out a permanent solution. We have biological engineering knowledge. We can build or grow a body for us to work in."

Technology you stole from someone else, said Rizzen.

"The same people we recently set free. We are the Almics who want peace. We don't need our bodies. We don't need our home world. All we need is to stop fighting so we can start living our lives. I have seen too much destruction. I want to make things better for everyone."

"This is insane," said Nelson.

"We need that ship," she said. She looked over at General Roy. "Do not take my word for it. I have shared everything with your leader. He agrees that this is the best plan for us. This is the best chance we all have to get what we want."

"How many people are on the *Kameyosek*? How many swarms, I mean?" asked Phillip.

"Four hundred and nine."

"You're willing to kill billions of your own people and save only four hundred and nine? You're talking genocide."

"I'm talking about a chance to redeem ourselves. They had their chance to do the right thing and now we have a chance to survive. If it means ending them then that's what we need to do. It's the only thing we have left."

"It's not," said Ryan. He wasn't in charge but he couldn't let it drop. "It's not the only thing *you* have left. You are winning this war. In a matter of hours you guys will have taken Ronos. This time next year all the humans in the galaxy could be dead. You could already be on the winning side of the war right now. All you need to do is get to Ronos and pretend like killing all humans is what you always wanted."

"We have broken the trust of our people. We have violated their laws. There is nothing any of us on this ship can do to avoid punishment unless we eliminate the punishers."

"They're going to kill you once you reach Ronos?"

"They won't even let us reach the surface. They'll put us in a cube and then hurl it into the sun. There is no forgiveness for our rebellion. I have no choice but to help you. It seems unnatural to you that I would help you, but the only way I can survive is if I help you survive."

Something about what she said rang true to Janelle. When she looked around the room, besides little Daniel, she saw nothing but soldiers and trained killers. These people were ready to fight. They were trained to fight. They were the ones that were going to get on the last Almic ship and take control. Not her. She wanted to see things through like everyone else and there was only one way she would be able to do that.

"Aleeva, I'll host you," said Janelle.

"Come on, Janelle," said Ryan. "Do you even know what you signed up for?"

"This is our chance. This is our only chance. How can I not volunteer to host?"

"I'm in, too," said Jazlyn.

"We can't take enhanced humans. We need to be in complete control of the host."

Phillip spoke up. "If you think we are just going to sit by while you do all the work—"

"There's more work to be done," said Aleeva. "No one is getting on that ship if we can't get to it. Because of you four the swarms know about enhanced humans. You won't be able to sneak around behind enemy lines undetected like you could before."

"Wait until the fleet gathers. Then we will have one last showdown to decide all our fates," said General Roy.

"The fleet that was left back on Earth?" asked Phillip.

General Roy gave Rizzen a knowing look.

I've been organizing the prisoners and their ships. The Invaders were able to take down each civilization one at a time. Soon we will see how they do against all them combined.

Mac and Volmere were on the Almic command deck when they got the message from Phillip's group.

We have a plan. You ready? said Phillip.

No, said Volmere. He turned to his crew and looked them over. Then pointed to two young officers, *You two, come with me. Mac, follow.*

They left the command deck and walked to a part of the ship Mac had never seen. It looked like the brig. There were rooms sealed off with force fields. Mac wondered if these young officers had done something wrong Mac hadn't heard about.

What's going on? asked Mac.

The plan was about to be given to us.

I know.

The plan that would help us destroy the Invaders and win the war.

I know.

We have swarms inside of us.

Oh.

Both young officers stepped forward. They understood what needed to be done and they knew that if the plan failed they were dead anyway.

Volmere, I don't know what your plan is but I found a weakness in the enemy's forces, said one of them.

I helped him find the solution. The war could be over by this afternoon. It's complicated but it will work, said the other one.

Mac wasn't sure what was going on. Both of them reached out to grab him and Volmere. They were all standing in one of the holding cells. Mac could feel movement inside his body as the last remaining swarms left. The same thing was happening to Volmere. When it was over he quickly pulled Mac out and then turned on the force field, trapping the two men inside.

Didn't the swarms know you were tricking them? asked Mac.

Their pride couldn't let them not move to a new target. My men knew enough to come up with a complicated plan that would take a few moments for the swarms to realize was not going to work. These are two of the most intuitive soldiers I command. They knew what they needed to do. And now we can learn the plan without accidently leaking it to the enemy.

We need to come up with a plan B in case plan A gets leaked.

You don't trust the rebel swarms?

Just in case.

Once General Roy and Aleeva revealed their plan Volmere gave the order to evacuate the planet. The Ronos Almic ships were all prepared for space travel. At the time of their building the engineers no doubt had thought it was foolish to follow the schematics given by the colony ship for space travel. They couldn't understand why a ship would need to survive in a place with no atmosphere. They didn't understand the principles of a vacuum. But they had known that if they didn't follow the directions they would be fired, so they did as they were told.

Despite them being prepared not everyone followed Volmere's orders. Zaxxer was still on the surface and he was still trying to control what was going on. As soon as he found out Volmere had—as Zaxxer had put it—*abandoned them* he took control of anyone who would follow his orders and set up a resistance on Sanctuary to gather troops and to plan their next attack.

It is a lost cause, said Volmere.

We do not give up as easily as you do, said Zaxxer. Volmere couldn't see the man but assumed his tongue was flipping in and out of his mouth in seething anger. *You destroyed the colony ship and now you seek to destroy our home. We will win this war the way we have always won. With sheer force of power. We are Almic! We cannot be stopped!*

Volmere couldn't believe how blind Zaxxer was being. To try and persuade as many Ronos Almics as he could, Volmere broadcasted a message to the entire planet, *Ronos has been lost. If you want to survive you must evacuate. Ships will be down there evacuating as many willing people as possible. If you stay on Ronos you will die. Come with us and you have a chance.*

What about the Passengers? asked Mac.

We passed the message along. Nally is down there now helping them prepare as many ships as fast as they can. It will not be enough but it is the best we can do. We are also sending ships to their cities and transporting them to your space station. It still has a lot of room inside of it.

There are probably some Passengers who still don't believe what's going on. Like Zaxxer, they'll refuse to leave even though we are telling them the truth.

We don't have time to save people who don't want to be saved. They'll be given a chance. If they choose not to take it then they will seal their own fate.

I had almost thought about flying the Lendrum *into the beacon to see if that would do any damage.*

It wouldn't. And your station has no engines.

I know.

Our only hope is to take the last Almic ship.

Chapter 17
Rally Point

There was nothing for Mac to do until the prisoner fleet arrived. Not that there wasn't a lot going on; there just wasn't a lot Mac could do. The planet was under evacuation. Nally was down there making sure she could save as many people as possible. Volmere had said to only save the people who wanted to be saved but she was shoving everyone—willing or not—into any ship that could survive the vacuum. Mac had tried to talk to her a few times but she was busy. Using the ship's sensors he could follow the activity. The Passengers and most of the Almics looked passionate about getting off the planet. No Rays. They still thought they could save themselves.

Hey Lynn, Mac called out. *You're not on the surface are you?*

No. We're on the Lendrum. *Trying to figure a way to get it out of the line of fire. Someone told me you guys were going to destroy Ronos or something like that. How were you lucky enough find a ship made out of the same stuff as the beacon?*

I wouldn't call it luck. There's millions of swarms between us and that ship. You got any advice before we start the attack?

You won't be able to force your way on—they're too strong. Unless…you know, I was thinking about something. The beacon here on Ronos was broken in two.

Yeah.

But that ship up there is still working. It travelled across the universe to get here. It shouldn't be able to last that long.

So what're you getting at?

It had to have been repaired at some point. If they didn't have any Almic material than it had to be repaired with something more vulnerable.

Maybe you should just come with me. For old time's sake.

I'm not going to follow you on this one, said Lynn. *Scott and I will stay on the* Lendrum. *Try and get it out of the kill zone. Soldiers go to war. Not biological engineers.*

Thanks to me you've also almost died a dozen times.

I did get stranded on a planet with a man who wanted to kill me.

Sorry about that.

You're also going to be destroying the planet I was born on. You haven't apologized for that yet either.

It hasn't happened yet. When it does I will gladly say sorry.

Wouldn't hurt to do it now.

Were you really born on Ronos?

That's what my parents always told me. Except they called it Grenor. I don't know if it's true. I didn't need to be born here but they did need to bring me here at some point to see if I had enough of the same genes as my ancestor who reprogrammed the beacon to follow our family's commands. I was a baby so I don't remember and it had to have happened before Zinger found it and set up his base. If I was to have kids then I would have brought them here to test them as well. But that's not going to happen.

I won't apologize until tomorrow, said Mac.

Mac didn't want to say what he was thinking. They weren't in the same room but it was still possible that this was the last time the two of them would have a conversation. He wanted to deliberately save something for another conversation. It felt strange. She hadn't been in his life for very long but in that short amount of time he had changed so much—everything had changed. For the rest of his life, however long that was, she would be a major part of who he was and what he had become.

But right now it felt like they were saying goodbye. It felt like they would never see each other again. He didn't want to accept that.

Hey, said Lynn, guessing at what Mac was thinking. *Don't stress about goodbye. You kept your promise to me. You brought Scott and me back together. If I only live until the end of the day—*

Come on.

Whatever happens, you kept your promise.

Thanks for helping me. Thanks for not giving up.

You guys think you'll take that ship?

We have to.

Then we need to move this station. And tomorrow we'll all be able to tell the tale of how we defeated an invincible alien fleet and you can apologize for destroying my home world.

Lynn?

Yes?

Where did we make the wrong move?

What do you mean?

We are talking planet-sized destruction now. It wasn't supposed to be like this. I was just trying to find Janelle and you were just trying to get back to Scott. How did it get to this? What did we do wrong?

It's no good having the people we love and then immediately getting killed by aliens. Quit being so melodramatic. Goodbye, Mac. I'll see you tomorrow.

Goodbye, Lynn.

Mac didn't feel like he could return the promise.

General Roy was back in charge. Sure, Aleeva and the rebels were the ones who were going to lead the actual attack on the last Almic ship, but General Roy had command of everyone else. His second-in-command was, appropriately, Rizzen. Janelle had seen it time and time again in the mind prison—it didn't matter who it was or what they believed, Rizzen could turn them around and get them to trust him. The one glaring exception being the Invaders, who couldn't be talked out of anything.

Having spent so much time on the front line, General Roy wasn't leaving anything to chance. He paced the command deck, back and forth. That's what he did while he was waiting. If General Zinger had done the same thing he wouldn't have been the massive blob of a man he had been. Every minute or so he would stop and ask Rizzen for an update. The purple alien would answer in mind speak so that no one else could hear.

Ryan turned to Nelson. "Why doesn't he want everyone to hear?"

"Control of information. Just like the front."

"When we get taken the swarms know everything that we know. Right now the only ones who know the plan are the general and Rizzen. Any of us get taken and the swarms have no advantage."

"They would know that we are planning on taking the last Almic ship."

"But right now none of us except Aleeva and General Roy know how we're going to do that."

Ryan looked over at Aleeva and Durgan. "He doesn't trust them either."

"We have no choice," said Phillip.

General Roy stopped, but instead of looking at Rizzen he looked at Phillip and the other enhanced humans. First he pointed at Ryan. "Come with me, spacer."

They left for a few minutes. When they came back, Ryan was smiling. General Roy went over and spoke with Rizzen quietly in the corner.

"What was that all about?" asked Nelson.

"There's a plan," said Ryan.

"There's always been a plan."

"But I know the plan."

"Why did he tell you?" asked Nelson.

"I can mind speak with people who normally can't. I can help lead the freed prisoners when they get here."

"You're going to pass along the general's orders?"

"Me and Rizzen."

General Roy walked over again and this time pointed at Nelson. Just like with Ryan, they stepped off the command deck for total privacy and then came back.

"What did he tell you?" asked Ryan.

"I can't say. Control of information."

"Don't be that guy."

"I'm following orders."

"Seriously?"

Nelson was smiling. Normally that would be a good thing but the new Nelson only smiled when death was involved. The smile worried Phillip. What had the general told him?

Janelle stood on the command deck with the other humans. The mood had changed dramatically as General Roy started to take people aside to give them special orders. No one mentioned what the orders were and no one said much of anything to each other anymore. To add to the strangeness of it all, Nelson was smiling now. Janelle couldn't think of something that could make him smile that much. Only dark humor had elicited a response from him so far, so the wide smile on his face made her nervous. She wanted to know what was going on but no one was telling her anything.

Aleeva was still working the command console and getting information on the fleet and the last Almic ship. Janelle was avoiding going near her. She was the swarm she would smuggle on board so they would be interacting soon enough.

Bernadette was a sweet lady. Janelle would have pegged her as a sweet old lady, but then Bernadette would always say that you couldn't be old without grandchildren. She didn't have grey hair or any physical infirmities, but she was unusually nice and was always trying to take care of everyone in the prison. Never quiet, she was always in a conversation with someone about something positive and reinforcing. That's why it was so strange to see her body searching over ship schematics and planning an attack. It was disturbing for Janelle but she couldn't look away. And it wasn't just Aleeva; there were a dozen of the same body lurking about, working, preparing for the attack.

"Have you had a swarm inside you before?" asked Aleeva without looking up from what she was doing.

"No," said Janelle.

"There's something you will need to know about it then."

"What?"

"You won't have control of your body. You won't even be a passive observer. When I take over your body you won't see or feel anything. You won't know what's going on. It'll be like you're sleeping."

"What?"

"You won't see or hear what's going on."

"What if we don't win the war?"

Aleeva didn't answer but she didn't need to. Janelle had volunteered so that she could be part of the action and now she found that that she might never wake up. If things went sideways then she might never see anything ever again. She would never get back to Mac, she would never find out what happened to her family, she would never be able to rescue Bernadette.

It made sense that she wouldn't be able to observe what Aleeva would use her body for. When they were in the mind prison the same kind of thing had been going on.

If this were possibly her last moments then she should at least say goodbye.

It wasn't long before Aleeva made an announcement.

"It's time. We will reach the Invaders in fifteen minutes. They've seen us coming for some time now, so it'll be a fight right from the beginning. Everyone, get ready to carry out your part of the mission."

The room scrambled. Jazlyn found a place to sit down and put her head between her knees. The closer they got to the fleet the harder it was for her to concentrate. Nelson hugged Phillip and then went to leave but his uncle followed after him. Janelle could hear them arguing as they walked away. She didn't know what that was all about.

She must have looked nervous because Rizzen had come over, put a comforting hand on her shoulder, and quietly spoke.

There's no such thing as the end.

Aleeva nodded at Janelle: This was it. Bernadette's body broke into a billion different particles and rushed into Janelle. The takeover wasn't instantaneous. She could feel buzzing all over her body and it felt like she was vibrating so hard her bones would break—but when she looked down her body wasn't even moving. She started to get tunnel vision. The darkness crept in from the edges of her vision.

"Stop following me," said Nelson.

"You're going on a suicide run, aren't you?" said Phillip.

Nelson was running now, heading towards the docking bay. Inside there was a ship that looked like the tip of a spear. Nelson headed for the HAAS3—something more familiar—and started the power up.

"Don't do this," said Phillip. "Let me go instead. Tell me your mission."

"You don't know what I'm doing. It will be fine," said Nelson.

"I won't let you go alone. I don't care what I'm ordered to do. There's other people that can take my place."

"You don't know what I'm doing. You can't come with me."

The *Kameyosek* started to shake—they were under attack. Phillip almost lost his balance. The doors to the docking bay rushed open again as another person entered. It was another Bernadette; she was carrying a cylinder the size of a human arm. It was silver and completely smooth.

"Don't activate it until you are in position. The closer you get the better chance we have. You got it?" she said as she handed the device over to Nelson.

"Got it." Nelson grabbed it and headed for the HAAS3. Phillip charged after him, but Bernadette grabbed Phillip by both arms and held him still.

"That's not your mission," said Bernadette, or whatever alien was inside of her.

"I can't let him die," said Phillip.

Phillip couldn't get the image of the broken Earth out of his head. Nelson was the only family he had left. Maybe it wasn't rational, but the emotions of everything that had happened were finally catching up to Phillip, and he wasn't about to let any more family die. He shook off Bernadette's grasp and ran as Nelson's HAAS3 fired up.

There was one other ship—the spear ship. An alien ship, but he was going to have to figure out a way to fly it if he was going to protect Nelson. The inside of it was compact. The cockpit sat to the back of the ship. There was no viewport. On the outside it looked like a solid metal ship but from the inside he could see in every direction.

Phillip was a doctor but he knew the basics of flying. Most humans did. Flying was synonymous with driving, enough that he felt confident in getting from one place to another. Flying into a war zone was totally different—especially in an alien ship. The HAAS3 lifted off and flew through the bay doors. Phillip studied the controls of his spear ship. There was the stick for piloting and a touch screen that was not in Earth Common. He pulled up on the stick but nothing happened. He started pushing buttons until the engine turned on and then pulled on the stick to follow Nelson out into space. Instantly he realized he had made a mistake.

They were approaching the fleet. Phillip didn't know why the *Kameyosek* was so close when they were still waiting for their reinforcements to catch up. Then the lasers started firing. The *Kameyosek* wasn't coming to the fleet; the fleet was coming out to meet them. Nelson could pilot well enough but he wasn't going to last against the thousands of ships that were converging on them.

Nelson! I don't know why I followed you out here but we need to get out of here or we're going to die, said Phillip.

We're going to die anyway. Being inside the Kameyosek *isn't going to stop them from attacking.*

Where are you going?

I'm doing my part.

Phillip didn't care about his part. The only control for the spear ship was the stick he used to point in the direction he wanted to go. It was touchy and responded instantly to every movement. A slight nudge and he took off in that direction but only as far as the nudge. If he wanted to go barrelling off in that direction then he needed to hammer down on the stick as far as it would go. He did that to propel himself towards Nelson's HAAS3.

You'll never get anywhere in that Hawthree, said Phillip.

I don't know how to fly alien ships.

The Invaders were within firing range. Red lasers shot out of the ships as they streamed towards Nelson, who wasn't going to kill himself quite yet. Trained as a soldier on the front and not as a pilot, he had to rely on the "heavy armor" part of his Heavy Armor Assault Shuttle. The lazy panicked maneuvers he executed only got him so far but he made up for it by unleashing all the fury he could. It was a military shuttle—it was meant to make more than a dent. Missiles and lasers rocketed at the enemy. Nelson was hitting his mark more often than not but he still wasn't going to be taking out the whole fleet. There was no way that he was going to make it.

Phillip was his only hope and all he could do was some poor flying. He needed weapons. The screen in front of him had several alien words on it. He started pushing random ones to see what happened. One button revealed a heads-up display that put a target on all the ships around him. Every one was green except for Nelson and the *Kameyosek*. He wondered if they used the same colors for friend and enemy as humans did. The ship moved itself now. The stick jerked in his hands and pulled him towards Nelson. Another word appeared on the screen blinking. He touched it, hoping it would take him out of autopilot. Instead it locked weapons onto Nelson. A blue stream of laser cut through space and burned across the top of the HAAS3.

You trying to stop me from dying by killing me?

I don't know how to fly this thing! said Phillip.

Try aiming at the bad guys. That seems to work for me.

Nelson backed it up by downing another ship. Phillip had a good look at the enemy ships now. They were spindly, and fluid—always moving. He didn't know how they were piloted or where the cockpit was but the ribbons coiled and then lasers shot out the end. They didn't look like they had engines. In fact, if they had been in the atmosphere he would have thought they could be blown around in the wind. He watched one attack Nelson. It wasn't a laser that shot out at the shuttle. It was the actual ribbon itself. Before the attack it coiled and spun like it was winding up and then it would stretch out. The end was super-heated. It could stretch to ten times its length, so long that it looked like a laser coming out. Nothing about that ship made sense but he didn't need to make sense of something to be able to destroy it. These ships were attacking them right now. The rest of the Invaders would be there soon enough.

Phillip's ship was about to attack Nelson again. He could feel it charging up; the whole ship was vibrating. The same word was flashing on the screen—like the longer he waited to push it the more powerful the laser would be. There were other commands he could push and so he chose the word furthest from the fire button and selected it.

There was a beep and then another word appeared beside it. He pushed that one. The heads-up display went down and a progress bar in the shape of a circle straight in front of Phillip appeared. It was harder to see what was going on out there without the heads up display illuminating all the targets. Nelson was still close by but the ribbon ships were so thin that it was hard to see them unless they were attacking. A few of them burned up as Nelson attacked. Beyond the action, immediately in front of Phillip, was the rest of the Invader fleet. They were all scrambling, either jockeying to get on to the last Almic ship where they would then be taken in groups to Ronos, or they were surrounding the vulnerable parts of the fleet: the hilt ship and the emulators. Those were the densest parts, and where Nelson was heading.

There were multiple Invaders moving to reinforce the ribbons. The biggest of them was out in the lead. It didn't even look like a machine—it looked like an amorphous blob. It wasn't quite translucent enough to see completely through it, but it was still far away. Phillip couldn't decide if it was another ship or if it was a massive alien creature inhabited by a swarm.

The progress bar filled all the way up and the heads-up display sprang back to life. This time it showed Nelson and the *Kameyosek* as his allies. He hit the fire button again. The spear ship was doing most of the work. It was on autopilot—he could see the projected path moving through the oncoming ships and the stick was moving on its own. All he had to do was fire when the button lit up. He assumed that meant the ship had a lock on the next target.

Now things were moving. Now he was doing the job he had set out to do. The ribbons saw the new threat and charged to move against Phillip in the spear ship.

They teach you how to fly in medical school? asked Nelson.

Nope. I barely know what's going on.

Thanks for taking the heat. I'm going to make my move.

No, don't!

Keep up with me and draw their attention.

I don't know how to do that!

Well, I'm going anyway.

Phillip didn't have time to figure out what to do. He was quickly becoming engulfed by ribbon ships. The HUD was lit up with red targets. Behind them there was a distant green spec but Phillip didn't know how quickly he could get there. He pressed the fire button over and over. Ribbon ships exploded. Not in flame, but splattered apart. They were strange ships. His own vessel rocked under repeated attacks and lights were flashing. He had no idea how much damage he could take but he couldn't just stay put and get attacked over and over. They would destroy him before he could destroy all of them. He had to make a move.

The ship was shaped like the tip of a spear, so he was going to treat it like that. He nudged the throttle forward but hesitated to go full out. The tip of the vessel tore through the ribbons and sent them scattering. They chased after him as he quickly left a gap between him and them.

The *Kameyosek* was in range now and firing on the ribbon ships. Phillip looked up and saw the green indicator that Nelson was still barrelling towards the invading fleet. There was a moment of inspiration. Nearly everything else had responded to his touch, so he reached out and pressed his finger against the glass where Nelson's ship was lit up. The spear ship jerked to the side and moved to intercept.

An attack came from behind the spear ship. The ribbons were all coiling up—as tightly as possible—to build up their maximum energy. Sirens blared in the cockpit while Phillip struggled to see what he could do. He started tapping the screen again. Nothing happened. He pressed the fire button again and again but he got a weird beeping noise each time he did. He was still locked onto the ribbons but they were behind him and he could only shoot forwards. The ribbons were going to unleash at any moment. Phillip gripped the steering stick with two hands and tried to force it to move out of their attack path but he couldn't unlock it from following after Nelson.

The spear ship rocked back and forth as ribbons struck out as they flew past him. Alarms were going off— at least he thought they were alarms—and the shaking was getting worse as each blow landed. Once all the ribbons passed he was worried that they would come back for another assault.

But they didn't come back. They kept moving back towards the fleet. Or, more specifically, the giant amorphous blob that was emerging from the fleet. He didn't know what kind of species would invent something like that, let alone get inside and drive around. It didn't look like a machine or anything manmade. It looked more like a giant animal.

The ribbons were heading right for the blob, which was twice the size of the *Kameyosek*. When they reached it they attached themselves. Phillip didn't realize how many there were until they all returned to their mother ship. There were hundreds of the ribbons dancing below, attached at one end. It looked like it was swimming through space now. The ribbons—which normally were a light blue like the blob—all turned red and jumped out much farther than they would have been able to before. They could reach Phillip even though he was heading away from them. Instead of attacking they wrapped themselves around his ship and started pulling him in. Phillip reached out to Ryan on the *Kameyosek*.

What is that thing? It's pulling me in.

Rizzen thinks he knows what species it belongs to but he's still trying to figure out what to do about it.

The spear ship was sizzling. The super-heated ribbons weren't able to burn completely through the ship. When the ribbons were attached to the blob they had increased range but weren't as powerful. He had maybe a minute before they pulled him into the ship. And that was only assuming that's where they were pulling him—as if they were going to trap him inside. Could that thing digest metal?

Phillip needed to buy some time. He kept pushing the fire button over and over. The streaks of laser stung the side of the blob. It would ripple and then absorb the blow without leaving a mark. Phillip touched the fire button and one of the ribbons on his HUD at the same time. The laser tore it in half. He shot out at them again and again but there were so many it couldn't make a difference.

We know what to do! said Ryan in a panic.

What?

Fly full speed right through it.

What?

Rizzen talked to the species that created that ship. They think your spear ship can tear through it.

But lasers can't get through it.

I know. It's immune to lasers but if your ship can puncture it then it's all over.

Phillip didn't know how that was possible but it wasn't the first time he had been asked to do something that sounded impossible. That whole conversation *had* taken place in his mind, after all. He slammed the throttle forward and expected the spear ship to shoot forward, but it didn't move. The engines were going full bore but the ribbons were holding on so tightly that he couldn't escape.

It's no good, Ryan. I'll wait until they get me closer and then try and puncture it.

That won't work. They are trying to absorb you into the ship.

But isn't that kind of like what you told me to do?

Yeah, except I want you to do it faster. If you do it fast it will create a hole that will suck the insides out into the vacuum of space. If you do it their way, the slow way, then they will be able to wrap themselves around you and bring you in without compromising the integrity of the ship. You got it?

I got it.

But that didn't mean Phillip was going to be able to do anything about it. The engines were still on maximum and he still wasn't moving. The ribbons looked to be a darker shade of red, as though they were trying harder to hold onto him. His lasers cut through a dozen ribbons and the ship lurched forward. The lurching motion tore a few more ribbons apart. But they were all quickly replaced and he was trapped again. Phillip swiped again and again but he was never able to destroy enough to make a difference. The amorphous blob of a ship was getting closer. He couldn't see where Nelson was anymore. He was going to get himself killed because he was trying to stop Nelson from killing himself.

A thick stream of laser fire from the *Kameyosek* rained down on the ribbons, cutting nearly all of them away. Phillip didn't hesitate. He punched in the course to head straight through the blob. His ship shot forward.

The spear ship tore through the blue blob. Phillip couldn't see anything. It was like he had gone through a gooey car wash. He didn't even know if he had punched through to the other side—except when he tore through the ship the HUD had disappeared and a minute later it came back to life. It showed a million red dots surrounding one tiny green dot. At least that meant that Nelson was still alive. Phillip touched the green dot and headed towards him. As he went he fired at what he hoped were the closest enemies but he really didn't know how to tell. One of the red lights snuffed out so he assumed his attacks were doing something. The blue goo was still covering the ship like he had flown through a whale and gotten covered by blubber. It was going to be nearly impossible to defend Nelson now.

There was no way that Nelson could take on the entire invading fleet by himself in a HAAS3. But that's not what he needed to do. He only needed to get as far into the fleet as he could and then set off the device he had been given in the docking bay.

Truthfully, he never would have made it this far if it hadn't been for his uncle. Phillip's initial defense against the ribbon ship allowed him to blow past the outer layer of the fleet. Nelson's ship was small. His only hope to stay alive now was to fly as close to the other ships as possible. Maybe they wouldn't fire on him in case they blew up one of their own.

That worked for the bigger capital ships but the small fighters were starting to swarm and they would have no trouble running him down. He could see them moving on the sensors. As good a pilot as he was—and he was only so-so, being a foot soldier—there was no way he was going to last against dozens of fighters. They were closing in on him.

He put the HAAS3 on autopilot. The human autopilot equipment was not as advanced as the one Phillip was using on the spear ship. The assault shuttle could fly in a straight line and only moved when it detected an obstacle.

As the shuttle moved through the fleet, obstacles would become more frequent. He had to be fast.

He moved to the back of the shuttle and gripped the device in his hands. It looked more like a big metal pill. They had told him what it could do but he wasn't sure how it was possible. As instructed, he smashed it on the floor. The thin metal tubing cracked and green-blue liquid started to spill out on floor. It was swirling and pushing everything away from it, like it had a built-in force field. Nelson was supposed to throw it outside but now he couldn't even pick it up.

The tube had looked like it only held a couple of liters, but either the tube was bigger than it looked, or whatever the liquid was went farther than expected. The back wall of the shuttle was a door but Nelson couldn't get to it anymore. The liquid was pushing him away. The puddle spread and he was pushed farther away. The walls of the shuttle were creaking as the force of the liquid pressed against it. He ran to the cockpit to open the door from there.

As he sat down the autopilot threw the ship to the side as they approached a massive alien ship. It looked like a giant engine, circular with a glowing center. The glow was intensifying and the alarms in the shuttle were going off as the heat increased. Nelson couldn't feel heat like a normal person; if he could he would have been sitting in a puddle of his own sweat. The glowing engine—if that's what it was—was so big the *Kameyosek* could fit inside of it.

Nelson took back control of the HAAS3 and flew away from the big ship. The fighters were swarming in on him now. There were more alarms as lasers were locked on him. He couldn't see the attackers with the naked eye. There were too many ships around him. The ship started to rock. More alarms. He looked behind him to see the puddle had spread out over half the floor. The alarms were coming from inside as well. He reached out and pushed the emergency release to open the door while still in flight.

If he hadn't had his safety belt on he would have been thrown out into space with everything else that wasn't tied down. The liquid and the canister thrived in the vacuum of space. There the liquid spread like wildfire—pushing the Invader ships away from it.

Rally point activated, said Nelson.

What's a rally point? asked Phillip.

You're going to want to see this.

The puddle was already big enough for a ship to fit through—which is exactly what happened. The nose of a ship appeared at the center of the rapidly-expanding puddle and then a whole ship came through, guns blazing. More ships came right behind it. The rally point was a hole in space. Rizzen had explained it as a temporary manmade wormhole. It was growing so fast now three ships could come through at once, and then five. Each time something else came through it got bigger and bigger. The fleet from Earth—with all the escaped prisoners—was here now. It was happening fast. Dozens, then hundreds, of ships. Space was getting tight and the attention was off of Nelson. He made a run for it.

Then explosion after explosion sounded as the prisoner fleet opened fire. The Invader ships all turned their attention towards where Nelson had been. Where there had once been one small HAAS3, there were now thousands of ships all commanded by the recently released prisoners. Explosions came from collisions as ships smashed into each other to make space for the newly arrived ships.

How is this possible? asked Phillip.

The Invader fleet was now fighting against itself. There was mass confusion as everyone struggled to figure out who was on whose side. Each ship was firing wildly in every direction. Explosions caused chain reactions that destroyed whole segments of the fleet on both sides. The confusion was working in favor of the former prisoners because they didn't have nearly as many ships as the Invaders. It was thousands against millions. There was no way that the freed prisoners would be able to overpower the Invaders.

Chapter 18
The Last Almic Ship

Phillip landed his ship back on the *Kameyosek*. He was guided to a different bay and when he got inside there were people waiting for him outside of a human transport ship. Janelle was there, but from the way she was acting it was obvious Aleeva had already taken her over. Same with Jace and Daniel. None of them were smiling and they stood rigidly with their arms straight down. General Roy, Rizzen, and Ryan were there as well.

"What's going on?" said Phillip when he got out of the spear ship.

"First things first," said Ryan, and he held out a cube. The cube had the same blue light bouncing around inside of it that every cube had. Using his mind, Ryan commanded the light to leave the cube and zip around Phillip before heading back in. As it re-entered the cube it dragged all the swarms that had tried to take over Phillip and trapped them in the cube. Now they wouldn't be able to overhear any new information that he would learn.

"You have no idea how bad I want to trap Aleeva and the others in here as well," said Ryan.

"What's the plan?"

"We got nothing. The prisoner fleet is a distraction. A small group of us is heading for the last Almic ship. Aleeva is going to secure a bay for us and Mac is going to try and draw their fire."

"Draw the fire of the whole fleet?"

"He'll at least try and get their attention."

"Isn't their attention already divided?"

"Once they find out that we are after the last Almic ship we want them to think Mac is the one making the move, not us."

Phillip looked over at the others who were gathered there. He didn't like the vacant look on Janelle's face.

There weren't that many humans with them—even fewer when you considered that the enhanced humans like Phillip, Nelson, and Ryan couldn't smuggle swarms with them. There was only Janelle, Jace, and Daniel. General Roy was staying behind to run the operation.

"There can't be four hundred and nine swarms between these three people here," said Phillip.

"There isn't," said Aleeva. "That many swarms inside of one normal human would kill them. The rest of the swarms are staying behind until we need them."

Phillip did a count. It was him, Ryan, Janelle, Rizzen, Jace, and Daniel there so far.

"We aren't waiting for reinforcements? We're just going with the six of us?"

"Seven. Nelson is coming as well. In fact, we have to go on two different ships because if we go with the swarms they'll know something's up."

There's something going on here that we aren't a part of, said Phillip to Ryan so they couldn't be overheard.

What do you mean?

We snuck around behind enemy lines for days without being caught. Why would we suddenly be vulnerable now?

I know what you mean. I'll take care of it.

Ryan hefted his cube with both hands while sending Phillip a wink. As soon as they got on board the last Almic ship they wouldn't need Aleeva and the rebels any more. There were too many variables and they were already running out of time. Aleeva went past him and with the other possessed humans got on the transport ship to head to the last Almic ship.

Mac and Volmere saw the action in the fleet. They were amazed when the prisoner fleet appeared nearly out of nowhere and started destroying everything in sight. That was their cue to make their move. Volmere gave the order to split the ship. The massive bird-like vessel broke apart into two dozen smaller ships and, in formation, they took off towards the fleet. They were supposed to draw fire and help get Phillip and his team on board.

As the smaller bird-like vessels approached the Invader fleet Mac and the others got their first clear view of what had been mentioned as the hilt ship. It really did look like the hilt of a sword with the brightly-lit stream of lights coming out the end of it being the blade that stretched all the way to Ronos. How there were still lights coming out of it was amazing. There must have been way more swarms than Mac had realized.

As if on cue the hilt ship stopped spinning and the lights dwindled. A few hours from now nearly every swarm was going to be on Ronos. They would win by sheer numbers. Numbers that would never dwindle.

Mac focused on their target. It was in the middle of the fleet. The giant crescent-shaped ship had several ships docked to it. One of them was the human transport ship. It was near the top of the crescent so Mac and the Ronos Almics were to board from the opposite end of the ship.

Mac didn't know which button on the ship was intended for communications but he figured the swarms would use mind speak anyway.

Request permission to come aboard.

There was no response.

We are here to help fight the new enemy fleet. Open docking bay doors and let us in.

Again, no one answered.

Sellet spoke up. *My scans show no docking bay doors. It looks like everything is done with airlocks on the outside of the ship.*

She's right, said Volmere. *Then they know we aren't trustworthy. We need to force our way on.*

I'll keep scanning the ship, she said.

Mac had blown their cover already and they weren't even on the ship yet. He scanned the fleet to see if there was anyone heading their way but there were so many moving ships it was impossible to tell until someone locked their weapons onto them. The prisoner fleet was still doing their damage; they heard explosions consistently going off. It had to have been the most damage the Invader fleet had ever faced. He could see collector ships moving towards the rally point. These were the ships the Invaders had used against the humans. They were powerful ships that could take a beating.

There are several gaps in the structure of the ship. Too small for our ships but big enough for us individually to fit through, said Sellet.

Volmere said, *Sellet, send us that information.*

Mac saw seven ships peel off from the fleet and head towards their position. They were spear ships.

We have company, said Mac.

As he said that the spear ships opened fire and destroyed one of Volmere's ships. Mac was finally going to see what these bird-like ships were capable of. Despite the fact that they were out in space, there wasn't a lot of room to move around because of the fleet and their close proximity to the last Almic ship.

That didn't matter to the Ronos Almics. The ship could turn without losing speed. Mac let the ship unleash its full potential on the enemies. The targeting system was amazing. The actual piloting he did while in battle was minimal. All the sensors were focused on avoiding collisions so that being a good pilot was actually secondary. The pilot selected the targets and the computer figured out the quickest route between the two and executed it. The only time a real person was needed was to pull the trigger, which Mac was happy to do.

One of his companions went down in a ball of flame as more enemy spear ships joined the fight. Another explosion and another Ronos Almic went down. They were in the middle of fleet. There was no way they would be able to survive if they kept fighting.

Get close to the last Almic ship, said Volmere. Mac was glad to hear he was still alive. *Get close to their sacred ship. Maybe they'll think twice before they pull the trigger.*

Mac nosed his ship towards the massive dark crescent ship. It was relatively smooth—still with random nubs and indents in the plating, but it had no towers or things for ships to hide behind. The best Mac could do was flying random zigzag patterns while circling the ship. He was going so fast along the surface that it was nothing more than a blur beneath him.

We won't be able to do this forever, said Mac.

There are holes in the hull. We have to force our way inside, said Volmere.

Another Ronos Almic ship was destroyed. Its fiery remains scorched the outside of the last Almic ship. Maybe it wasn't as sacred as they were led to believe.

Mac got an incoming transmission from Lemnell's ship. It was a map of the last Almic ship with a target assigned to each pilot.

These are breaches in their hull. Fly your ships in there. The inside of the ship isn't as strong as the hull so you might be able to blast your way inside. But there won't be an air lock so keep your masks on and your mag boots ready, said Lemnell.

You're skin isn't going to freeze in the cold of space? asked Mac, who wouldn't need a mask.

We are durable.

Let's hope so.

Mac had well overshot his target and had to flip around and fly back along the sacred ship to get to his entry point. He kept his laser cannons burning bright. More alien ships had joined the fight. If Mac and the others didn't get inside soon then none of them would.

Mac saw his assigned entry point ahead of him, but it didn't look like one. There was a jagged opening in the ship along the inside of the curve where some damage had been done. If it was big enough for a ship to fit inside then it was only by an inch or two. Even when he programmed it into the nav computer it told him it was impossible. He decided to trust Lemnell's information.

The best way to approach it was head on so Mac flew away from the ship and then pivoted back towards it. As he flew towards his entry point he let the laser fly in front of him hoping to open the way a little more. The enemy ships weren't even bothering with him anymore. It looked like he was going on a suicide run.

The ship slipped through the opening. Well, the cockpit did anyway. The wings were sheared off. Mac killed the engines and what was left of the cockpit slammed into the last Almic ship.

The last thing Janelle had seen was the command deck of the *Kameyosek*. Aleeva was right—it did feel like being asleep. She wasn't aware of the passage of time. She felt nothing that her body was going through and she was completely unaware of her surroundings. One minute she was on board the *Kameyosek* and the next she was on the last Almic ship. It was disorienting to wake up and not be lying down in bed. She was suddenly awake and surrounded by the others. It took her a moment to realize what was going on. She was so happy that she had woken up at all that at first she didn't notice that something had gone terribly wrong. For starters, not all of them were there. She saw Nelson, Rizzen, Jace, and a swarm in the form of Bernadette.

They were all in a panic at one of the walls as it slammed shut. She looked around. They were in a small room. There weren't any visible doors. She shook her head. That wasn't right. There were blast doors that had come down. That's what the others were in a panic over. They had been walking down a hallway when blast doors activated.

"What happened?" asked Janelle.

Jace looked over at her. "She let you go, too?"

"What do you mean?"

"Durgan just let me go and re-formed as Bernadette. They have access to these emulators, I guess. Won't do us any good anyway. They know we're here. They trapped us. We didn't even get down the first hallway. This was pointless."

Jace was pounding on the door. His nephew wasn't with them. The blast doors had come down in the middle of the group. They looked for a way to pry the door open, or to break through it or the wall, but there was nothing. There were no panels in the roof or floor that could be pulled away so they could sneak through a vent. According to their map they weren't near anything that could help them. Nelson kept studying the small holographic image of the ship on his wrist projector and asking Durgan questions.

"How come the explosives on this ship didn't go off at the same time we blew up the Searchers Sphere?" he asked. "You said there was a plan to take the last Almic ship."

"Our men were apprehended before they could. "

"Why didn't the bombs get disconnected?"

"Because the other Almics didn't know about them. The people in charge of setting it off were not going to be given any information about it until they were right there in case they did get caught."

"Sounds convenient."

Nelson still didn't trust Durgan. More than once Durgan had turned into a swarm and searched for a way to escape and each time he claimed there was no way. Nelson didn't buy it. Janelle didn't know what to think. She felt powerless. Any moment the wall was going to open and swarms were going to come in and kill them all.

Rizzen sat against the wall next to her. There was nothing left to do but wait. Jace still hadn't given up and was pounding against the wall separating him from his nephew.

"This was a bad idea," said Janelle.

Maybe, but what other choice did we have? I would rather die trying to do something then spend any more time in that prison.

"Do you think Bernadette is on this ship somewhere?"

I don't know. For sure she is somewhere in this fleet. Rizzen was talking to Janelle but he was looking at Jace. He had stopped banging on the door and was simply standing there facing it, like he had fallen asleep standing up.

Something is wrong, said Rizzen.

Jace turned around with a blank expression on his face and walked over to where Janelle was sitting on the floor. He bent down and grabbed her around the neck, lifting her off the ground.

"He's possessed!" said Nelson.

He rushed to tackle Jace to the ground but was straight-armed. The impact looked like it would have hurt both of them, considering Nelson's strength now that he was changed, but the man with his fingers wrapped around Janelle's neck didn't look fazed.

Rizzen was the only one thinking. He grabbed his cube. The ball of light bouncing around inside flew out and zipped around Jace, pulling the swarm back in with it. Janelle was too heavy for him now and she fell to the floor while he stumbled away, confused.

"What happened?" he asked.

"You got possessed. Despite the fact that Durgan told us it was impossible for a swarm to get in or out of here," said Nelson.

The humans and Rizzen clumped together in a group. Each of them had their cubes out waiting for another attack.

The swarms could be nearly invisible if they wanted to be so there wasn't really anything they could do unless it was obvious an attack was coming.

Nelson had no more trust left in him. He pointed his cube at Durgan and tried to trap him.

Durgan took swarm form at the same time the ball of light leapt out of the cube. The light went to where Durgan used to be and then immediately went back into the cube.

"Did that work?" asked Jace.

"I don't know," said Nelson.

They waited for an uncomfortable moment, all of them standing in a circle with their backs against each other and their cubes out. There could have been swarms in the room right then and they wouldn't have noticed.

Janelle felt a breeze—how that was possible in the middle of a ship she didn't know—and her world went black. For a minute she saw nothing and when she came to she was on the ground and Nelson was standing over her with a cube. Jace was gritting his teeth and holding his arm.

"What did it make me do?" asked Janelle.

"Break my arm."

"Why is it only going for me and Jace?"

"Because you two are the most vulnerable. When a swarm comes in me I still have control over my body so I can just use the cube and suck it out," said Nelson.

Same with me, said Rizzen.

Jace stopped holding his arm and charged at Janelle. He jumped and tried to land feet first on her face but she rolled away. Nelson sucked the swarm out of him and he started to nurse his arm again.

"Did I hurt you?" he asked.

Before Janelle could answer she felt a tingle around her feet and went black again. This time when she came to Jace had a bloody nose and Rizzen was holding her against the wall, as far from Jace as she could get. Nelson was doing the same to Jace.

Jace's face went to stone as a swarm entered his body but Nelson held him still and sucked the swarm out. They could do this until they ran out of room in the cubes. Janelle looked at her own. The cube hadn't changed. How were they going to be able to tell when they ran out of room?

"The others?" asked Janelle.

They are doing the same as us. Aleeva is helping them, said Rizzen.

"What about Mac?"

I do not know what happened to him.

Mac's eyes opened. That honestly surprised him. He was still in the cockpit and the cockpit was in the hallway of the last Almic ship. The walls around him were charred and he could smell smoke in the air. He looked around him and saw that nothing was floating. That had to mean there was atmosphere. He had made it successfully inside the ship.

Volmere, you still alive? asked Mac.

Yes. But there is something wrong. No one has come to investigate us infiltrating the ship.

That *was* odd. Mac had passed out but he didn't know for how long. Swarms were fast. There should have been a few there to greet him when he woke up. Unbuckling his seat and reaching back for his Ronos Almic cutter, he got out of the cockpit. He wondered if his weapon would make any difference. If not the first thing they needed to do was get their hands on some of the cubes Phillip had told him about.

He stood with the weapon out in front of him, waiting for trouble to show up. Out of the corner of his eyes he saw a body form out of thin air. He spun around and fired his weapon but the body evaporated and came together in another spot behind Mac.

I'm on your side! said the being.

Who are you?

My name is Durgan. I'm working with Phillip right now. I left their group to come find you.

Where are they?

Causing their distraction. We need to go now.

To find Volmere and the others, right?

Yes. Right.

All the doors opened to Durgan's command as he led them through the ship. When Mac tried to do the same they did nothing. Durgan claimed it was because he was an Almic and the ship could tell the difference. They got to another crash site and Sellet was waiting there, with her weapon out in front of her, much like Mac had been.

You made it, said Sellet, happy to see him. She was definitely the kindest Ronos Almic he had come across so far. After all, she was able to connect with kids despite having an alligator head.

He's with us, said Mac about Durgan. She didn't lower her weapon.

He's one of them, she said. Mac could sense that the conversation was just between the two of them.

He helped us come up with this plan.

And many have already died because of this.

We don't have any other choice, said Mac. *He's the only one who knows the way.*

Sellet reluctantly went with them. She shared her suspicions with all the other Ronos Almics that had survived. There had been twelve on this mission at the start and now there were only seven, and Mac. Volmere still wasn't with them but he said he was looking for a stash of cubes.

I've been in touch with the other team. They are pinned down and under attack, Volmere said.

Under attack? Mac looked around at the empty halls they were walking through. They hadn't seen an enemy swarm since they got on board. Something was wrong.

What do they say about this Durgan? asked Sellet.

He is not to be trusted.

Then why are we following him?

Their evidence of his betrayal is sketchy at best. There is still a chance that he will lead us to the command deck but it is also possible he is leading us into a trap.

Mac spoke up. *If he wanted to kill us then we would be dead already.*

There is betrayal in him, said Sellet. This would have sounded like prejudice coming from anyone else, but Sellet saw the good in everyone and even she didn't think Durgan was trustworthy.

Durgan hesitated before opening the next door. The group waited, sure that he had somehow been listening in on their private conversation. He looked back at them seriously. *There are swarms on the other side of this door waiting to kill us all. They think that I am working with them but I am not. Are your weapons effective?*

We don't know, said Mac. Volmere still hadn't caught up to them.

Durgan shook his head. *Ready your weapons.*

As Durgan turned his back to them Mac brought his weapon cautiously up. He had Durgan in his sights for a moment and wondered if he should pull the trigger. Was it worth the risk if Durgan was a bad guy? It wasn't worth it. The weapons might not even work, and if they didn't, then Durgan would have a reason not to trust them.

Mac also hesitated because of the last Almic he should have trusted but didn't—Vlamm, the alien impersonating Major Jace Michaels. Vlamm had worked with Mac to try and find the truth about who destroyed Northgate but as soon as Mac found out he was really a swarm he turned his back on him. Vlamm only wanted to help and Mac hadn't trusted him.

Durgan insisted that he was trying to help and he'd already had plenty of opportunity to kill them all.

The door whooshed open and the Ronos Almics had their weapons pointed out in front of them, waiting to fire. The room beyond was round with several hallway doors leading off of it. It was a major intersection on the ship. No one fired because no one could see any worthy targets. Sellet started to move her weapon towards Durgan when he shouted.

Fire!

Where? said Mac.

Everywhere! They are in swarm form.

He had no idea where any of the bad guys were but he fired into the room. Every bolt of his scorched the wall on the opposite side. Except one. One hit an invisible cloud particle in the middle of the room, but from what they could see it did no damage to the swarm, same as the humans' weapons.

The swarms were no longer passive. They moved to attack. As they moved the particle clouds became easier to see. Laser fire filled the room. The weapons didn't do anything but they couldn't just stand there doing nothing. There were shimmering clouds everywhere and the group fought to keep them at bay.

The swarms gathered into a cloud in the middle of the room and began spinning violently. The spinning cloud rushed across the room and smashed into Mac and the Ronos Almics, knocking them all to the ground. Mac fell and his cutter skipped across the ground to land at Durgan's feet. He picked the weapon up and threw it back to Mac.

Follow me! Durgan ran into the intersection and through another door.

Mac was about to stand up but he saw Sellet and another Almic stand up in the thick of the swarm cloud. The Almic that Mac didn't recognize started to roar and thrash about as his skin vibrated. Then he stopped and pointed his weapon at the others. Sellet had gotten to her knees before her feet. Mac reached out and pulled her back to the ground. Swarms had entered her body but it wasn't enough to take it over completely. She crawled out of that hallway to join Durgan, firing behind her as she went.

Mac had to roll and dodge the attacks of the soldier who had been taken over. He shot the weapon out of the infested Almic's hands but that wasn't going to stop him. The possessed soldier charged at Mac to kill him with his own hands, forcing Mac to put him down for good. Two head shots and the swarms left the dead body to try and go after him. He ran to meet up with the rest of the group while everyone covered him with laser fire. Once they were all in the hallway Durgan closed and locked the door but kept everyone moving quickly.

Hurry, he said. *These doors are not swarm proof. They will follow us.*

Janelle and the others were still trapped and she and Jace were still constantly being bombarded with swarms. Nearly every minute her vision would go black and she would snap out of it with no memory of what had happened. The swarms weren't letting up, as if they were just keeping everyone busy so that the invasion of Ronos could go on uninterrupted. There was no way they were going to be able to take over the ship at this rate.

On the plus side, they had discovered a way to tell when the cubes were getting too full to pull in any more swarms. The ball of light inside of it moved more slowly the more swarms it contained. It was slow enough now that the gaps in Janelle's consciousness were getting longer by a couple minutes each time. It was getting harder to hold her down while the cube did its work because it took so long.

The cube was also getting ridiculously heavy. Rizzen couldn't keep holding it up anymore. He had to put it down right beside him between attacks but that only made it harder to hold Janelle down while he used it. They had already gone through her and Jace's cubes. They were too heavy to budge now. They could still be activated but to use them both handles still needed to be gripped and the light moving inside would take over ten minutes to pull a swarm inside. Not that long in the grand scheme of things, but an eternity to a swarm-infested body. Janelle could have easily killed Jace in that amount of time if Rizzen wasn't there to hold her back, and vice versa for Jace.

Janelle's vision went black as she saw Rizzen putting the cube down from the previous attack. As the darkness closed in Jace was being held back from his own possession. The darkness drowned her and for several minutes she wondered if this was it and she wouldn't come back at all. But then she did come back. She was on the ground and her arm was broken in two places. Jace was limping away from her with a look of terror in his eyes.

"I'm sorry. I didn't—" But he was possessed before he could even finish the sentence. Nelson and Rizzen struggled to lift the lightest cubes to stop the swarm—even though Nelson had superhuman strength. Jace punched Rizzen in the face, causing him to drop the cube. Then the darkness returned to Janelle. The only good thing about that was the pain in her arm was gone. She waited for Rizzen to suck up the swarm and return her control over her own body but it didn't come. She kept waiting.

And waiting.

Mac and the Ronos Almics were attacked by four other groups of swarms. Each time they used a new method and each time they lost another soldier. At this rate they were never going to make it to the command deck.

How is plan B going? asked Mac.

Nothing yet, said Volmere. He said it with anger. He didn't want to have to resort to plan B. It meant using his own daughter.

Lemnell was in constant communication with Vissia, looking for where the last few emulators were being kept.

The long range sensors on the Almic command ship were much better than Vissia's smaller scout ship. But hers was faster so she had the best chance of flying in there, destroying the emulators, and getting out without dying. Seeing how many ships were still left in the fleet, the "without dying" part was not likely; hence Volmere's hesitation to see his daughter go on a suicide run.

How about those cubes? asked Mac.

I'm trying to get through all the swarms you're running from.

Mac and the others came to another group of swarms. This time, instead of staying in a group the swarms scattered and attacked from all different angles. They all focused on the same target, Sellet. That threw everyone off. They had been trying to defend themselves, not just focusing on defending Sellet. Swarm after swarm entered her body before they were able to get away. She couldn't hold her weapon up anymore. If any more swarms went into her body she would be gone. Her skin was vibrating.

I...can't...feel, Sellet started to say.

Conserve your strength, said Volmere. *Focus on keeping control of your body. I am almost there.*

She stumbled as she walked. Durgan was ushering her ahead. The attacks were getting less frequent the closer they got to the command deck. This didn't sit well with Mac. The command deck should have been the most secure place on the ship. The way to it should be getting harder, not easier.

Sellet came stumbling up to Durgan. He put a hand on her arm to see if she was okay and then vanished inside of her. She stopped struggling and stood straight up. Durgan, in Sellet's body, continued to lead the group.

This way, said Durgan's male voice.

You took over Sellet's body! said Mac.

We don't have time for this.

You can't just do that for no reason.

302

You guys are planning to destroy the emulators. This is the only way I can protect myself.

Mac brought his weapon up and pointed it at Sellet.

Stop, he said.

You don't realize what's happening, said Durgan.

You aren't taking us to the command deck, are you?

No. But we never needed to go there.

You're messing with us.

I'm taking you to the engine room.

Why?

There is a bomb hidden there that we need to disable before it is used against us to immobilize the ship.

Mac knew about the old plan to destroy all the important ships in the fleet so that the rebel Almics could take over. If anyone knew about how to destroy this ship, it was them. But if the beacon couldn't be destroyed after 20,000 years of fighting on Ronos then he wondered if it was actually possible.

If the rebels had the technology to destroy a ship made out of the same material as the beacon then the right course of action was to use that weapon on Ronos. Not to take over a ship and crash it into the beacon.

There were heavy footsteps behind them as Volmere finally caught up. He was carrying six cubes and he passed them out to everyone who was left.

We can't keep following this guy, said Mac.

I agree, said Volmere. *The other group may have been right not to trust him.*

They all took a couple steps away from Sellet.

There was a rush of swarms moving past them. Mac felt more of them enter his body. He looked around him and saw all the remaining Ronos Almics under similar attacks. Sellet was running down the hall. Volmere still had enough control of his body to run after her. One of his men was already taken completely and was firing at his leader. The others were trying to free him with the cubes but it wasn't happening fast enough. The lights leapt out of the cubes and brought swarms back in but it was only one at a time. The cubes were not effective. Mac lay flat on the floor, concentrating on not losing himself. The swarms were moving like a current through the hallway. They must have figured Mac was down permanently because he was ignored.

Or they could see that he was already taken. The swarms moved past him. The infested Ronos Almics—all of them except for Volmere were taken now—followed after Volmere and Durgan in Sellet's body. Once he thought he was alone, Mac rolled over. All his movements were slow. He still had full control over his body but he was vibrating with all the swarms inside of him. He forced his legs to move as fast as they could, which was little more than a trot. If Volmere was attacked by everyone chasing after him, he would be dead before Mac could get there to help.

Chapter 19
Last Chance

Mac was all alone with the swarms trying to pull his body apart. He kept walking down the hallway, hoping the engine room would be an obvious place so he wouldn't accidentally walk past it. Up ahead of him he heard gunfire and shouts. Well, more like growls, which is what an Almic sounds like when it yells.

Volmere! I'm coming, said Mac.

Hurry. They almost have me.

Mac got to the engine room. It was full of machinery and loud noises. It looked like an industrial shop—two levels tall and packed with a bunch of metal machines that looked almost like garbage instead of an engine. Mac didn't see anyone at first.

There is only one way out of this, said Volmere.

Mac didn't realize he was talking to him at first.

What? What do you need me to do? said Mac.

Lemnell will help you get the ship to Ronos. I can clear the room and buy you some time.

What do you mean?

Mac was panicking. Volmere was backed against the far wall. Sellet, her weapon out in front of her, lead a thick swarm cloud moving closer and closer to him. They didn't jump out and attack him because he was pointing his weapon at a bomb to his side. The bomb that the rebels had planted ealier.

That bomb isn't going to damage the ship enough to stop it, said Mac.

Volmere was slowly backing to the far end of the room where the mechanical humming was at its loudest. The machinery back there was a different color metal than the hull of the ship. Mac remembered what Lynn had suggested about vulnerable points that were made with non-Almic material.

An explosion from the inside will cause enough damage to help you get this ship to Ronos, said Volmere. *You see that terminal to your left?*

Yes.

That's what you'll use. Follow Lemnell's guidance and make it count. This ship is our last chance.

Volmere was going to sacrifice himself—detonate the bomb to kill all the swarms. The room wasn't so big that Mac knew he was going to be safe. He went over to the terminal and tried to operate it, but it wasn't in Earth Common so he had no idea what to do. This was a bad idea. It should be the other way around. Mac needed to sacrifice himself to get Volmere to the terminal.

Mac pointed his cube at the swarm cloud and sucked one in. Sellet turned towards Mac.

This is the only way I can regain standing with my people. Aleeva is too foolish to see that you are a lost cause, said Durgan. *The human race will be extinct.*

No! said Volmere.

Sellet ran. The swarm cloud streaked across the room to attack Mac, leaving Volmere free. He knew that there was only one choice for him.

Hold on to something, Mac, said Volmere.

Mac turned away from the swarms and held onto a tube beside the terminal. Volmere pulled the trigger of his weapon and an explosion burst forth, immediately enveloping Volmere. The strength of the ship was sure but there were still weaknesses. The engines weren't destroyed but a seam that had been patched by non-Almic material burst, releasing the atmosphere in the room. Sellet and the swarms were sucked through the breach before they could get to Mac.

If Mac hadn't been holding onto the tube he would have been sucked out with them. As it was he was struggling to keep his grip with all the swarms inside of him. After several painful moments he heard a buzz behind him. He dropped to the floor while a hiss of air indicated the atmosphere was returning to the ship. The rip in the hull had been covered by an emergency force field.

Lemnell, I need help putting in a trajectory for this ship, said Mac.

You won't be able to plot a trajectory from there. Activate the engines and I'll tell you which way to point the ship.

I don't know how to read anything on here.

One moment.

An image entered Mac's mind. Some beings who could mind speak could also send images. The Ronos Almics knew the language of the colony ship, which was the same language as the Invaders. Mac was sent a series of symbols. A straight slash next to a wavy slash, a circle with a triangle in the middle, three lines stacked on top of each other.

This is the word for turning on the engine. Do you see it anywhere on the terminal?

Mac studied the screen. It was full of odd symbols but he didn't recognize any of them. It was like doing a word search in a different language. He ran his finger over the screen and looked for the straight slash under the squiggly slash. He found a couple but the next symbol after them was incorrect.

Then he saw it and pushed. The whole room started shaking as the engines turned on and the ship started to move. Volmere's bomb had done a lot of damage to the room but at least the engines still worked.

I need to lock the doors, said Mac.

No time. You are heading in the wrong direction. The engines take a bit to warm up and you need to have the right trajectory before you take off, said Lemnell.

Mac studied the screen. It had changed when he activated the engines. There was a dial in the middle of the screen that responded to his touch. He reached out and subtly turned it. If it was moving the ship at all, it was so small it was imperceptible.

That's good. You're at least facing the planet now. Wait while we calculate.

Getting to the planet wasn't going to be good enough. Mac needed to collide head on with the beacon if this was going to work. While he waited he kept one eye on the entrance of the engine room to see if any swarms were coming. He wouldn't be able to take on too many more swarms before he was overpowered.

Mac? It was Phillip, not Lemnell.

What?

We got free. Where are you? The swarms stopped attacking us.

The lights in the room switched from red back to a normal hue. The ship wasn't on lockdown anymore.

I'm in the engine room, said Mac. *Get back to your ship and we'll all get out of here.*

We can help.

There isn't really anything anyone can do now. It'll all be over soon.

Okay. But we won't take off until you get back here.

Lemnell came back. *You need to readjust. Ever so slightly. You are close.*

Mac turned the dial and waited for feedback.

You went the wrong way, said Lemnell.

Mac turned the dial the other way. While he waited for Lemnell's response he studied the screen. The other group wasn't being attacked anymore. That meant the swarms were all moving to his location—he was the one they had to worry about. The hum of the engines was getting louder as they warmed up. Soon they would be up to full speed.

Once that happened, whoever was on the ship was going to stay until the impact.

Okay, you're good. Lock it in, said Lemnell. He sent another series of symbols to lock in the coordinates.

Mac pushed the buttons and they lit up in green.

Now get out of there, said Lemnell.

Mac was about to leave when the symbols turned red. They weren't locked in anymore. Mac touched them and turned them green but they didn't stay that way. This wasn't going to work. The swarms could change the coordinates from the command deck. There was nothing Mac could do to keep them out of the system.

Mac, Janelle is gone, said Phillip.

What do you mean?

She ran away. I don't think she wants to leave without you.

There was no way for Mac to tell her to get back to the ship. If she was running to get to him then she would be dead, either from the swarms or because she would still be on the ship when it hit the beacon. He couldn't understand why she would risk her life.

Lemnell, it won't lock in the trajectory, said Mac. *They keep overriding it.*

There's a way to get around that.

Is it fast?

No.

Then send me the symbols quickly.

Mac was sent a dozen Almic words at the same time that needed to be pushed in a certain order. He looked for the first one but it was already taking too long. This wasn't going to work.

How much longer before the engines engage? said Mac.

Two minutes.

What's the trajectory now?

Away from Ronos.

Has Vissia found the human prisoners being emulated?

Yes. They are in the middle of the fleet. Very well protected. Nothing we can do.

Mac watched the dial and felt the hum of the ship powering up. He was only going to have one chance if this worked.

How far off am I from going right through the middle of this fleet?

He was sent another image—the dial and how far he needed to turn it. Lemnell knew exactly what he was thinking.

Ten seconds until the engines fire up, said Lemnell.

Mac got ready to hit the dial. If he could change the trajectory to blow through the fleet and destroy the emulators, the swarms would be useless. Well, most of them would still be. The ones buzzing around inside of Mac would still be functional but they could use cubes on them later.

Now! said Lemnell.

Mac spun the dial as the engines kicked into gear. The ship lurched and spun around. The force of it threw Mac to the ground. The last Almic ship charged through the fleet at incredible speeds. Ships crashed against the hull and exploded. None were powerful enough to bounce off unharmed. It was total destruction. The massive old ship was moving at full power now and it was too fast for any of them to get out of the way. Mac didn't know which ship it was but one of them had the emulators.

Did it work? said Mac.

Yes. The ships are immobilized, said Lemnell. *But the Invaders on Ronos are still going. And the emulator machine is still bringing them all back to life. There are billions of them on the surface.*

This was all going to be over soon. He walked over to the computer and with Lemnell's help he reset the coordinates to ram the ship into Ronos. Before he started the engines up he heard someone call his name from the doorway.

"Mac!"

It was Janelle. She looked the same as the night she was taken. She was wearing the same clothes and she hadn't aged a day. It was the same way she had looked when he had seen her body being emulated on the collector ship on the front—but this was no emulation. Her hair was tousled and there was sweat on her face from running all the way there. This was real. This was really Janelle, in the flesh. After five years he had finally found her—finally, here at the end of the war. All he had to do was push a button and then the two of them could run to their ship and escape.

But Janelle wasn't Janelle. From behind her back she pulled a gun out. The laser burned Mac's chest and threw him away from the terminal. When he landed he felt another burn on his back as she kept pulling the trigger. She had done this before—or the swarms had tried this before, using Janelle to gun down Mac. She walked towards him and kept pulling the trigger.

It really was her but there was a swarm inside of her. If he attacked then he could hurt her and one of her arms already looked injured. Each blast from the laser made it harder to think of a solution where he could save everyone without having to kill her. He rolled to duck behind some equipment. She was still across the room so he had room to look at his wounds. She wasn't using a human weapon. It had done some serious harm. He could smell his own flesh burning. The healing was slow to happen, either because of the swarms inside of him or because he didn't have enough Mac Gas in his system. If she kept gunning him down he wouldn't last much longer. He grabbed a nearby wrench and threw it.

The wrench knocked the weapon out of her hand and he charged at her. Even with a swarm in her there was no way she would be able to physically overpower him. He made contact, touching her for the first time in five years, and he felt the swarm inside of her go into him. His hand let go of her and he stumbled back. His vision was cloudy as the swarms fought to subdue him. She stumbled back and looked lost, like she had no idea where she was or how she had gotten there.

"Mac, what's happening?" Once she realized how close he was she stepped towards him.

"No." Mac tried to say. But he didn't have full control over his voice. It came out as an angry gurgle. He was kneeling with one hand on the ground the other grasping at nothing. It felt like he was having a seizure but if he concentrated he could slow down the tremors. He tried to calm himself down, keep his body his own.

But he couldn't do it fast enough to stop Janelle from touching him. Swarms moved from him to her. He didn't know how many, but he had control over his body again. He pushed her away before the swarms could make a move and ran over to the terminal. He moved the ship into place and started the engines. The familiar hum returned.

Is the ship still on course? Mac asked Lemnell while Janelle got to her feet.

Yes. The engines don't need as much time to power up. You need to get out of there now.

How much time?

Five minutes. Probably less.

Behind the terminal he pulled out the wires. Sparks shot into the air and the screen went blank. The engines were still humming.

Janelle looked at the blank screen and said, "What have you done?"

"I'm not done yet," said Mac and took off running. He hoped that the swarms would chase him so he could get her on Phillip's ship. All he had to do was get to the ship. Use cubes later. He ran faster.

Mac's body had been changed so that he was faster and stronger than any human should be. The swarms inside of him were slowing him down a little bit, but he had adrenaline and the quickly-dwindling timer ticking in his head. It was a big ship and five minutes wasn't a lot of time. He worked against the swarms and pumped his legs faster.

Then it dawned on him that Janelle couldn't run as fast as he could. He turned around and couldn't see her down the hallway. There was the distant echo of her footsteps but he couldn't see her. Once the swarms figured out he wasn't going to the command deck would she keep following him? She could ruin the whole plan by going to the command deck and turning off the engines.

Mac set his gun to continuous laser. It wasn't as powerful in this mode but would keep going until he took his finger off the trigger. He burned a message on the wall: *Don't touch me. Get to the ship.*

Then he waited for her to catch up. It would look suspicious if he was simply standing there waiting for her so he lay down like he had been hit. Her footsteps got louder as she caught up to him. Her steps slowed, cautious. Mac sprang out and grabbed her ankle. The swarm moved into his body—they thought he was the bigger threat so controlling him was better than controlling Janelle—and he let go. He flung himself in front of the message on the wall and then he lost control of his body.

Janelle was in a hallway now. Mac was on the ground, vibrating. On the wall behind him was a message. He was trying to save her. The swarms were transferred by touch. She didn't understand but she listened and kept running down the hall.

"Nelson! Jace!" she yelled out. She didn't know where she was or where she was going. Her only hope was for someone to hear her.

There was a distant yell. She was getting close. Nelson, Jace, and Phillip were running up to meet her.

"We need to get out of here," said Jace. "The ship is about to take off. Lemnell says we only have a minute or two."

"But Mac—"

"There's no time!"

"What about Mac?" asked Phillip.

"He's possessed. He can't make it."

Nelson looked down at the cube he was holding in his hand. The light inside was still bouncing around freely. There was plenty of time to save Mac. Phillip shook his head.

"There's no time," he said.

Nelson didn't agree or he didn't care. He may have been still feeling suicidal. He ran back the way Janelle had come. Phillip ran after him. Janelle moved to go with them but Jace held her back.

"They're not going to make it," said Jace.

"I have to help," said Janelle.

"There's nothing the two of us can do. The cubes run on mind speak. Come on."

Jace led her back to the ship. If the three soldiers didn't get back in time he would have no trouble taking off without them.

Nelson got to Mac and started taking swarms out of him.

"What were you thinking?" said Phillip.

"That Mac would have done the same for me," said Nelson.

Three swarms had been taken out. Mac got slowly to his feet. Phillip dragged him down the hallway while Nelson kept pulling swarms out of him. Lemnell's voice echoed in all their heads.

Less than a minute, he said.

Undock, said Phillip.

What? said Ryan.

We won't make it in time. Go now.

Mac was moving quickly now. He looked for another alternative. The three of them could survive in space. He started randomly opening doors to find a way out. Nelson tapped him on the shoulder and showed him his holo wrist display. There was an airlock close by.

Twenty seconds.

They were at the door. But it was locked while the engines were being used. The three of them started punching the door. They hit it all at the same time, causing it to fold it in on itself. Mac grabbed an edge and ripped the door open. Then he blasted through the thin outer layer and all three of them were sucked out into space at the same time the last Almic ship took off towards Ronos.

Mac floated through space, looking back to where Ronos was. The planet itself was too far away to see. The ship's engines glowed bright but were quickly swallowed up by the vastness of space. If it made it to the planet Mac was going to have to hear about it second-hand.

The last Almic ship shot through space at full speed. The Invaders knew there was something wrong. All the ships that were piloted by Almics who already had their bodies back moved to attack it, maybe even board it and turn the engines off, but there wasn't enough time. Millions of them flew into the upper atmosphere to stop it from crashing into the planet but the crescent-shaped ship cut through them.

Lemnell's trajectory was right on. The last Almic ship collided with the surface at the bottom of the crater. It struck the beacon, easily piercing the hull. The two ships folded in on each other and then tore themselves apart. The speed at which it happened was so incredible and so powerful that the planet ruptured. Crags appeared across the mountains and plains of the horseshoe continent. The abandoned Passenger cities sunk into the ground.

Large segments of the planet started to break away from the core and the oceans began to bubble and boil. The planet lost its atmosphere. Everyone still on the surface was killed as Ronos broke into a dozen large pieces; those pieces then shattered into thousands.

The transformation from planet to space rubble was so complete that there was hardly anything left to recognize as a planet. It happened so fast—it was over in seconds.

On the *Lendrum*, Lynn and Scott watched as the war ended. The *Lendrum* was pummelled with rocks but the hull was strong enough to deflect the barrage. She had lived on that planet longer than she lived on Earth. It felt more like home and yet she wasn't sad to see it go. The beacon had been destroyed. It was impossible for the Invaders to keep their swarm forms and all the Invaders who already had their bodies had been destroyed on impact.

Everyone who had wanted to be evacuated had been. Most of the Rays had stayed—their reasons weren't known. Now they never would be. Lynn knew they were better off without them. And it's not like they weren't given the option to save themselves. They chose their own destruction.

Scott looked over at her, smiling. "It's over."

"Yeah," said Lynn. "Wanna know something crazy?"

"Crazier than Mac blowing up a planet?"

"I wasn't sure I would survive."

"What?"

"I'm a swarm. I thought that I would disperse into nothing. The colony ship is the reason I'm able to do that and it's gone now."

"But you said swarming came from harnessing energy emitted from the colony ship. We didn't destroy that energy. That's why you can swarm."

"And anyone else who was possessing a body, as well. Considering the vast majority of the Invaders were on Ronos, it might just be me."

"How long will the energy last?" asked Scott.

"I don't want to wait around and find out."

"We need to get you a new body."

"Yeah, Genny Hunter is in for a surprise when she gets hers back. Any ideas about where I should end up?"

"Android?"

"They're illegal."

"Not anymore. Those are the old rules. Who knows what the laws are now."

"It might work if we use enough organic components. It might take some time to get it right. But I don't want to use Genny to figure it out. I stole her body without permission. We'll ask permission."

"Nally made it, right?"

Lynn reached out to her with her mind.

"Yeah, Nally made it. I'll ask her for help later."

"Is it really over?" asked Scott.

"It's really over."

Chapter 20
After

Mac couldn't sleep. He hadn't been able to sleep since Ronos had been destroyed. Except that he never thought about it that way. At two in the morning—he had no idea why they still kept Earth time, but it was so ingrained in humans it would probably stick around for a while and the next generation would be very confused—it wasn't "since Ronos had been destroyed," it was "since I destroyed Ronos." Everyone who called Earth home had the Invaders to blame for its destruction. The only one to blame for the destruction of Ronos was Mac. He had brought the planet out of obscurity. He had tried to raise an army there to fight a war for him. He had told Volmere to evacuate. He had been on the last Almic ship that destroyed the planet. He was responsible.

And at two in the morning it was a lot to take in and made sleep impossible. Despite how many people were crowded on the *Lendrum*, Mac had been given his own room. People treated him like a hero, which also didn't help him sleep. Everyone knew his name. That meant he was going to be known to history. His name was being written down.

Even though Mac and sleep were never in the same room at the same time, he still lay down in his bed every night and hoped to be reunited with it. Every night he'd really tried to fall asleep but tonight was different. Tonight he lay on top of the covers with a flight suit on. He hadn't left the space station in over a month and it felt like the walls were starting to close in on him.

There was always a night shift working but most of the Passengers and refugees—they were all refugees now until they got used to calling ships home—were asleep. It was only humans on this ship. The Ronos Almics had their own vessels. Mac left his room and walked down the hall, past Lynn and Scott's room directly beside his and Janelle's on the other side of that one. His steps were light so that none of them would wake.

There were a few refugees sleeping in the hall as he walked to the closest docking bay. A massive space station like the *Lendrum* had several, and right now they were all packed with as many ships as possible. None of the refugees woke up as Mac passed, which he was grateful for. Most people knew his name by now but he wasn't sure how many knew his face.

The docking bay was being guarded by a group of five soldiers in Earth military uniforms—the kind of uniform that Mac used to wear. The men were low-ranking and three of them had their weapons holstered. The other two didn't even have any on them. They didn't even notice Mac walk up to them.

"I need to get inside," said Mac.

"Sorry," said the leader whose name tag said Stallmer. "General Roy's orders. No unauthorized people in the docking bay for now."

"Why?"

Stallmer spoke slowly as he studied Mac's face like he had trouble thinking and speaking at the same time. "Can't say...Hey, do I know you?"

"No. Thanks. I'll head back."

"You're Mac Narrad!" said one of the other men and rushed forward to shake his hand. The other men were equally excited about seeing Mac.

"You saved us all," said Stallmer. "I was on the front when I was captured. We had no chance of winning this war without you. Thank you."

Mac couldn't bring himself to say anything so he smiled instead.

Stallmer continued, "We aren't supposed to let anyone

but there's no way I could keep you out. Whatever you need, sir."

"Why is General Roy keeping people out of the docking bay?"

"The council is deciding how to divide up all the surviving property. Since there are no habitable planets left ships have become extremely valuable. But some people don't own any and some people own dozens. Others live on space stations like this that can't even move. They are trying to decide how to give everyone a place to call home and not just the humans. There's dozens of alien species out there that need somewhere to go as well. Laws need to be passed so that we can all get along and stay out of each other's business. Shouldn't be too hard for now. No one seems eager for any more fighting."

"Are there enough ships for everyone?" asked Mac.

Stallmer shrugged his shoulders. "I have no idea. I'm just passing on the rumors I've heard. Either way, it's going to be a long time before normal happens for us. No need for you to worry. If anyone gets a ship it's going to be you. Pretty sure you can kind of do whatever you want."

Except go home, thought Mac to himself. *Except be with my family.* And really that's all he wanted. Stallmer opened the docking bay doors and Mac squeezed inside. There wasn't even room between the ships to walk through. The only way he was going to fly out of there was to pick a ship near the doors to outer space. He climbed on top of the ships and started walking over them to the other side of the massive room. Out of curiosity he started counting and got to two hundred and three. Walking across the tops and wings of the ships reminded him of when he had been floating out in space while the pull was going on and he had to avoid getting crushed by all the ships that were being pulled to the same spot that wasn't big enough for more than one. They ended up as one big ball of metal and

Mac had almost been crushed more than once. Another story that would become part of the history books.

Near the front of the docking bay was exactly the kind of ship he had been looking for, a HAAS3. The look of the ship was comforting. The scarred armor was inviting. It reminded him of his days in the military, where his only problem was trying to find Janelle. Before he became a major player in the destruction of planets.

He went inside and momentarily flashed back to being trapped in the cave with Lynn and Raymond, and listening to the Mac Gas burn away the armor. He took a seat in the pilot's chair and turned the ship on. The lights came on and the display, controls, and console all lit up. The switch to activate the engines was right in front of him but he hesitated to flip it. He should ask Stallmer to open the docking bay doors before he started the engines— Stallmer had said he would need to if he wanted the doors opened. But Mac also couldn't bring himself to open a channel to Stallmer.

Mac was frozen in inaction when the door to the HAAS3 opened and Janelle came in. She sat down in the co-pilot's seat and put her safety belt on.

"Where are we going?" she asked.

"You following me?"

"I couldn't sleep either. You should have come to get me instead of trying to sneak past my room with heavy boots."

"I just needed to get out."

"Then let's get out," she said. "You spent five years trying to find me. It's probably best we don't get too far from each other now. Just in case."

"In case another alien fleet abducts you?"

"There are dozens of those out there now. I know a lot of them, but still I don't want to go anywhere else without you."

"You sure?" It was a genuine question. Everyone treated him like a hero but he didn't feel like one.

"I was in the prison for a long time. Out here it was only five years but on the inside it felt ten times as long. There was no way to measure the passage of time. We didn't age. And the humans were the newest members of the prison. The others had been there for decades, maybe longer. Rizzen—who knows how long he's been there. You saved all those people. You brought entire civilizations back from extinction and gave them a chance. Stop focusing on whatever it is that's dragging you down and see the good. We have all been given a second chance. Maybe we can avoid making the same mistakes as last time."

"I don't want to be in charge of making any more big decisions. I found you and now I'm done. I just want to be normal now."

"Normal is a pretty flexible word right now. But I'll go wherever you go. I don't have anyone else left in the world."

"We should probably start saying 'in the galaxy.'"

"And you don't have anyone else in the galaxy either."

"No family, anyway. I'm sorry I never figured out what happened to yours. They kind of just disappeared."

"If everything about the war was secret and my abduction was the start of the war, I'm guessing they looked for me in the wrong places. You're lucky you didn't disappear as well."

"They might still be out there," said Mac. "Maybe on a prison ship on the front. Or maybe they were thrown in the Invader prison and you didn't notice."

"It's possible." She said the words but did not believe them. Even though the Invaders had taken a lot of humans to be emulated before they destroyed the Earth and the colonies, a lot of humans had still been killed. Taking a census of the survivors was a top priority and the data was still being compiled. It was possible Janelle's family would show up on that list—possible but not likely, and they both knew it.

"You used to be older than me," said Mac.

"I'm still older than you."

"You haven't aged in five years. I passed you a while ago."

"But time was ambiguous in the prison. I never slept there. I'm probably close to fifty in mental years. A wise old woman."

"That much closer to being senile."

Janelle laughed.

"I don't want to stay here," said Mac.

"Where?"

"With the fleet. Living in the shadow of a broken planet. I can't do it anymore. I know that I had to destroy it, and I know it saved billions of lives and ended the war, but I can't stay."

"Where are we going?"

"I want to find a new home. A place for humanity to feel soil under their feet again. A new planet to replace the one I destroyed."

"You didn't destroy the Earth, you know."

"I know. But that doesn't change anything."

"So you're going to travel the galaxy looking for a new Earth."

"Galaxies. Might have to go pretty far."

"We might get lonely."

"We might. I wasn't going to take this Hawthree. I was going to go ask the general for a bigger ship and then look for volunteers. See if maybe the others wanted to come with us. Scott, Lynn, Phillip and those guys. Maybe even Nally or some Ronos Almics."

"I'd like to ask Rizzen as well."

"I bet he would prefer to stay. He is a helper. Lives to serve the people."

"I'll still ask. Are you going to ask the general for one of the capital ships?"

"Too big and too powerful. I've been thinking about this for a while. This isn't me running away because I can't handle everyone knowing who I am, or because I have such bad mental health now. I'm going because this is the way it needs to be done. The fleet waits here and rebuilds society while I go look for a new home. One ship goes out, not everyone. And that one ship can't be a military ship loaded with weapons."

"You're worried we'll turn into the Invaders. Burning through the galaxy, looking for our new home."

"Yes. We can't become what we fought to destroy. One ship, minimal weapons. A mission to find a new home. Not steal someone else's."

"I like that idea," she said as she leaned over to kiss him. A continuation of the night she had been abducted.

Mac reached out and pushed the button to ask for the bay doors to be opened. The ruins of Ronos were behind the station so all they could see were endless stars. He had heard that on a clear night on Earth it was possible to see 2,500 tiny sparkles in the sky. In the whole Milky Way galaxy there were actually billions of stars. That was a lot of possibilities to explore.

THE END

What I Know

I know that this book would have been unreadable without my test audience, including my wife, and editor Hillary Barton. Thanks for your honesty (The test audience had to tell me the first draft was terrible. Not an easy thing to do). I was able to completely rewrite the book—twice—to get exactly what I wanted out of it. Just a hint of what the book could have been, in the original draft the only people who survived were Mac and Janelle. Grim. It wasn't even a little bit fun to read and most of the test audience didn't even finish. I know better now.

I know that this book wouldn't have been as easy to sell if it didn't have such an amazing cover. Chris Pratt is awesome. What he has done with these books is beyond what I had hoped for. For this book I told him I wanted an eviscerated planet. The end result made me giddy.

I know that this book would not exist without you. That's right, you. The person holding this book right now. 2014 was the worst year of my life. Our daughter was still born at thirty-four weeks. My wife went into labor, we went to the hospital thinking we would be adding a happy healthy baby girl to our family, and they told us there was no heartbeat. She was born a few hours later. That is something that I can never forget. For weeks and months after it was something I couldn't stop thinking about. The memories of losing my daughter prevented me from writing. On bad days I didn't care about anything, especially things that made me happy, like telling stories. Even on good days, when I sat down to try and finish this book my mind immediately went back to the night Rosie was born and no writing would happen. There was a long time when I honestly didn't think that I would ever finish and that I would never write again.

But you guys wouldn't let me give up. It started with my wife, who kept telling me I needed to write, and that I needed to finish the story, because she wanted to know how it would end. Random people at church would ask me how writing was going and when they would be able to find out how it ends. Then people at work started asking me how it would end. Each time someone asked me I would try to sit down and write to see what would happen, and each time I was disappointed with the results and got angry and sad—angry and sad were my dominant emotions for that year.

The tipping point came when my nephew Clark told me that he was reading my book and that he really liked it. That changed everything. I remember being that little guy. When I was his age I was into Animorphs. I remember staying up all night reading about those kids fending off an alien invasion. To young Tyler, those books were the most entertaining things on the planet. I fell in love with reading immediately. The feeling of seeing the characters in fiction overcome insurmountable obstacles gave me goose bumps. I loved it. I don't know if that's exactly what Clark felt when he read my books but that's what it reminded me of. That feeling is why I wanted to be a writer myself. I wanted to give readers those good feelings, those goose bumps. His excitement for my books helped me get back to writing. Thanks, Clark! Now you're famous because I mentioned you in a book.

I know that I wouldn't have been able to get through the hardest year of my life without my family. Just like I know that Joseph Smith was a prophet of God, that the Book of Mormon is a true book, and that Jesus Christ is the Savior of the world, I also know that Rosie still exists, that families are forever, and that I will see her again someday. I'm sure that by then we will have a lot of stories to tell each other. Family is the most important thing in the world. If you are still reading this, please go and do something today that will help strengthen your family.

About the Author

Tyler Rudd Hall is a member of the Church of Jesus Christ of Latter-day Saints. He grew up in the small farming community of Rosemary, Alberta. Because of this he had to use his imagination and VHS copies of *Star Wars* to keep himself entertained. After graduating from Rosemary High School he went into the Professional Writing program at McEwan University in Edmonton, Alberta. There he met his beautiful and talented wife who was enrolled in the same program. Both of them are now pursuing their professional writing goals in Edmonton.

Find more books by Tyler Rudd Hall on
goodreads.com/tylerruddhall

Manufactured by Amazon.ca
Acheson, AB